WHILE ROME BURNED

A NOVEL OF THE ROMAN REPUBLIC

THE SERTORIUS SCROLLS
BOOK SIX

VINCENT B DAVIS II

For Avery.

Your mother and I are so proud of the bright young woman you've become. Never stop smiling. You have a beautiful heart and an incredible future ahead of you. Ashley and I will be here to support you every step of the way.

THE SERTORIUS SCROLLS
READING ORDER

Although this book can be read and enjoyed on its own, The Sertorius Scrolls series is intended to be read in chronological order:

1. The Man with Two Names
2. The Noise of War
3. Bodies in the Tiber
4. Whom Gods Destroy
5. Sulla's Fist
6. While Rome Burned

DRAMATIS PERSONAE

Apollonius—freed *servus* of Quintus Sertorius, close friend, and mentor

Arrea—wife of Quintus Sertorius, freed slave

Barca—former gladiator, *lanista* of a successful gladiator school

Caecilia (Metella)—sister of Metellus Pius and daughter of Metellus Numidicus. Betrothed to Lucius Cornelius Sulla

Caesar, Gaius Julius—a child at the time of the Social War, nephew by marriage of Gaius Marius. Son of man by same name. Future dictator

Catalina, Lucius Sergius—brother-in-law of Marcus Marius Gratidianus, a military tribune under Gnaeus Pompeius Strabo

Catulus, Quintus Lutatius—elderly statesman and former consul of the Roman Republic. Serving as the father of the senate (*princeps senatus*) during the Social War

Cicero, Marcus Tullius—serving as a junior tribune under Gnaeus Pompeius Strabo. A friend of Gavius Sertorius. Later becomes famous as an orator, writer, and statesman

Cinna, Lucius Cornelius—former ally of Gaius Marius, a political nonentity with ties to both senatorial parties during the Social War.

Crassus, Marcus Licinius—the son of a wealthy patrician family with growing ambitions. An ally of Lucius Cornelius Sulla

Cluentius, Lucius—a former friend of Lucius Cornelius Sulla. A leading statesman of the Italian city of Pompeii

Didius, Titus—former consul, serving in the Social War. Quintus Sertorius served under Titus Didius in Greece

Gratidianus, Marcus Marius—nephew of Gaius Marius, cousin of Marcus Tullius Cicero, brother-in-law of Lucius Sergius Catalina. Serving as a tribune under Gnaeus Pompeius Strabo

Hirtuleius, Lucius—childhood friend of Quintus Sertorius. Served alongside Quintus in the war against the Cimbri and Teutones, and in Greece

Insteius, Aulus—childhood friend of Quintus Sertorius. Served in Greece alongside Quintus. Twin brother of Spurius

Insteius, Spurius—childhood friend of Quintus Sertorius. Served in Greece alongside Quintus. Twin brother of Aulus

Juba—prince of Numidia, who has been held captive by the Romans since his youth. Captured by Gaius Papius Mutilus during the Social War

Lucullus, Lucius Licinius—*tribunus laticlavius* (senior tribune) under the command of Lucius Cornelius Sulla during the time of the Social War. Friend of Gavius Sertorius

Marius, Gaius—former consul (six times previously) who was considered the "Third Founder of Rome" for his success in defeating the Cimbri and Teutones. He retired during the Social War, but seeks command of the war against Mithridates. Uncle of Gaius Julius Caesar. Bitter rival of Lucius Cornelius Sulla

Mithridates—King of Pontus, a powerful kingdom in northern Anatolia. He is mounting a war against the Roman Republic which is expected to begin soon. Mithridates' riches make command of the war against him desirable to many Roman generals

Mutilus, Gaius Papius—a Samnite noble who was elected "consul" by the rebelling Italic League during the Social War. He leads the main Samnite army in southern and central Italy

Pius, Quintus Caecilius Metellus—a Roman statesman from an important family, serving under Gnaeus Pompey Strabo. Son of Metellus Numidicus, the enemy of Gaius Marius

Pollux—dog of Quintus Sertorius, brought back with him from Greece. Named after the twin gods Castor and Pollux as a reference to a friend, Castor, who served with Sertorius in Greece.

Pompey, Gnaeus—son of Gnaeus Pompeius Strabo, and important officer under his father's command

Rhea—mother of Quintus Sertorius, grandmother of Gavius Sertorius.

Rufus, Quintus Pompeius—cousin of Gnaeus Pompeius Strabo, political ally and friend of Lucius Cornelius Sulla

Rufus (Minor), Quintus Pompeius—son of Quintus Pompeius Rufus, an ally of Lucius Cornelius Sulla

Sertorius, Gavius—a son of Titus Sertorius by birth. After his father's death in battle and his mother's suicide, he was adopted by his uncle Quintus Sertorius. Raised by Arrea, wife of Quintus Sertorius, while his adoptive father was away at war

Sertorius, Proculus—deceased father of Quintus and Titus Sertorius, husband of Rhea. An influential local magistrate in the village of Nursia

Sertorius, Quintus—protagonist of The Sertorius Scrolls. Son of Proculus Sertorius and Rhea, brother of Titus Sertorius. Husband of Arrea and adoptive father of Gavius Sertorius. Former officer of the legions with over a dozen years of military service

Sertorius, Titus—deceased brother of Quintus Sertorius. Son of Proculus Sertorius and Rhea. Birth father of Gavius Sertorius

Strabo, Gnaeus Pompeius—a prominent member from a noble family in Picenum. Despite being a "new man," he levied a large army from those local to Picenum and fought against rebel tribes there. Elected Consul during the Social War

Sulla, Lucius Cornelius—a rising politician and military commander. Born to a tarnished but patrician family. A legatus at the time of the Social War. A bitter rival of Gaius Marius

Sulpicius, Publius (Rufus)—an ambitious young man from a patrician family who seeks a political revolution and the alleviation of his many debts. Ally of Gaius Marius

Toria—daughter of Quintus Sertorius and Arrea, short for "Sertoria"

TRIBES OF THE SOCIAL WAR

TRIBES LOYAL TO ROME OR NEUTRAL

Campanians—Comprised the area and peoples around the important city of Capua. Comprised the most fertile soil in Italy, this was an area Rome was determined to protect at all costs. In addition, Campania was considered to rear the best horses and cavalrymen in Italy. Many cities within Campania, including Pompeii, which did not have citizenship, quickly joined the rebellion.

Etruscans—The Italian tribe of Etruria, which was delimited by two rivers: the Arno and the Tiber. Etruscans, the dominant civilization of Italy previously, had fought many wars against Rome but had altogether assimilated with Roman culture. Whether or not they would join other tribes in rebellion wasn't settled until the end of the war and was a matter of great importance to the Romans who relied on their support.

Latins—An Italic tribe in central Italy and along the western coast, including the city of Rome and the surrounding territories.

Umbrians—an Italic tribe in central Italy, situated close to Rome. They did not support either side during the Punic Wars. Unlike the Etruscans, most of their people lived in small villages rather than cities. They were heavily integrated with Rome in the third century BC. Whether they would remain loyal to Rome was not a foregone conclusion, and Rome would continue to be concerned about their possible defection throughout the war.

ITALIC LEAGUE TRIBES

Apulians—An Italic tribe in the southeastern peninsular section of Italy. Although they were reluctant to join the rebels, they were surrounded by many tribes who opposed Rome and therefore would be a target if they stayed loyal. They were one of the last tribes to join the rebellion. The Roman colony of Venusia within Apulia was one of the only Roman colonies that joined the rebels, primarily out of fear of being destroyed by those already supporting the rebellion.

Frentani—An Italic tribe on Italy's southeastern coast. Closely connected with the Samnites. They were particularly important because they controlled the Adriatic seaboard of Italy.

Hirpini—A Samnite tribe in southern Italy, sometimes lumped in with other Samnites and considered a distinct and independent tribe. Their name in Oscan, the language which they still spoke during the Social War, means "wolf." Their land surrounded the important Roman colony of Beneventum.

Lucanians—A tribe in southern Italy that was closely connected with the Samnites. They spoke Oscan, the same tongue as the Samnites and other rebelling tribes. They supported Pyrrhus and Hannibal Barca during their wars against Rome. In the Second Punic War, they were ravaged by both Rome and the mercenaries of Carthage and never fully recovered from these disasters.

Marrucini—a small tribe very close with the Vestini who were one of the earliest to join in the war. They fought alongside the Marsi in many battles.

Marsi—The first tribe to take up arms against Rome in the Social War. Along with the Samnites, they were the most active leading tribes during the conflict. They were situated very close to Rome by the Via Valeria, less than sixty-five miles from Rome itself. Their primary leader during the Social War was Quintus Poppaedius Silo.

Paeligni—a mountain-occupying tribe near modern Abruzzo. They were close in proximity and affinity to the Marsi and quickly joined them in rebellion. One of their cities, Corfinium, was named the capital of the Italic League and thus renamed "Italica."

Picentes—fought Rome several times previously and instigated the Social War by killing all Romans within the city of Asculum, including a relative of Caepio's. The city of Asculum would be a main objective for both sides throughout the war. Pompeius Strabo (and his son, who became known as Pompey the Great) were native to Picenum and raised locals to fight back against their tribesmen.

Samnites—Rome's oldest enemies, they had fought many wars against Rome before. Most recently, they joined Hannibal during the Second Punic War, and Pyrrhus of Epirus during the Pyrrhic War before that. Rome held hatred for the Samnites for battles they lost to them in the past. It was a foregone conclusion that they would join the rebellion once they began, and they led the rebel efforts throughout. Their primary leader during the war was Gaius Mutilus Papius.

Vestini—a Sabine tribe forced by the Romans into an alliance in 302 BC. They were one of the first tribes to join the war effort against Rome after the rebellion at Asculum.

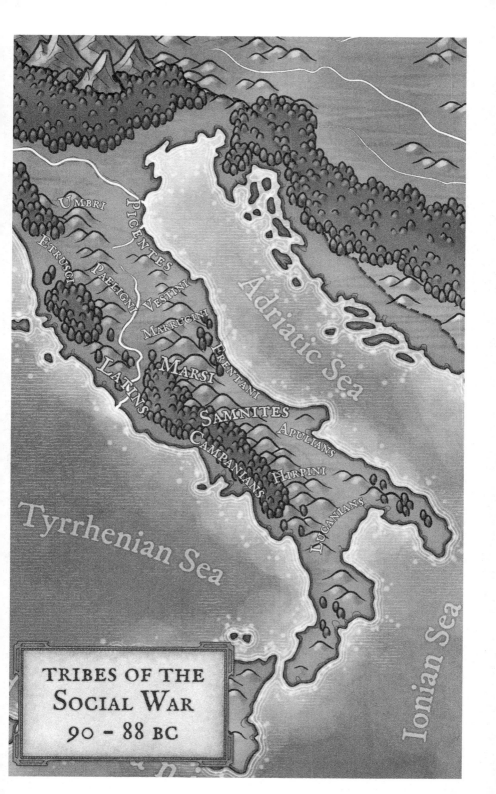

TRIBES OF THE
SOCIAL WAR
90 - 88 BC

CITIES OF THE
SOCIAL WAR
90 - 88 BC

Join the Legion to receive Vincent's spinoff series "The Marius Scrolls" for FREE! Just scan the QR code below.

PART I

SCROLL I

QUINTUS SERTORIUS—THE Nones of March, 665 Ab Urbe Condita

I brought the blade down with as much force as my aching body would allow. It failed to hit the mark. With a groan of effort, I tried again. The stubborn root finally broke under the effort of my mattock.

I set the tool down by my feet and wrapped a fresh strip of cloth over the palms of my hands. The blisters had burst sometime that morning, and red blood clotted with my farm's soil.

A raspy laugh rang out a few paces behind me. "You aren't as young as you were in Greece, legate. The effort's likely to kill you if you keep this pace."

I turned and found him sitting cool and comfortable atop the oxen-drawn *aratrum*.

My voice was hoarse from thirst. "Your tongue is likely to get you killed, Silvanus. Keep working." I picked up a clod of dirt and threw it up at him.

The crunch of the heavy wheels accompanied his laughter. "I don't understand why you're determined to do all this by hand. We're breaking up the earth just fine, me and my oxen."

"If we aren't prepared for cultivation, it will be my responsibility," I said.

He shrugged and clicked for the oxen to keep moving. "As you wish, legate."

But he was wrong. That wasn't my title. Not anymore. I wasn't a quaestor either. I wasn't even a legionary.

The moment I heard my wife was with child, I knew something had to change. I needed to be there for her. I needed to be *here* with her.

As war season ended, I relinquished command of my legions and finished my term of office as quaestor. With what little I earned for the previous year's efforts, I purchased a plot of land outside Nursia, the village of my birth.

Twenty-one *iugera* in size, it was small by most standards, but still as much as I could manage with the help of Silvanus and my other two workers, Priscus and Atilius. The fields sprawled out before us like a blank scroll, waiting to see what story we'd write during our first harvest. The Apennines stood watch around my barren plot of land, a familiar guardian from my youth. Last winter's snows still hooded the peaks.

Silvanus had served under me in Greece. Young, reckless, and without ambition, but a loyal man and a good friend. He was discharged from the legion after taking an arrow to the knee, so he sought me out for work, knowing his old legatus had a soft spot for his legionaries.

I turned my attention back to the work before me. The earth was still hard from the frost fall of winter, but it was now relenting under my effort and the burgeoning sun. We had only weeks to prepare the field for planting, and I did not know if we were on schedule.

I had no idea what I was doing at all.

But I felt a connection to the earth each time I brought down my mattock. I was used to only enemies being on the other side of my blade. Men. Despite my exhaustion, aching limbs, and bloody hands, I found the work refreshing. To create rather than to destroy.

A large clod of dirt burst beneath my blade. Every foot of the field needed to be softened and rotated before planting began. Breaking a single spot still hard from winter's kiss was a small victory, but a victory nonetheless.

"I believe I'm catching up to you."

I turned to find Priscus, his face sheen with sweat. He used the sickle in his hands to take up the grass and weeds that plagued the field.

"I'll wager ten denarii I finish the day's work before you," I said.

The former legionary *medicus* smiled, but as always, there was sadness in his eyes. Part of him never returned from Gaul.

"I'll take you up on that offer," Silvanus shouted from his ox cart.

We both ignored him.

I shaded my eye with the back of my hand and looked at the sky. It was nearly midday. Arrea and my mother were in our villa and would have *cena* prepared soon. Hunger eluded me while I focused on my work, but refuge from the heat was alluring. A few more strokes and I would rally the men to join me for some bread and watered-down wine.

"Sertorius," the third worker, Atilius, shouted. He was the youngest of our group, the son of my father's oldest friend. What he lacked for in strength, he made up for with his mind. Atilius constantly read books on agriculture and crop farming, and he put the knowledge to good use. I placed much of my hopes of an adequate harvest on his shoulders.

"What is it?"

"A rider," he said.

Despite myself, I felt a knot of apprehension develop in my stomach. I'd dreaded the arrival of a messenger each day since I arrived on my farm. Some emissary bringing news that would draw me back to war and away from my wife. What ripple would this rider introduce to the tranquil pond of my newfound peace?

I threw the mattock on my shoulder and hurried to the fence line. Atilius was nearly finished with its construction.

I strained my eye to make out the rider's features, naturally expecting to find a golden eagle or a legionary standard hoisted up behind him. But even at this distance, I could see that wasn't the case.

"Expecting visitors?" Silvanus asked, as he and Priscus joined me.

"No. Nor do we need a welcome party, gentlemen," I said, but neither hurried back to work.

As the horseman drew nearer, I could see by the skill of his riding that he was a Numidian. His dark skin became apparent beneath his armor and a fox fur cloak. I knew at once this must be my closest neighbor. He rarely made social visits.

"That the gladiator?" Silvanus asked me.

I leaned against my fence. "He's not a gladiator any longer, Silvanus. Won his freedom, his citizenship, and now owns a school of gladiators himself."

The Numidian rode without a saddle. Instead, an intricately woven African carpet draped over the horse's back.

"I may have gone into the wrong profession," Silvanus said with a quiet whistle.

I waved to the rider. "Greeting, *amice*."

He halted before us, a cloud of dust rising like a mist beneath his steed.

"I'm told this word means friend. Am I your friend?" he asked.

There was a childlike innocence in the way he awaited my response, but there was no mistaking this man for a child. He bore a deep pink gash atop his clean-shaven head. It was old and healed over, but it was a wonder he lived through the initial wound. Spider-webbed scars covered his sinewy arms, calluses lined his palms. He was, perhaps, the only man in Nursia who had shed as much blood as I had, both his own and that of his foes.

"We're neighbors now," I said. "I'd like to think we are friends."

He placed a fist over his heart. "I am honored then." The rider assessed my fields. "You have much work to do."

Silvanus laughed.

I gave the barren fields a look myself and nodded. "We do. But a few weeks remain before planting can begin. We'll be ready."

"Why do your slaves stop working?" He glared at the three men beside me. "And why do they not avert their gaze?"

I smiled. "These are no *servi*, but free Romans."

This perplexed the rider. "You are a great warrior. You have conquered many foes. Why no flocks of slaves working?"

I decided not to lecture the former gladiator on stoicism, slavery, and how my father taught me to reject the institution when possible. "Why should I need slaves to do work when I can do it with a few friends?"

My words confused him, and perhaps he was trying to remember his Latin. Eventually, he smiled. "I like you, warrior. Your name is Quintus, yes?"

"Quintus Sertorius." I said. "And yours?"

I noticed more men arriving on the dirt path to my home a few hundred paces in the distance. Their intricate and exotic armor proved they were gladiators. My grip on the mattock tightened.

"All Romans name their sons Quintus." He swept off the horse with feline precision. "My name, in my tongue, you cannot pronounce. Your people call me Barca."

Atilius perked up. "Any relation to Hannibal?" He was unfit for warfare by nature but enjoyed hearing the stories the rest of us told. A gleam appeared in his eye when we spoke of battle. I was glad he didn't know the reality.

"No," Barca snapped. "But name drew crowds."

Silvanus pointed at the nearing gladiators. "You take them with you everywhere you go?"

Barca raised his chin. "I killed many fathers and many sons in the arena. I made many enemies."

"Surely a man like you can defend yourself?" Silvanus asked.

Barca stared with an intensity uncommon to Romans. "The first rule of battle is to never fight unless you can win," he said. "I cannot know who will attack or how many will come. I only know they will, eventually. When they do, I will kill them."

Atilius was enraptured, Priscus listened with absent curiosity, and Silvanus balked. Legionaries and gladiators often look down on one another, considering their own form of combat to be superior to the other.

"What can I do for you, Barca?" I asked.

The Numidian warrior smoothed out his horse's coat and allowed her to nibble a stick of celery in his hand. "I seek to invite. To offer invitation." He considered his words. "I am preparing a feast. I'm told Romans dine together to forge alliances."

The six heavily armed gladiators stopped just behind Barca's horse, but their demeanor was peaceful. I released my grip on the mattock.

"I'm honored," I said. "I would be grateful to join you, but I must speak with my wife first."

His brows furrowed, an old scar running through one of them. "Romans must seek permission from their wives to break bread?"

My companions laughed.

"Not exactly," I said. "She is with child. The baby could arrive any day now."

He nodded, but a look of confusion remained in his eyes. "This is for women to handle, no?"

I smiled. "I'll not interfere, if that's what you mean," I said. "But I'd like to be there to usher my child into the world."

Barca raised a fist. "He will be strong warrior."

"Yes," I said. I felt the smile fade from my face.

I already had one son, Gavius, who was a warrior. Even now, he served under Lucius Cornelius Sulla, counting down the days for war season to begin again. I prayed my child with Arrea would never experience war.

I extended my hand, which Barca accepted with the strength of a retired gladiator, his grasp as unwavering as his stance had once been in the arena.

"Let me speak with my wife, and I'll return momentarily."

"I do not know what this word means, but I shall wait," he said. "My men are thirsty. May we seek water?"

I gestured to Silvanus. "Will you show them to the well?"

He raised a finger. "Yes, I, as a free man, shall choose to show these men to the well."

Barca grunted. "You talk much for little man." He turned to me again as I began my way back to the villa. "You may bring your woman. I have no wife. But my cook is expensive and cooks well."

"I'm sure we will enjoy it." I let the mattock fall to my feet and picked up my pace.

By the time I reached my villa, my mind returned to Arrea, and the child we would soon meet.

My mother, Rhea, opened the door before I even knocked.

The crisp smell of freshly baked bread wafted out to greet me.

"Hello, mother," I said.

She embraced me despite the film of sweat and dust covering my arms and back.

Mother said, "Are you hungry?" She helped me take off my muddy boots. "If your companions intend on eating with us every day, they should help prepare it."

I smiled. "I think Arrea is eating more than all of us combined."

My pregnant wife peered into the atrium, a look on her face that could terrify the bravest of legionaries. Gallic women were famous for their temper, and I was careful not to provoke it. I could levy a joke at her expense from time to time and get away with it though.

"You're eating for two, my love," I said.

Her face softened as she melted into my arms.

Despite swollen ankles and a rotund belly, Arrea had never been more beautiful. There was something divine about her, creating life before my eye.

I kissed her head and whispered, "How are you feeling today?"

"Like I could burst," she said. "Whether from the seams or into tears, I do not know which."

The flower scent of her hair contrasted with the sweat and smell of the field clinging to me.

Mother stood close by and admired us. There was a look of contentment ever present in her eyes. She'd endured much hardship in life. Two stillborn births, the premature death of my father, losing my brother in combat, and the subsequent death of her daughter-in-law by suicide. I could tell that to see something good come of it all brought her immense joy.

Just like the rest of us, the only thing which remained was for my son, Gavius, to return. Each day he did not was greeted with fresh disappointment, but we still held out for hope.

"We have bread and we have figs. Silvanus ate what little cheese we had left yesterday, so we'll need to ride into market," mother said. "I'll bring some tomorrow."

She still resided within my ancestral home a brisk walk from my new farm, but she spent most of her time with us, and promised to do so until our child was safely born.

"That should be enough for today," I said. "And I want the wine heavily watered. I don't need Atilius getting drunk in the field again. He'll spend all day asking about old battles."

I followed Arrea into the triclinium. It lacked the size and trappings of the dining room of our domus in Rome, but it had everything we needed.

I half expected to find my old friend Apollonius asleep on the couch there, an old copy of Aristotle's *Nicomachean Ethics* in hand. But he was gone.

He'd wanted to join us in the field when we first settled in, but I refused him. He wasn't a young man any longer. His old bones were weary from all we'd endured together, so he departed a few weeks prior for a holiday in Greece. With our dog, Pollux, beside him, he set sail to visit his niece in Athens.

I was happy Apollonius could enjoy some time with his only remaining family, away from the toil and strife that seemed to follow me. But I missed his wisdom tremendously. I needed his sage advice and calming presence with a baby on the way.

Arrea brought me a glass of wine and I sipped gratefully.

"You have something you wish to say," she said. Despite the burden of pending birth, she was as perceptive as ever.

"We have our first visitor." I wiped the wine from my lip. "A neighbor has invited us for dinner."

"Oh?"

I nodded. "The Numidian. He arrived on a fine steed with six armed men, but as friendly as a farmer."

She shrugged. "A gladiator would make for interesting dinner company."

"He's not a gladiator any longer. Won his freedom some years ago and now owns the largest gladiator school north of Capua. I've seen his home only from a distance, but I'm not sure if Rome's richest noblemen could afford it."

Raised voices carried in through the open shutters.

"Is your new friend causing trouble?" she asked.

"He has a brash manner of speaking," I said. "I rather like him. But perhaps he's offended one of my boys. Let me take care of it."

The voices continued to elevate in volume and aggression.

I made for the exit but paused before a marble column by the door. My sheathed gladius rested atop it, as it remained like a relic of the ancient past since we arrived here.

My hands lingered above it.

"Take it." Arrea gingerly cradled her belly.

"Just in case." I grabbed the sword and tied its belt around my waist, the weight as familiar to me as my wife's embrace.

The shouts grew louder. I wasted no time. Laughter accompanied the voices now, and I wondered if that was good or bad.

I ran down my dirt path. The landscape was hazy until I drew nearer, but I immediately noticed more men present than when I'd left them.

As I closed in, I noticed Atilius, Silvanus, and Priscus standing side-by-side with the gladiators. Across from them, a dozen men faced them, their armor glimmering in the midday sunlight. Weeks had passed since our last visitor, and now it seemed all of Nursia arrived on my farm.

"I won't tell you again, peasant," one antagonizer shouted. "You can give us food and water of your own free will, or we can take it with our swords. Your choice."

Barca stepped away from his gladiators and my companions. "Call me a peasant again, and I'll carve your tongue out and feed it to my pigs." With a swoosh, his cape flew backward, and he brandished a curved *khopesh*.

"Your ornamental swords and arena showmen do not frighten us, whelp."

I said, "What is the meaning of this?" I hurried to Barca's side, sword sheathed, but firmly in hand. "I am the owner of this property, and I demand to know why you chastise my guests."

It was plain to see these were no ordinary bandits. These were soldiers. They each wore a bronze breastplate with a blue tunic beneath. Round shields with the same bull painted on each rested by their side. All of them bore bronze helmets not dissimilar to those issued to legionaries, though one of them had a horsehair plume fixed onto his, designating him as an officer of distinction.

This man stepped forward and sized me up. From the look on his face, I didn't impress him.

"Look here, peasant," the warrior began. "We are with the army of consul Papius Mutilus of the Italic League."

I gripped my sword.

Six months previously, we'd killed one of the Italian rebel "consuls" and annihilated the Marsi tribe, alongside many of their allies. The fight was far from over though. Samnite armies under the command of Papius Mutilus were still at large, and apparently farther north than any of us realized.

The rebel smiled at the look of realization in my eye. "We're in winter quarters. Food is short. Mutilus sent us to get what we need. Now, I've told your mongrel companion here that charitable alms would be enough. Give enough water and food for my men here, and a place to stay for the night, and we'll be on our way."

The rebel spoke with the accent of Rome's urban poor. I wondered if he moved to Rome like many others—seeking opportunity and prosperity—only to find crippling poverty and resentment.

"Winter was hard," I said. "I have barely enough to feed my own people, and I have no rooms to share." I made eye contact, but the rebel commander studied the scars along my arms, perhaps assessing how difficult it would be to kill me.

He clicked his tongue. "Come now. We are simple soldiers. Not asking for a feast, are we? Just a little sustenance. Mutilus will remember those who aided his men when he brings Rome to her knees. You would do well to make a kind gesture."

If only he'd known that I was a Roman senator. A former quaestor, tribune, and legatus of the Roman legions. Still, I could tell they'd already made their decision.

"Go on your way," I said.

Barca stepped forward. "And come nowhere close to my home. My gladiators will use your headless corpses for training."

Immediately, and on both sides of us, swords sliced from their scabbards.

"Hold, hold!" I shouted. I lifted my arms, and fortunately, both sides waited. Perhaps there was the chance to stop bloodshed after all.

I looked back at my companions, who wielded their farm tools with courage and indignation in their eyes. But even with the fierce gladiators at their sides, we were no match for a dozen veteran rebel soldiers.

"War season has not begun," I said to the rebels. "Your 'consul' agreed. Rome agreed. There is to be no bloodshed until four days after the Ides of March. We have nearly three weeks until the fighting can commence."

Silence followed for a moment until the rebel commander laughed. His men quickly joined in.

He shook his head at me. "I've been trying to figure it out since you arrived," he said. "I can't tell if you're twenty or sixty. Your naivety points to you being too young to understand the subtleties of warfare. Either that, or you're so old you belong to a bygone era."

Barca shouted, "Quintus Sertorius has seen more war than all of you combined. Fix your tongue."

The rebel commander's brows raised when he heard my name. He seemed to consider the glory he'd earn by taking my life.

I exhaled.

"What did you say your name was?" the rebel commander asked.

Before anyone could respond, he lunged at me.

I stepped back. His blade cut through the air with a deadly hiss.

The Samnites let loose a war cry, a haunting ululation, and charged in.

The commander stabbed at me. I let my scabbard fall to the earth and raised my blade to deflect his.

Soldiers are good at spotting weakness. Two of them charged Atilius, who let out a yell. His voice quavered but he didn't back down. Perhaps he'd learned something from our war stories after all.

Barca jumped in to protect him before they arrived. With a flourish and spin, his *khopesh* slashed through one rebel's neck as easily as a scythe through harvest wheat.

I parried another blow from the commander and stepped forward to meet him. He stabbed down at my left knee. I stepped back in time to avoid it and thrust my blade forward with an attack of my own. Off balance, I couldn't generate enough force to mortally wound him, but my blade struck his breastplate and forced the breath from his lungs.

He recoiled to compose himself but wasted no time returning with another wild slash. I ducked to avoid it and dodged past him. I sent my elbow into the back of his neck. With a grunt, he stumbled to the dirt.

I turned and lifted my blade, preparing to end the rebel's life. But from the corner of my eye, I saw Barca being swarmed. His swords slashed like a hungry viper, striking with precision at the exposed flesh of their legs and arms.

Atilius sought to help him. He brought the hammer down on the back of a rebel's neck. The Samnite warrior grunted with pain but threw his sword back. It ripped through the flesh of my young friend's chest.

"No!" I bellowed.

The rebel commander took advantage of this distraction. He stabbed up at me and caught me just above the hip. The blow wasn't deep, but pain reverberated down my leg. I grabbed his wrist and turned it back until the sword fell from his grip. He kicked up at me until I brought my gladius down through his neck. A rattle escaped his lungs and blood sputtered from his lips.

By the time I looked up, Atilius was on his knees.

Silvanus was hobbling toward him as quickly as his bad leg would allow, a plow in hand.

Barca fought off three rebels at once, evading, spinning, and ducking like a wild dance. He clearly hadn't lost a step since his time in the arena, but mangy dogs can bring down a lion if they attack as a pack.

His gladiators fought around him, embroiled in combat of their own, some twirling tridents in hand, others tossing out nets to capture their prey as they did in the arena.

One lunged forward with a spear and missed his mark. That failure cost him his life, as the evading Samnite stepped in and thrust his blade through the gladiator's exposed belly.

I rushed to help Barca.

Before I arrived, and without pausing, he shouted. "No, go to your friends." He jumped into the air and hooked his curved *khopesh* around a Samnites neck, beneath the rebel's helm, and severed the head cleanly.

"Atilius!" I shouted.

But the boy, now on his knees, did not look up. His fingers ran errantly over the cavernous cut through his chest.

Silvanus stepped forward to protect him. He brought the plow down on a rebel's head, the clank against his helm reverberating throughout my field. The Samnite was stunned enough to fall back, but another was there to take his place.

Before I could reach them, the second Samnite stabbed deep into Silvanus's thigh, just above the knee he'd spent so many years rehabilitating. He collapsed beside Atilius as another blade ripped through his stomach.

I let out a war cry to rival the Samnites and jumped toward the killer. He attempted to dislodge the sword from my companion's stomach but couldn't do so fast enough. My sword punctured his cheek and tore through soft tissue until it crushed the bones of his face.

He screamed, but the din of arms swallowed it up.

Three gladiators had fallen now. Blood dripped from Barca's arm, but whether it was his own or a fallen foe's, I did not know.

Silvanus was lifeless on the ground, save the twitching of his lips and fluttering of his eyes. Atilius was still breathing, and blinking rapidly, but the rebels must have considered him dead already, for they ignored him.

I searched for Priscus and found him engaged with two Samnites. He wielded his sickle like a legionary's sword.

The old *medicus* handled himself well, but he would be the third of my friends to fall if I didn't act fast.

Ignoring the pain and the blood seeping down over my leg, I sprinted to his aid.

"On your right!" I shouted.

He wheeled closer toward me. As one rebel charged him, I thrust my blade into the exposed flesh of his underarm. As he writhed, Priscus slashed the sickle across his face, leaving a jagged gash through the man's forehead in its wake.

The other attacker stepped back. I lifted my sword and stamped my foot, enticing him to strike. Instead, he turned to run.

The sound of battle silenced behind me.

"Dimitrius, finish him," Barca said to one of his gladiators.

A pilum went sailing into the air. It ripped through the back of the fleeing rebel, who stumbled forward a few steps and collapsed.

I turned to find all the Samnites dead or dying. Four gladiators lay on my virgin fields in the same manner.

Atilius remained on his knees.

I ran to his side. "*Amice*, speak to me," I said. "Can you breathe?"

He said nothing, but I could hear short, sharp, raspy breaths wheezing from his lungs.

"Priscus!" I shouted. "Come swiftly, he needs aid!"

Before I finished speaking, the old *medicus* was at my side.

"Hold on, boy." Priscus's bloody fingers fumbled through a leather satchel at his hip. "Hold on."

A decade had passed since Priscus was discharged, but he remained vigilant. He quickly found what he needed.

He handed me a small vial. "Give him this quickly."

I didn't ask questions but brought the tiny bottle to Atilius's lips and tilted his head back for him to drink. Atilius neither complied nor resisted but continued to stare forward with rapidly blinking and wide eyes.

Priscus materialized another bottle, slightly larger than the first, from his pouch. "This will hurt worse than Jupiter's lightning," he said.

Wasting no time, he helped me lay Atilius back on the ground and poured the contents of the bottle over the wound.

Atilius's eyes narrowed, and he emitted a groan.

"That's acid vinegar," Priscus said. He was clearly concerned by the lack of a reaction. "Atilius, stay with us. Now, this will stop the bleeding."

He passed me a handful of white flower petals and kept the rest for himself.

"Pack the wound," he said.

I did as he requested, and pushed the tiny petals into the flesh, which now boiled and hissed from the acid.

Priscus did the same, and as his fingers packed the flower deeper, he stopped.

He felt something which confirmed the worst, perhaps a severed artery or a punctured organ. The old *medicus* looked at me and shook his head.

"I was too slow," Barca said, standing behind us. "I could not save the boy."

"Give him this." Priscus handed me another vial. "Opium. It will ease his passing."

I poured the liquid over Atilius's trembling lips.

Was there no way I could have prevented this? I thought of Atilius's parents, my father's old companions, and shame overcame me. Their boy had died under my protection.

I ran my fingers through Atilius's bushy hair. "You fought in a proper battle, *amice*," I said. "And you fought bravely."

Something akin to a smile appeared on his lips, but I'm

unsure if he could even hear me. His body convulsed, his hands shaking beneath the weight of ours. Then he fell still.

I laid his head back on the field we'd been preparing for planting and closed his vacant eyes.

Standing, I found the gladiators had gathered the bodies of their own and placed them together with their arms folded across their chests.

"I could not save him," Priscus whispered to himself. Tears streaked through the dirt of his face.

I helped him up and put my hands on both his shoulders. "You did all you could."

Barca's face hardened. "I could have prevented this. I should have challenged the commander."

"They would have denied your request and proceeded as they did," I said. "We did what we could."

Barca was unconvinced. He knelt by a dying Samnite. "May I?" he asked.

I was unsure what he meant, but it didn't matter now. "You may."

He positioned his *khopesh* before his face and stared forward. "Look here, Baal Hammon. Look here. This man I sacrifice to you for the safe passage of our fallen. May you delight in his death. May you bathe in his blood." He brought the blade down and sliced through the rebel's throat, who was too weak to stop him. Barca ran two fingers through the wound and painted his forehead with it. "We must prepare a funeral pyre."

I looked around at my barren fields. We'd gathered weeds and debris for days now, but there was little wood to be found nearby.

He seemed to notice this as well. "I have great collection at my *ludus*. We burn them there."

There didn't seem to be a fitting alternative. I thought about ways we might preserve them long enough to prepare a proper Roman funeral. I considered relatives we might invite. But Silvanus had no one, and Atilius was an only child and his parents were long dead. Neither married. We were the only ones left to mourn them.

"Thank you," I said.

"We will gather them." Barca nodded to his gladiators. "We will burn them at sundown, and drink to their memory."

I looked around at the carnage on my farm. Bodies covered the earth where my crops should grow. Blood drenched the soil where rainfall should nourish my fields.

I thought I'd found somewhere safe. A haven, somewhere away from war I could bring my child into the world and live with my family in peace.

But war found us. And it was at our very doorsteps.

SCROLL II

Barca and his gladiators were experts at crafting funeral pyres. It was likely a routine occurrence for combatants of the sand.

We gathered in Barca's *ludus*, a sandy gladiator's training ground enclosed by high stone walls. The bodies of Silvanus, Atilius, and the fallen gladiators rested on a pyre in the center. The *lanista* bore a torch and touched it against the oiled wood.

As the flames billowed up, Arrea took my hand. I'd encouraged her to stay behind, but she refused. She and my mother both donned a black shroud and joined Priscus and I in the carriage to Barca's home.

Elevated stone benches rested along the walls, where spectators could view Barca's gladiators and consider investing in his *ludus*. But they were empty now. Only the gladiators, my family, and a handful of wooden dummies with shredded leather armor stood witness to the funeral.

"Valiant fallen," Barca lifted his voice. "We honor you."

The gladiators formed a circle around the training field. They beat their chests in unison, a reverberating thud that echoed along the high walls of the *ludus* with the crackling of the fire.

My eye remained fixed on my companions as the flames slowly overcame them. It was my responsibility to protect them and I'd failed. I was keenly aware of the child in Arrea's belly beside me, and I prayed I'd be more capable of protecting it than I had been of my friends.

"Who will speak on behalf of the fallen?" Barca asked.

I released Arrea's hand and stepped toward the fire. "I."

There was no time to organize a proper funeral. We hired no mourners to honor them. We made no death masks of their faces. But the solemn gladiators and the marvelously high funeral pyre would have made them proud.

"Atilius and Silvanus were good men. Good Romans. They served, each in their way, for the betterment of the Republic, and for those they loved."

The flesh of my cheeks burned as sparks swirled around me.

"They will know peace in the afterlife as a reward for their character in life," I said. Bracing against the heat, I leaned in. "Goodbye, *amici mei*."

As I stepped back, Barca thrust a jug of wine into my arms and said, "We drink to their lives. We drink to their deaths. We drink for their safe passage." He lifted a jug of his own and drank deeply.

I took a swig and offered the wine to Priscus. The old *medicus* cast down his gaze and shook his head.

"We will miss them," Arrea said.

In the days up until now, she had bickered with them like siblings, but their concern for one another was real.

My heart ached. We were on the verge of creating new life, and still death plagued us.

Barca raised his jug and beat his chest in rhythm with the gladiators. "Gladiators who have fallen, you fought bravely," he said. "We salute you!"

"We salute you!" his warriors bellowed in reply.

The gladiators eventually ceased their drumming and began to share wine. Despite the deaths of their friends, they appeared unperturbed. Certainly, they cared for these men who trained and fought beside them each day, but death was so common in the arena, it must have been as natural to them as falling asleep or waking up.

Even after all my years fighting, I'd never grown accustomed to death. In fact, it burdened me now more than ever. I wondered if I could even tolerate the battlefield at this point in my life. Could I endure the losses as I had before?

The setting sun cast a golden hue over us, with patches of sky turning a deep shade of twilight blue. The air grew colder as evening neared, accompanied by a gentle breeze to stir the sands.

We watched as the fire raged on. I'd burned enough of my men on the battlefield to know it would continue for six hours or more, before we could mix the teeth and bones with wine and fill their funerary urns. I didn't relish the thought, but I would ensure they were honored properly.

"Why don't you ride back with mother?" I said to Arrea. "We could be here until late in the night."

She placed a hand on the small of her back to steady herself. "They were my friends, Quintus. I will gather their ashes with you."

Barca joined us and saved Arrea from my rebuttal. "You fought like lion today, Roman," he said.

If I'd fought better, perhaps my companions would still be alive. If I'd been prepared. If I planned for such an event, perhaps they would be sharing wine with me, and by a campfire, rather than a funeral pyre.

But I quieted those thoughts and said, "You as well, Barca. Your combat prowess may have saved all of us today."

He nodded at the wine in my hand and encouraged me to drink. "Will they return?"

I considered that. Would Mutilus's forces retaliate if they

determined who killed their scavenging soldiers? Perhaps. But Barca and his gladiators wasted no time disposing of the rebel bodies, and not with a grand funeral pyre.

"We must prepare for the possibility, even if it is unlikely."

I kept my eye on Arrea for any reaction but found none.

"My gladiators are not simple showmen," he said. "They are the finest warriors from Numidia, Carthage, Greece, and Gaul. We will come between you and death. Your family and . . ." He pointed to Arrea's belly. "Safe."

I nodded. I considered why this man, so recently a stranger, would take such a vested interest in us. But I perceived from the look in his eye that he was a simple man. The kind who lives by a code and does not deviate from it. We were part of his tribe now, and he would sacrifice for us the way he did beside his fellow combatants in the arena. Whether this was because of his respect for my skill in battle or the proximity of our farms, I did not know. But it didn't matter either.

"Thank you, Barca," I said. "We must rely on one another in these tumultuous days. With war raging in Italy, we must stand together."

He placed himself between Arrea and I for a moment. "Could I share word?" He gestured away to a more private area on the training grounds.

I looked at my wife, who gave me a nod and rested on my mother's arm.

Barca led me to an area just out of earshot between a few training dummies, bundled hay in the form of a human torso filled with punctures.

"You will not be safe now," he said.

A rather odd declaration, I thought. "What do you mean?"

"In your home." He gestured past his *ludus* walls toward my villa. "You can come here and be safe. My gladiators protect your family."

I patted his shoulder. He responded to the gesture of friendship with confusion but didn't resist. "You are very kind to offer such hospitality," I said. "But I cannot abandon my home."

He frowned and shook his head. "Your home will burn down around you with your family inside." His voice rose, defeating the purpose of leaving the group. "You have no slaves, no guards to protect you."

I wasn't sure how to respond. He was right. If the rebels did return, in any manifestation, we would be powerless to stop them. The Samnites could take what they want and leave us for dead or enslave us at their will, regardless of my personal abilities with the sword.

And how could I prepare for planting with only Priscus and me left to do the work? Even if we readied the fields, how would we tend to it? How would we harvest?

"If you were in my position, would you abandon your home?" I asked.

He leaned back and considered it. He was a proud man by nature, and he likely understood me. Then he said, "I never had a home. From one *ludus* to the next, from one arena to the next. I never had family, except these men." He gestured to the quietly drinking gladiators. "If I had pregnant wife, I would scorn everything else to protect."

I exhaled and nodded. I hadn't expected such wise words from a retired gladiator with a poor command of Latin.

I considered my response, but my mother's shout interrupted me. "Quintus!"

Turning back toward them, I saw she was pointing to Arrea. In the light of the blazing flames, I saw clear liquid pooling between her feet.

It was time.

My mother had prepared me for this birth as if it were a battle. We'd held nearly daily briefings over Arrea's state, and what I could expect when the process began. I knew that once the water broke, the baby could arrive within an hour, or it could be days. With this being Arrea's first child, the latter was more likely.

Either way, despite my mother's training, I felt woefully unprepared.

"Now it is time to celebrate!" Barca clapped me on the shoulder.

But my eye was locked on the nervous face of my wife. Perhaps my Numidian friend was simply an optimist by nature, but there would be no celebration for me until the baby was safely in my arms.

"What do I do?" I asked my mother.

She gave me a curt nod but mostly ignored me as she ushered Arrea inside the gladiator's home.

Barca seemed unperturbed at the prospects of a birth taking place in his home. "What a momentous occasion," he said. "The gods have ordained this."

I shouted to Priscus, "Ready the carriage."

Barca appeared confused. "Why? You must have child here."

"We should return to our home. Arrea has all her things there, which will help her remain comfortable," I said. "And we need the midwives. There are three villagers who are prepared to come."

My mother returned to the *ludus* training grounds. She bore the same calming demeanor I'd relied on throughout my life, but she moved quickly.

"Quintus, it will not be long. We will not have time to return home," she said. "I've brought quite a few children into the world, my son, and this one is coming quickly."

Barca smiled triumphantly before a sharp whistle escaped him. Several of his gladiators ran toward us. "Send them. They will fetch your midwives."

I contemplated what to do. I found it easier to formulate my thoughts on the battlefield, more frightened of this moment than being surrounded by a dozen swords.

My mother laughed. "A few burly gladiators arriving at their door will give them the scare of a lifetime."

Barca smiled as well. "I assure you they will arrive quickly."

I told them the locations of each midwife's home, and the gladiators wasted no time mounting up and riding toward the city.

"Quintus." Mother took my hands as they departed.

"What do I do? What does she need?"

"Quintus." She soothed me. "Everything is well."

"When I was born, I was breached."

"Yes. Your legs came first because the gods—"

"I know, I know, mother," I said. "But the birth was difficult. What if it . . . runs in my blood? What if this will be a difficult birth?"

We'd discussed this before, a dozen times or more, but I needed to hear my mother's reassurance again.

Priscus's grasp on medicine was of some comfort to me. Men weren't permitted anywhere near a birth, but if something went wrong, his knowledge could prove invaluable. Still, Asclepius himself couldn't alleviate my concern for Arrea.

She squeezed my hands. "This is *my* arena, Quintus. I will handle it."

My mother was the expert. The hands that now held mine had ushered a dozen or more Nursian children into the world. I took a deep breath to collect myself.

"I trust you," I said.

She kissed my cheek and returned inside.

The sun was long since set now, but the funeral pyre painted the training ground with a divine orange glow. The smoky air tinged with the scent of loss as the ashes of my friends danced in the wind.

"I keep my best wine inside," Barca said. "Come."

I nodded for Priscus to follow us, but the *medicus* remained behind.

Two enormous iron doors opened to Barca's home. Despite the time of night, the interior was well lit with braziers, heat pouring from them like a furnace.

Warm, dark hues covered the walls. I wasn't certain whether it symbolized the sand of the arena or the deserts of Numidia. It invoked both.

Unlike most Roman atria, which are lined with the death masks of respected ancestors and busts of inspirational figures from history, trophies of Barca's many victories lined his entry-way. Shields, helmets, and weapons taken from his defeated foes, a testament to his legacy as a warrior of the sands. Brightly colored frescoes depicted the scenes of Barca's triumphs, each image a frozen moment of time with the death and glory that enthralled Rome's masses.

It was a strange place—one honoring death so profoundly— to bring new life into the world. I wondered how many halls could be adorned with the arms of those I'd slain. If it existed, I wouldn't want to visit.

Barca seemed to read my thoughts as he led me deeper into his villa. "Your wife gives birth in my room," he said. "Away from this."

I shook my head. "You are a gracious host, Barca, but we couldn't do that."

"The blood of birth is fortuitous." He snapped his fingers, and two more gladiators stepped out from the shadows to join us. "Lead the women to my chambers. Best manners."

They nodded and spun on their heels as if receiving battle orders.

"Here is for dining." He led me into a large banquet hall.

It was comparable to a Roman triclinium, one large enough to host the most lavish, opulent dinner parties. But ornate textiles, woven with threads of gold and vibrant colors, adorned each couch and table, their patterns reminiscent of the sweeping landscapes of Barca's ancestral home. Sculptures and pottery, both Roman and African style, filled most of the empty space.

Barca's home lacked a woman's touch, but the vast fortunes he'd spent on acquiring these trappings was apparent.

"Bring the finest. Vintage from Lentulus's year," Barca ordered one of his *servi*. He pointed to a couch. "Last chance for prediction," he said. "Boy or girl?"

The couch's fabric was rich and supple.

"Well, my parents had two boys. My father was one of three boys, although the other two did not live long. My grandfather . . . well, you understand. Males run in the family."

I prayed I was wrong. All Roman fathers want a son to carry their name and their legacy. I had Gavius, of course, but he was my brother's son by birth. Most men would want a son of their own. I did not. A boy would know warfare and strife, no matter how much I might seek to spare him. It was the way of the world. I might give a girl a better life.

A clamor sounded from the atrium as the midwives apparently arrived.

"Where is she?" one of them asked in a hushed but anxious tone.

Barca smiled. "Many have died here," he said. "Never has life come. Perhaps this is good omen," he said. "For both your family and my *ludus*."

"I should offer a sacrifice," I said. "Do you have any Roman altars?"

"I have many altars to my gods. They would not mind if you used them."

I nodded. Although roman priests would be upset with me to be certain, my wife needed a god's protection now. I was more concerned with that than with protocol.

Barca pointed to an altar in the corner of his crowded dining room. As I approached it, wails rang throughout the home's long corridors.

My mother's voice rose above it all. "The child is coming quickly."

I broke off in a sprint toward the sound of her voice. Men were not permitted to witness the process of birth. Not allowed to be present until the child was cleaned, oiled, and healthy. But I no longer cared about social conventions. I wanted to be there at its first breath. Even if my child was a stillborn, I would lay my eyes on it. And if something happened to Arrea, I would not let her go through it without me.

I took the stairs up to Barca's chambers and followed the sounds of the midwives' hushed chatter.

Before I could reach the room, Arrea's cries had ceased, and utter silence replaced them.

I burst into the room without a delay.

"*Dominus*, we're not ready!" one midwife shouted.

But my mother and Arrea seemed not to notice. They focused on the bloody, slimy child and nothing else.

"Our child, Quintus," Arrea said, her voice fragile and soft and on the verge of tears.

My heartbeat pounded against my breast like a ravenous lion in a cage. I fixed my gaze on the babe, my stomach dropping until a faint, shrill cry rang out. Piercing and primal and healthy and real. The child squirmed now, seeking to roll back up into a ball.

"You have a girl," one midwife said.

I stepped forward, ready to embrace my daughter for the first time, but I halted.

"She should go to her mother first," I said.

The helper handed Arrea the baby, carefully cradling her head into Arrea's delicate hands.

Death followed me closely all my life. I'd come to expect its intrusion. Relief flooded me as I realized it would make no appearance today.

She held the child as naturally as drawing air. "Quintus,

look," she said. She ran her thumb gently over the girl's fore-head. "These dark eyebrows belong to you."

The breath caught in my lungs as I knelt beside them. All I'd ever worked for, ever hoped for, was before me. My eye could hardly behold it.

I ran my fingers through my daughter's hair, the calluses of my hands starkly contrasted with the smooth, unmarred skin of her head.

The baby's wails settled down now as she nestled against Arrea's breast.

"Congratulations, my son," mother said. She departed with the midwives to give Arrea and I a moment alone with the child.

"Are you disappointed?" Arrea asked.

I hadn't spoken of my desire for a daughter. She must have assumed I wanted a son, like most Roman fathers.

"I have never been happier in my entire life," I said.

Tears welled up in her eyes. "Would you like to hold her?"

I'd grown accustomed to small children growing up in a communal village like Nursia, but I'd never held an infant. So fragile, delicate, precious. Fear gripped me at the prospect, but I couldn't resist.

I held out my arms and accepted my daughter into them for the first time. Nothing ever felt so natural.

She began to babble and pucker her lips.

"Shh . . ." I soothed her and bobbed her gently in my arms as if I knew what I was doing.

"Sertoria is a cumbersome name for a girl." Arrea dried her eyes. "Perhaps we can call her Toria?"

I whispered. "Is your name Toria, little one?" I peered down at her scrunched little nose, her wrinkly eyelids.

I was prouder of my daughter than all the accomplishments, decorations, and honors I'd achieved throughout my career. All the sacrifices were worth it. All of them.

Despite my joy, something else dwelled in my breast. Perhaps it was the loss of my comrades, whose funeral pyre was likely reduced to a smolder by now. But I believe it was something more.

Here in my arms was the most precious, innocent thing I'd ever laid eyes upon. More divine than the Oracle of Delphi, more valuable than all the gold of Tolosa. And I had to protect her. The world outside Barca's *ludus* was war-torn and grief-stricken. Rebel forces were on our very doorsteps.

I would stop at nothing to ensure Toria was protected from it all.

SCROLL III

There were times on campaign when I'd be required to remain awake for multiple nights in a row. Sometimes we would have briefings and officer's meetings to plan our strategy in the middle of the night. I fought the Battle of Burdigala with less than two hours of rest. When I infiltrated the camp of the Cimbri, I once stayed awake for four nights in a row for fear I'd be assassinated in my sleep.

But I'd never been this tired before. Although Toria slept soundly and without disturbance for much of the day, I wouldn't allow myself to do the same. I felt the constant need to watch her, to remain vigilant, as if I were on night watch in enemy territory.

Arrea fed the child every few hours. Time, and days in particular, seemed to hold little consequence for us now. They blended seamlessly with a few moments of nodding off, followed by frantically working to ensure Toria received everything she needed.

The first several days, Arrea could not get the child to latch onto her properly. It was a source of immense grief for Arrea, but mother insisted this was normal. After a week of fretful days and nights, Toria fed properly, but this created problems of its own. Arrea's breasts swelled up and caused immense pain.

"This is harder than the birth, Quintus," she once lamented, with tears in her eyes.

Despite this, she bore it with a strength reminiscent of a hardened centurion. Nursian women arrived at our doorstep with increased frequency, offering their services as wet nurses. Despite her pain, Arrea laughed and claimed we went into the wrong trade. We refused them, and she soldiered on with increasing pain every few hours.

But despite the difficulties of these first two weeks, we'd never been happier.

The looming threat of war remained. Gavius was still serving in the legion, and war season was about to begin. Two of my companions and workers were now reduced to ash and bone, their remains in two urns in my tablinum. I had no prospects of being prepared for planting season now, and Toria allowed me no time to address this. The burden of our villa's cost would be harder now than ever.

But we did not care. Or perhaps we cared, but all of this was infinitely unimportant compared to the child in my arms. She was here. She was healthy. And despite the waning wealth of her family, she would always be fed, and she would always be safe. As long as I could do anything about it.

I was considering all this, rocking Toria in my arms, when Arrea pulled me back to the moment.

"I love these little folds." She pointed at the pudgy flesh around Toria's elbows, her arms stretching out toward us. She lost weight after the birth, which at first terrified Arrea and me. Mother ensured us this, too, was normal. Now that two weeks had passed, she'd reached the weight of her birth and showed no signs of slowing down.

"Such weight distribution would be unseemly on an adult," I said. "But they suit her just fine."

Arrea rolled her eyes and mother, who reclined on a couch behind us, laughed.

"You looked a bit like this when you returned from Greece," Arrea teased. "But a little bit of rustic cooking from your Gallic wife got you back into shape." She patted my belly.

"Wait a few more weeks," I said. "I haven't exercised once since Toria arrived. I'll be crawling on all fours by the time she learns how to."

Even from the triclinium, we could hear the front door open. The old rural villa creaked in many places, but nowhere as loudly as the entrance. Arrea often said it was as effective an alarm as buglers at the gate, and she wasn't wrong.

Arrea rubbed her weary eyes. "What now?"

On Toria's eighth day, my mother hosted a celebration for all of us. Dozens of citizens of every class and background from around Nursia attended. Many of my former legionaries joined us and had to be reminded how to behave in civilian society. Even a few of my senatorial colleagues—who were on holiday in the countryside—attended and spared no expense in the gifts they presented us.

But other than that, we desired no visitors. Newborns were exhausting enough without guests, and the slightest disruption to her sleep or feeding schedules could set us back by a matter of days.

"If it's another wet nurse plying her services, I'm going to hire her to work the fields with me instead," I said. "If I can hire all of them, I'd have more farmhands than a rich man's latifundium."

Priscus peeked into the room. "Quintus, you have visitors."

"Send them on their way as amicably as you can," I said.

He shrugged. "These are too stubborn, I'm afraid. You'll have to fight them off yourself."

I weighed his words, but assumed it was probably Barca.

He'd visited nothing short of a dozen times since the child was born to check on her progress, never failing to offer a plethora of Numidian girl's names he thought would suit her.

I passed Toria to my wife and gave the babe a kiss on her soft forehead. "I'll handle it."

"Better you than me," Arrea said. "Remind them a Gallic woman's temper is legendary."

The moment I exited into the hallway, two men rushed at me. Sunlight, pouring in from the open door behind them, created a silhouette around them but darkened their faces.

They were upon me before my mind could catch up to the moment. I struggled to defend myself, but the two had already seized me by the arms and ruffled my hair.

"You thought you could bring a child into the world and we wouldn't come to visit?" one said.

"She's too young to be tarnished by our poor manners," the other said. "Nothing to worry about."

As soon as they released me, I threw my arms around them.

"You mad dogs, what are you doing here?"

Lucius Hirtuleius was my first friend in this world. I loved him like my kin.

"Visiting my niece!"

I released him and turned to my other childhood companion, Aulus.

"I don't know whether to call you brave or stupid for traversing Italy with rebel armies all about," I said.

Aulus Insteius and his twin brother, Spurius, had been constant allies of ours since we were children. We bathed together in Nursia's frigid rivers, played games of legionary with wooden swords, and wasted time debating over who would marry the prettiest girls in Nursia. After outgrowing foolish adolescence, the Insteius brothers fought beside me in Greece for eight years and again the previous year against the rebels.

But his brother had betrayed us the year before. Spurius

supported the rebel efforts and sabotaged our own. I would have killed him myself had he not rescued Arrea from capture. Instead, I sent him into exile.

At the time when I told Aulus all this, I'd expected him to become irate, or perhaps even attack me for casting out his only brother. They'd been inseparable their entire lives. But Aulus had only looked down and gritted his teeth. "My brother is dead to me," he'd said.

"We didn't come alone," Aulus said. "Thirty head of cavalry wait for us outside. I expect you to have them all fed and bathed properly."

"I'd allow the horses to use my baths before those ruffians," I jested. "How are they? How are my men?"

I led them to the triclinium.

"Your men? Are they still his men, Lucius?" Aulus asked.

"Hmm . . . I'm not sure. Seems to me Aulus has been leading them since October. I think they might be his men?"

I laughed. "Just tell me how they are and lower your voices or my wife will pose more threat to you than all the rebels in Italy."

The smiles faded from their eyes as we walked. "We'll talk about those things," Lucius said. "But for now, please introduce us to our niece."

Of course, they were not brothers of mine or Arrea, but they were uncles nonetheless. I intended to raise Toria to consider them as such and expected them to embrace and protect her as if she was their kin.

Mother hurried to embrace the boys when we entered, though she remained silent as if she walked on cat's paws. Lucius lost his mother at an early age, and his grandfather raised him. Aulus had good parents, but ones who constantly found themselves vexed by their twin boys' mischief. My mother helped raised them both, and the love between them was still apparent.

"Rhea, you have not aged a day," Aulus said, ever the charmer.

Lucius, however, turned his gaze on Toria the moment mother released him. His mouth hung open, and his breathing seemed to stop.

"She is perfect," he said, his voice less than a whisper.

Both had been at war without pause for nearly ten years. Lucius had barely known a time without warfare since he was old enough to shave. New life is beholden as more precious and beautiful to such men, even the gruffest and most grizzled of old veterans.

"Would you like to hold her?" Arrea asked, her voice expertly leveled to be heard but not disturb Toria.

The question stunned Lucius. He looked down at his arms. One of his hands was still strong, but the other was missing. He'd lost it in Greece and was lucky to escape with his life.

"Oh come, Lucius, you can hold a child with one hand," Aulus said.

"May I sit?" He swallowed.

I gestured toward a couch, and once he found himself seated, he accepted Toria into his arms.

"Just cradle her head there." I showed him how, and although awkward at first, he settled in. He'd never been around children much and wasn't old enough to remember his mother modeling this behavior.

Toria squirmed in his arms but was otherwise content.

Lucius shook his head. "Arrea, I want to know right now who the real father is," he said. "There is no way Quintus Sertorius produced something so beautiful."

I smiled. "The beautiful comes from her mother. The strength in her grip is my own."

Lucius continued to admire Toria until he begrudgingly passed her off to Aulus. Unlike Lucius, Aulus naturally took Toria into his muscular arms and cooed and bobbed her until she fell asleep.

We enjoyed this time, but soon she would need feeding and an undisturbed nap.

"Would you like something to eat before you leave?" mother asked them.

Aulus shook his head. "We have rations back with the horses. Perhaps you'd like to join us, Quintus? Legionary food might not sate you any longer, but you might enjoy feeling like a man again."

I watched Arrea as she took Toria to the darkness of our room. "Lead the way, you ruffians."

We exited my home and entered my barren farmland. I'd barely seen the sun the past few weeks, and the heat was considerably hotter than when I last worked my fields.

"I see your fields are . . . unprepared," Lucius said.

The dirt crunched beneath our feet as we made for the cavalrymen in the distance. "You must be planning on returning to camp, then?" Aulus asked.

I shook my head. "Unfortunate events have delayed planting. But I'm not returning. Not yet," I said.

"I only jested," Aulus said.

Lucius added beneath his breath, "We could certainly use you though."

I stopped in my tracks. Did they have another intention for visiting beside meeting my daughter?

Lucius reached out and patted my back with his nub. "There is something you need to see."

The riders were lounging in the shade of a few old oaks as their horses grazed when we arrived.

"On your feet!" Aulus shouted. "Officers afoot, boys."

The riders groaned from the heat but stood in unison and saluted.

I returned the gesture and greeted several I remembered from the year prior.

Lucius snapped, and a rider led three horses to us.

"It's not far, but the journey will be easier on horseback," Lucius said.

"We don't want you passing out from the heat in front of the men, now do we?" Aulus jested as he swept up on one horse's back.

"And where are you taking me?" I said and mounted up.

"Seeing is better than hearing, I believe," Lucius said.

We trotted off, at first toward Barca's home, but eventually we broke off toward the north.

Still early in the year, the terrain around us was already rolling and lush. Vibrant green grass covered the hillsides, punctuated by clusters of wildflowers in early bloom. The white-capped Apennine Mountains surrounded us in the distance.

Lucius led us down a well-trodden dirt path through the winding hills, bordered by moss covered fences built long ago. Intermittent groves of olive trees provided occasional shade from the midday sun.

"You said you'd tell me how things are in camp," I said. "I'd like to hear."

I reminded myself that it didn't matter. There was nothing I could do about the state of the legion or the war efforts. But I levied many of those legionaries myself and shed blood along-side them. I couldn't resist the desire to know.

Lucius continued to lead the way. "Fair," he said. "Restless from winter, but not ready for battle either."

The conversation was punctuated by the chirping of birds, the rustling of leaves, and the gentle thud of horses' hooves on the earthy path.

"I assumed Marius would have them in fighting shape by now," I said.

Aulus chuckled.

From his side profile, I could see Lucius's jaw tightening. "Marius retired from the war. Bought a home in Baiae and now spends his days in the bathhouses. This year's consuls are commanding the legions."

We picked up the pace, the breeze now overcoming the heat. The wind blew the overgrown locks of hair on my forehead.

"You'll have to remind me. Who are our consuls?" I said.

Aulus shook his head. "You really are behind, aren't you?" he said.

"You should know, *amice*. News travels slowly in Nursia," I said.

"An aristocrat by the name of Lucius Porcius Cato," Lucius said. "And a ludicrously wealthy nobody named Pompeius Strabo."

Aulus chuckled. "They say Strabo is the most hated man in Rome."

"Some say he's also never set foot there," Lucius added.

"One can gain Rome's highest office with coin now, I suppose," I said.

I'd given up on politics before even stepping away from the legion and was rather disinterested in the personal backgrounds of powerful men.

"Are they suited to lead? Can they win the war?" I asked.

Neither responded for a moment, and that told me enough.

"Strabo is greedy and coarse, from what I'm told." Lucius blocked the sun from his eyes as he scanned the steep hill passages before us. "I've heard he doesn't even join his men on the battlefield but lets his officers command for him. That's problematic because the quality of the officers is lacking."

"And Cato?" I asked.

Lucius determined the proper path to wherever he was leading us and quickened the pace.

"There aren't many old aristocrats who lead armies well," Aulus said.

I sighed. "I've learned from experience."

"Sulla and his legion . . . what do they call themselves? 'Sulla's Fist'? They are under Cato's command, as are we. But Sulla reports to Cato in name only. He's utterly autonomous. The war efforts rest more on his shoulders than anyone."

My stomach churned. A yearning in my breast. There were many men in the legion who were as capable as I. They could handle this. Rome would prevail with or without me, I told myself. But there was a certain pride that remained within me, an arrogance perhaps, that believed I was the only one who could save the Republic.

I thought of Toria's scrunched nose and tiny, wrinkly feet, and forced the thought from my mind.

"Are we almost there, brothers?" I gazed up at the sun and estimated the time. "I should not tarry much longer."

Lucius dismounted and tied his horse's reins around a large, jagged rock. "Nearly there, but we should go the rest of the way on foot."

My curiosity was marked with a sense of apprehension. Something was off.

It wasn't long before we reached the precipice of the hill.

As we neared the top, Aulus said, "Best we keep low now."

They crouched, and I did the same.

Once at the top, they lowered their bellies to the dirt. I crawled beside them.

They came to a stop. Lucius pointed down to the valley below, where a massive fortress was constructed. Countless thousands of soldiers trained. Some marching, others practicing with pila, others with swords on straw dummies with Roman helmets.

The Samnite army.

"The legions of Papius Mutilus," Lucius said.

"Vast, aren't they?" Aulus said.

I thought back to our journey here and the conversations we shared along the way. The ride hadn't taken a full hour.

The rebel army of Rome's oldest and most formidable enemy was within an hour of my home. It was almost incomprehensible to me that they were so close.

"Well?" Aulus said.

I lacked words. What could I say? What could I do? The

foragers who attacked my home indicated the Samnites were close, but I had no notion of the degree.

My farm, where my infant daughter now slept on the breast of my wife, was only a steep but scalable hill and a brisk march away from Mutilus and his legions.

"Why have you brought me here?" I asked.

"We thought you should know. What you do with this knowledge is your choice alone, of course," Lucius said.

Orders in the Oscan tongue rose from the camp, as did the echoed shouts of the commander's men.

"Foragers attacked my home," I said. "We killed them." I spoke almost to myself.

"When one has come, more will follow," Lucius said.

Aulus frowned. "Especially if they seek vengeance for their fallen."

"War season will be upon us in days," I said. "They'll likely move on."

Lucius sighed. "The question is whether they will squeeze the area dry before departing," he said. "Rome has a vast empire to draw resources from to feed their armies. The rebels have only the land around them."

"We just want you to be safe, Quintus," Aulus said, in a rare moment of utter seriousness.

My mind returned to the cremation of my comrades. And to Barca's *ludus* and his promise.

We would be safe behind his walls. Raiding armies usually spared gladiators—like priests and men of medicine—from their plundering and destruction. Whoever won the war would need entertainment to appease the masses when reestablishing order.

"Let's return," I said. "Scouts could swarm these hills."

I'd seen what they wanted me to see, so they offered no resistance.

Lucius said they didn't intend to convince me to return to war, but he must have known Mutilus would do that for him.

I'd drifted into a false sense of security in my new home. A feeling of safety and peace I'd desired all my life, but one that was as fragile as a whisper and as false as a lie. The foragers proved that. Mutilus's legions proved that.

Most of the ride back to my home was in silence. Only a few times did they speak up.

"Rome passed legislation giving citizenship to any Italians not currently under arms," Lucius said.

Usually, I would have welcomed such news with joy. This would stop more allies from betraying us, but it would do nothing to stop those currently at arms. It would do nothing to protect my home and my family.

"Without new tribes lending their support to the rebels, we can win this war," Aulus said.

"We have few obstacles left," Lucius said. "The first is to take Samnium. They will fight until the last man otherwise."

"And the other?" I said. "What is the other obstacle?"

"We must take Asculum," Aulus said. "The city that started this war. It is a beacon of hope to every man who harbors hate for Rome. It's been under siege on-and-off since the beginning of the war, and yet it still holds strong."

"Until Samnium is taken, until the city of Asculum falls, we will have no peace," Lucius said.

When we returned, I offered to feed Lucius and Aulus, and I offered them a bed if they'd like to spend the night. But I had no shelter for their men, and they both agreed it was safer, paradoxically, to travel under the cover of night. War season would begin soon, and they could not delay.

I bid them farewell with a firm embrace, but one much less joyous than I'd greeted them with.

Toria was waking and fussy when I entered. I gave Arrea some rest and rocked my daughter back to sleep in my arms.

But as soon as she'd fallen back into sleep, I swaddled her up and placed her back in the small bed beside mine. Then I gathered our things.

No matter how much I sought to resist it, war was upon us. And we were not safe. Despite my desire for safety, despite all the sacrifices I'd made to earn it, my wife and daughter were still in danger.

SCROLL IV

Gavius Sertorius—Four Days after the Ides of March, 665 Ab Urbe Condita

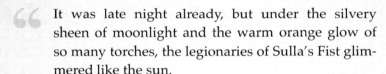 It was late night already, but under the silvery sheen of moonlight and the warm orange glow of so many torches, the legionaries of Sulla's Fist glimmered like the sun.

We'd grown over the winter. My commander's power and authority had expanded, as did the troops under his control. We numbered more than twenty-thousand strong now. And that vast sea of Roman soldiers stood in formation like an army of statues.

The night's silence was punctuated only by the soft rustling of chain mail and the occasional snort of a horse. The deep rhythmic breathing of thousands of men underpinned the soft hum of the priest before us.

I ran my fingers through the mane of the horse beneath me, but otherwise remained as still as the others. We'd been here for hours now, but Sulla insisted we do everything the proper Roman way.

A priest of Mars stood before a temporary altar a hundred paces or so before the formation of legionaries. Clad in robes as white as our Sulla's Fist tunics, the priest searched the entrails of a sacrificial ewe lamb.

The city of Pompeii waited in silent anticipation a mile behind the toiling priest. They'd taken up the rebel cause, and now the time for their punishment had arrived. With the war god's blessing, their fate would be sealed.

I tightened my grip on the hilt of my gladius, the leather-wrapped handle now slick with sweat. With bated breath, I awaited the confirmation of war season. I was hungry. All of us were. Not just for battle but for victory. Not just for victory but for glory. To be admired. To win favor and praise and decorations. To be remembered. To be eternal. And most of all, to have our indomitable commander, Lucius Cornelius Sulla, glance our way with a nod of approval.

I saw the weight of what war does to a man in my father's eye the last time I'd seen him. He'd grown battle weary, bearing the weight of loss and endless toil. I wasn't bound so. I'd tasted war for the first time the previous year, and I'd yearned for it since winter's arrival. It was almost time.

The priest, the harbinger of death and chaos, stepped back from the sacrificial lamb and raised its bloody liver above his head.

"The gods have spoken!" His voice cut through the cool night air like a knife. "War season has begun!"

As if a dam had burst, the legions erupted in a

deafening roar of cheer and applause. So loud I couldn't distinguish my voice from the rest of the twenty thousand. One unified voice.

Sulla emerged from our rapturous forces, and we all watched him with the same reverence usually reserved for gods. He hoisted a pilum above his shoulder.

We watched and waited as Sulla drew back the pilum with a warrior's grace. With a swift and fluid motion, he hurled it away from camp and toward enemy territory, the symbolic declaration of war. It whistled through the night air, its silver tip glistening in the torchlight. The pilum's arc was a vow of intent, it's landing a promise of conquest. It plunged into the earth as if it were a lightning bolt from Jupiter himself.

Pompeii. The rebel city that stood defiantly in the darkness before us. We would besiege the city, and we would conquer it.

Sulla turned back to us and unsheathed his sword. Thrusting the blade toward the pale moon, he shouted "Mars!"

"Mars!" In repetition we chanted and shoved our own swords toward the heavens.

My gaze fixed on the high walls. My father earned his first military decoration by being the first to scale the walls of an enemy city. I would do the same if Sulla would let me. The sharp teeth of the barricades wrapping around the stone walls taunted me, but I'd prepared myself. I could defeat my fear.

"Mars!" I shouted with them again.

The weight of legacy, of the shadow of my father's reputation, of Sulla's expectation, all rested on my shoulders. But I was ready. I would carve my name into the annals of Roman history. I would earn my place beside legends like Achilles.

War season had begun.

 After our war chants reached their crescendo, the proper celebration began.

The festival of the Agonia had begun. The feast of Mars, ushering in war season the only way it should be, with feasting and a week's ration of wine in a few hours.

Mars was a god who fought hard and drank harder. A festival in his honor would require the same, and Sulla was not one to offend the gods.

"Drink to the final year we aren't known as the saviors of Rome!" Sulla roared.

He dismissed our formations, and the celebration began. I and the other officers waited only to take our horses back to the stable.

The next morning, we would roll out of bed with splitting heads and groaning stomachs, and begin the siegeworks around Pompeii. But tonight was for celebration.

Our senior tribune, Lucullus, found me soon after Sulla dismissed the formation. He clapped me on the shoulder and thrust a jug of wine into my arms. "To victory!"

"To victory!" I drank deeply.

I enjoyed legionary wine now. Despite the heavy spice and poor quality, it was becoming easier and easier to drink. I needed to be careful lest I lose control of myself.

"Are you ready?" he said.

"To get drunk or to fight?"

He laughed. Lucullus was a serious man by nature, always focused on whatever task lay ahead. But tonight, he was cheerful. "Both."

"I'm ready. It's been two hundred and thirty-one days since our last battle."

He seemed impressed. "You've been keeping count."

We watched the legionary musicians as they ceremonially cleansed their instruments for war. The priest of Mars, still bloody from his haruspices, helped them.

"I've been waiting. I'm ready for my next opportunity."

"You'll receive that, and much more," Lucullus said. "I only wish Cicero was still here to experience the same."

Despite the song-singing and laughter of the surrounding legionaries, we both lapsed into momentary sullenness. Cicero was a fellow tribune of Sulla's legion, and he'd become a close friend. He was a poor soldier by any measure and had a squeamish disposition toward violence and bloodshed. Still, Lucullus and I relied on his wisdom and insight.

During the winter, the senate ordered Cicero to serve the remainder of his tribunate under Consul Pompeius Strabo. Nominally, this was because Strabo needed officers who were native to the area he commanded. But I wondered if Sulla orchestrated it all. Unlike Lucullus and me, Sulla had little tolerance for Cicero's cynicism and inadequacy in battle.

The musicians raised their newly purified trumpets.

Lucullus smiled. "If we aren't sleeping tonight, neither will the citizens of Pompeii." He gestured to the musicians. "Let them resound throughout Italy, boys!" he said.

The trumpets blared out. As legionaries are required to lie down their swords for winter, trumpeters also store their instruments until war season. Despite this, they were right in tune, and louder than ever. Pompeii would not be sleeping tonight.

I leaned closer to Lucullus and raised my voice. "Sulla gave me an exceptional vintage as a birthday gift. I've been saving it for a special occasion, but tonight seems as good as any. Let me fetch it," I said.

I navigated through crowds of drinking legionaries toward the tribune's quarters. I entered through the back entrance, avoiding the bed that used to belong to Cicero, its emptiness a constant reminder of his departure. When I arrived at my cot, I found a letter on my pillow.

The seal itself looked marred, but I didn't get letters often, so I eagerly opened it without inspecting further.

The handwriting within was ornate and familiar. My father's.

Dear Gavius,

I've been wanting to write you for some time but waited until I could provide you with good news. You are Rome's newest older brother. Arrea gave birth to a healthy child. A girl. Your sister!

When you look at her, you can see reflections of our entire family. Without stealing too much credit from her mother, little Toria, as we've been calling her, is undeniably a Sertorius. She has plentiful, dark hair like when you were born. Her eyes remind me of your grandmother's, and Rhea doesn't deny it.

We all miss you and eagerly await your arrival. Toria longs to meet you. I know you have many responsibilities, and your mother and I are both so proud of you and what you're doing. Still, I hope you can visit soon.

Follow the gods. Follow your heart. Do as you are called to do. And we will wait, with eyes cast on the horizon, for your arrival.

Your father,
Quintus Sertorius

I rolled up the letter and burst back out into the camp.

"Where's that vintage you promised?" Lucullus called out when he spotted me.

"I completely forgot it," I said. "Do you know where I can find the commander?"

He pointed toward the edge of camp, where Sulla continued to stare out over the land he would soon conquer.

I hurried to him.

"Gavius, my boy, look how the stars have come out to usher in our victory." Sulla placed an arm around my shoulder and pointed to the sparkling sky.

"The gods are with us, legate," I said.

"That's right. The gods hate traitors."

"May I steal a moment of your time?"

He turned to me, a serious look in his eye. "Of course," he said.

Despite his position and everything required of him, he never failed to give me his full attention when I needed it.

"I received this letter." I extended it to him. He accepted it but kept his eyes on mine. "My parents just had a child." I smiled as I spoke the words aloud for the first time.

"Boy or girl?" he asked.

"A girl. Healthy and strong from the sound of it."

He smiled. "That's good for you," he said.

I considered those words.

He continued. "I'm happy for your family. I'll sacrifice twenty doves to the child's good health and to your father's good fortune."

Vague rumors about the animosity between my father and Sulla had abounded for years. Some said they were political enemies. But even if their views differed, perhaps they still respected one another. Sulla never failed to speak fondly of my father and offer his favor.

"Thank you, legate, truly," I said. "I thank you for your sacrifice, as I'm sure my father would."

A strange look passed over his eyes as he turned back toward Pompeii. "I suppose you mean to ask me for leave?"

His response caught me off guard. "I . . . well. Yes, I suppose. I'd like to visit my sister. When I'm able of course."

The average legionary wouldn't be granted permission to leave for something as sentimental as the birth of a sibling, but I was an officer. One of Sulla's chosen. Perhaps it wouldn't be unreasonable if I took a brief holiday before the fighting began.

He nodded. "Certainly. I will not restrict you," he said. "Go with fortune."

I'd expected something more. Resistance, perhaps? Or at least . . . I'm not sure. But something.

"Thank you, legate," I said. "I will not be long."

"I only hate that you'll miss the battle," Sulla said, eyes still fixed on Pompeii. "I know you long for glory. This would be your chance to earn it."

I deflated. "Yes . . . I have desired this."

More than glory, I yearned for Sulla's approval. Despite his blessing, I could feel his disappointment.

I'd hoped I could make the journey to my father's home and back before the battle, but Sulla didn't seem to think this was possible. And I couldn't expect him to delay plans for the entire legion because of my personal desires.

"You must do what is right. Follow the gods. Follow your heart," he said.

Strange, I thought. That was precisely what my father wrote. The gods must be trying to tell me something.

But if so, what would that mean? What did the gods desire of me? What direction would my heart lead me?

"When will we fight the Pompeians?" I stalled. I knew he would need an answer, and now I wasn't certain what to do.

"Soon. The rebels will send reinforcements, and we'll defeat them first. Then the city will fall to us. If they don't surrender voluntarily, I will give Pompeii over to the men for plunder."

Pompeii's wealth was vast. I cared little for taking trinkets off the battlefield's dead, but what I could earn in a siege like that was unfathomable. I was nearing my twentieth year, and by the time we won the war, I would be expected to buy a home. Land, slaves, furniture . . . it would be a costly venture. Missing an opportunity like this would be costly.

"If I travel by horse, I could be there in five days of hard riding. I could make it back in ten."

Sulla shrugged. "I suppose, though, that wouldn't leave you much time with your sister," he said. "We'll see battle many times in the next two weeks, I believe."

I couldn't fathom the men fighting without me. It didn't feel right. No, it was wrong.

"But there will be many more battles." He clapped me on the shoulder. "Do what you must, Gavius."

I thought of my sister. I wondered what she looked like, what she would feel like in my arms. Arrea would be beaming. Father would be at peace, more like the man I knew from childhood than the one I last saw on the battlefield. I yearned to see all this, to experience it.

But I couldn't do it.

"I'll remain," I said.

Sulla couldn't restrain his smile. He kissed my head. "You won't regret it."

"It won't take long to end this war," I said. "I'll visit then."

He cupped his hands round his mouth and shouted toward Pompeii. "You hear that? I'm coming for you, Pompeians, and Gavius Sertorius is coming with me!"

The legionaries behind us cheered.

I'd made the right decision.

It didn't feel like it as I woke with the sun and twenty thousand hungover legionaries. We sweated the poison out under the beating Italian sun as we began siegeworks. It was here scouts arrived and informed us of a Samnite army arriving within a day's march to aid Pompeii.

"Wonderful!" Sulla clapped at the news. "A few thousand left behind can maintain the siege. Pompeii will offer little resistance. Let's greet the Samnites!"

The blood from the sacrificed ewe lamb had yet to dry. Our trumpets still dripped with ceremonial oil.

War season had just begun, and battle was upon us. This would be a bloody summer. And I was ready.

SCROLL V

QUINTUS SERTORIUS—FIVE Days after the Ides of March, 665 Ab Urbe Condita

There was a nip in the air as we loaded the wagons, but by the time we reached the road, it was gone. With war season, even the mornings would soon fill with heat.

Mother and Arrea sat beside me, Toria swaddled between them. Priscus sat behind us, staring off at the horizon. So much had changed since he signed up to work on my farm.

I flicked the reins, and we set off for Barca's *ludus*.

After I spoke with Arrea and my mother, they both agreed going to Barca's was the only sensible thing to do. Perhaps some would find it cowardly to abandon your home, but I wasn't concerned with the opinions of others. All of Rome could insult me if it meant my family was safe.

Overgrown trees cast shadows over the road for most of the journey. A gentle breeze rustled the leaves. Nursia's countryside was peaceful, even with an enemy army so nearby.

Two of Barca's gladiators guarded his gate, each of them

heavily armed and wearing helmets useful for fighting and entertainment but limiting for sight.

"State your business," one of them said, as both raised their spear tips in our direction.

"My name is Quintus Sertorius, I am here to speak with—"

"Apologies, *domine*," the first gladiator said. He must have remembered me from the funeral. "Right this way."

He and the other gladiator pulled two horsehair ropes to swing the heavy wooden gates open.

The sounds of sparring combatants flooded out to greet us. As we entered the *ludus*, I was both surprised and unsurprised to find Barca standing in the middle of three combatants.

"Come, come," he taunted them. "Attack at once. I surely cannot defeat you all?"

The three warriors nodded to one another and lunged at him, all at once.

Barca stepped forward, narrowly dodging one sword while the two gladiators on his flanks crashed into each other. Fortunately, the swords they used were wooden, otherwise the blows might have been fatal.

"Your first lesson today: never listen to your enemy. He is lying. Deception is easiest way to kill foes." He swung his training weapon around and cracked the third gladiator on the back of the head. "You may deceive, but never be deceived."

The three gladiators stood and nursed their wounds. Wooden or not, the swords still left splinter-laced cuts.

He turned and caught sight of me. Without pause, he thrust his sword into the sand and bowed. His gladiators did the same.

"I should pay for such a spectacle," I said.

Barca raised, but the others remained on one knee, as disciplined as any Roman legion I'd ever seen.

"For you, always free." He made his way to the cart but looked past me to the sleeping babe in Arrea's lap. "My little warrior." He smiled.

"We're sorry to arrive unannounced, but—"

"Nonsense." He shook his head. "You are welcome. This time, any time. Come, come." He gestured toward a place I could station the carriage and dismount.

Only now did he notice the crates in the back of our carriage.

"To which god should I sacrifice for your arrival?" he said.

I wondered if that was the Numidian way of asking why I'd come.

We shook hands, and I looked him directly in the eye. "I've come to you for shelter, *amice*."

He straightened when he heard the Latin word for friend. "You have it. Women and babe may stay in my finest rooms." He turned and shouted to another gladiator. "Dimitrius, fetch cook! Roasted peacock and Sardinian oysters."

"That's quite unnecessary . . ." I said.

I'd expected, for whatever reason, more resistance. I'd planned out a speech and several things I could offer him in return for his protection. Clearly, he wasn't interested in compensation.

"Romans like feasts, yes? Let me give one."

His straightforward mannerisms forced me to smile. I placed a hand on his shoulder. "We're a simple people, truly. We would not inconvenience you if it wasn't for the looming threat of rebel armies."

His jaw flexed. "They will not threaten us here. Nothing to gain. Much to lose."

I nodded. "That's why we've come."

I was unaccustomed to asking for charity. I found it difficult. Only Barca's affable nature put me at ease.

"Stay as long as you like," he said. "I keep my men in line."

I offered a hand back to Arrea to help her down. Barca helped my mother down.

"If there is anything I can do for you in return, just say the word."

"Teach these pups to fight." He threw a thumb back at his gladiators.

"Gladly."

I wondered why Barca was so charitable. Romans enslaved him, and now he offered shelter to a Roman he barely knew.

Barca ordered his gladiators to carry in everything we brought with us. He showed us to our spacious and luxuriously furnished rooms. Once we settled in, he organized a feast.

He presented many delicacies—more lavish than a patrician's symposium—but I could eat very little.

Why? We were safe now. There was nothing more to fear if we remained within the *ludus* walls. But still something gnawed at me like a parasite. It wasn't in my blood to hide while Romans fought. I didn't know how long I could stay here.

The room we stayed in contained an expensive mattress of feathers and threaded sheets. It was the softest I'd ever felt, save perhaps in the opulent home of Gnaeus Caepio when I was a young man. Still, I couldn't sleep.

I rocked to my feet and sat on the corner of the bed. Toria was sleeping in a crib there, and I watched her in the pale moonlight pouring in through the open shutters above the bed.

Her nose wrinkled; she puckered her lips. I wondered what she was dreaming.

I placed my hand inside the crib, and as carefully as I could manage, I ran a finger over her cheek. It was softer than any fabric sheets.

Toria was safe. At peace, because she was protected and loved. That's all that mattered.

A soft voice cut through the night silence.

"I know you must go," Arrea whispered.

I turned but could barely see her in the darkness. I thought she might be dreaming. Since Toria was born, the sleepless nights had led to some interesting conversations with my half-awake wife.

"Go where, my dove?" I humored her.

"Back to war. To your legions." She sat up in the bed now, and her eyes were clear and alert.

I couldn't find the words to reply. I continued stroking Toria's cheek.

She continued. "You must end this."

I shook my head. "Rome has other officers. Many are just as capable as I am."

She made her way to the edge of the bed and sat beside me. "We both know you are gifted," she said. "Gifted or cursed. The gods gave you the ability to lead. To command. Rome needs you."

I couldn't resist any longer and pulled Toria from the crib. Fortunately, she only babbled for a moment before falling asleep again in my arms.

"I cannot leave her," I said. "I cannot leave you, not again."

"This is different," she said.

"Why?" I peered at Toria's innocent face. "For once, no senator has ordered me to take up arms."

"And that's precisely why you must go," she said. "This time you control your fate."

After so many years of distance, and the struggle we'd endured to protect our marriage while I was away, these words surprised me. But she was right. Whether the gods had blessed or cursed me, I knew I wouldn't be able to remain in safety and comfort while my men fought and died.

"If the rebels win," she said, "there will be nowhere in Italy safe for a senator and his family. Not even behind the walls of Barca's *ludus*."

Toria stirred. It was that time in the night she usually became hungry. I cradled her head and passed her to Arrea.

"What of us?" I said. I knew the answer wouldn't be enough to keep me from my duty, but I had to ask.

"Toria and I will wait for you," she said. "You will come back to us."

Her eyes shimmered in the moonlight. There was more resolve in her now than I'd ever seen before. She was making a sacrifice and I vowed to myself that it would not be in vain.

"I will return to you," I said.

The longer I waited, the harder the departure would be. The more time I spent behind Barca's walls, the more tempting it would be to remain.

I could not tarry.

Fresh air always cleared my mind. I needed to think. I needed to decide what to do next, and preferably come to a conclusion before daybreak. Once Arrea and Toria fell back asleep, I got out of bed and threw a cloak over my shoulders.

I made my way out to the *ludus*, where gladiators were still sparring under the light of a few torches and a silver moon. Most *lanista* would keep their men in cells overnight, but Barca was not most *lanista*. He was almost like an older brother to them; that much I could see.

I watched as the gladiators laughed, chugged sour wine, and sang songs about their many victories. The gladiator's life was not an easy one, but I admired the way they accepted their lot.

"Their skill is quite impressive, isn't it?" My mother appeared beside me.

"Can you imagine a legion full of men like these? They could conquer entire nations." I rested on a wooden railing. "Are they keeping you awake?"

She smiled. "You know I could sleep through an earthquake," she said. "But a mother always knows when she's needed. Toria is fast asleep, so I could only assume *my* child could use some assistance."

I placed a hand on her back. "That's a remarkable skill, mother," I said.

"What's on your mind?"

I took a deep breath. "Arrea and I just spoke. We both agreed

I need to serve Rome again. I need to help finish this war, or none of you will be safe."

She nodded. "I knew you wouldn't be able to stay here for long. Your father and I always knew the gods destined you for greatness."

The gladiators threw down their swords and wrestled one another into the dirt, laughter filling the night air.

"I just want to end the war," I said. "Rome will always have more battles to fight, but if we pacify the rebels, at least Italy will be safe. Foreign nations may threaten our borders, but lifetimes might pass before citizens are at risk again. That's all I desire. I want Arrea and Toria to be safe. I want you to be safe."

She rested up against me and wrapped her arm around mine. "Where will you go?"

"That's what I'm trying to decide," I said. "Where could I serve Rome best?"

"You are a great warrior. None can deny that. You are as powerful on the front lines as you are orchestrating tactics across the battlefield. But your father and I . . . we always believed you would leave your mark in Rome. Perhaps you could serve best through political position?"

"I've considered that," I said. "If I pass a law offering citizenship to any rebels willing to lay down their arms, the war will swiftly end."

"To Rome then?" she said.

I sighed. "The elections are still months away. And besides, we can hardly take the entire family to Rome. The roads are treacherous and a single cry from Toria could bring rebel scouts down on us. I will not go to Rome without all of you with me, and Rome must win the war in the north before we can make the journey," I said. "Rome will have to wait."

A shadow passed through the torchlight beside us. "Ending wars is what Quintus Sertorius does best." Priscus joined us at the wooden railing.

"Somnus eludes you as well?" I said.

Dark bags hung under his bloodshot eyes. "Every night since Atilius died. When I close my eyes, I see his face. I hear Silvanus's puerile quips endlessly."

There were no words I could offer to comfort him, so we remained in silence until he stepped past the wooden railing and began drawing in the sand with the toe of his sandal.

"This is Italy," he said.

"You're quite the artist, Priscus," mother said.

"We're here in central Italy," Priscus continued. "Cato's armies are camped nearby. They are mainly cleaning up the vestige of defeated tribes. Consul Pompeius Strabo besieges Asculum in the north, and Sulla leads his men in the south, currently near Pompeii. The real fighting takes place on those two fronts."

"The men I levied last year serve under Cato. That's where Lucius and Aulus are currently," I said.

Priscus shrugged. "Seems like a natural fit, then. You were inseparable from Lucius Hirtuleius all those years in Gaul."

Mother didn't seem convinced. "I'm sure you'd like to return to your men and your companions."

"I would, but the war efforts hinge elsewhere," I said. "I have no intention of leaving my daughter to spend the year wasting time in camp."

A few gladiators began singing, another pounded on his shield like a drum.

"Two choices then," Priscus said. "Go south to join Sulla, or ride north and fight under Pompeius Strabo, whoever he is."

I hopped over the wooden railing and grabbed a nearby torch to illuminate Priscus's crude rendition of Italy.

The thought of serving under Sulla revolted me, but at least I could reunite with my son. I could keep Gavius safe.

But Rhea was right, as mothers often are. If I ran for office, the tribunate perhaps, I could pass legislation to stop the war faster than by winning any number of battles. Nothing would spare more Roman lives nor offer the Republic a greater chance of rehabilitation.

Attempting to end the war would create animosity in those who wish to continue waging it. This would make me enemies among the people and the aristocrats in equal measure, but I would sacrifice any amount of prestige and reputation for the good of the Republic. Even if it destroyed my career, it would be worth it.

"I should go north," I said. "If I can help Strabo take the city of Asculum, passage to Rome would be safe. We can travel to the city, and I can stand for election. I have no desire to be a magistrate, but it's where I can serve Rome best."

"You'd have my vote," Priscus said.

"Hear, hear!" mother cheered.

The gladiators shouted their approval as well, although they likely had no idea what they supported.

"Do you know anything of Pompeius Strabo?" I asked them both.

"He's Picentes, if you can believe it, but his family have been Roman citizens for generations. Now, he's leading an army against his own people," Priscus said. "Unlikely to make local friends with the strategy, but it earned him the consulship."

"Lucius and Aulus said he's . . . unliked."

"You can help him win," mother said.

I turned to Priscus. "Will you join me? You can patch up my wounds, like old times."

His gaze fell. "I cannot," he said. "I don't think I can witness the death of another comrade."

I smiled. "I'm not planning to die, *amice*."

"No, you have a habit of evading death. But everyone else."

"We'll benefit from your presence here, Priscus," mother said.

After a moment of silence, Priscus shook his head. "I cannot join you, Sertorius, and I also cannot stay. I'm called elsewhere, to wander for a while. Perhaps I'll find my way back to Gaul."

I could see my mother's disappointment. She'd come to look

after our three helpers as sons of her own. Now two of them were dead and the other was leaving her.

But neither of us offered any resistance. I understood all too well how the past haunted Priscus. Perhaps leaving Italy was what he needed most.

"Be safe on the road, will you?" I said.

He smiled. "How many times did we scout Gallic hills swarming with Cimbri warriors and Teutone bandits? I'll be fine," he said. "Worry not for me. Your journey is far more important. You have a Republic to save."

I took a wooden sword from a nearby weapons rack and shoved it into the sand where Priscus marked the rebel stronghold of Asculum.

"To battle then."

SCROLL VI

GAVIUS SERTORIUS—SIX Days after the Ides of March, 665 Ab Urbe Condita

"The field of battle lay stretched out before us, a vast expanse of grassland blanketed with a heavy dew and rippled by the morning wind. In the distance, the banners of the Samnite army stood defiantly before their endless ranks. A golden bull stood out among the rest, meant to imitate the Roman eagle, which rose above our own ranks.

My horse's restless energy surged beneath me. He was ready, along with the six hundred other warhorses beside us, to charge the enemy flanks. He saved my life in battle the year before, and I vowed to ride into battle on no other steed as long as we both lived. I named him Bucephalus after Alexander's steed. Prebattle jitters developed in my hands and feet, but Bucephalus always had a calming effect on me.

So did my commander's presence. His silver

breastplate shined in the morning sun like Vesta's flame. The winter had not dulled him whatsoever. He was just as prepared for this battle as he was the last. Somehow, his distinct aroma of oils and perfumes overcame the scent of sweaty horses, freshly sharpened steel, and the musk of leather.

The leader of the Numidian cavalry leaned over and clapped me on the shoulder. "Ready, Roman?" Maharbal asked.

We'd rode into battle together many times before. I'd come to rely on his spear and *khopesh*, and Sulla did as well. The Numidian riders were the greatest I'd ever witnessed. We were blessed by the gods to have them fighting beside us.

Maharbal's eyes revealed the same insatiable hunger I felt.

It was a yearning to enter the fray. To prove oneself and earn the respect of ancestors. To step into the horrifying, breathtaking, exhilarating threshold between life and death and remain there until . . . victory.

"I'm ready," I said, and meant it.

The clinking of bridles, the soft thud of hooves on the earth, and the murmured conversation of our cavalry filled the air, a dissonant prelude to the chaos awaiting us.

The memories of last year's battles flooded back to me like a maelstrom. Deafening roars, the screams of the dying, the taste of iron and blood and dust. Part of it horrified me. Turned my stomach, made me sick. Yet something else, something more powerful perhaps, drew me in. It bade me come. The agonizing months of waiting were at an end.

Trumpets and buccinae rang out, clear and

resounding throughout the battlefield. The cavalry ranks opened as Sulla charged to the front of our formation.

His voice carried as effortlessly as the instruments. "Legionaries of Rome! Today, we meet our oldest friend in battle. Our oldest friend, and our oldest enemy." His words sharpened as he spoke them. "The Samnites have betrayed us at every opportunity. They've spit on our hands each time we've extended them. And perhaps we can fault our ancestors. For all their mercy, grace, and wisdom, they failed to see we must remind these stepsons of Italy of their place. That lesson begins today. We will punish them as we must until they fall to their knees and beg for forgiveness."

The legions erupted.

Were I in the Samnite army, I'd be terrified.

"We, we are Sulla's Fist! Rome's most elite, courageous, and deadly defenders! We will bring forth justice; we will spread the glory of the Republic from one end of Italy to the next and then . . . *Roma Invicta!*"

The war chants escalated. We'd been just five thousand the year before, now Sulla's Fist contained twenty thousand men, and our collective cries made that clear.

"*Roma Invicta!*" we roared back at him as his horse reared up. He thrust the tip of his sword at the Samnite army and the centurions bellowed out commands.

As the commander galloped back into our ranks, the legions marched. One step, all in unison, like a great machine of war crafted by Mars himself.

Sulla led the cavalry at a brisk pace. The world seemed to blur before me, and then sharpen. Blur, then sharpen. The smell of the grasses, the wind on my face, the rhythmic pounding of thousands of feet and hooves on the ground. Clearer, then nonexistent.

I tightened my grip around the reins with one hand and brandished my sword in the other.

The dance of death had begun, and this time, I was its most hungry participant.

The rebels vastly outnumbered us in every battle we'd fought against them the year prior. And yet, we prevailed. This time, we matched them man for man. None of their Samnite gods could hope to save them. And even if they could spare them the wrath of our legionaries, we had our most powerful weapon to wield: the Numidian cavalry.

Superior riders and superior steeds to any to be found in Italy, the Numidians joined the war out of loyalty to Sulla for his part in suppressing a war there years ago. And there was nothing the rebels could do to stop them.

Instead of collapsing on the exposed Samnite infantry, we passed them by. Flanking maneuvers were effective, and we used them often. But this time, Sulla had a different strategy. We would take out the enemy riders first. They were no match for the Numidians. Once they scattered, we could harass their legions without repulse.

The Samnites ignored us in the cavalry as they clashed with the legionaries of Sulla's Fist. The cacophony of war began. It was familiar to me now.

The rebels were no longer nameless, faceless

figments of my imagination. They were flesh and blood now. Men with names, families, desires, aspirations. I could see their faces as we galloped past them.

I leaned into the charge, pushing Bucephalus as hard as he allowed me. The wind was a fierce gust now, pushing my helmet up on my forehead, whipping my cloak, and rippling in my ears.

The ground beneath us quaked as we thundered forward. My heartbeat pounded to the same erratic rhythm.

Horsemen appeared on the far side of the enemy flank. Probably no more than three hundred to our six hundred, but they were still more than enough to inflict grievous casualties. Sulla said to never underestimate a man with a sword, and here there were hundreds of them on horseback.

To my surprise, the Samnite cavalry charged in our direction. I hadn't expected that. This was suicide, surely?

They careened toward us, a sea of horseflesh and sharpened steel.

I shouted. "Whoa, boy!" I tightened my legs around Bucephalus as if he wasn't doing exactly as he was supposed to.

Then, we clashed into them. The world seemed to rend in two as we met.

Horses screamed. Men shouted, cried. Metal clanged.

One enemy rider flew past me. Fortunately, he was thrusting his sword in the other direction, or it might have been my death. My sword sliced through the air just enough to nick his arm, but it wasn't deep or lethal. I had been unprepared. He kept riding, and more Samnites replaced him.

I desperately clung to my reins, feeling less sure of my grip than I remembered being the year prior. With my other arm, I extended my sword. It ricocheted off the blade of a rebel rider, cold sparks flying by as fast as the horses.

Sulla's voice rose above the tumult like a clearing of trumpets. "Send them to Dis!"

He was right there, fighting with us. I would not disappoint him.

The next rider to pass me was losing some of the speed from his initial assault. His blade was caught against the *khopesh* of a Numidian. I took advantage of the distraction and brought down my blade. It cut cleanly through the wrist of his left hand. It severed and fell, still clinging to the reins. The rider cried out, almost loud enough to make out above the screams of the horses. But he fell silent as the Numidian hooked the curve blade around his neck and sliced through in one swift, sickening motion.

The head toppled to the earth, mouth still agape and eyes in agony. The horse trampled it as it galloped off.

I felt a weakness in my limbs as I continued riding. Had the winter made me weak? The horrifying display continued to play before my eyes.

Distraction. I needed to focus. The battle was not over.

The Samnite riders mixed with our ranks. Fortunately, Numidians made up most of our cavalry, or I wouldn't have been able to distinguish friend from foe. The enemy were the ones that looked most like me.

Another rider careened forward. He aimed the dripping tip of his sword at me. His gaze was on me. Or was he glaring at another rider? He looked angry with me. Why?

Get out of your head, Gavius.

The enemy charger collided with Bucephalus and me. I swung back and forth atop him as we both struggled to keep our balance. He let out a cry, and that woke me up.

Harm me if you will, but do not injure my horse.

Once the enemy and I had both recovered from the collision, we were side by side. So close we could barely angle our swords to injure each other.

He brought his gladius overhead. I released the reins and grabbed his wrist. I attempted the same maneuver, but he caught my arm as well.

We wrestled there, seeking any kind of leverage over each other.

If possible, my heartbeat pounded even faster. Ringing in my ears. Breathless.

My eyes darted in search of a nearby ally to assist me. Everyone focused on their own skirmishes.

Without thinking, I threw my head against his. My helmet cracked into his nose. Blood dripped from the rim.

My vision sparkled like the night sky, but the Samnite's strength waned.

I gritted my teeth and roared through them as I bent back his wrist until the sword dropped from his hand.

In a moment of panic, he released his grip. My left hand now free, I clutched his throat and held him off me. I reared back and drew my sword.

I made the mistake of meeting his gaze. His eyes

were wide and wild. Anger was no longer present. It was something more akin to hunger.

Hunger for what? To kill me? To live? To say one final word before he drew his last breath?

Stop thinking. Just act.

I thrust the sword forward with as much power as I could generate, twisted up as we were.

It was enough to puncture the exposed flesh of his armpit. The blade entered easily enough. The resistance came when I reached his ribs.

With another groan of effort, I put all my weight behind the sword and forced it through.

He writhed and collapsed from the horse.

If he wasn't dead now, he would be soon.

I looked up; the world expanding as if I were exiting a tunnel.

The Samnite riders scattered. We'd broken them entirely, as expected. I was almost angry with them for such a haphazard assault. Had their commander no concern for their lives?

I spotted Sulla among the deluge of cavalrymen, his face smeared with fresh blood. "To the line!" he bellowed.

We echoed the call, the other officers and I in Latin, the Numidians in their own tongue.

Pouncing over the bodies of horses and their riders, the writhing and the dead, we rode toward the exposed back of the Samnite line.

They saw us coming.

Their line broke long before we arrived. Their centurions barked orders just like ours did, but no one heeded their commands. They scattered in all directions.

The legionaries of Sulla's Fist pursued them with vigor.

The cavalry and I chased down any who escaped the legionaries.

Thousands evaded us to the distant forests marking the boundaries of our battlefield. One would not know it by looking at the carnage on the battlefield.

Our first battle of the new year was a victory, and a decisive one.

Knowing Sulla, we would soon celebrate, but there were many more battles to fight, and I couldn't truly rejoice until we won them all.

SCROLL VII

Leaving Arrea and Toria was the hardest thing I'd ever done. With every step I made toward the siege of Asculum, the groaning in my heart deepened. I didn't have to do this. Turning around was still an option, but I refused.

I pressed on. I slept under a banner of trees and stars and never lit a fire. The light and smoke could draw unwanted attention. I stayed off the main roads when I could and always listened for the sound of rebel scouts in the distance.

I'd relinquished my command with the first snow of winter the previous year. The Roman consul in the north, a man I did not know named Pompeius Strabo, could tell me to turn right back around. He had no obligation to bring me onto his staff. If he resisted, I would have to volunteer for whatever position he had available, even if it was a demotion. I couldn't turn back now.

On the fourth day, I reached Asculum. Before me stood the citadel itself, surrounded by a vast wall of Roman siege works.

Lookouts announced my arrival long before I reached the gate.

"*Salvete, amice,*" I shouted.

"State your business," one said, his accent thick and unfamiliar.

"I am Quintus Sertorius, former quaestor and legatus of the Roman legions."

One guard eyed me curiously and spit a glob of yellow mucus by his sandals. "You the one they call 'The Hero of the North'?"

People rarely used the moniker these days, and it surprised me. "Some have called me that."

He looked to the other guard and shrugged. "Commander will want to hear from you, then."

They opened the gate and I stepped into a labyrinth. Rows of legionary tents, workshops, stables. Legionaries busied themselves in every direction, sharpening weapons, practicing marching drills, testing out the strength of their shields and pila. This was the least organized military camp I'd ever seen.

I turned back to the guards. "Where can I find the commander?"

One shrugged. "He's around."

Finding Strabo took about as long as the walk there that morning. I wandered aimlessly throughout the camp searching for officers or someone friendly enough to point me in the right direction. Most of the legionaries just stared. I was an outsider.

I eventually found the commander by chance. There was a large tent on the eastern side of the camp that caught my attention. I navigated in its direction, and upon reaching it found a rotund man whose armor shone unlike any I'd seen before. The gold breastplate glared in the sun, not a scratch or cut on it. Someone who could afford equipment like that could also afford his own army. That had to be Strabo.

If I could tell by their unique crests, several officers stood behind Strabo as he hovered over a few ballistae.

"These are the latest models, consul. Approximately double the force of the weapons we had last year." A legionary gestured to the device. "Recently constructed by Greek engineers."

"I don't trust the Greeks," came the nasally voice of the commander. "And I don't like being the first to use new equipment. What if they fail in the middle of battle?"

I positioned myself at attention just behind him.

"Well, we've tested them a great deal. They're as reliable as the model of ballistae we used last year, perhaps more so."

"And what if this happens . . ." Strabo brandished a dagger and sliced through the ballista drawstrings. "What if that happens, soldier?"

The legionary stared back, eyes wide.

"Move! I'm counting. One, two!"

A few others joined the legionary as they worked to fix the ballista with a new drawstring. It took them a long time to adjust the tautness properly, their fingers fumbling as Strabo continued counting.

"That's far too long, legionary. Far too long." Strabo shook his head. "If that happens in battle, this contraption is useless to us."

I said, "It's unlikely the strings will break in battle if they're prepared correctly." I took a careful step forward. "It's more likely that a structural fault in the timber could fail if we don't bolster the mainframe."

Everyone turned to me.

Strabo's eyes were little more than squinty slits in a ruddy, fleshy face. "Who's this then?" he said.

He positioned himself directly before me, close enough I could smell the olive oils he'd used to shave that morning.

"My name is Quintus Sertorius, former quaestor and progenitor of the XIV legion—"

He held up his hand. "Yes, yes. I'm familiar." He sized me up. If possible, his eyes narrowed even further, doughy eyelids flapping over what little was visible. "They say you were quite instrumental in the victory of the Marsi last year. That true?"

He had a peculiar manner of speaking, remarkably like the guard who'd allowed us entry.

"I commanded a flank in the battle, yes," I said.

He frowned. "They said you retired?"

"I took the winter to prepare my farm." I met his gaze. "I've returned to pledge my service."

He laughed—a sardonic and condescending chuckle—and turned back to his officers to ensure they did the same. "We've a regular Cincinnatus here," he said. "Tell me, why have you returned?"

I thought I already answered this question. "I will always serve Rome when she needs me." The words filled me with strength, but they failed to impress Strabo.

"I don't have any positions for someone of your rank. Try another army." He turned his back to me.

"With all due respect, consul, I have extensive experience with siege works and with the enemies we're fighting," I said. "I can serve with utility in whatever position I'm given."

He clasped his hands behind his back. I could tell he was smiling even as he looked away. "Must not be much money in farming." His voice trailed off as if he were thinking. He spun back toward me. "It turns out I'm in need of a new camp prefect. Last one was more useless than a plump arse on a Vestal Virgin. It's a pay decrease and demotion, but the position is yours if a senator's pride won't get in the way."

Camp prefect is an honorable position, third in the legion behind only the senior tribune and the legatus. It was still a matter of grave importance and would give me the authority to make a meaningful difference in the war effort. But having served in as a legatus and a senior tribune multiple times in the past, this was undoubtedly a demotion. He tested me.

"I accept," I said. Strabo would learn soon enough how little power and accolades motivated me.

He nodded. "Fine. Don't get yourself killed like the last one." He threw a thumb over his shoulder at a mound of dirt near the siege works tent. There was humor in his eyes as he said, "I told him to mind himself, but he stumbled too close to the enemy walls and ended up with three arrows in his chest. I've buried him here to remind him in the afterlife he should have heeded my instructions."

It was a horrible portent to bury the dead within a camp or city. Romans entomb all our dead outside the city walls for that reason. Perhaps the Picentes had different beliefs, or perhaps Strabo really wanted to make his point.

"I don't have special quarters available for you," Strabo said. "You'll have to stay with the other junior officers."

Another test.

"Of course."

"Pompey!" He shouted. Another of the officers stepped up to his side.

The young man bore an uncanny resemblance to Strabo but was more striking and in better shape. He had a round face and nose like the commander, but his eyes were wider and striking. Thinly pursed lips rested above a dimpled chin. Curly hair billowed up around the brim of his helmet.

"Yes, father?" the young man said. I noticed a touch of hesitation in his voice.

"Show our newest prefect to your tent. Ensure he's settled in and return to me presently. We have a lot more equipment to inspect."

"Heard," Pompey said. I thought this was a rather strange response, another idiosyncratic manner by which the Picentes speak, I supposed.

The younger officer said nothing to me directly, but I followed him away from the siege works.

I didn't expect this, but I suddenly missed serving under Gaius Marius, or even Titus Didius. This was going to be a long campaign.

The junior officers' quarters must have been on the complete opposite end of the camp from the siege works. We traveled in silence through parade fields of drilling legionaries and unorderly rows of tents for quite some time.

The young man didn't look back, he just assumed I was following.

"Commander Strabo is your father?" I said.

"Yes." Pompey continued. "But I didn't receive this position as a favor. I work twice as hard as the next man to earn my father's respect."

He clearly was in no mood for conversation, so I declined to reply and continued following until we reached a large tent near the eastern gate.

Pompey stopped at the entrance and held back the tent flap, allowing me to enter.

Only the soft glow of a few oil lamps lit the interior, and it took my eye a few moments to adjust.

"Here it is." Pompey entered behind me.

The smell of fresh wax and burning wicks mixed with the earthy aroma of straw, leather, and the unmistakable metallic scent of polished armor. Officer's quarters or no, this was unmistakably a barracks for young men, accompanied by all the usual body odors to prove it.

Shadows flickered on the canvas walls. A few officers lounged in their personal space. One, a lanky fellow with a mop of curly hair, strummed a small wooden lyre, filling the tent with sad melodies. Another worked diligently on a letter under flickering candlelight and didn't seem to notice us.

"The free bed is on the far side. The former occupant died of fever during the winter." Pompey spoke without emotion.

"Thank you, tribune," I said.

I unbuckled my helmet and set it on the free bed, the unspoken language of claiming your space in a legionary camp.

"Gentlemen," Pompey said, "this is Quintus Sertorius. He will be joining us."

For the first time, the two officers looked up. The musician set aside his lyre and stood.

"We're fortunate to have such a warrior join us," the man said. He extended his hand. "Gratidianus. It's a pleasure." There was something as melodious in his voice as in the songs he'd been playing. Something sad, deep, resounding, and thoughtful.

"Gratidianus . . . I believe we've met?"

I knew the name sounded familiar, but I couldn't recall his face.

The young man smiled. "I think you're correct," he said. "I believe I was with my uncle."

I finally registered it. Gratidianus was a nephew of Gaius Marius, a man whom I'd served with as much as any man over the past fifteen years.

I nodded. "Your uncle is Gaius Marius."

The officer who'd been writing the letter made a noise. "He's a distant relation of mine as well, but I chose not to claim him."

Gaius Marius was a polarizing man. There were many who disagreed with his politics, with the petty and personal squabbles he often inflated as matters of the state, his boundless desire for power and praise. Still, it was surprising to hear a relative of the six-time consul speak this way.

Gratidianus smiled. "I rather like Uncle Marius. Say what you will about his politics, what he's accomplished for Rome is unmatched."

They both looked at me, expected me to weigh in.

"I served under General Marius in many wars. We fought the Marsi together last year."

That was the least committal I could be. What I'd have to say about Gaius Marius, the good and the bad, wouldn't please either of them.

"This is my cousin." Gratidianus gestured to the other officer. "Marcus Tullius Cicero."

The young man cooled the ink on his parchment before rolling it up. He took his time before standing and offering his hand.

Cicero's grip was weak compared to his cousin. He was several inches shorter and lacked the muscles typically acquired in Rome's legion, but there was a resolve in his gaze.

"It's nice to meet you, Cicero," I said. "Perhaps we've run into each other previously as well."

He shook his head. "I don't believe so. I've spent little time by Gaius Marius's side, and that's where you usually are. From what they say."

There was a certain edge to his voice. Perhaps it was the officer's ego, or perhaps he considered me a threat.

"Well . . . it's a pleasure to make your acquaintance for the first time then."

"I've heard so much about you, I feel as if I've known you my whole life."

He brandished a cloth, and for a moment I thought he was cleaning his hands after touching mine. No, he just had to dab his nose.

I was uncomfortable with so many of Strabo's officers knowing about me. I'd rather arrive in camp with no expectations other than for bravery and service to the Republic.

"Whatever you've heard, I'm sure it was exaggerated, if not outright invented."

Cicero tapped a finger against his lip. "Interesting. You're saying your son doesn't know you very well?" he said. "Gavius told me many stories I believe to be accurate."

Hearing my son's name sent a shiver down my spine. Here was the friend Gavius had mentioned to me. Cicero.

I wanted to bombard him with questions, but I knew I shouldn't. That Cicero seemed to dislike me did concern me, though, if most of what he heard came from my own son.

"I'm sure he spoke true."

"He said you didn't write him." His eyes narrowed as he watched my response.

My jaw tightened. I'd sent him letter after letter, and never heard a response. Gavius said he never received them.

Before I replied, Cicero waved me off. "Don't worry. I know Sulla was surveilling our correspondence."

Gratidianus shook his head. "Didn't he congratulate you on my sister's betrothal before we announced it publicly?"

Cicero kept his eyes on me. "He certainly did. I let him know I didn't appreciate the invasion of my privacy, and it's likely the reason he transferred me to this legion." He returned to his chair. "The pressing question, however, is why Sulla would want to deprive a son of letters from his father."

I'd been wondering the same thing but didn't mention it.

Sulla and I had served together in the past but were usually at odds. He'd extended his hand in feigned friendship, but I refused to accept. I didn't trust Sulla, his motives, or his desires. If Marius was driven by a lust for power, Sulla was consumed by it. That sort of ambition within a man as capable as Sulla was dangerous.

When I refused to cooperate with his designs for power, to offer my loyalty to someone so unscrupulous, he attempted bribery. Then threats. When I made it clear he couldn't purchase me or frighten me into submission, he enlisted my son in his ranks while I was fighting in Greece.

He claimed to look after and protect my son. If so, I was grateful for it, but I never forgot the purpose of this arrangement. Gavius was leverage. He held my son in his fist, with power over his life and death like the Fates. Where money and threats failed, Sulla hoped my son's life would guarantee my compliance. The only question was: compliance with what? What was he planning that required a low-ranking senator and military man like myself to not intervene?

Light burst into the tent as another officer walked in.

"Speaking of my sister's fortunate husband, this is Cataline," Gratidianus said.

The light from the lamps became more erratic as Cataline entered. Perhaps it was just the wind, but the casual, congenial air between us became taut.

The young officer looked like a Capitoline statue. His coifed dark hair framed a strong jaw and Roman chin. His armor, the same standard issue as the rest, somehow seemed more tailored than the others.

"Lucius Sergius Catalina, at your service," he said. He extended his hand.

My father said you could tell a lot by the strength of a man's handshake. If so, I was uncertain what to think of Cataline. His hands were like a vise grip around mine, and I wondered if this was effortless or an effort to intimidate me.

His piercing eyes, almost predatory, fixed on me.

"Quintus Sertorius," I said. I met his gaze.

"Your name is spreading through camp like a fire in the Subura." Cataline smiled. "We're fortunate to have you among us if the stories are true."

His tone was jovial, unassuming, nonchalant. Yet his gaze remained fixed, unblinking. There was something enticing about his presence. And something unsettling.

"Well, I'd say it's about time for some *cena*, wouldn't you?" Pompey said, perhaps noticing the shift in the room.

"I dried out some meat for jerky, and rebaked the bread for biscuits," Gratidianus said. "I'll put on some porridge."

We ate around a campfire outside our tent. They shared some wine and oil with me since I'd yet to receive my own rations.

They were friendly enough. Even Cicero seemed to warm to me as the night went on. Cataline was clearly the most talkative of the lot, dominating most of the conversation by regaling us with stories of his ancestor's exploits or bawdy tales of his youthful misadventures. Gratidianus was a keen listener, always laughing or responding at just the right time, but nothing more. Cicero chirped up with a quip or two from time to time.

Pompey didn't speak. He ate quickly and cleaned his bowl, dagger, and spoon extensively. He continued to sit with us but didn't appear to hear a word of Cataline's oratory. He stared into the fire before us, transfixed by each crackle.

There was a sharp contrast in the way we all communicated. Gratidianus and Pompey had a rural accent not dissimilar from Strabo's. Cataline spoke with the refinement of an aristocrat, even if the words themselves were vulgar enough to be spoken by a drunkard on the Aventine. Cicero was more difficult to determine, but he placed emphasis on his words in a way that reminded me of the newsreader in the Forum, someone whose every word was measured and calculated with precision.

The biggest difference wasn't in our backgrounds or heritage but in age. I was much older than these men, and I'd never felt older than when I failed to understand their jokes.

I used the excuse of age to retire early. "I'm going to visit Somnus." I stood as soon as Cataline finished one of his stories.

"So soon?" Cataline said. "The sun's just setting."

"I come from the farm," I said, "where one always rises before the sun and sleeps with it."

"Careful, prefect." Cataline smiled. "You're not in the fields any longer."

I returned to my cot, took off my armor and placed it neatly in the chest by the foot of the bed. I lay down. Tomorrow would be my first full day in this legion, and I'm sure Strabo had much planned for my orientation.

I needed to get a few hours' sleep before Toria woke up.

My eye shot open as realization struck me. Toria was back in Nursia. I was in camp. I couldn't rise with her any longer. I couldn't fall asleep with her on my chest.

Longing tightened my chest. When I closed my eye, I saw only them. Arrea, as clear before my eye as a play in the Forum.

She hummed a song to our daughter and rocked her to sleep. Then they were giggling. Toria discovered her feet for the first time and tugged at them.

I slept this way fretfully for an uncertain amount of time. A nervous vibration was coursing through my body. There was no point in trying to sleep any longer. I sat up on my cot.

Cataline and Cicero were on the beds closest to me, snoring quietly. It was impossible to know for certain, but I assumed it was the middle of the night.

I stood, doing my best not to wake them. I grabbed my sword and buckled it around my hips and exited the officers' quarters.

Roman camps are never truly silent. Snoring and farting continuously belted out from the rows of legionary tents. Pack mules brayed in the baggage camps. The chain mail of guards on watch jangled as they ascended and descended to get various vantage points.

But other than that, the camp was quiet. With no wind, even the cohort and century standards refused to make any noise, as they usually did. The air was heavy and warm. It seemed to have a presence all its own.

I formulated no plan of action other than stretching my legs and easing my mind. I wandered aimlessly up the wooden stairs to the walls. Perhaps surveilling the surroundings of my new station would bring me some measure of comfort.

The walls weren't broad, but enough for three men in armor to walk abreast. They clearly constructed this camp for battle. The signs of damage to the crenellated battlements indicated it'd seen plenty.

Reaching the top, I expected to find a few guards whispering about what they missed most of their homes, while keeping their eyes on the dark horizon.

Instead, I found one guard. Seated with his head back against the leather of his chair. A cup of wine in hand.

My fists tightened. Perhaps this was how Strabo ran his

camp. But at war, surrounded by hostile rebels, this was unacceptable.

"Legionary, on your feet!" I said.

The guard didn't stand. He slowly rotated toward me, and gave me a simple nod.

"Good evening, prefect. Have you come to join me?"

I didn't recognize him at first, without his armor and high-plumed helmet. Yet his Picentes accent was unmistakable. The "guard" was none other than Strabo's son, Pompey.

"I apologize for the intrusion, tribune," I said. "What are you doing here, of all places?"

He turned his gaze back toward the dark abyss outside our fortress walls. "I could ask you the same thing."

"Fair," I said. "Sometimes I have trouble sleeping."

He kicked a stool toward me. "I'm communing with old ghosts."

I sat beside him. He offered me his wine and poured himself another cup.

"Thank you." I accepted it.

I weighed his words. Rural Italians, like myself, are more superstitious than our urban counterparts. Perhaps he was speaking literally. But there was something in his eye, a sadness in the flickering starlight. He spoke like many veterans I'd met over the course of my career, ones who'd fought for more years than young Pompey had been alive.

"Who are these ghosts you speak with?"

He brought the cup slowly to his lips and sipped gingerly. "The dead." He didn't appear interested in further explanation. "Do you ever look at the stars?"

I noticed then that he fixed his gaze not on the horizon, but the sparkling sky above us.

Pompey was a hard man to read. Even his age seemed impossible to estimate with any precision. I was a swift and accurate judge of character, but Pompey was no simple figure.

"I suppose I do as much as the next man."

I listened closely, curious what this all was about.

He took his time before replying. He lifted a hand and pointed to one of the brighter stars. "That's the Pleiades," he said. "The seven nymphs. Orion chased them across the earth for seven years until they beseeched Jupiter for aid. He transformed them into doves so they could seek refuge among the stars."

I squinted. "I can see only one."

"There are seven if you look long enough. Your eyes don't see clearly without careful inspection."

Still confused why this was a matter of discussion in the middle of the night, I kept my gaze on the star Pompey pointed out. Almost like magic, the one became three, and then five.

A smile spread across my face, a feeling of wonder men my age rarely received. "They're coming into view." I squinted and strained, the light star bursting in every direction as a result.

"Some say the stars can speak to you." He took another sip.

"Consul Strabo must have given you an impressive education for you to know so much about astronomy."

He chuckled, a low and unhappy laugh. He took another sip. "Not by Roman standards," he said. "Philosophers know little about the stars compared to fishermen, soldiers, and farmers. Fortunately, I've spent enough time with all three to learn what I have."

I took a sip of Pompey's wine. To my surprise, it was a cheap *posca*, the same vinegar swill legionaries drank. I would have expected a richer *passum* for a Consul's son.

My belly warmed from the first taste. "You are an interesting fellow, Pompey."

He chuckled, shook his head, and his lips curled like he wasn't enjoying the wine. "*Pompey*," he said with derision. "Pompey."

I wondered for a moment if I had said it wrong. "I apologize," I said. "I thought that's what you go by."

He leaned back farther in his leather chair and stretched out his legs. "A childhood name, given me by my father," he said.

"I've fought in six battles, killed fourteen men, and led a flank to win a decisive battle. Yet still I am just . . . Pompey." His voice grew softer, speaking only to himself. "It's as if I'm still not worthy of my family name."

I wondered if the wine was talking for him. Any man knows Bacchus is capable of it. But his eyes, still focused on the Pleiades, were sharp and focused.

"Would you prefer I call you Pompeius?" I said. "Or something else entirely?

He seemed to recall my presence. "Pompey for now," he said. "Perhaps I'll go by something else when I've earned it."

The young officer took the amphora of wine and tilted it in my direction until I placed the cup beneath it for a refill.

"Anything else noteworthy in the sky?" I said.

"There's too much to count," Pompey said, his voice a bit more cheerful now. "The moon is new. Without its light, you can see everything else more clearly. If you look close enough, you can see the Taurus." He directed my sight with his index finger. "Another wonder Jupiter placed in the sky."

I stood and walked over to the edge of the wall, as if that would improve my vision.

"I'm not sure what to be looking for exactly," I said. "Perhaps it's my lacking an eye."

"No, no," he said. "One is good enough. Look for the two bright stars, they're the horns."

I squinted, but the light I saw came from closer to the earth.

"On Jupiter's Black Stone . . . maybe it's my eye, or maybe my age. But . . ."

"Find the Pleiades again," he said. "That serves as the tail."

"No," I said. "I think there is fire."

Pompey stood and made his way to the battlements.

"Rebels," he said.

I took a deep breath and shouted, "Sound the alarms! Rally the defenses!"

My voice carried effortlessly throughout the camp, echoing throughout the high, silent walls.

One eye or not, by the times the trumpets rang out, I could see a body of armed men, moving under the shroud of darkness with the help of nothing more than a few torches.

Their number was impossible to calculate, but one thing was certain: we were under attack.

SCROLL VIII

QUINTUS SERTORIUS—SEVEN Days before the Kalends of April, 665 Ab Urbe Condita

The carved, menacing face of the battering ram gleamed in the torchlight as it made toward the gates beneath us. Before I could give that much thought, ladders crashed against the walls. The rebels were planning two points of entry.

Our legionaries were still climbing out of their cots and scrambling in the dark to dress themselves for battle. I'm sure Strabo had trained his legionaries for this possibility a hundred times or more, but simulations can't capture the mind-numbing chaos of a real attack in the middle of the night.

I jumped toward the nearest ladder. Pompey did the same to the one closest to him. The wood splintered in my hands as I pried them from the wall, but no matter how much I strained, I couldn't lift it. Was it already weighed down with several men clambering up?

Pompey had no better luck.

"They're on dollies! We cannot topple them," he shouted.

A dozen quicker legionaries and those who'd been on guard duty joined us on the walls.

"Steel will have to be enough then," I said. "Shields on me!"

Pompey and I drew nearer. The horns continued to sound from our sentries and the enemies at our gates.

Still there was no sign of Strabo.

"Three deep, three deep," Pompey ordered and fell in beside me. Another contubernium joined us.

The rebels groaned with exertion as they hauled themselves up the ladders. We needed more warriors to join us on the walls, and quick.

I narrowed my eye and scanned the enemy. They were many, but how many? Did they outnumber us? Were they more skilled than us? Better equipped? Why would they attack in darkness when losses on both sides would likely be severe?

The light of morning was breaking behind rising silver clouds, but I could discern little about the force assaulting us. It was like trying to count a swarm of bees in the hive.

One brave rebel reached the top of the ladder. I once attempted the same feat in my first battle as a young man. Unlike this rebel, I wasn't skewered with four Roman blades immediately.

His blood sprayed my face as I pulled my gladius from his neck. It'd been months since I last killed a man in combat. The feeling was both foreign and familiar. Unnatural. Inevitable.

By the time his body plummeted to the earth, three new ladders reached the walls on either side of the first, and more rebels climbed up to replace him.

They outnumbered us in a matter of mere moments.

"Shields on me!" Pompey shouted.

There was no use. Proper organization was impossible, and our line merged with the rebels' into one chaotic fray.

"Pompey, where is your father?" We fell in alongside the few legionaries who attempted to form up.

"We will lead the defense." He said nothing else.

"Three deep, three deep," I ordered.

The rebels wielded short swords, much like ours, and it was clear they were just as skillful with them. They would likely overrun us unless more legionaries joined us on the walls without delay.

Why wouldn't the commander be an active participant in the defense of his own fortress? Perhaps he was drunk? Or maybe he was—

No time to think. A rebel lunged for me. Even without our armor, the rebels seemed to know Pompey and I were officers, and that made us their first targets.

I sidestepped the sword aimed at my chest and kicked his knee. He stumbled, but quickly recovered as if he couldn't even feel the pain.

"Here!" Pompey shoved a shield toward me just before the rebel attacked again. He now had one as well.

I couldn't turn to look, but I hoped the shields meant more legionaries were arriving with extra arms.

The rebel stabbed toward Pompey and me. He made the same mistake I made when I hunted as a boy. "Don't aim for the flock, aim for the bird," my father would say. His sword jabbed errantly between us.

Pompey sent an elbow into his chin, and as he recoiled, I thrust the blade into his eye. His mistake cost him his life.

I turned to see how many had arrived. Somehow, among the crazed scramble to the walls, I spotted Cicero trying to fasten his helmet securely.

"Tribune! Tribune!" I shouted. "Go tell the quaestor we need pila, and we need them now!"

He complied without hesitation.

The walls shook then. Again, harder. Warriors of both forces stumbled. A third time caused a few men to fall off the ledge.

The ram had reached the gates.

Steel crashed against my shield. Pain reverberated through my arm and centered on the elbow. The attacker raised the sword again and pierced down over the shield, just as Romans do. Either he served with the legion, or those who trained him had.

Before the sword could reach me, I thrust my shield into his chest.

He gasped as wind and spittle was driven from his body. I narrowly dodged the gleaming tip of his sword. I was not wearing my armor. Even a superficial wound could be fatal.

The rebel collected himself, and I poised to strike. Before I could, a spear wedged through the man's belly. The Roman holding it drove it deep and pushed the rebel back into his allies.

It was Cataline. "Welcome to the siege of Asculum," he said. "A fitting welcome!"

Before I could thank him for the assist, the walls trembled again, stronger than before. We braced ourselves against one another, and the rebels across from us did the same.

The gates would soon collapse.

Pompey shouted, "You two, defend the walls. We must hold here at all costs. I'll lead the Third to defend the gates." He raised his sword toward the Pleiades. "Legionaries of the Third, on me!"

But before Pompey could make it down from the walls, the gates splintered and collapsed. The rebels poured in like water through a crack in an aqueduct.

Pompey and the others moved quicker to the broken gates as Cataline and I steeled ourselves against the attackers on the walls. Our numbers were thinner there now, and the fighting only grew harder.

Cataline was a skilled warrior, though, I could tell that much. Of all the patricians I'd fought beside, he was the most capable. He was very brave or very reckless. The line between the two is thin. He fought as if he were the only man on the battlefield, offering no orders and heeding none himself. He either cared little for preserving his own life or didn't believe losing it was possible.

"Prefect! Prefect!" I heard Cicero's voice cut through the fighting.

He arrived beneath the gates with bundles of pila, a dozen legionaries beside him with more.

I gave instructions on their disbursement and use. "I want death raining down from above," I shouted.

The first line continued to hold off the rebels as those behind were given pila.

"I want every rebel preparing to climb to think twice."

I grabbed one myself and hurled it over the ledge. It splintered the armor and wedged into the shoulder of a rebel. He cried out. The wound wasn't lethal, but he wouldn't be able to use his sword arm for the remainder of the battle.

"Now, now!" I ordered, and those who were able threw pila below, aiming or not aiming, it did not matter.

The enemy on the wall thinned out. Pompey was holding at the gates. If we could rout a few rebels, we might end this battle soon.

The now-familiar sound of wood splintering erupted through the fortress. Why? The gates were already down. But this booming came from the other direction.

The Asculum army had joined the fray, and we were now being attacked on both sides.

"Pompey!" I shouted.

He looked up, and we made eye contact. We shared a nod, an unspoken agreement that I would lead the defense of the other gate.

"Cataline, you hold here," I said. "First cohort, on me!"

They acknowledged the order with a stomp of the foot, and they followed me down from the walls, once again leaving the legionaries atop it thinner and thinner. I feared how long they could hold, but Cataline only nodded and continued fighting, unperturbed.

We could spare no time, so we sprinted toward the Asculum gate before we properly formed up.

The ram's silver head ripped through the splintering wood. A few more strikes and they'd break through.

Before we could reach them, however, another cohort of Romans arrived.

I caught the gaze of their leader, a legatus if I could tell from his crest and plumed helmet.

He appeared surprised to see us, or unhappy, I could not tell. He seemed vaguely familiar.

No time to be concerned with that. The gates collapsed.

"Onager!" the officer shouted.

I stepped out from formation as my men collided with our attackers.

"Catapults?" I said to myself. Siege weapons were for taking cities and fortresses. Perhaps our enemies could use them right now, but if we employed them . . .

No. No officer would do that.

The ground rumbled as the siege equipment rolled out.

"What are you doing?" I shouted at the officer.

"Saving the Republic," he replied without looking in my direction.

I moved toward him. "Those projectiles will kill as many of our men as it will rebels!"

"Acceptable losses if we repulse the attackers." He raised his arm. "Fire on my order."

I've never seen a more ludicrous use of siege equipment. Those boulders could destroy stone walls, what level of destruction would they cause to our ranks?

"If these losses are so acceptable, join the front line yourself, and I'll give the order."

This irritated the officer enough to delay him for a moment, but it didn't change his mind.

"Fire!"

Each onager required eight legion engineers to crank down the ropes. They strained with all their might and struggled to pull the device to a horizontal position, and then it was released in an instant.

"No!" I shouted, but it was too late.

The earth shook from the recoil. The crash deafened out all other noise.

Dozens of men fell in the wake of each projectile, each as heavy as an ox. Those fortunate enough to have survived a fatal blow screamed out and clutched the nubs of destroyed limbs. Strings of viscera like spiderwebs dangled from the ends.

Most of the wounded and dead were Asculum rebels, but some were Romans.

The next onager fired, and this time I watched several Roman legionaries die at the hands of their own countrymen. Another fired.

I sprinted away from the line toward the siege equipment.

The engineers stepped into my path.

"Move!" I shoved them apart.

Other legionaries loaded the next projectile and cranked it into position. But I arrived before they could finish.

I grabbed the thick skein of twisted cord that propelled the device and severed it in one swift motion. The onager sagged to the side as the engineers cursed me.

I moved on to the next.

"By order of your legatus, I command you to stop!" the officer shouted.

I did not obey.

Sacrifices were required in battle. I'd personally implemented tactics that I knew would result in many deaths of my men. But this was more than that, it was slaughter. It was barbarity. A total disregard for Roman lives.

Another legionary jumped in my path to stop me, more force-fully this time, with arms outstretched.

I threw an elbow into his jaw, his helmet barely clinging on as he staggered to the side.

I'd pay for that, I'm sure. Strabo would have something to

say about it, but he wasn't here, and we were killing our own men. I had no choice.

A few more severed ropes and the second catapult collapsed.

I'd handle the consequences later, but I needed to get back to the line. Immediately.

I lost my vision.

Something hit me. I could hear fighting, but it was distant now. Muffled. The sensation of weightlessness overcame me. I felt no pain. Was I dead?

No, no.

My wife and daughter needed me.

No!

I could still hear the fighting and legionaries running, cursing. I could smell the death, steel, and fire. I only needed to focus on that, and I would wake up soon.

But then I lost those too. And all was black.

I woke to a ceaseless dripping. Water falling on concrete and soggy wood.

My head throbbed, pounding to the beat of each water droplet.

I reached up and felt the back of my neck. There was blood there. I followed the substance up to the source, a sticky scab, not fully dry. I hadn't been unconscious long. Good.

My eye adjusted to the darkness. I could see iron. Iron bars. I was in the carcer. Why? Was I captured? Was this Asculum or a rebel fortress?

Everything flooded back to me. The battle. The officer and the *ballistae*. The crack against my head.

Anger burned in my chest. Had that officer truly detained me? Either way, I didn't regret it. Roman soldiers will die for the Republic, but it should never be their own officers who kill them. I would do the same again if it meant saving a single Roman life.

Red light poured into the brig from a cramped hallway nearby. I winced and looked away. Apparently, it frightened my cellmates—two hairy, bloated rats—who scurried into cracks in the wall for cover.

Footsteps neared. It was at least three men. I pulled myself to my feet. Whoever it was, I wouldn't give them the satisfaction of seeing Quintus Sertorius in the dirt.

I spotted Pompey's face in the growing torchlight.

He exhaled deeply when he saw me. I could not tell what his reaction meant.

"It is him, father," Pompey said, and moved the torch closer to my cell.

"Why was he without armor?" Strabo said, as if I weren't there to answer for myself.

"For the same reason as I," he said. "I'm grateful to find you alive, prefect," Pompey said. "I thought you may have died in the fighting, but when I heard . . . well, I thought it might have been you."

"You as well, tribune," I said. "Did we win the battle?"

My vision was growing into focus and accustomed to the light. Beside Pompey and his father was the legatus from the battle, the man almost certainly responsible for my arrest.

"If we'd lost the battle, it'd be the rebels finding you here and not us," the legatus said.

I met his gaze. "There are many ways to lose a battle," I said.

"And one of them is to arrest your prefects mid-battle," Pompey added.

The officer clasped his hands behind his back and nodded. "What happened was unfortunate," he said. "How was I to know he was an officer? He looked like nothing more than a crazed madman running around destroying Republic equipment."

It's true that I hadn't been wearing anything to designate my rank, so perhaps he honestly didn't know, but one shouldn't need to be an officer to stop a legatus from callously betraying his men.

"Father, we should honor the prefect with a military decoration for the bravery he showed today, not keep him here like some prisoner of war." Pompey didn't wait for a reply. He nodded to a guard who appeared from the darkness with iron keys in hand.

"Did we win the battle?" I asked again. I wanted a full answer.

"Yes," Strabo answered. "With heavy losses. The rebels fought like Achilles with his balls on fire, but we forced them back."

The guard swung the gate open and hung his head. "I'm sorry, sir," he said.

I patted his shoulder to reassure him. He was simply following orders. My quarrel was with the officer.

"Don't you want to know what happened to you?" Strabo asked.

My chest burned with a desire to ask what happened to *him*. Why hadn't he been defending the fort? I resisted. For now.

"I think it's fairly obvious, consul," I said. "I was trying to stop a reckless officer from needlessly sacrificing our men. He had one of his troops crack me over the head with the hilt of a gladius and locked me up in here for doing so. Is that the nub of it?"

The legatus shook his head, venom in his eyes. " Needlessly? We were surrounded. Breached. We had to use every weapon at our disposal to repel them. If we failed, many more would have died, many more," he said. "And that blood would have been on your head if we failed. You clearly don't possess the stomach to make the difficult decisions required of an officer."

"Every battle feels like the most dire ever fought. If there aren't limits in place, one can justify any amount of betrayal in the name of victory. I've fought in many battles more disastrous than this, and I've never seen a Roman general turn weapons on his own men in the name of expedience. And still they were able to achieve victory."

"I agree with prefect Sertorius," Pompey said. "A great general can always find another way. Did Scipio use his legionaries as fodder to defeat Hannibal?"

The officer finally tore his gaze, with all its vitriol, away from me. "You have much to learn, son of Strabo. Sacrifices like this have always been required during war, only no one records them for posterity. They do not make it into your annals of history, but they've always happened, and always will."

Strabo gestured for us to follow him from the carcer. "Well, before we're included in any annals, we have to win the war," he said. "Metellus Pius was right. Victory at all costs. Besides, what's the lives of a few Mules if it means . . ."

I stopped listening. I already knew what he was going to say because I'd heard arrogant commanders make such claims to justify their incompetence before. They'd never been a legionary, they'd never served on the front line. If they had, they'd know the cost of each man serving under them is valuable beyond compare.

But as Strabo droned on, my mind returned to that name . . . Metellus Pius.

It struck me like the sword hilt earlier.

I'd met him many years ago when we were little more than children. He was the son of Metellus Numidicus, leader of the senatorial party and the sworn enemy of my then-mentor Gaius Marius.

His recklessness made more sense now. One can never underestimate the value rich men place on the lives of the poor.

"Isn't that right, Sertorius?" Strabo's voice cut through my thoughts.

"What's that, sir?"

He stopped pacing and turned to me. "Did that blow to your head render you slow, or are you simply not listening?"

I did not respond, so he continued.

"I said that the assault, although costly, may yet prove useful," he said. "We gained a vast amount of intelligence about their capabilities, and I believe we should be able to complete the siege of Asculum soon, once we destroy the army seeking to liberate them."

Pompey added, "We estimate that less than ten thousand of their men survived, and many of the living bear wounds."

Strabo spoke. "Right you are, *Pompey.*" He said his son's name with a hint of derision. "Whining like kicked dogs though they may be, we must deal with them before we conduct the final assault."

"I agree," I said. "Their reinforcement would have us surrounded while we attempt to take the walls."

Strabo smiled, but it wasn't a happy smile. "I'm delighted we have your blessing," he said. "That is why I am ordering you and Metellus here to lead an army to obliterate them."

Metellus's jaw dropped.

Strabo lifted a finger before either of us could respond. "I've made up my mind. If you succeed, perhaps you two can learn to work better together. If you fail, then I will have gotten rid of two quarreling officers and bought myself enough time for our reinforcements to arrive."

"Consul, I beg you to reconsider," Metellus said. "The prefect is clearly not well after the . . . he isn't thinking straight. Allow me to—"

A glare from Strabo was enough to stop him mid-sentence.

"I will follow your orders, consul," I said. "Though, as Camp Prefect, I don't believe I have battlefield authority, if my injury hasn't scrambled my memory."

"You would make a poor politician, Quintus Sertorius," he said. "Allow me to explain. You destroyed siege equipment and got yourself locked up in the carcer. I must either reward you or punish you but cannot remain neutral. So, I'm going to appear pleased with your courage and give you a battlefield command rather than have you crucified." He shrugged. "Don't think I didn't consider the alternative. But although you'd make a poor politician, you're clearly a talented commander. So, I've taken the shit-covered grapes you've given me and I'm making it into Falernian wine."

"I'll prepare myself accordingly," I said. "I would ask that you allow me to bring along someone I know and trust as an advisor."

"You cannot take Pompey," Strabo said. "He has much to do here. And I can't think of anyone else here you know."

"I would take tribune Cicero, if you can spare him," I said.

Strabo laughed. Even Metellus stopped his fuming for a moment and chuckled. Pompey hung his head.

"You clearly don't know the lad well enough at all if you're asking to take him with you," Strabo said. "As useless in battle as a plump arse on a vestal virgin."

Despite noting Strabo's apparent shortage of analogies, it was clear how they felt about Cicero. Regardless, he was a friend of Gavius. I considered Cataline, but there was something about him I didn't trust. No, I wanted to ride into battle with a young man my son had fought beside.

Metellus's face was redder than his cloak. I'd met many like him in my campaigns. He loathed the idea of sharing authority with a man of lower rank, militarily and socially.

I'd seen this before. And the last time resulted in the deaths of ninety thousand Romans.

I wouldn't let that happen again.

SCROLL IX

GAVIUS SERTORIUS—SIX Days before the Kalends of April, 665 Ab Urbe Condita

 The thousands of legionaries in Sulla's Fist lined up in formation. Across from us were the members of our fleet—marines, oarsmen, crewmen, and all.

Both sides were eerily silent.

We faced one another like we were about to enter battle, but of course we weren't. Regardless, a lot of blood was about to be spilled.

Atop his tall, white stallion, one man remained in the chasm between us. Sulla cast his gaze on the fleet in judgment. I couldn't see his face, but I knew his famous, infectious smile was absent.

His joy had been present three days prior as we celebrated our victory over the Samnites. We drank wine and sang songs like we'd already won the war, but before the blur was gone from our eyes, we received the news.

Sulla's fleet commander, Albinus, had been murdered. Stoned to death by his own men.

The salt-tinged breeze from the sea wafted past us. It would have been a pleasant day if not for what was to come. Despite the open space between the legionaries and the fleet, the atmosphere felt stiflingly close, each breath laden with dread.

Behind me, the subtle clinks of armor adjusting, and the shuffling of feet painted a tapestry of unrest. Every so often, a muffled cough or choked-back sob would pierce the silence.

Sulla's shadow seemed to stretch out and dominate the entire beachfront, where we besieged Pompeii from both land and sea. After our victory, we expected to return and triumph over the rebel city, but first Roman judgment would have to be meted out on our own.

The commander's voice cut through the silence like a piercing arrow. "Since ancient times, since Chaos formed the heavens and the earth, there has been no crime so repulsive and incomprehensible as mutiny." His horse came to a halt before the fleet. "This act is cowardice of the highest level, treason, and patricide, all in one." The white stallion bucked, but somehow Sulla seemed not to move. His gaze must have been more paralyzing than Medusa's. "There is no punishment this side of Tartarus truly befitting this betrayal. But our ancestors tried . . ."

I advanced with several other officers. We'd received instructions on what to do now. It made me sicker than warfare ever did. No one desired this responsibility.

The officers spread out, and we began to count. I pointed to every tenth man.

Sometimes they wept, sometimes they hung their heads, but none said a word as every tenth man stepped forward.

"Our ancestors developed an answer: decimation."

Those words lingered in the air as they echoed. It invoked memories of nightmares, haunting stories we were told as children. Dis Pater must have created a special place of torment for the minds who contrived such an idea. But after its creation, how could we not use it when faced with such betrayal?

"They demanded every tenth man should step forth." Sulla's voice revealed sorrow, but unwavering resilience. "And kneel."

Centurions followed behind us and forced each of the chosen to their knees. Four thousand men belonged to the fleet, so four hundred were called forward. Some required more force than others, but none resisted. The hope in their eyes had already died, and they had no one to blame but themselves.

"Rome decrees traitors must die."

A centurion handed me a bundle of clubs wrapped in a leather tarp. I struggled under the weight.

Passing the chosen men, I laid the bundle down before the formation of sailors. I unraveled the tarp, and they stepped forward.

"Not only should the tenth man die, but it should be his own brothers who slay him, so that they may share in his death and bear shame of their survival for the rest of their lives."

"Up arms," I said, and the other officers joined me.

The chosen men wept, but not as much as those

who would soon kill them. These marines, sailors, and oarsmen would go on living, but more like ghosts than men. Without honor. Without the possibility of redemption. Without purpose. A curse to their families, to their names. Damned.

"Take position!" I shouted.

Circles gathered around the chosen. Four hundred men were about to die; the 3,600 men who mutinied beside them would deliver the death blows. The twenty thousand men of Sulla's Fist could only watch.

"Our ancestors commanded this," Sulla said.

Drums began, slow and booming at first, but their rhythm quickened. When it ended, the thudding of clubs was expected to replace them.

I fell back in line with the other officers. None wanted to be close enough to taste the blood. We couldn't get far enough away to avoid the screams. We would all have to experience that.

"They may have commanded this," he went on, "but we are no more compelled to obey than a dog is forced to sit."

The bowed heads and misty eyes looked up at our commander.

His voice was steel. "Let this be the day each of you dies and is born again. Never forget, this is the day Sulla gave you back your lives."

The fleet dropped their clubs and fell to the Italian soil, lying prostrate before the commander, weeping and praising him. I felt like doing the same. I didn't know a single man in the fleet across from me, but I didn't want to see them die in this sordid manner.

Sulla raised a hand and his voice over the supplication. "Now only fight the enemy with as much tenacity and bravery as you fought your commander, and Rome will conquer."

The legions of Sulla's Fist erupted in applause. There was a persistent and ancient rivalry between the fleet and the legion, but no one wanted to see Romans decimated. That memory would seer into our minds like a cattle brand.

I made eye contact with Lucullus, and we shared a nod. We broke away from formation in Sulla's direction. The legatus would have new orders for us to relay to the centurions, who would pass them along to the men.

Sulla dismounted from his steed and passed his horse's reins to a *servus*.

"How was that for unexpected?" Sulla said. His grin returned.

"Unexpected yet favorable, legate," I said.

"Agreed." Lucullus nodded. "Yet I would be remiss if I did not mention that the senate will be furious with your decision. Admiral Albinus was a client of the Claudii. They will demand his murderers to be held accountable."

"Did you ever wonder why they did it?" I asked.

Sulla shrugged. "Men rarely come together to slaughter their leader except for good reason. I've never had to fear my own men."

Lucullus swallowed. "Legate, they'll likely put you on trial. Your mercy may be mistaken for complicity."

Sulla placed a hand on the young tribune's shoulder. "We are Rome's best chance of survival, my boy. I'm immune to such concerns. I could impregnate the consul's wife and get away with it, if I had a mind to."

"What about after the war, commander? What about after we've won, and we lay down our arms?" Lucullus said.

I knew nothing of the courts, but trusted Lucullus as an expert in these matters. The concern in his eyes burdened me.

Sulla didn't answer.

A rider was drawing near and quickly.

The rider cried out in a shrill voice that cut through the shouts of the still-celebrating men. "Legate, legate!"

Sulla stood in the center of the rider's path. I feared the rider might trample him, but Sulla remained still and unafraid.

Dirt flew up and barely missed him as the steed skidded to a halt before him.

"*Salvete,*" Sulla said.

I could not tell from the sound of his voice whether he was angry, curious, irritated, or amused.

"*Domine,* are you the one they call Sulla?" Closer now, I could see the rider was a woman. A thin cloak covered her head and shielded her face. I could not tell if the dark staining was from hard riding or blood. Perhaps both.

"I am Sulla," the commander said.

"I come with news from Nola." The woman was breathless.

"We have representatives there. Official emissaries. Why did Nola not send one of them?" Lucullus asked me beneath his breath.

But Sulla heard him. "Because they're all dead."

The woman tilted her head like a confused dog. "Yes, but how did you know?"

"I didn't until now." He sighed and lowered his voice. "How?"

"A Samnite army."

We rarely spoke when Sulla was in a conversation, but Lucullus shook his head and said, "That's impossible. We just defeated their primary force a matter of days ago. They couldn't have regrouped so quickly."

"It wasn't their primary army," I said.

Sulla nodded. "You must be right, Gavius."

"All I know is that Nola has been taken," the woman said. "All men have been put to the sword. Women and children have been taken."

"The force we fought was merely a distraction." I rubbed my forehead. "They wanted to take the city but knew we would stop them if we weren't occupied. Nola will be a powerful stronghold for the rebels."

The prospects of taking Pompeii remained daunting, but Nola was well-known for its impregnable walls and powerful defenses. With a well-stocked army stationed there, it would be unconquerable, at least without starving them out, which could take years. Rome did not have that long.

"A distraction . . ." Lucullus shook his head.

"What I'm wondering is what kind of general we're dealing with. The man sent out twenty thousand of his men to die as a distraction," I said.

"A dangerous one, Gavius," Sulla said. "A very dangerous one."

"One last thing," the rider said. "Juba, prince of Numidia was staying in Nola when the city was taken. The rebels now have him in their possession."

I wondered why this was worth mentioning in

the same breath with the news we just received, but I watched as fear and dread grew over Sulla more than the words of Nola's defeat had.

"I will take my leave." The woman wheeled her horse around.

"One last question," I said to her. "If all the men in Nola are dead, and all the women and children are captive, how did you escape?"

"Who sent you?" Lucullus added.

She stared back blankly for a moment, then her eyes narrowed. "Mutilus sends his regards."

Italian soil and small rocks kicked up at us as the horse raced off.

 Rhea always said my father suffered from sleepless nights. I thought she meant something like the nightmares I suffered as a child, but now I understood.

My mind was still fighting the Samnites. Still celebrating the salvation of the sailors and marines. Still reeling from the news we'd received.

Tossing about in my itchy woolen sheets did me no good. I cursed Somnus's name and rose.

The midnight air was not cool, but the dampness of my tunic from today's efforts left me with a chill. I shivered and pulled my cloak around my shoulders.

The moon was a silver crescent, a thin eyelid barely open. Its light did little to illuminate my way. But my feet knew how to navigate the labyrinth of tents and supplies to the stables.

Even the torches seemed unable to conquer the

dark shroud of the April night. Their shadows cast strange shapes, making the familiar camp foreign.

The smell of camp was different at night. Cooler, tinged with the sharpness of dew and the musk of still smoldering embers from recently extinguished campfires. Regardless, the unvarying earthy scent of the stables beckoned me on, as if calling me home.

I found the stable doors ajar as I arrived. Odd. We kept them locked as tight as Vulcan's vault at night. I'd been prepared to climb through a window, but I passed through the open doors.

My hands brushed against the wooden posts as I counted down toward Bucephalus's stall.

I expected to find him snorting and snoring, as he usually did after as much riding as we'd been doing. Instead, I found him alert, his massive head poking over the slat in his door.

"*Salvete*, boy." I stroked his forehead. "Were you expecting me?"

He nestled his nose against me, begging for a scratch behind his ears.

I ran my fingers through the coarse hairs of his mane, a grounding sensation. The other officers might mock me for it, but I knew I'd sleep better with his calming presence, and perhaps he would as well.

I reached from the stall door, but there was a disturbance. A subtle break in the nocturnal rhythms of camp. The stables were oddly muted. There was an emptiness—a void where the presence of many horses should be.

Bucephalus quieted with me, as if both of us were listening for the cause.

The soft clatter of hooves. The jingle of bridles being fastened.

I grabbed the nearest lantern and ran toward the sound. In my heart, I already knew what was happening.

I burst from one stable into the next, where the Numidians kept their steeds.

Lifting the lamp, I could see the empty stalls. Riders were leading their horses through the barn doors.

They were abandoning us.

"Why?" the words, breathless, escaped my lips, but I already knew the answer.

Their prince was with the rebels now. And they were going to him. Our most potent battlefield weapons—the six hundred Numidian riders who'd fought with us from the beginning—were abandoning us.

I ran toward them. They ignored me.

"In the name of Rome, I order you to halt!" My voice cut through the morning air.

Most of the riders continued their slow departure. Only one turned back toward me.

He was mounted and could make a quick escape but chose not to. Was it arrogance? Respect? I did not know.

"You understand," he said.

The rider's heavily oiled hair was bound into a single, tight braid as thick as a mallet. The bronze breastplate glimmered in the torchlight.

"You cannot abandon Rome. You cannot go back on your vow," I said.

I grabbed the hilt of my gladius with my free hand, although I knew from witnessing their skill over the past year that they would kill me before I could draw it. The Numidian cavalry were among the finest warriors the world had ever known, and they could make quick work of me if they desired.

"My first allegiance is to the prince," he said, his Latin crisper than usual.

The voice belonged to their commander, Maharbal. I'd rode into battle beside him numerous times. The strength and courage of the Numidian riders had been an enormous comfort to me since I first joined the legion.

I released my hilt but stepped closer, a horse brushing up against me as it departed with its rider. "Why not fight back and destroy his captors? You could be his liberators!"

He sighed. "Messenger arrive. Prince Juba supports rebels now, calls for aid," he said. "We must answer."

"With one shout, I will alert twenty thousand legionaries. We will slaughter you, and your prince will not reward your sacrifice."

He shook his head. "No," he said. "You won't. We are armed; your men sleeping. We cut down many, and ride away faster."

I swallowed. He was right. But I couldn't just watch them walk away. Sulla may have spared the sailors, but how could I escape punishment for allowing our allies to betray us in silence?

Sulla stepped into the light of my lantern. "He's right, Gavius," he said.

From his tremor, Maharbal was just as surprised as I was at my commander's arrival outside the stables.

"We shall let them pass."

Maharbal's jaw dropped, unable to find the words.

"Oh, spare me, Numidian," Sulla said. "The moment we received the news, I knew you would betray us. I could have had you all killed in the night if I'd wanted."

"Why spare us now?"

I'd never seen a look as cold as the one now in Sulla's eyes.

"The same reason I spared the marines today," he said. "Because it pleases me."

"And you know we fight against you?"

"I do. And you know—or should know by now —that I will kill you," Sulla said. "Every last one of you will die by the sword. Not in your cots, but as warriors on the field of battle. That is my parting gift to you."

Maharbal's eyes danced as he considered the threat. "Romans tell story of one called Alexander. They say all earth was not big enough for his ambition, but in the end, coffin was enough," he said. "Will be enough for you?"

Sulla smiled. "Oh, Maharbal, have you learned so little of me in our time together?"

I didn't understand the response, but Maharbal seemed to. He clicked his tongue in the peculiar way Numidian's do and turned his horse.

"Commander, you're letting them go?" I asked.

Only then did I see the sweat beginning to develop on his brow.

"They will lead us right to their prince. And I have plans for him." That was all he said.

We didn't speak of the Numidian cavalry again.

SCROLL X

Quintus Sertorius—The Kalends of April, 665 Ab Urbe Condita

I stood alone beside Metellus on a hill, grassy valleys on either side. Behind us were two full Roman legions of 4,800 men. One I would command, and Metellus would command the other. We both had six hundred cavalry under our authority as well. Before us was the Picentes fortress.

"I think we should just attack them in camp. They're packed in like fish in an Aventine net," Metellus said. "They can't retreat."

"We have no siege equipment, and when men have nowhere to run, they fight harder and to the last man," I said.

I refused to allow this battle to be a war of *dignitas* between Metellus and me. It would cause the deaths of too many Romans. But I also couldn't give in to his arrogance.

"They have many skirmishers," I said. "Half our men would die before the walls are breached."

Surprisingly, he didn't resist. I thanked the gods for that but wondered how much longer he would tolerate a variance in opinion.

A single scout rode up behind us.

"Orders?" he said.

"Go. Tell them to meet us on the field of battle, or we'll burn them out," I said.

The scout complied and galloped off down the hill.

Metellus crossed his arms. "I am the senior officer, so I'll command the center." He was looking for a way to regain dominance, that much was clear.

His reasons may have been self-serving, and I didn't like the idea of dividing my legion, but I wouldn't object. Veterans know you win or lose a battle on the flanks.

"Agreed," I said. "You only need to hold the center. If you can maintain position, I can secure the edges with our superior cavalry."

"I know how to win a battle, prefect," he said.

We watched as the scout arrived at the gates of the rebel fortress. Two officers rode out to meet him. After a moment of speaking, their gaze turned toward us. I wondered what they would say. Luckily, they couldn't see the size of our force in the valley below, or they may well challenge us to attack them there.

I studied Metellus for a moment while we waited in silence. He wasn't more than a few years older than me, but he carried himself like one of the old breed. Taller than the average Roman, and with a barrel chest that comes from one who eats well rather than trains hard. His bovine face featured a short, well-maintained beard. The legionaries were expected to shave to the skin each morning, but there was no such restriction on officers. Politicians like Metellus often wore beards to identify themselves with the Roman ancestors of myth and legend. Perhaps he expected to find his face on a coin or a statue in the Forum one day.

The scout's meeting did not last long. In a matter of moments, the scout was riding back toward us.

"One hour, one mile east. They will fight us there."

Metellus put on his feathered-plumed helmet. "Let's get on

with it then." His shoulder collided with mine as he began back toward the legions. "I'll show you how to win a battle too."

I found Cicero in camp, reading over a scroll used for training young officers. If he didn't already know what to do in battle, it was too late to learn now, but I appreciated the effort.

"We have one hour," I said. "You're going to lead the left flank. Don't worry, just follow the commands and all will be well."

He rolled up the scroll and leaned back against a stack of shields.

"You know, I heard you speak in Rome once," he said.

"Oh?"

"I did. I was a small lad, but even then, I could sense the weight of the political decisions being made." He looked at me with a curiously blank expression. "I've since listened to many speakers in the Forum. Of all the crude, rabble-rousing, pandering, and coarse orators, you were the worst."

The harsh accusation was leveled with such calmness I could hardly be angry.

I laughed. "Well, perhaps you can offer some education in the matter."

He nodded. "I most certainly could. I said none of this to Gavius, of course. It's clear he admires you," he said. "I'm beginning to understand why."

Cicero was a curious lad. Everything about his physical appearance seemed meek, inadequate, out of place. But there was a strength, a certain resolve in his breast I was coming to admire.

He continued. "You seem to have a good heart, as they say. I cannot think of another reason you would have chosen me for this task. I don't much desire it, to tell you the truth. But I will lead as admirably as I'm able."

I clapped his shoulder. He stared at my hand as if soldierly affection was totally uncommon to him.

"You were the right man for the job," I said. "Although I'll accept the compliment, and the criticism in stride. If Gavius trusted you, so do I."

I hoped that measure of trust would be enough to win the battle. We would soon find out.

The rebels were good on their word and met us an hour later.

The battlefield was an open, grassy valley just wide and deep enough to host both our armies. Forests lined the hills above us, as if the gods specifically designed this location for nature to bear witness to the chaos and brutality of battle.

I stood three rows from the frontline on our right flank. As I aged, many would expect me to lead from the rear, where I could see the battle develop with more clarity and leave the fighting to those younger and more able. That's certainly what Metellus was doing, stationed with his cavalry far behind the infantry lines of our center.

But I had a few good years of combat prowess left at least, and I meant to use them. Besides, I did not know these legionaries or their tendencies. I would lead better beside them, feeling their pulse and sensing every shift in momentum.

I had no choice but to trust Cicero to maintain on the left flank. Since I couldn't be on both sides at once, we devised a flag system to relay orders down the line.

It was a simple system, something we used at Vercellae with Gaius Marius when I was young, and no one questioned my presence on the front line.

Two *signiferi* propelled flags high above the formation—one white, the other red. The latter signaled to the legionaries, the former to the cavalry. When the flags were pointed vertically, the respective units were to maintain position. If the flags dipped forward, the signal was to advance. Backward meant retreat.

The left flank had flags of their own, which would mirror

ours. We kept two flags of each color in reserve in case the bearers died or the originals were damaged.

Three short trumpet blasts would signal a change, ensuring no one missed their orders.

Time to see if the system would work.

I raised my arm with two fingers extended, and let it fall. The first red flag dropped forward, and the trumpets blared. It took a moment for the centurions to perceive and for the signal to pass along to the left flank, but it did so properly and the legions on both sides marched forward—silent and methodical.

I whispered a prayer beneath my breath. "Diana, watch over me and keep me. Bring victory to us today. Protect my family until I can be with them again."

I raised my arm again, this time with one finger extended. The bearers heeded my order quicker this time. The white flag fell forward and our cavalry began a unified trot, away and behind our infantry lines.

Our enemy charged forward at twice our speed. The rebels had the luxury of fighting with hatred in their hearts. We had only the desire to protect our homes and restore the Republic. Which would be more useful remained to be seen.

Centurions ordered the first line to prepare their pila. They hoisted them over their shoulders, somehow keeping step with those behind them.

From the ranks of the advancing Picentes, skirmishers emerged. I knew from scouting reports they had about twelve hundred of them. Though in the moment, that number seemed woefully understated.

"Volley!" the centurions shouted.

Pila split the afternoon air, but it was no use. The skirmishers were spread out too much for the volley to be effective.

Most of the spears plunged into the earth. A handful found their mark, but the skirmisher onslaught was undeterred.

"Shields! Shields!" I shouted. I gave the signal for our infantry advance to halt.

"*Testudo!*" the centurions bellowed.

I fell into the shield formation and waited as arrows, spears, and stones pelted our line.

Lightly armored spearmen pounced on our shield wall like angry mountain lions. Some jumped over and hurled themselves down, doing anything they could to break up our line.

"Hold your positions!" I shouted.

They had no other options, of course. But I shout orders like this so the men could hear the sound of my voice and know I'm there with them, nothing more.

I felt an enormous weight crash down above me. It would have broken my hold if my arm wasn't sturdied by the surrounding shields. But as the rebel above began stabbing through the cracks in our shields, we had no choice but to separate and let him fall through.

He crashed into the earth with a thud, already slashing wildly at our ankles. He got a good slice at my heel, but I couldn't feel it yet. I stabbed down through his thin breastplate.

The wind was driven from his chest, unable to even cry out. He stopped slashing.

The assault seemed to slow for a moment as the skirmishers regrouped. I took advantage and signaled for the cavalry to hasten. The white flag dropped farther, and the hoofbeats grew louder.

"Maintain your spacing!" I shouted.

My legionaries were bunching together. It was natural to seek safety in the proximity of one's brothers when the battle gets going, but it could cost many lives. It revealed the lack of experience in Strabo's troops.

They tried to follow my command and space out as the rebel skirmishers began their second wave of assaults.

Several men on our front line collapsed, but the second rank admirably filled in the gaps.

I hoped Metellus was holding the center—all I needed him to

do was maintain position long enough for my men to win the flanks.

The cavalry arrived—as clear by the nearing hoofbeats as the stalled skirmisher attack.

"*Tecombre!*" the centurions shouted, and we broke the shield wall.

The skirmishers were running back toward the line. Our riders quickly swallowed up the wounded and the slowest among them, but the rest escaped.

I raised my hand with one finger out and tilted it back. The white flag shifted, and the cavalry retreated. I could have pressed the advantage, but with only six hundred cavalry at my command—three hundred behind me and three hundred with Cicero—I couldn't afford to lose any of them so early in battle.

As soon as the skirmishers disappeared into a rolling cloud of dust, the Picentes' heavy infantry emerged from it.

They looked just like Romans, with pila lifted over their heads.

Pila?

Gods.

"Shields! Shields!" I ordered.

Our first rank raised their *scuta* just in time to block most of the pila. But the rebels had constructed their pila just like ours. They wedged deep in our shields and forced us to discard them.

"Second rank, pila!" the centurions bellowed, but it was far too late for that. The Picentes infantry was already crashing into our line.

Shieldless, the front line collapsed.

"Rotate! Rotate!" I yelled.

Some were still hopelessly trying to prepare their pila for launch.

Strabo and his officers failed to prepare the men, and now many would die for it.

"Drop the damned pila!" I pushed my way forward. "Rotation, now!" I led by example and wedged my way into the front rank, many in the second joining me. The few survivors of the initial first line fell back to safety.

Two enemy shields bashed into my own, steel short swords poised atop like a ravenous wolves' teeth.

I finally felt the wound to my heel. The entire leg felt cold save for the searing heat of the wound itself.

One sword shot forward and caught me in the shoulder. A jolt of pain rippled through my arm from the impact, but it didn't pierce the chain mail.

The other rebel stabbed as well, but I sidestepped this attack.

I thrust my gladius over the shield wall and connected with the first attacker. I'd struck his chain mail as well. If I pushed harder, I could split the rings and tear his flesh, but I'd seen too many arms severed at the wrist, still clutched to hilts. So I recoiled quickly.

The second rebel jabbed again. His blade passed right beneath my arm. He failed to recover as quickly as I had. I trapped the sword between my arm and breastplate and severed his arm.

He let out a piercing cry. The rebel's shield stopped pressing against mine as he fell away, his sword and arm falling limp and cold by my feet.

"Rotate!" I bellowed. "Rotate, now!"

This was an order the centurions were supposed to be giving, but they were too slow in the delivery. At least they took up the order and rallied it down the line.

I fell back with the rest of the front. As difficult as it was to leave the fray, I needed to survey the battlefield and make sure everything was proceeding according to plan.

A junior officer intercepted me as I made for a vantage point. "You're limping, sir."

"I'm fine," I said. "Any word from the left flank?"

"Advancing properly, prefect."

I trusted the young man but needed to see for myself. I

pushed out of the formation and began up a small hill at our backs.

The field stretch out wide, but I could see most of the field clearly now. The left was slowly winning the battle of the trenches.

Cicero was doing well for his first time leading. Not much longer and the rebel flanks would fold. Then we could reinforce the center.

The center . . . I turned my gaze on Metellus's troops.

What was the fool doing?

His troops were advancing, thinning out.

He overextended his line!

Maybe he didn't notice or was too arrogant to see the risk, but the Picentes were catching on and moving their reserves to the center. That's why we were winning so easily on the flanks.

Metellus remained with his cavalry far behind his lines. I could run to him and beseech him to halt the advance and reform before it was too late.

But I knew better.

Metellus wouldn't change his strategy based on the suggestion of a provincial. Instead, he'd further entrench himself in this folly.

Instead, I ran to my own cavalry that was waiting in reserves nearby.

"A horse, give me a horse!" I shouted to the first man who met my gaze.

The rider jumped off. I ignored the pain shooting up my leg and hoisted myself up.

All the horsemen turned their eyes on me. I aimed my dripping sword down the middle of them.

"Those to the left of my blade, follow the flag. Those to the right, stay with me."

They blinked in confusion, but eventually nodded.

I rested my shield on the horse beneath me and raised my hand, one finger extended.

The flag bearer had fortunately been following me and dropped the flag forward at my order. The trumpets burst three times.

Approximately half the cavalry broke into a gallop. I stayed planted with the remainder.

I said the same prayer as before. "Diana, watch over me and keep me. Bring victory to us today. Protect my family until I can be with them again." This time, I added a silent, unspoken prayer for the rebels to fall into my trap. If they did not, and Metellus's center collapsed, it would be impossible to salvage the day.

The cavalry advanced with speed and freshness, just as I'd hoped. The flags couldn't communicate who I wanted them to attack, but I didn't need them to.

They would instinctively crash into the rebel-heavy infantry.

At worst, it would sow terror into their ranks, and the rebels assaulting our flank would retreat.

At best . . .

The rebel cavalry chased after my own horsemen, only a few hundred yards away.

I thanked Diana.

My cavalry adjusted and aimed straight for the enemy riders. They numbered something like three hundred, which I knew was the total they could field. The left and center wouldn't have to deal with mounted reserves any longer.

But they were crashing against one hundred and fifty of my own, while the other one hundred and fifty remained with me.

Our forward riders wouldn't last long, even if they were better trained than our Picentes enemies.

Cavalry engagement is always the loudest part of any battle. Between the blood, the dust, and the rearing and screaming horses, it was impossible to know what was happening. There was no way to assess the losses, to know if one side was winning decisively.

I wouldn't wait to find out.

I raised my hand, one finger extended, and let it fall back.

The flag bearer and trumpeter took a moment, but eventually complied.

At first, the riders did not move. Were they still watching and listening for the signals?

Then they wheeled about. Once freed, they galloped back toward us.

Only then did I perceive the losses. But this was the only way. I hoped it was worth it.

The rebel cavalry, perceiving a victory, charged after them.

I thanked Diana again, knowing I wouldn't be able to offer prayers again until the battle was done.

I raised my sword and hand simultaneously and sent them both forward.

"Charge!" I shouted.

The cavalry beside me echoed the cry and set off, perhaps beginning to perceive my gambit.

We rode hard. The others, galloping back toward us, began to understand as well.

I raised my arm again, knowing full well this was the last time I'd be able to offer orders directly.

The white flag fell forward at my command. The riders who had so recently been retreating now turned, and we crashed into the Picentes horsemen together.

It was all a blur. My blade connected on the right, then the left. My horse collided with another but managed not to collapse. The rebel rider nearly fell into my lap.

I struggled to contain him as he squirmed. I gave him a quick death, one swift blow to the back of his neck, and he was with the ferryman.

I shouted, "Repel them! Fight!" I pushed the man back and his horse galloped off into the chaos without him.

The Picentes were scrambling. Perhaps their leader was dead, but I heard no orders given. If there were commands being offered, they did not heed them.

Their horsemen were outnumbered and scattered about with ours.

My horse screamed and wheeled about violently to the side. With a fistful of mane, I held on and saw the rebel who'd struck her.

His bloody spear tip was now poised at me.

Nothing could anger me in battle like the sound of my horse's pain.

With all the strength afforded to me with my injured leg, I lunged from my steed to his. I wrapped my arms around him like a Grecian wrestler and we collapsed into the mud.

It was a wonder the melee of horses didn't trample us to death immediately, but the fray had thinned out. The Picentes cavalry was retreating, at least in part.

The warrior beneath me shot his head into my nose with a crack. Darkness crept in like when I'd received the blow to my head, but I refused to give way to it. If I did, it would mean my death.

I reeled and he ran his fingers through the disturbed earth for his spear. He found a grip and tried to angle himself for a killing blow. But while the spear is an excellent weapon from horseback, its range is less effective in a scrummage like this. My short sword suited me just fine.

I threw an elbow to stun him. The blood of his lips mixed with that dripping from my nose. With my left arm, I caught his wrist and held the spear aloft. Straining the way I was, I couldn't get the proper positioning, but I managed to place the steel tip of my sword against the nape of his neck.

He released the grip on his spear, and it fell to the mud. He stopped squirming.

His eyes met mine. The warrior said nothing, but waited, accepting his fate.

I stood and grabbed his spear before he could and snapped it. I kept his gaze as he crawled to his feet and sprinted away.

Enough blood had been spilled that day, and I was in no condition to give chase.

My leg was numb, cold as ice now. The wound to my steed was superficial, and he had remained just where I'd left him, frightened perhaps, but as brave and loyal as any legionary had ever been. I threw my arms over his back and hoisted myself up with the last bit of effort available to me.

Straightening, I looked out across to the flag bearer. As if divined by Diana herself, he met my gaze. The tall plumes of officer's helmets aren't just to intimidate enemies.

"Send the reserves to the center! Reinforce the center!"

I shouted this again and again, praying some break in the chaos would allow him to hear me.

My cavalry was already charging on past me, chasing after the fleeing Picentes before the flag bearer understood. There was no signal for this maneuver, but he passed along the orders to the centurions. The back third of our right flank backed away from the line and marched to the failing center. Metellus would have something to say about this, but so would I.

I chased down my riders and joined them.

"To the line! To the line!"

They were reluctant but followed orders. We let the remaining Picentes riders escape the battlefield. Our focus was the rebel infantry now.

The rest of the battle is a faint memory. Steel. Blood. Limbs.

I fought until the end. I would have died otherwise.

But I can remember little more than hazy visions, like watching myself from a cliff far above the battlefield.

With my reinforcements, Metellus's center held. No enemy cavalry was present to impede Cicero, so he won the left flank by the time we were victorious on the right.

Together we crashed down on the Picentes center, and we quickly routed them.

Thousands of them survived, but too few to field an army. Many would quietly disband or flee somewhere safe from

Rome's wrath, if such a place exists. Others would seek out remaining rebel forces and pledge their services to them in the hopes of revenge, but that was a problem for another day.

"*Roma invicta!*" some of us shouted, while others resorted to vulgar insults and curses on the fleeing rebels.

As our officers surveyed our losses and our men collected the dead, I found Metellus on his horse. Not a drop of blood was on his sword or hands. His armor and flesh were unmarred.

"I told you to hold your position," I said.

He balked. Whether from the forwardness of my words or the crudeness of my appearance, I did not know. "I do not take orders from you, prefect."

He wielded a weapon for the first time that day, but it was just an angry patrician's finger pointed in my direction.

"We had a strategy, and you failed to maintain it," I said.

"You frog-spawned prole! Mind your tongue."

Perhaps I would have governed my words more carefully if I wasn't hazy from a shattered nose and an injured leg. But he had risked the lives of our men twice now. For greed, incompetence, expedience, or ambition, I didn't know which.

"If you ever again risk the destruction of our men to seek more glory for yourself . . ." I blinked the blur from my eye so I could see him clearly. "I will kill you myself."

For once, he was astounded. He heard me, and so did his retinue.

But I had measured my words carefully. "Go and tell Strabo that," I said, and then turned back to my men. "Prepare the pyres! Let's give our fallen the farewell they deserve. Then we leave this place."

SCROLL XI

ARREA—TWO DAYS before the Nones of April, 665 Ab Urbe
Condita

Less than a month had passed and already Toria fell
asleep to the sound of their training. She slept more
soundly on the training grounds than in the silk
sheets Barca provided us.

I tucked the cloth under my daughter's chin as I
bounced her in my arms, careful to shield her from
the sun when I could. Philosophers say the sun in
Gaul is the same in Italy, but even after years of
living in Rome, it still oppressed me in ways I never
experienced before. Toria shared my blood, so I
assumed she'd feel the same way.

She made a babbling noise but did not wake. I
smiled and wondered what she was dreaming
about. Perhaps the sting of her father's beard
against her cheek or the strength of his arms around
her. I prayed she would not have to dream of it
much longer.

The gladiators continued their training in various areas around us, each fenced in by wooden posts. There was a chorus of grunts, groans, shouts, insults, and a cacophony of vulgar language that endlessly amused me. The wooden swords of sparring partners cracked against one another. The more experienced among them added to the music with the clanking of steel.

I whispered, "One day, you can teach them how a real warrior fights."

I resisted the urge to kiss her cheeks or stroke her hair—a desire I couldn't seem to satiate.

"What do you think of my gladiators?" Barca's coarse but sharp voice cut through the melee as he neared.

He trained with his men most days, constantly berating them for minor weaknesses in their stance or the flaws in their strikes. But they didn't seem to begrudge this. The way they teased and taunted one another, they were all like siblings and Barca was the eldest brother.

Technically, they were Barca's slaves. But he treated them as kin, and their eyes revealed love and admiration when they gazed at him.

Deep old scars crisscrossed Barca's body in too many places to count. I was no doctor, but by the looks of them, no one tended to them properly.

I kept my voice quiet so as not to wake Toria, which was ludicrous considering the clamor of sparring gladiators. "I would give you my honest opinion, but it's an untrained one."

He smiled and drank deeply from the same stale, tepid well water his gladiators drank from. Barca reserved the good water from Nursia's aqueducts for his guests. "I steel myself in preparation."

"You seem to train some of them to win and some of them to die." I bounced Toria and rocked her in a particular method I discovered she liked.

"Explain," he said.

I nodded toward one of the training areas. "These you don't expect to live."

There was a rack of weapons and armor in between us, and he leaned up against it. I'd seen racks like this in the legionary camps Quintus served in, but Barca's were much more diverse. Not only swords and shields, but tridents, *murmillo's* helmets, *retiarius' manica*, and nets rested here, waiting to be used.

Barca's eyes flickered in a peculiar way, something they often did when he thoughtfully considered something.

"Why would you suppose that?"

"You teach them only how to kill," I said. I nodded toward another pen, where the men were training with steel rather than wood. "These you teach to win. To entertain. I think you expect them to last longer."

He crossed his arms. "You are perceptive. Some say this is why women shouldn't be allowed in *ludus*."

"Perception is neither helpful nor harmful," I said. "It matters only what you do with it."

Toria's little hand emerged from her swaddling cloth and stretched out, but she soon fell back into her dreams of Quintus.

"Should I alter my training regimen then?" He came around the weapon rack and gestured to a backless stool nearby.

I sat, and he dragged a wooden barrel nearby and joined me.

"Only if you want your gladiators to live longer," I said.

"I want this," he said. "Gladiators are expensive. Investments." He looked over at them, and a certain weight fell over him. "And I . . . care for them."

Barca was ageless, in a way. Youthful, but old. He'd lived many lives, I supposed, and was fortunate to still be alive at all. But I could not discern his age.

"When I was slave, I wanted to fight in great wars," he said. "Battles. Glory. Honor. Purpose. But sands always call me back, even after freedom."

Rhea walked toward us and silently gestured for Toria. I passed her along. Usually, I had a hard time letting her go, but the conversation intrigued me.

"Have you tried?"

He turned back to me. "Tried?"

"Tried to leave the sands. Tried to fight in battles."

He made a gesture akin to a nod, but different than a Roman's. He used unique head bobs like this to communicate often. Yes and no were imperceivably alike.

"I moved back to land of my fathers." He slouched. "Numidia. Deserts are in my blood. I expect to feel home. I married. Had child . . ." His gaze returned to the sands, and he seemed then to speak to himself. "But all is dull compared to roar of adoring crowds." He stood and clapped his hands.

I wasn't sure what that meant, but Barca was not one to remain still for long.

"I returned dowry. Left much to her and child. Then returned."

Barca and I had few things in common, but a past of slavery was one of them. I grieved for him, for whatever he may have lost. I mourned the man he might have been and what he might have accomplished.

"You should not burden yourself with this now," I said. "Although, you may have found an adoring child to be just as satisfying as the crowd if you'd given it some time." I smiled to ensure he didn't take the words too seriously, but he didn't look my way.

"I should like to create life." He nodded his head in that peculiar way again. "I should like to create life. Not take it. But not my lot. Tanit designed each for purpose. This is mine." He pointed to his *ludus*, where dark bloodstains marked the sands.

"Protecting life is almost the same as creating it," I said. "And you have protected ours. I cannot thank you enough for your hospitality, Barca."

He frowned and nodded in a way I believed meant no. "Your husband is great warrior. Your presence honors me."

Barca was a simple man. His code wasn't one I completely understood, but I respected his unwavering devotion to it.

"I should like to learn how to protect life," I said. "And take it if I must."

Barca threw his scarred head back and belly laughed. "Like to join me on the sands?"

"Perhaps there will be a time when Quintus is not there to protect me. Perhaps there will be a time when I can't rely on your high walls and gladiators.

If the Fates weave such a thread, I want to be able to defend myself and my daughter."

The laughter fell from his face and he became quite serious. "You want to learn?"

"I would."

He clicked his tongue. "Then I will train you, but I require compensation."

"I have little with which to pay you. I already owe you all I have."

Barca shook his head in that odd manner. "Not coin. I require skill. I want to read." He uttered the words without the usual confidence and bravado. "I never know how."

I smiled. "I just learned how to read and write Latin a few years ago myself . . ."

"Who better to teach me?"

I extended my hand. "It's a deal then," I said.

Barca shook it with the same strength and respect he would a man's. He turned and looked at one of the training pits where a gladiator was being dragged away with a wound to his leg.

"Ready?"

I turned to check on Toria, who was still sleeping soundly in the adoring arms of her grandmother.

"Let's begin."

SCROLL XII

GAVIUS SERTORIUS—TWO Days before the Ides of April, 665 Ab Urbe Condita

" Bucephalus and I rode alongside Sulla and the remaining cavalry, and behind us were eighteen thousand legionaries of Sulla's Fist. Two thousand remained at Pompeii to continue the siege, but we were still the strongest of all Rome's legions at arms.

Regardless, we no longer had the Numidian cavalry riding with us. We could no longer rely on their strength. I didn't mention it to Sulla, and he didn't mention it to me. But I was thinking about it, and I knew he was too.

Sulla's Fist marched in columns that stretched back as far as the eye could see. They moved as one entity—as they did in battle—a snake of iron and flesh winding through the Italian landscape.

But they moved differently than they used to. There was a reluctance in their step, a somberness to their songs. For good reason, I suppose. The rebels outwitted us, not once but twice. We looked like fools.

For the first time since the war began, we'd be riding into battle without our Numidian allies. And not only without them, but against them. Fortuna was a fickle goddess by all accounts, but she'd so recently been our bride and was now our tormentor.

The road ahead bent around a copse of cypress trees, their dark silhouettes stark against the pale morning sky. It was here that I first spotted them.

Riders. At first, I supposed there were a few hundred. Then a thousand. As they continued pouring into view, I gave up trying to count.

The centurions ordered a halt.

"Who on Gaia's earth is that?" I said to myself.

"Do not worry, young Gavius," Sulla said, high and resolute on his white steed beside me.

I caught sight of a grin on Lucullus's face. "Don't you know Romans when you see them?" he said.

Sulla and Lucullus swept by me.

"Are you not coming?" the latter cried back.

I still failed to fully comprehend what was happening, but I refused to be left out.

"Yah!"

Bucephalus galloped after them and we arrived before they exchanged introductions.

"*Ave*, sons of Rome!" Sulla shouted.

"*Salve*," was the only reply from the leader. He was a young man, barely out of his teens, but carried an assertive posture that belied his years. His face bore not a single wrinkle—from hardship or laughter.

Battle had yet to mar or weather the leader's armor. The breastplate's gleam was stark against ours. I could see nothing on the young officer's face that indicated exposure to combat, but the riders flooding in behind and alongside him made up for any doubts I had. These riders were ready for war.

The officer raised his right hand. I discerned from this small gesture the man's lineage. He was a noble, a patrician, someone born of powerful men.

"My name is Marcus Licinius Crassus." He allowed each word to linger.

Crassus meant "fat" or "well-fed." Oddly enough, he was tall and thin, but the name signified wealth more than dining habits, and so the name was apt.

"It's a pleasure to meet you. I believe I know your father," Sulla said. "I suppose you know who I am? Who we are?"

"Indeed," the man said.

The cloak draped across his shoulder was a deep, unblemished red. He adjusted it.

"Just out for a stroll, then?" Sulla questioned.

"I am here to fix your problem."

"And what problem might that be?" Lucullus asked.

Crassus kept his eyes on Sulla as he answered. "Your Numidians have abandoned you. The news has reached Rome already."

I looked down.

"You need cavalry. I have brought them." He gestured to the riders behind him. "Seven hundred equestrians from Campania. The finest horsemen Italy has to offer."

"Did the senate send you? Are you a magistrate?" Sulla asked.

Crassus didn't blink. "No. These are my employees, and I am their employer," he said. "If you know my father, then you know my family is quite . . . wealthy. And what is the purpose of wealth if you cannot afford your own army?"

We stared at him in silence for a moment, waiting for him to smile or laugh. He did neither. Instead, he waited patiently for Sulla's reply.

"You speak truth?"

"I have no time for lies, legate."

Sulla shifted on his horse. "What can I do for you in return, Licinius Crassus?"

"Nothing. I and my cavalry are here to pledge our loyalty to you," he said. "I ask only that you allow me to command the men I've brought you."

The calmness in his eyes punctuated the dry manner of his speech. The man seemed to be totally oblivious or completely unconcerned that we marched to face the rebels' most dangerous army in an impregnable stronghold.

"Done." Sulla clapped his hands twice as if the gesture were a sealed contract. "Anything else?"

"Only this." Crassus raised his right hand again, an oratorical gesture of those who'd recently gone through rigorous training for a political career. "Two rebel armies are converging on your position. One from the northwest, the other from the southwest. They will meet us within two days. They are not expecting you to have sufficient cavalry support. We can use this to our advantage," he said. "And slaughter them."

Sulla smiled. "And slaughter them, we shall! Welcome to Sulla's Fist, Licinius Crassus. We have many battles ahead."

SCROLL XIII

QUINTUS SERTORIUS—SIX Days after the Ides of April, 665 Ab Urbe Condita

It only took me a few weeks in my new camp to realize what was different: the men were disgruntled.

Not because they were fighting their own countrymen. Not because of the sweltering heat we toiled in each day. No, the cause of their discontent was that old terrible curse that had brought about more wars than the gods, love, and patriotism combined: money.

Well, money and land.

Strabo raised an army so quickly the year prior in part due to the many promises he made. So far, most agreed he had under delivered.

As the men grumbled, Strabo's promises continued to grow and expand, with more and more vowed to them after we took Asculum.

But, while his men ate meager meals and received less than what he'd promised them, Strabo continued to host lavish dinners for his officers.

I now understood why my friends told me he was the most hated man in Rome.

I did not attend a few of these dinners as a form of protest. This ostentatious display would alienate our men from us at the time when we needed to rally closest together. But six days after the Ides of April, Pompey came to me and addressed the matter.

"My father conducts his business at these feasts. If you want any input at all in the attack on Asculum, you need to be there."

There was shame in his eyes as he spoke those words. He probably felt the same way about his father's actions as I did, but his family loyalty or honor kept him from addressing it.

"I'll be there," I said, and I refused to break a promise.

So, I joined them. Stitches still held together the wound to my ankle. I still struggled to breathe through my swollen nose. My head continued to throb. But for Rome and for honor, I would have joined Strabo and his officers in the latrines if I had to. I refused to let an officer like Metellus Pius devise the battle plan for taking Asculum.

The transformation from the exterior camp to the interior of Strabo's praetorium was disorienting. From the ruggedness of a military siege to the opulence of a Roman villa. The tent was a world unto itself, an island of luxury among the harshness of warfare.

Sumptuous fabrics of rich purples and deep reds hung throughout. Ornate vases, decorative silver plates, and finely carved marble busts lined the space. Whether these were spoils of war, or brought from Strabo's home, I didn't know. Either way, they had no business in a praetorium.

"Greetings, prefect," Gratidianus said with a smile. "I'm delighted you've joined us."

At least the first face to greet me was a friendly one. I'd grown to like Gratidianus, his cousin Cicero, and Pompey as well. The rest, I didn't care for.

"By Hera's tits!"

The friendliest of them all, Cataline, came and threw an arm around Gratidianus's shoulders.

"You told me he'd join us, but I didn't believe you. Brother Sertorius, good to see you."

Nothing about his delivery appeared disingenuous, although I did detect the slur of drunkenness on the edge of his words. Still, I didn't trust him. Something in the eyes.

"*Ave, ave.*" I shook their hands.

Lavish couches, arranged in the Roman style of villa dining, were scattered around behind them. Plush cushions and fine linens accompanied each one, as if this was a symposium rather than a military meeting.

"Come, come. Let's get you some wine," Cataline said. "I've seen that swill you've been drinking. Strabo serves only the finest Greek imports here."

Rather than a desk filled with maps and military ledgers, the centerpiece of the praetorium was a large table. It groaned under the weight of the extravagant feast being prepared. Roasted meats, assortments of baked bread and expensive cheeses, and fresh fruit, which I knew couldn't grow anywhere within a hundred miles of Asculum.

It was no exaggeration to say this meal may have cost more than a monthly supply of grain for my entire legion. This greed stirred rage in my chest, but I quelled it. I needed to keep my mind clear.

Fine wine flowed freely, served in goblets that glinted in the light of oil lamps, casting a golden glow over the proceedings. Cataline snatched one of these from a *servus* and poured me a cup himself.

"Gratitude." I found an empty couch and sat, rather than making the rounds to speak with everyone directly.

Cataline and Gratidianus sat across from me, though, and Cicero soon joined. I wouldn't be able to escape conversation.

"Your recovery goes well, I assume?" Cicero asked.

"Well enough," I said. "I've received my fair share of battle-field injuries. These are no different."

The surrounding officers engaged in lively conversation. The occasional bout of laughter punctuated the clank of silverware and the gentle clatter of plates.

"You and Asclepius must be old friends," Gratidianus said.

"I've sacrificed a lot to him over the years, and he's always healed me." I sipped my wine. It was a high quality, in the style I'd sampled during my campaign in Greece. Still, soldier's swill suited me more on campaigns. None of this was right.

I caught sight of Pompey across the praetorium. He reclined on the couch beside his father, plucking at a simple plate of bread and cheese. He must have felt my gaze for he looked up and gave me a curt nod.

"Who is that?" Strabo's voice silenced all else in the tent. He was pointing in my direction.

Metellus leaned over and whispered, "Prefect Quintus Sertorius."

"What an honor, gentlemen!" Strabo said. "Our illustrious, victorious prefect has joined us."

I stood, placed my wine on the ground, and saluted him. "Consul."

Officers around the praetorium snickered. Clearly, Strabo didn't require proper military decorum at his feasts.

"Come, join us. Perhaps you and Metellus could tell us some stories of your time in battle together."

I made my way to them and took my seat on the couch across from them. I kept my eye on the commander, but I could feel Metellus's presence beside him. His glare might burn holes in my flesh if it lasted any longer.

We'd not spoken any more than necessary since our confrontation on the battlefield. I'm sure he immediately reported my threats to Strabo. The commander likely found it amusing, although Metellus and I both knew whose side he would defer to if Metellus and I found ourselves at odds.

"Tell me, why have you joined us?" Strabo leaned forward on his couch. "You've refused my generous offers in the past."

I weighed the words. "I'm healing more and more each day. And I hear that the attack on Asculum may begin soon. I wanted to assist in preparations."

Strabo exchanged a look with a few of his officers. "You are an interesting creature, Sertorius. Morose is how I'd describe you. Always focused on the next battle . . . don't you see we've already won the war?"

"I do not see that, sir," I said.

He sighed. Explaining this was apparently bothersome. "The senate passed legislation offering citizenship to any Italian who doesn't take up arms against us. Without fresh tribes arriving to their aid, the rebel forces will dwindle. We, on the other hand, have an empire to draw resources from."

Officers around him nodded. That explains why they took their duties so lightly. They didn't need to initiate battle. They only needed to hold off for the rebel cause to fail.

"There are still battles to be fought. Like Asculum," I said. "Unless we intend to wait and allow starvation to do the work for us?"

Perhaps we could win the war by waiting year after year, sustaining countless losses, and draining the state coffers. But he would gain no glory by doing so.

I didn't know him well enough to know whether glory, money, power, or something else motivated him. But as the smile fell from his face, I knew the insinuation upset him.

"Oh we will take Asculum," he said. "And soon. I mean only that smiling occasionally would not be so damaging to the prestige and safety of Rome as you seem to think."

Hearing those words, I did smile. One battle. One city. We could end the war in the north. Then I could take my family to Rome, run for office, and end the war in the south with legislation. No more bloodshed.

"See? Not so hard, is it?" Strabo said. "Get him another cup of wine. I want to see what he's like when he's more satiated."

A *servus* brought me another cup without delay.

"Thank you, consul," I said. "If you would forgive my morose and battle-focused ways, I have been thinking about the attack on Asculum, and I have some ideas to share with you."

That was an understatement. I'd prepared a strategy for the entire battle, such that I could lead it myself if asked. Strabo's previous absence from the battlefield made that a distinct possibility, but I knew the honor would go to one such as Metellus Pius unless I convinced him otherwise.

Strabo placed a hand against his forehead as if he was growing very weary. "Oh, prefect. Before I discuss strategy with a man, I like to get the measure of him first. Tell me, tell me of your family."

"I have a wife. Her name is Arrea," I said.

Strabo slapped a *servus* behind him with his pudgy, ringed hand. I paused, but no one else seemed to notice. Strabo himself offered no explanation, and the *servus* sulked away without dabbing the blood from his split lip.

"Go on," the consul said.

"We've been married for ten years now, though I've been away and fighting for many of them."

"I do not recognize the name," Strabo said. "I'm assuming she's not of notable stock?"

I cleared my throat and considered my response. It was clear Strabo was testing me, and the other officers were listening closely to see how I'd handle it.

Arrea was unashamed of who she was, and who we were, so I refused to be ashamed either.

"The most noble stock of all."

"And what is that?"

"She was born with great character and courage," I said, "and then enslaved."

Strabo chuckled along with several other officers. Metellus laughed the loudest.

"You aren't the first Roman—nor will you be the last—to fall in love with his slave," Strabo said. "Jupiter knows I've made the mistake a time or two myself, although I usually return to sanity after spilling my seed."

The officers laughed harder.

"She wasn't my slave," I said. "She was a slave in Gaul. I killed her master and liberated her on campaign."

Strabo nodded as if he understood entirely. "A trophy of war then?"

My grip tightened around the stem of my wine cup, but otherwise I didn't move. "A gift from the gods."

"Well . . . who can blame the man," Strabo said to his officers before turning back to me. "Is she beautiful?"

"Yes."

"A wife can never be perfect." Strabo clapped his hands and accepted another cup of wine from the bloody-lipped *servus*.

"And so is my daughter."

"You married a slave, but a beautiful one. She may be a detriment to your career, but at least she's pleasant to look at. Nay?" He gulped his wine. "Have you seen my son's wife?"

"No." I turned my gaze to Pompey.

His strong jaw twitched.

"Well, she was no slave. In fact, she was relatively highborn. Good family, good name. The dowry was impressive. However . . ." He paused, but I already knew where he was going. "She looks as if she were hit in the face by a sack of hot denarii, to put it plainly."

I'd never heard the expression before, but I assumed it was another crude Picentes metaphor, this time to describe someone unattractive.

"Father, please." Pompey exhaled. "I ask you not to speak of her this way."

"See, this is what I mean," Strabo said. "Even with a hideous wife, they say my son actually loves her."

Pompey stood. "I'm going to the *latrina*."

As the consul's son departed, I said, "Marriage can be the bedrock upon which a man builds his greatness. Or it can lead to ruin. I applaud your son for making his marriage a happy one."

Strabo rolled his eyes. "Why applaud him? I was the one who found the girl, brokered the marriage, and sorted out the dowry."

I decided not to respond to that.

"So, what else?" Strabo said. "Have you any begrudging children of your own?"

"I have two, a son and a daughter. The girl is too young to begrudge me. She is less than two months old."

"Ah." Strabo clicked his tongue. "Now I understand your haste to finish the war. And your son?"

"A man now. He's a tribune under Legatus Lucius Cornelius Sulla."

No one laughed at that.

"Sulla, you say? That is a lucrative command. You must be heavily indebted to your son's commander," Strabo said.

I met his gaze. "My son earned the position. It was not a favor."

Strabo didn't appear to hear my answer. There was mischief in his drunken eyes. "They say Sulla might run for consul next year. They say he is the favorite to win command of the war against Mithridates. Perhaps you mean to join him and your son on the adventure east?"

I took a sip of wine. "I have fought in many wars, commander. Each has been to protect Rome for a real and present threat. I have no interest in fighting foreign wars of conquest and plunder."

The laughter returned. How horribly naive they must have thought me. How horribly misled I found them.

"After Asculum falls, I intend to return to Rome. I will run for office, and if elected, will pass legislation to quicken the end of the war in the south."

"Either way, you're clearly influenced by your desire to end this war as expeditiously as possible," Metellus said. "Desire can betray you."

"Anyone fighting a war should be seeking to end it."

No one seemed to refute me, but I knew they disagreed. They wanted to milk their positions like tired old heifers until they had nothing left to gain from it.

"Well, tell us of your *plan*, then." Strabo threw himself back on his couch, preparing for boredom.

I spoke of Asculum's defenses, and what our guards had estimated their numbers to be. With little feedback from the consul or his officers, I explained our own capabilities and where I thought we could find strategic advantage. Without the use of maps or a sandbox to draw in, I used empty cups of wine to illustrate the various maneuver elements, and a bowl of figs to display the high walls of Asculum.

"They cannot sustain two points of attack, general," I said. "They do not have the manpower. If we send the bulk of our forces against the main gates, if we delay long enough, we should be able to send a single legion to the weak point along the northeastern wall. If we move swiftly, we can scale the wall there with no resistance."

"And I suppose you desire to lead this flanking force?" Metellus interrupted.

"Who leads the force is immaterial," I said. "The commander will have a heavy weight to bear whoever he is. My desire is simply to win this battle."

"Very interesting." Strabo wiped the blur from his eyes. "You've thought this through even more than I expected, and I didn't suppose that to be possible."

I didn't know whether that was an insult or compliment, but I didn't care. "If the city walls have even one more point of exit, the rebels could execute a flanking maneuver of their own. This strategy is sound, but it only works if—"

"I have done all the required surveillance," Metellus interrupted me again. "There are no other exits this side of the river. They cannot flank us."

"It's settled then." Strabo guzzled the rest of the wine. "Sertorius, you may lead this expeditionary force of yours, and my son can lead the assault on the main gate, along with Metellus here. We will assault Asculum's walls on the next auspicious day," he said. "Now, finish that drink of yours, Sertorius. Your advice has been taken and your words heard. Nothing else to be sullen about now."

The fate of Rome depended on our victory. My wife and daughter waited for me. I would win the battle, and then I would end the war.

SCROLL XIV

AREA—SIX DAYS before the Kalends of May, 665 Ab Urbe Condita

" Unlike the rest of the arena, our chairs were cushioned and shaded by a canvas awning, yet that offered little respite from the summer heat. *Servi* waved us down with large, colorful ostrich-feathered fans, but still the sweat clung to my skin like a blanket.

Barca told me I could remain at the *ludus*, but after training with him for the past nineteen days, I was eager to see real gladiators in combat for the first time in my life.

A *lanista* and his guests could access these special seats during the games, alongside the wealthy patrons who invested heavily into their gladiatorial schools.

"You're putting on a good showing today, Barca," one of the old aristocrats said.

Barca's eyes remained fix on the combat before us.

I imagined everyone would enjoy the spectacle of the arena. But Barca had remained on the edge of his cushioned chair the entire day, and not once had his peculiar smile appeared. He wore an expensive toga and jeweled bracelets rather than his training armor. That made him uncomfortable.

But there was something more. Perhaps he feared for the safety of his men, or he simply yearned for his school to be victorious. Maybe both.

"Come, Barca, we have earned a lot of denarii today, you and I." The aristocrat took a heavy pull from his wine. "I'll place another two thousand on the *murmillo*," he said to a nearby record-keeper.

I couldn't fathom the amount of money these patrons had won and lost throughout the day. But if one could tell by their purple-teethed grins, they were on the winning side of the ledger.

Barca did not reply to them. Instead, he leaned over to me. "Are you comfortable?"

"Yes." I lied. He seemed unfazed by the heat, and I refused to show him weakness or slight his hospitality.

If I was not sleeping, eating, or caring for Toria, Barca expected me to be practicing a particular movement. He took his role as teacher seriously. He treated me the same as his gladiators, save the insults and vulgar language. He expected much of me. That honored me. I refused to let him down.

In turn, I also expected much of him. "What does that say?" I pointed to a leather canvas hanging down beside one of the far arena gates.

He strained his eyes, and I could see his lips moving as he sounded out the words.

"Red . . . team . . . combat . . . comba*tants*," he said. "Red team combatants."

His lack of progress often frustrated him. But he was as dutiful in his lessons as he was on the sands, and he learned more each day.

"Did the color of the dye aid you?" I jested.

He shook his head. "I know these words."

I pointed to a tarp on the opposite end of the arena. "And this one?"

"Green team combatants," he said. For the first time that day, I saw a stifled smile. "This time, dye helped me."

I rewarded him the same way he rewarded me when I performed an exercise correctly: eye contact and a nod of the head.

The platform where we sat was elevated so that I could see the entire arena. A vast circle of sand surrounded by rising tiers of seats, each row teeming with spectators. The entire structure seemed to vibrate with the weight of their cheers and jeers, a cacophonous symphony that ebbed and flowed with the tide of the battle below.

We were still close enough to the sands to experience it all. The tang of sweat, the sharp stench of fear and blood from the combat, mixing with the heady aroma of perfumed nobles.

The crowd erupted as one combatant fell to his knees. Everyone jumped to their feet except Barca and me.

"Damn it," he swore under his breath and held a clenched fist to his lips. "How many times have I taught him to evade maneuver? How many times?" He spoke to himself.

The patron closest to him slapped him on the shoulder and leaned close to be heard over the crowd. "Oh, come now, Barca. He was one of your weakest entrants." I could smell the sour taste of wine on his breath from where I was sitting. "That did just cost me two thousand denarii, though, so I expect your next man to win."

Barca's jaw twitched. "Dimitrius will not fail."

"Live! Live! Live!" The people chanted.

"See? Your man lives to see another day," the patron said. "Four thousand on the next bout, on the *secutor*."

I felt as if I could evaluate combat sufficiently after training with Barca for a few weeks. Before, it was simple chaos to me, like watching someone play a game without knowing the rules. Now, I could almost see the beauty in it. Not so much a display in strength but in skill, preparation, and desire. I recognized many of the feigns and parries Barca taught me. It was more akin to a dance now. A dance that doesn't end until blood is spilled.

Still, as a former slave, I was acutely aware of the barbarity of it. I was intrigued but horrified. I wondered how Barca truly felt. He knew intimately what the combatants experienced on the sands. It was all he'd ever known.

The presiding magistrate spared the defeated gladiator. The crowds cheered as the victor raised his fist in triumph.

After the two gladiators departed through their respective gates, *servi* rushed out to rake over the sands to prepare for the next battle. Still, they could not eradicate the bloodstains.

"Only one battle left today," Barca said.

"You seem relieved," I said.

He nodded his head in that peculiar manner, and again I did not know what he meant.

A hush fell over the crowd suddenly, more so than in the brief interludes between previous battles.

I looked to Barca and noticed his keen eyes narrowing, he perceived something different as well.

There was a clatter and shouting coming from the bowels of the arena.

Rather than the next round of combatants, a band of soldiers strode out onto the sands.

They looked like Romans to me, wearing armor like my husband's. But the crowds were silent. If these were Romans, the crowds would be cheering.

One soldier stepped out from the shields of the others. The light glinted off his breastplate and plumed helmet, casting a brief, blinding flash across the arena.

The man was average height, but strong. Fleshy bags hung under his eyes and deep lines etched the flesh between his brows. He might have been fifty years old, but it was clear he had the vigor of a man half that.

The man rested both hands on the hilt of his sword and scanned the crowd with piercing, dark eyes. The silence did not disturb him.

When he spoke, his voice carried effortlessly to the silent spectators. "My name is Papius Mutilus, Consul of the Italic League."

He allowed these words to linger and echo throughout the arena. This was the commander my husband feared. The man all of Italy was concerned about, and he was here in this arena. Why?

Barca was again on the edge of his seat, glaring at the soldiers and their leader. The wealthy men beside him slouched over in their cushioned seats, as if hoping to disappear. They'd heard of what Mutilus did to Romans. We all had.

"I have not come to speak to Roman dogs. You know what I would have to say to you. I am here to speak with those of more substance. Those of will and strength." He scanned the arena, where gladiators were flocking to the edges of the barred gates and listening intently. "You warriors fight for the greed and entertainment of your captors. They become rich off your scars. They benefit from your every victory and benefit from your swift and cruel death."

My heart pounded and my mouth ran dry. I could not bring myself to move an inch, or I would have drank more honey water.

"I offer you another fate. Cast off your chains! Stop killing one another in the mere hopes that one day you'll be 'freed.' Trust me, as one who has fought many battles for Rome. The fallen Republic will *not* reward your sacrifice. Even if you're fortunate enough to survive or earn your citizenship, they will *never* count you as one of them."

He brandished shackles from his cloak and lifted them for the crowd to see. He threw them to the bloody sand.

"Instead of waiting for Rome to free you . . . free yourselves! Join me. Slay your captors rather than one another. Seek revenge. Seek justice. I founded the Italic League to punish Rome for her iniquities and her transgressions against my people. With me, you can exact vengeance for what Rome took from you and those you love." He raised his fist and his soldiers pounded their shields.

"But don't just listen to me!" Mutilus grinned. That charming, easy, confident smile had convinced entire tribes to betray Rome. "I know many among you are Numidians. I speak to you now. There is someone I would like you to see, someone you're far more likely to trust."

Mutilus waved back to his soldiers. They parted, and a young man joined the rebel consul.

"I present to you Juba, Prince of Numidia!" Mutilus pulled the prince forward for all to see.

Juba's skin was youthful and chestnut colored. His black hair was shoulder length and bound in thin curls. The young man's attempt at a beard was beginning to develop on his chin.

Only the silver crown on his head distinguished him as royalty. I might have doubted Mutilus's claims if not for Barca's reaction. He knew the young man before us was the heir to the throne of his people.

Juba scanned the crowd with anxious, darting glances.

"Go on, your highness. Tell them," Mutilus said.

Barca trembled with repressed emotion. The wine in his cup spilled over his hands.

The prince cleared his throat. "Mutilus liberate me. I am free now, you can be too." Juba's voice was high and shaky. He looked at Mutilus to see if that was enough. Apparently not. "Join us, and we punish Rome."

Mutilus, satisfied, ushered Juba back into the ranks of his men. "Sons of Numidia, six hundred of your warriors have already joined us. You, too, can fight beside your prince. Not only may you punish Rome, you can share in the forging of our new empire." He raised his ringed hand as an oratorical gesture that he'd reached his conclusion. "I've stationed my army in the stronghold of Nola, but

I'm currently camped two days ride from here. Head south on the Via Flaminia, and you'll find us. But I will rejoin my forces on the Ides of May. This is your only opportunity to join us. The choice is yours. You must decide your fate. Now."

He and his warriors departed.

The crowd remained silent as the iron gate crashed down behind them.

I turned to Barca, hoping he would have something to say, or some reassurance to offer. But he simply gazed down at the empty arena.

For the first time since I'd known him, uncertainty was in his eyes.

SCROLL XV

 Battle in May was hot, but it was nothing compared to the bathhouse.

"If there is a better way to celebrate victory, I've never encountered it." Sulla slipped off his cloak.

Steam rose from the sunken stone of the baths, obscuring the other officers as they discarded their armor.

Lucullus said, "Bring wine, figs, cheese, bread . . . anything else you can find."

A *servus* bowed and sprinted off to do Lucullus's bidding.

I untied my breastplate and let it clatter to the ground. I slipped the chain mail over my head and peeled off my sweat-soaked tunic like a snake shedding its skin.

The breath caught in my lungs as I dipped my toes in.

"It's quite pleasant once you're submerged." Crassus sunk down to his shoulders.

"I've not seen a bathhouse like this before," I said.

"Stabiae is known for its opulence," Sulla said. "Now it is ours to enjoy."

I settled into the water and was able to breathe again. The warmth of the sunken pools embraced my battle-weary limbs, soothing the abrasions from my armor and the cuts I'd received in the day's battle. Steam kissed my skin, softening it until the pads of my hands and feet grew pink and pliable. Smooth rocks and pebbles lined the inside of the pool, gently massaging my muscles.

It would have been one of the more restful moments I'd experienced since joining the legion if it weren't for the incessant screams and pleas for mercy coming from outside the bathhouse. The occasional crash of an expensive vase or glass shattering added to the cacophony as some officers looked through the discarded belongings of the bath's former patrons. They must have scattered the moment they heard our war horns.

"Ah, there is the wine." Sulla splashed water over his face. "I have never been so parched."

The *servus* was effective in his orders. He brought us no less than six amphorae of wine and a basket filled with delicacies to enjoy. He must have been afraid for his life, but slaves needn't fear us. The citizens of Stabiae, however, had every right to be afraid. The turmoil outside was evidence of that.

I accepted a cup of wine and drained it quickly. Water would have suited me just fine, but stupefaction was as desirable after battle as quenched thirst. The tart vinous liquid dried my already parched throat, which was hoarse from shouting commands at our men and insults at our enemy. Still, I snapped for another cup.

"You were true to your word, Licinius Crassus," Sulla said. "Those riders of yours are some of the finest I've commanded, and I've commanded many."

The dour man nodded. Even in victory, I rarely saw him smile. "They should be, for what I paid them."

Crassus had certainly been good on his word. Within two days of his arrival, we'd completely routed a Samnite army. Within a week, we'd conquered a rebel stronghold. It'd been almost a month since Crassus arrived with his cavalry reinforcements, and we'd taken three Samnite cities, Stabiae being the third.

And we didn't just take the rebel cities, we destroyed them. It seemed like a waste to burn down such beautiful cities when we simply could have occupied them, but Sulla insisted it was important to demoralize the enemy. As a result, the men fought harder than ever. As fiercely as they battled in a pitched engagement, they were even more determined when taking a rebel city, imagining the women and plunder awaiting them on the other side of victory.

Nola would have to wait, Sulla said. He compared this war to a poem and said the destruction of Nola would be the resounding line he finished on.

"Well, whatever you've paid them, they've doubled their investment since joining," Lucullus said. "Can you imagine the spoils the men are claiming as we sit here soaking?"

"I will make the men of Sulla's Fist richer than all the senators in Rome before I'm done," Sulla said.

When we'd arrived, the perfumed air contained traces of lavender, rose, and imported spices from the East. Now, the pungent, metallic odor of freshly spilled blood took over. The acrid stench of burning buildings oozed in through the arched rafters. Crimson blood permeated the bath, clouding the underwater mosaics depicting Jason and the Argonauts.

Crassus swept back his wet hair to cover the premature balding of his head. "Legate, I heard rumor you plan to run for consul in the upcoming elections," he said. "Is that true?"

Sulla concealed a grin behind his cup of wine. "You should never believe the rumors you hear about me, young Crassus," he said. "Although this one is true."

Crassus nodded, the strongest indication of pleasure he'd ever revealed. "In all Rome's many years, this might be the most lucrative year of all to be made consul. You've chosen your time wisely," Crassus said.

My ears perked up.

"Why do you think so?" Lucullus wondered the same thing I was.

Crassus took a delicate bite of a fig. "Because the war with Mithridates is bound to begin as soon as we've finished with these rebels. The most qualified consul is likely to lead the war."

"Well, no matter who Rome elects alongside Sulla, he will be less qualified than our general," Lucullus said.

One might have assumed Lucullus was vying

for favor the way he praised Sulla, but there was nothing but conviction in his voice.

"And why is war against Mithridates so desirable?" I asked at the risk of sounding stupid.

"Because he's the richest king in the world, as far as we can tell," Crassus said. "The wealth flows so freely in Pontus his men imbed diamonds in their shields." His eyes contained a peculiar glimmer when he spoke about money. "Or so they say."

Sulla watched Lucullus and me for our responses.

I tried to hide my greed better than Crassus, but it was no use.

"You're beginning to understand it." Sulla winked. "If I'm elected, Sulla's Fist will lead the war against the king of Pontus, and we'll come back with riches greater than Rome has ever seen. Italian cities like Stabiae will appear as little more than thatched villages by comparison to the great citadels we'll claim. I want each of you alongside me."

I smiled. How could I refuse such a generous offer? Sulla shared the spoils freely with his men and his officers. I would likely earn more in one war than my father earned in his entire military career.

But who knew how long the campaign would last? My father served in Greece on a peacetime mission and didn't return for eight years. I'd heard little about this Mithridates outside of rumors and speculation, but I imagined defeating him would be no small feat, even for legions as powerful as ours. I still longed to meet my sister and wondered how

old she'd be before I could do so if there was no
time before our departure.

"That actually brings up a matter I want to
discuss," Sulla said. He pointed to the *servus*. "You,
boy, more wine for each of us."

We accepted refills and waited for Sulla to
speak.

"I will return to Rome to announce my bid for
consul on the Kalends of June. The journey should
take no longer than a few weeks."

"Your accomplishments speak for themselves.
I'm sure a few weeks will be all that's required,"
Lucullus said.

"My thoughts exactly. In the meantime, I want
each of you to continue leading in my stead."

"I would be remiss if I did not ask who you
intend to place in command while you're away."
Crassus settled into the water up to his chin.

"You'll command the legion by committee.
You'll all work in conjunction with one another.
Unorthodox, I suppose, but I need to know you all
can cooperate."

"We'll see it done, legate," I said.

Sulla took a sip of wine. "Actually, Gavius, I
meant the others. I would like you to come with me
to Rome."

The waters rippled as Lucullus crossed his arms.
"Why Gavius?" His words slurred, and I could tell
he was becoming drunk.

"I trust you all to accompany me, and I trust
you all to lead. But I need Gavius for a special
purpose."

"A special purpose?" Lucullus said.

"A special purpose." Sulla met his gaze,
ensuring Lucullus asked no more questions.

Footsteps echoed through the long, dank bath-house corridors. Two centurions arrived and saluted.

"Report."

"We've rounded up the captives, legate," one centurion said.

"Three hundred and fifty-six fighting men in total," the other added.

"So few?" Crassus said without emotion.

"Many . . . took their life before we could disarm them."

I took another gulp of wine, well on my way to joining Lucullus.

"And civilians?" Sulla asked.

"Too many to count," the first centurion answered.

"I suggest you try," Crassus said. "Ledgers require exact numbers."

"You heard the man." Sulla shrugged.

"What shall we do with them?" I asked.

There had been no consistent policy with the previous cities we'd taken. We burned each city to the ground and executed every fighting man, but Sulla's orders for the women and children had been vastly different. One group we sold into slavery, and we released another with promise of sanctuary in Rome if they sought new homes. I could find no explanation for the variance aside from Sulla's whims.

Sulla tapped his chin. "Hmm. What do you think, Gavius? You decide."

The officers and centurions looked to me, awaiting a response. This felt like some sort of test. I assumed there was a right answer, a wrong answer, and a clever answer I couldn't think of.

"Free them," I said.

I watched for signs. Lucullus seemed pleased, or perhaps he was simply too drunk to care. Crassus shook his head and pursed his lips.

Sulla simply nodded. "The tribune has spoken," he said. "Do as he says."

The centurions saluted and spun on their heels, their boots clopping on the wet stone as they departed.

Crassus said, "Why release them? Do you have any idea the coin their sale would have brought in?"

Because it's what my father would do, I thought.

Instead, I said, "Let the people of Italy know there is no greater friend than Lucius Cornelius Sulla, and no worse enemy. Today, we reveal the fruits of friendship. Tomorrow, we show the entire world what it means to be his enemy."

SCROLL XVI

Quintus Sertorius—Four days before the Ides of May, 665 Ab Urbe Condita

Oftentimes the hardest part of any battle is waiting for it to begin. This task was made more difficult as we watched the legions assembled under Pompey beginning their advance on Asculum's walls.

Clouds swept over the verdant hillside, darkening our faces as we remained in formation under a thick patch of trees. I could feel the weighted thoughts of the men behind me.

Would they be brave? Cowardly? Would they die? Would they kill? Would they be overcome with bloodlust or over-whelmed with dread?

Pompey's forces were nearing Asculum's gate like a vast and angry sea crashing against an island. And what a formidable island it was. The crenellated battlements were wide enough to host four rows of men at deeper points, each armed with a bow, slingshot, or javelin.

We would not spring into action just yet. The men could use some distraction.

I turned and locked on the first man who met my gaze.

"What's your name, soldier?"

"Marcus," he said.

"Have a nomen, Marcus?"

"Fronto. Marcus Fronto."

"What did you do before joining the legions?" I asked.

My men's leather creaked and their mail rustled as they shifted anxiously, but they were listening now.

"I was a hunter, and a hunter killer."

"Care to elaborate?"

"I hunted anything with four legs or wings," Fronto said. "And then I hunted my competitors—wolves, wildcats, anything you can think of."

"Were you good?"

He straightened. "Show me wolf piss and I can tell you whether it belongs to a male or female."

The men laughed, just as I hoped.

"I suppose that's a good thing." I turned to the next man. "And you?"

"My name is Hybrida, and I'm a glassmaker. I helped my mum run a shop in the Forum. She's run it since my father died at Arausio."

I declined to mention that I survived the same battle. It was honey and spice seeing the son of one of my fallen brothers here, taking his place.

"I'm sure your mother misses your assistance," I said.

"Mum's the one who made me join," he replied. "Said I'm no good at selling glass and I'd have to start selling my arse to bring in coin. Said I could sell it at the brothel or to the legion."

More laughter.

"Seems like a fairly obvious choice," I shrugged.

"Depends on how this battle goes, prefect," another legionary answered. "I'd rather take it from a drunkard in the Forum than an Asculum rebel."

The men were cackling now, just in time for Pompey's battering rams to touch the walls.

"We'll be just fine," I said. "Stay with me. Protect your brothers. Fight for Rome. All our mothers will be proud, and everyone's arse will be spared, even Hybrida's."

I turned back to the assault. All was going well. A bit longer and we would rush to the western wall. No siege equipment needed. Three ladders would be enough to see the three hundred of us to the top, as long as the rebels remained focused on the main gate.

"That was smart, getting the men to laugh." Gratidianus came to my side.

He technically outranked me as a tribune, but Strabo had ordered me to lead this flanking party and placed a few officers under me regardless. I was glad he was there. I found his presence calming.

"I'll steal that tactic in the future if you don't mind."

"It's all yours." I clapped him on the shoulder. "I hope this is my last battle, the last time I'll have need of any tricks except the ones that grow my crops."

Cataline was the other officer placed under my command, and his laugh now cut through the barrage of the ram against Asculum's gate. "A regular Cincinnatus, are you?"

"I believe Cincinnatus was a dictator before he returned, tribune," I said. "I'm just a provincial, the son of a horse breeder and the father of a baby girl."

He held up his wineskin and squeezed it until the last drop fell on his extended tongue. "I'm no soothsayer," he said, "but I know your future isn't that of a simple farmer. A man like you? Who believes in justice and peace and the good of the Republic? Bah! I have better odds of bedding Aphrodite than you do of leaving the battlefield. Rome will always need you, and you'll never be able to refuse Her."

He spoke in jest, but the words stung. I remembered the words of Apollo's oracle when I visited her in Delphi years before: *"War will beset you all the days of your life. Battles you do not seek, cannot win, and do not desire. You will feel the gods have cursed you, but in fact you are their chosen. Their tool, their sacrifice, their vessel."*

I tried to block the words from my mind as the wood of Asculum's reinforced gates began to splinter.

"If you really want a peaceful life, you should develop a taste for oysters," Cataline continued. "Flamingos, flocks of slaves, beachside villas . . . That and a lack of concern for Rome's safety, and you might just find your peace."

"Can you believe this?" I winked at Gratidianus.

He smiled and shrugged. "You do have a habit of making other people's problems your own. Until you find someone you trust to protect the Republic more than yourself, Cataline might be right."

"I'll keep teaching you my tricks then," I said. "And send you two to fight all my battles for me. Failing that, I'll send Cicero."

They both laughed.

But our candor was cut short.

All of us turned our attention to the rebels materializing outside the city walls. They seemed to spring out directly from Hades.

I was too perplexed to say anything at first. Where had they come from?

The success of our entire strategy hinged on forcing the rebels into one singular place: the gates.

"Metellus swore he surveyed the walls!" Gratidianus shouted.

I ground my teeth. "He swore there was no other gate."

But there must have been some hidden exit, a tunnel even, but something large enough for several hundred men to escape from quickly. And what was it they were carrying?

"See, prefect?" Cataline tossed away his empty wineskin and unsheathed his sword. "You can't trust anyone else to protect the

Republic for you." He raised his voice. "We'll have to take it into our own hands won't we, boys? Let's get them!" He sprinted off, expecting us to follow or not caring if we did.

"Cataline, wait!" Gratidianus said, but it was too late.

"Abandon the ladders," I ordered. "We have no use for them now."

We needed to reach the rebels quickly. It wasn't just a few Picentes attempting a suicidal flanking maneuver. No, they brought with them something far more dangerous than swords.

Fire and oil.

Vases shattered onto the battering rams and ballistae. Torches followed and acrid smoke filled the air.

I wasn't quick enough.

"Pila!" I ordered, and the ranks behind me hurled them mid-stride.

But the rebels were already scattering. They'd done their part and they would only die needlessly if they tried to fight. They couldn't lead us back to their hidden entrance either, so they fled in all directions.

Few lived. History would remember them as great heroes if the rebels were victorious.

"Put out the flames! Water! Water!" everyone was shouting.

The damage to the siege equipment was already complete though. There was no salvaging it now.

In the midst of the chaos, piercing screams rang out.

I turned in time to see the last of three massive cauldrons turning over, scalding hot liquid falling from each. It engulfed those unfortunate men who'd recently been slamming the battering ram against the walls, and those closest to them.

They fell to the ground, writhing, their flesh melting. Their unharmed comrades tried helplessly to save them, but the poor legionaries were boiling alive inside their chain mail.

"Watch the men," I said to Cataline and Gratidianus.

I sprinted off toward Pompey's cavalry at the back of his formation. Fortunately, I spotted his blue-dyed horsehair plume and shouted until he saw me.

"We must pull back from the walls, now! We cannot take them this way."

"No retreat!" Metellus was nearby and answered before Pompey could. "The walls are almost down. Retreat means defeat and will set us back for months! Pompey, send in the reserves and crash down that wall with their skulls if you must!"

I saw the turmoil in Pompey's eyes as he watched the dying legionaries.

I said, "Pompey, we need not retreat but simply pull back from the walls. Your men are dying!"

"Dying is part of battle, prefect," Metellus spit. "It is unavoidable."

Perhaps he was right. Had I grown soft?

The screams of the burn victims faded as most died or fainted from the pain, but more wailing replaced it as arrows and rocks rained down on the front lines. Their suffering pulled me away from my thoughts.

Metellus wheeled his horse closer and towered over me. "What do you suggest then, prefect? This was *your* plan."

"Sappers. We'll use sappers to destroy the walls where they have no battlements to assault us."

It's what I would have suggested if I'd known there was another point of exit along the walls. I wanted to shout this in Metellus's face, but it would serve no purpose. The damage was done, and we had a battle to win.

"Fall back! Fall back!" Pompey shouted and the centurions rallied the orders. He turned to his aide. "Go, fetch the sappers. Hurry!"

Metellus may have missed the enemy's hidden escape route, but I soon realized he had learned a great deal about the construction of Asculum's walls.

We needed that knowledge now.

While waiting for the sappers to arrive, we planned our actions. There were three weak points along the walls, and we would begin working at all three.

When the sappers arrived, we dispersed them among our legionaries and shielded them under a *testudo*. They would normally march under the protection of a mantlet, but we had no time to construct them now.

They began their work at midday, and we knew it would last hours. Asculum rebels continued to pelt us with whatever they could find, but the battlements at these weak points were too shallow for them to use such maneuvers as pouring hot oil on us.

I kept my eye open for the secret passage, careful to spot any materializing rebels, but none appeared. We were too close to the walls now—they would give away the location and risk greater harm if they tried.

The sappers began digging and worked more tirelessly than the Marathon runner for the remainder of the day. We focused on protecting the workers as best we could, but otherwise kept our men away from the walls and enemy projectiles.

The yellow half-moon was high in the sky and covered in a smoky cloud by the time the sappers finished digging. We'd been waiting in formation all day, and the rush of rage had long since dissipated, which usually made for a poor battle. But Metellus was right about one thing: we could not retreat. It would set us back months and cost us coin and lives we couldn't afford to lose.

No, it had to be tonight.

The sappers came and found Pompey, me, and the other officers where we waited beyond the reach of the walls.

Soot stained the leading sapper from head to toe, his eyes strained and wild from hours of diligent work digging and laying explosives.

"We're ready to breach, tribune," he addressed Pompey.

The young man took a deep breath and looked up at the moon. "No more delays," he said to himself. "Let's go."

"I'd instruct your men to back up even further," the sapper said. "There's no telling what that wall will do when the fire is lit."

Pompey passed along the orders to the first spear centurions. "Anything else?"

"The resistance at the point of entry will be fierce," I said. "We should order the *evocati* to enter first."

We usually held our cohort of *evocati* in reserve, but they were the finest veterans in Strabo's legions, many of them having been centurions themselves earlier in their career. They were better equipped and more skilled than any other cohort under our eagles, and they alone could bear the initial assault.

"This is wise, I think," the sapper said.

"Let it be done then," Pompey said.

The sapper saluted and sprinted back toward the walls.

"Have you ever done this before?" Pompey asked me quietly. "I've never seen it."

I shook my head. "Never. But I've read about it."

He looked at me like I was mad for a moment, but then forced a smile.

"I'll lead the *evocati* from the front, if you'll allow me," I said.

He chuckled. "For a father striving to end this war and make it back home alive, you seem to love putting yourself in harm's way."

"It's the only way I know."

Cataline came and plopped an arm on my shoulder. "I'll

march with the prefect. And Gratidianus here will, too, won't you, brother-in-law?"

Gratidianus swallowed. "We make for good company. I'll march with you."

Pompey raised an arm as if swearing an oath. "If our men are half as brave as you three this day, Asculum is already ours."

The *evocati* were already inching closer toward the walls.

"Let's go," I said.

In the darkness, I made out the sappers charging back toward us, arms over their heads in anticipation. "The fire is lit! Lit!"

All became silent. We waited. Every legionary in Strabo's army was still. The city of Asculum seemed to take a collective inhale.

Then the night shattered. The ground beneath the wall erupted in a thunderous roar. The deafening roar shook Gaia's earth to the core. Flames burst forth from the tunnel's mouth, as if from Vulcan's infernal forge, consuming the wooden supports in a fiery blaze.

Flame and force devoured the foundation of Asculum's walls, that ancient structure so tall and proud.

The heat came in waves over us, a signal as clear as any trumpet.

"Forward!" I roared as the *evocati* fell in line behind me.

Warriors on both sides shouted their war cries.

The fire cast a hellish glow, illuminating the smoke and dust that billowed upward, forming a ghostly cloud over the battle-field. There was a gaping wound in that recently impregnable wall, and we headed directly toward it.

The heat was nearly unbearable at the point of entry, but we leaped up onto those smoldering rocks regardless and swiftly moved past.

Rebels awaited us. Endless scores of them.

The smoke partially concealed us just as it partially concealed them. It was enough to choke the lungs, but it was of little concern compared to the spear tips glinting in firelight and moving our way.

Brutal and chaotic, that's what the initial assault was. Even with the experience of our *evocati*, the rage of the defenders nearly shattered our formation.

Arrows rained down on us. I could not see the source through the smoke, but I assume the archers had climbed on the tops of houses, temples, and any other high point they could reach.

We were packed in with the enemy infantry like sheep in a pen. Their men were just as at risk from the arrows as us, but they must have decided there was no other choice. Or perhaps they had a "Metellus" of their own.

"*Testudo*!" I shouted, and others rallied the order. We raised our shields and ducked into tight order as the rebels crashed into us.

I thrust my sword through the small gap between our shields. There was no way to discern what I was striking against, but I pierced something.

We were collapsing in on ourselves as the flood of defenders continued. We needed to thin them out soon.

"Ignite! Ignite the second tunnel!" I shouted back.

The message was rallied back to Pompey. Soon, the explosion of another sappers' tunnel filled the air.

Fear spread through the ranks of the rebel defenders, but they couldn't abandon their post. They kept their attention on us.

"Push forward!"

We dug the studded pads of our legionary boots into the scorched earth and pushed the attackers back as best we could, if only to allow more of our men to enter behind us.

They resisted with strength and courage, but they could not break the line of our shields and wouldn't hold back for long.

It felt like we'd advanced only a few feet before legionaries began pouring in on either side of our formation.

"Tecombre!" I bellowed, and we broke the shield wall to assume a more offensive formation.

I stood. A spear ricocheted off the cheek guard of my helmet. A bit to the right, and it would have taken my life.

The attacker struck again, but this time I was ready, and batted it away with sword. I thrust my shield forward and caught him in the throat. A gob of spit flew from his lips as he struggled for air. Two of the *evocati* warriors beside me took advantage of his recoil and ended his life before he could recover.

An arrow hit me in the shoulder but failed to pierce the chain mail.

I thanked the gods as quickly as I could and asked for continued protection.

As if to say I'd not praised them well enough, a spear careened over my shield and connected with my ribs. The strike failed to splinter the chain mail, but the wind was driven from my lungs.

I stumbled back to catch my breath.

Cataline took my place. "I'll protect the Republic for you, prefect!" he shouted.

"Make room," I ordered. I pushed him to the side to reach the front line again, determined to retaliate.

The same rebel who'd struck me must have desired to finish the job and aimed his spear for me again. This time, I raised my shield in time and deflected. The spear flew from his hand and landed somewhere in the mob of soldiers around him.

I brought my blade down on his arm. The tip slicing through the interior of his biceps. He discarded his shield to hold back the blood.

That was the last thing he should have done, and it was the last thing he would do. I stabbed with what weight my injured leg allowed me to generate, and it was enough to wedge through his breastplate. It wasn't deep, but enough. He collapsed.

I struggled to free my blade as two more attackers pounced toward me.

I ducked beneath my shield to protect myself from one rebel, but watched as the other raised his blade to deal the death blow.

I closed my eye. I prayed another instant, wordless prayer for my family to be protected. When I opened it again, the attacker was missing an arm and his head drooped to the side. Cataline's blade dripped as he stood over the defeated foe like a triumphant gladiator.

The full force of a sword crashed against my shield from the other assailant. I swept my gladius to the side. His leg separated above the knee, and he collapsed, soon on the ground beside me.

I silenced his cries before they could truly begin.

The enemy ranks were beginning to thin out. Perhaps they were retreating to seek shelter with their families, or to take their own lives in whatever way they saw fit. More likely, some were heading to defend the other entry point. I knew in my heart the rebels of Asculum, the same ones who started this war, would fight to the last man.

By the time I stood, the third explosion boomed out. It was farther away this time, but just as devastating for the rebels. They could not defend three points of entry. There was no siege equipment to burn, no secret exit to save them now.

"Repel them and move into the city." My words were breathless but rallied to the men all the same.

The battle was almost over.

SCROLL XVII

Quintus Sertorius—Three days before the Ides of May, 665 Ab Urbe Condita

Charred flesh, metallic blood, and smoked shit.

That's what the city smelled like now. The smoke and ash hung in the air so thick my throat clenched. I would have torn a strip from my cloak to breathe through but had no time to set down my sword or shield.

Crackling flames spread and devoured wooden beams supporting humble homes. The collapse drowned out the blood-curdling cries from within. The fires were raging now, and not just from the walls and its surroundings. It was almost as bright as the daytime, despite the half-moon being shrouded by the billowing smoke. Searing waves of heat licked my blistered skin.

Battle waged deeper into the city.

Asculum's destruction clearly began long before we ever breached the walls. They'd long since shuttered and boarded up most of the buildings. There were no fruit or vegetable stands. Rotting corpses of those who died long before our arrival littered the streets. The bones of house pets and livestock were strewn about, likely eaten as a last resort as the city ran out of supplies.

But Asculum couldn't very well eat their gold, so there was bound to be plenty of that. The men were restless for plunder.

I continued to lead the *evocati* through the smoky streets. "Stay in formation! Stay in line."

"What harm is there in letting the boys have a bit of fun?" Cataline said.

"There will be more resistance," I said but was unsure if that was true.

Gratidianus lowered his voice. "The *evocati* do usually receive first rights to women and spoils."

"These people were our allies once. This is not some barbarian village to plunder as we see fit. They should be treated with dignity."

Cataline said, "Afraid that's not your call to make." There was a gleam in his eyes, and it wasn't just the reflection of flames.

"Advance and meet resistance," I said. "Those are our orders."

"I believe enjoying the fruits of victory are implicit orders," Gratidianus said, perhaps less eager than his brother-in-law.

A roar sounded from the smoke, followed by the clopping of hooves against cobblestone.

"Pila!" I ordered.

Those who still had a javelin raised them.

"Release!"

The pila ripped through the fire's fog. Riders catapulted into view and horses collapsed. Others continued on.

A final, futile ride to defend their city.

"Brace!"

We hunkered down beneath our shields as the surviving rebel riders crashed into and over us.

They did not last long but made a heroic exit.

I silenced the cries of the horses as swiftly as I could. The sound was more piercing and haunting than any other, even the dying words of men.

"Advance," I said as we dispatched the remaining enemies.

"No, wait," Cataline said, and the men listened to him.

"What? We need to reach the inner city. The battle isn't won until the Capitol is taken."

He pointed with his sword toward Asculum's heart. Smoke rose above even the tallest temples. "The Capitol is burning to the ground as we speak."

"We cannot halt the advance until we confirm. Rebel leaders are to be apprehended."

"They will be, the ones that aren't already dead, that is," Cataline said.

"Let's keep moving then," I said.

Cataline shook his head. "No."

His jokes were famous, and I waited for him to make one, but his eyes were as sober as I'd ever seen them.

"Strabo placed me in command of our flank," I said, "and Pompey gave me command of the *evocati*. My order is to advance."

"You were given command of the battle, yes. But the battle is over, and I outrank you." He feigned a smile. Cataline turned to the men. "Besides, you boys want to sack the city and have some fun, don't you?"

They cheered.

"Go on, then! Drink all the drink, take all the gold, and enjoy every whore you can find."

They split in every direction before I could say anything else. Cataline gave me a wink, threw off his helmet, and joined the chaos.

Gratidianus alone remained at my side. "I should have warned you he would do that," he said.

"You knew?"

He shrugged. "He's my brother-in-law. I know him well. He lives for this." He gestured to the burning buildings, fleeing children, and rampaging soldiers around us. "You could only delay him for so long."

I sheathed my sword. "Go and join them if you wish," I said. "I am going to the Capitol."

"I'm a good soldier," he said. "I follow your orders. Lead on."

The two of us walked alone through the chaos. I did everything I could to drown out the screams, to breathe freely in a city clogged with smoke.

But it was no use.

Cataline was correct about the Capitol. Other legionaries had broken rank and made it there faster than we could. Every temple and state building there was ablaze.

We met no more resistance. Most of the rebel fighters were dead, but the rest had likely sought shelter with their families, a fool's hope that the torch would spare their homes.

I stood in the middle of Asculum's Forum. I imagined it filled with shopping families, shopkeepers peddling wares, flute players entertaining the crowd for a few coins. They were all dead or dying now.

"You should be pleased, prefect," Gratidianus said, reminding me of his presence. "The battle is over. The war in the north is finished. You can return to your fields and your flocks."

I unbuckled my helmet and let it fall to the stone beneath me. "I should be pleased, but I'm not," I said.

"Any idea why?" he asked.

I shook my head. "I fought beside these men. A few years ago, I might have broken bread with the women you hear screaming now. The children being rounded up for a life of servitude might have called me 'uncle.'"

"It is war," he said.

"It is war." I nodded. "Today it is Asculum, and one day it

will be Rome." Visions haunted me. Raging fires consuming temples and state buildings. Senators rounded up and crucified. Insulae set ablaze with screaming families inside. Our priests slain. Our coffers and relics of victories past taken. My wife and daughter . . .

He winced. "I'd be careful who you say that to, prefect. That's treasonous talk."

"No, tribune," I said. "It is war."

A woman and a young boy in tattered rags ran toward us. Three legionaries were in close pursuit behind them.

When they looked up to see us standing in their path, the boy unsheathed a sword much too large for him to wield and threw away the scabbard.

"Close your eyes, boy, you don't want to watch this," one legionary laughed, catching his breath.

"Halt," I ordered.

The legionaries looked at me as if I were mad.

"What's your name, boy?" I said.

The young man lowered his sword. He lifted his chin to conceal quavering lips. "Bassus," he said. "Publius Ventidius Bassus."

"This your mother?" I gestured to the crying woman huddled behind him.

"Yes. Your men have widowed her and orphaned me."

I stepped toward him as the legionaries glared in my direction. "Yes, but they haven't left your mother childless. Lay down your sword. You may fight one day, but do not throw away your life needlessly."

He studied me to see if I was trustworthy. He didn't blink as he lowered to a knee and laid his sword on the bloody cobblestone.

"Fight or not, we're still going to share his mum," the legionary said, "and kill the boy after if he so much as sheds a tear."

"No you won't," I replied. "His father, Gaius Ventidius

Bassus served with the auxiliary at Vercellae. I saw his courage with my own eye. He was a hero. His wife will not be your plaything, and you'll bring no harm to his son."

The legionaries sulked, but they didn't perceive the lie. The boy, however, seemed keenly aware of my duplicity.

"Shackle them," I said. "Strabo can display them in his triumph, and the boy can fight for his freedom and citizenship, to Rome's glory." The words stung me as I uttered them, but it was their only hope for survival.

I could not save all of Asculum's citizens, but at least these two would not weigh on my conscience.

The legionaries reluctantly pulled out leather straps to bind them.

One said, "You should erect a shrine to the prefect and worship him 'til the day you die. He's the only reason you're going to see tomorrow."

I lowered my voice and addressed the boy. "Remain strong for your mother. Justify your father's sacrifice. Rome gives you a second chance at life. Earn it."

He blinked tears away from his resolute eyes and nodded. I stepped away as the legionaries bound them, grumbling all the while.

"Did you really serve with his father?" Gratidianus asked, more perceptive than most legionaries.

"I served with many fathers, brothers, and sons of Asculum."

Amid the chaos unfolding around us, I heard the laughter of opulent men nearby. I turned to find Strabo walking with the cortege of officers who never left his heel.

He'd been absent from battle, but I was not surprised to find him now that we'd claimed victory.

I should have left the city, the flames, and the dying behind. I should have returned to camp and waited for my formal discharge. But I couldn't.

"Whatever you're considering," Gratidianus said, "It is unwise."

I ignored him and stepped toward the officers. "Your troops are breaking Roman law, consul," I said.

My voice cut through his persiflage. He turned to the closest officer and asked, "Who is this speaking to me so disrespectfully?"

I walked closer. "Prefect Quintus Sertorius," I answered for him.

His nose scrunched like my name smelled worse than the roasting dead. "I should have known," he said.

"This is Asculum, not some barbarian village you can do with as you like. The senate has ordered the defeated rebels to be treated with respect," I said. "If this is how you show respect, I shudder to think how you would show apathy."

"Senate? What senate?" he snarled. "Out here, I am Rome, boy. And this is war."

I was tired of hearing that.

"Rome is trying to encourage the rebels to lay down their arms. Is that what you are doing?"

He laughed and nodded. "Precisely. When the world hears of what I've done to Asculum, they will come trembling to kiss my hand."

"On the contrary, they will fight harder to cut it off."

"Let them!" It was difficult to make out the faces between the smoke and the blood on the faces of all but our commander, but the voice unsurprisingly belonged to Metellus. "We shall defeat them too."

"It's just us officers now, consul," I said. "You can tell the truth. You've given your men liberty to sack the city, despite our orders, because you have woefully under compensated them since the war began. You have no way to pay them what they're owed, so you intend for Asculum to pay on your behalf."

"You impudent, frog-spawned whelp!" Strabo roared. "Here I thought you were a battle-hardened veteran, instead I find a weak-hearted peasant. Return to your fields then if you have no thirst for blood!"

I raised my crimson hands. "I have no fear of blood if you can't tell. I've shed as much this day for Rome as any man here," I said. "But this, this is not simply bloodshed. This is annihilation. And that is contrary to the dictates of the Senate and People of Rome."

Metellus laughed. "I've never met a soldier so naive." He pretended to wipe a tear from his eye. "Sulla is doing the same in the south. Every conquering Roman army takes its liberties, and the senate understands this. I should know." He flashed his family's signet ring, which gleamed in the firelight.

"Sulla does many things; that does not make it right."

If Metellus spoke true, I wondered about Gavius. Did he partake? Did he revel in the misery of our kin like Cataline? Or did it repulse him?

"We are trying to end a war." Strabo waved me off, making it clear he was done with this conversation.

But there was still a foolish part of me that thought if I could speak some sense into the consul, further bloodshed could be avoided. "If we end the war by destroying every once-great city in Italy, Rome will be crippled for it. Mithridates and other foreign kings will crawl out to pick apart what little meat remains on our bones."

"Wise Sertorius with all the answers," Strabo said. "Go then! Go to Rome and tell them about the horrors you've witnessed. Stand for election and create the change you wish to see."

"Perhaps I will."

Strabo snatched a bag of coin from his hip and threw it my direction. The silver scattered across the cobblestone. "Go with my blessing, peasant. You're discharged, quick as Mercury. Get out of my legions."

"Save your coin. Use it to feed your men."

I turned my back on them, as Strabo hurled Picentes insults my way.

Perhaps they were right. Perhaps this was simply the cost of war. Unavoidable. Inevitable. Preferable.

But in Rome, I could create change. Perhaps I could save more Italians from sharing Asculum's fate. A single piece of legislation could end the war and restore the Republic, even if it made me enemies and destroyed my political career in the process.

I found Pompey standing in solitude before the scorched gates.

"Congratulations, tribune," I said. "You've won a glorious victory today."

His eyes were stark against the blood and soot covering his face. "I have you and many others to thank for that."

"You have new ghosts to commune with as you look up at the stars," I said.

He lowered his gaze and squeezed a rag around his wounded forearm.

"So, what's next for the mighty Quintus Sertorius?"

Strabo and the others would soon tell him the story, with their own twists added to be certain.

"Your father has discharged me," I said.

His eyes revealed more pain at the words than from the wound he nursed. "Why?"

I took a deep breath. "Your father and I don't see eye-to-eye on many things. Besides, with the northern resistance broken, I can return to Rome and run for office, as I've planned."

His jaw tensed. "My father is blind. Or nearly blind. Did you know that?"

It explained his absence from the battlefield. I now recalled the way he looked through those he addressed.

"He hides it as well as he can," Pompey continued. "Rome will tolerate cowards before the physically impaired." He sighed. "But it seems my father's deficiencies aren't limited to his sight. Our legions will suffer more from your departure than any man who fell this day."

I placed a hand on his shoulder. "You are a great leader, on and off the battlefield. The legions are safe in your hands."

"Perhaps we'll draw swords together again one day," he said.

"As long as we're on the same side of the battlefield, I look forward to it."

I gave him a final nod and set off. In two days' ride, I would be back with my wife and daughter. With the war in the north effectively concluded and the roads safe to travel, we could now return to Rome. I would run for office and, once elected, pass a law offering citizenship to any rebels who laid down their arms. The war would end, Italy would be secure, and the Eternal City could prosper once again. That was my plan.

My farms would have to wait a little longer.

SCROLL XVIII

Toria was as punctual as her father. Each night, she'd wake exactly three hours after her previous feeding and fuss until I pulled her to my breast.

"Shh . . . mum is here." I massaged my weary eyes with one hand and stroked her back with the other. Her hair was growing so fast, before long she'd have a mane to rival Venus. She may have had her father's nose and shimmering eyes, but it was my curly Gallic hair on her head.

She cried and refused to latch.

"Toria, shh . . ."

Barca hadn't complained a single time since we arrived, but I still did everything I could to keep Toria from waking him in the middle of the night.

She kept whining. It was then I noticed the *ludus* was silent.

It wasn't uncommon for Barca's men to train through the night. Fueled by cheap wine and dreams of grandeur, the gladiators often found themselves unable to sleep. Toria was accustomed to it.

I smiled and kissed her head. The sound of gladiators training was as soothing to her as my lullabies. Her tears were protesting the silence.

I bobbed her up and down as a means of distraction and moved toward to shuttered window.

Rhea appeared in the doorway. She could sleep through war drums and a full-fledged battle if she wanted to, but a single babble from a child, and she was up and alert.

She whispered. "Can I help?"

I shook my head. "She's just a bit fussy," I said.

"Fresh air always worked with Quintus," she said. "I think he enjoyed being closer to the horses."

I rubbed Toria behind her ears to sooth her. "I wasn't aware there was fresh air in Italy."

"Even the fetid, humid air of this *ludus* can hush a child right up."

"I trust your experience. If only—" I lost the words when I peered out at the training ground.

The gladiators were out there as usual, but they were not training. No, they were packing. Gathering swords and shields by torchlight.

Rhea must have noticed the fear in my eyes. "What is it?"

"Take her, take her." I passed Toria to her grandmother and hurried from the room, not bothering to put anything on over my night tunic.

Barca was on his feet the moment I opened his door, alert as a fox. I could find few words to say, but all I had to do was point and he inferred the rest.

He grabbed nothing but a dagger and sprinted toward the commotion.

"Dimitrius!" Barca shouted as he burst out into the heavy night air.

The gladiators stopped in their tracks, and I stood by the door. I knew I should retreat inside and find somewhere safe to hide, but I found myself frozen in place.

Dimitrius, Barca's champion gladiator, pursed his lips. "*Domine.*"

"In middle of night? That's how you betray me?"

"We thought it best." Dimitrius turned and closed the lid of a chest filled with weapons. "We did not want to fight you."

"Ever since Capua, I expected treachery. But not from you."

More and more gladiators exited their cells and entered the sands. The confused look in their eyes revealed not all were privy to Dimitrius's plan.

Dimitrius's shoulders tensed when he noticed them.

"What have I done to deserve this?" Barca's voice teemed with anger, but it was a thin veil over the pain he felt.

"You've been a good *dominus*," one gladiator answered.

"I share with you everything I have. *Ludus* is your home. Do I lock you in cells? Do I beat you? Do I not share all I gain with you?"

"You do." Dimitrius's jaw flexed.

"I treat you as kin. You repay me with betrayal."

"Barca, be reasonable!" Dimitrius shouted. "We would fight to the death for you, but we're tired of fighting one another. This is an opportunity we cannot ignore. We can take the fight to the Romans who cheer for our deaths."

Barca was without words.

Dimitrius approached and put a hand on Barca's shoulder. To my surprise, he allowed him to do so.

"Enough warriors are staying behind. This *ludus* will grow strong again, and one day it will be the greatest in Italy."

Barca turned toward a *retiarius* on the far side of the training ground. "Mago, shut those gates!"

Mago did not move.

"He is coming with us, Barca," Dimitrius said. "I'm sorry, *domine*."

"I cannot let you leave," Barca said. "Romans find out my gladiators are joining rebels. They will kill me. They will kill all. They will kill our guests."

"Then join us, *domine*, I beg you." Dimitrius looked past Barca, directly at me. "You owe nothing to these Romans."

My heart dropped into my stomach and my knees threatened to buckle as Barca's silence lingered. I contemplated running to my daughter and fleeing. Still, I could not move.

Barca followed Dimitrius's gaze to where I stood in the shadow of the doorway.

"One last chance to stand down," Barca said. "Go sleep well. Tomorrow, we forget."

"There is no need for bloodshed," Dimitrius said.

Barca brandished his curved dagger.

Several other gladiators grabbed weapons of their own. Brothers were about to kill brothers, the very thing these traitors sought to avoid.

Dimitrius backed away and pulled a spear from the wagon behind him.

"You leave no choice," he said.

Barca positioned himself the same as he did before training and awaited the attack. Dimitrius did the same as combat ensued around them.

With a roar, Dimitrius lunged forward.

Through the midst of the melee, a single rider galloped through the open gate. He launched a Roman pilum.

Dimitrius collapsed to his knees with the bloody tip of the pilum exiting through his abdomen.

The one-eyed Roman swept off his horse and finished Dimitrius with a swift cut through his throat.

"Quintus!" I shouted.

"What is happening?" he asked Barca.

"Treachery!" Barca answered. "To me, hurry."

My husband threw his shield up instinctively, and just in time to deflect a throwing axe aimed for his head.

He joined Barca along with a few other gladiators who rallied to protect their *lanista*.

"Arrea?" he shouted as I ran up behind him. "Go inside! Hide!"

"No." I shook my head. "I can help fight."

"Arrea, inside now. Please!"

I hesitated, but eventually turned and ran back inside the house, faster than I knew I could.

"What is happening?" Rhea bobbed Toria in her arms, who was now fast asleep.

"Help me gather our things," I said, my voice shaking. "We need to leave."

"Leave? What do—" She stopped herself and helped me.

We all had many questions. Why was Quintus here? What would we do now? Where could we go?

But all that mattered now was Toria's safety. We packed all our belongings and hid in Barca's guest room and waited for a signal.

PART II

SCROLL XIX

"It's my turn, love," I said. "Bid me fortune."

She squeezed my hand one last time. "You won't need it, but I will." Arrea leaned up on her tiptoes and kissed me.

Before I began ascending the steps to the rostra, Rome's oldest and most important speaking platform, I embraced Barca.

"I wouldn't be here if it wasn't for you," I said. "None of this would be possible."

It'd been two weeks since I returned to Barca's *ludus*. We fought two dozen or more of his gladiators and had no choice but to kill them all. My friend was not one to show weakness, but I could see the pain in his eyes.

Barca's gladiatorial school was in shambles after so many deaths, but it wasn't the loss of profit or prestige that burdened him. To lose so many at once, to take their life with your own hand . . . it was enough to break the stoutest of hearts.

Despite that, he refused to let us leave his *ludus* without escort. He and a half dozen of his surviving gladiators accompanied us to Rome. We'd been back for six days, but still he remained. "I stay," was all he said, without bothering to explain why he cared so much for our safety. Arrea and I didn't object. We were as grateful for his company as his protection, even if we didn't understand why he offered them so freely.

"Many gods watch over you today," Barca said. "Your gods and mine, and Arrea's old ones too."

I turned to the rostra and prepared myself with a deep breath.

The speaker before me was a disgraced senator of some repute whose name I don't remember. He was announcing his bid for praetor under the campaign slogan of "Rome for Romans." He spent most of his time talking about the influx of Jews and eastern influence in the city. There were a few vocal supporters among the massive body of Romans who'd gathered in the Forum on this occasion, but nothing more.

I took the first step up the old wooden steps to the platform, rehearsing in my head the speech I'd prepared.

My mother taught me rhetoric when I was a boy and hired accomplished tutors as well. I remembered so little of it now. But Apollonius taught me how to render effective speeches: introduce myself, state my intentions, reveal how it benefits the listeners, and close with a lingering statement.

The newsreader on the platform craned his head to see me and shouted. "The noble Quintus Sertorius will address you next!"

The crowd erupted. I reached the top of the platform and faced the people. It'd been ten years since I'd spoken before the Roman people, and the sight was once again just as breathtaking.

At least a thousand citizens had gathered. The packed throng stretched back past the Temple of Castor and Pollux to the *Regia*, and all the way to the rostra steps. Only in Rome could so many congregate, save on the battlefield.

The cheers continued. Were they mistaking me for someone else?

"*Roma Invicta!*" someone shouted.

"Hero of the North!" a young boy shouted from the first row of listeners.

I raised my hand to quiet them, and they shouted even more.

In truth, I was thankful for the delay. I'd anticipated this moment for so long. The siege of Asculum, ending the war in the north . . . it was always about getting to that very spot. For once, I could end a war with my voice rather than my sword. I could stop the endless cycle of violence between Rome and my Italian brothers.

"I . . . I . . ." It took a moment before I could speak. "I intended to introduce myself to you today, but it appears many of you already know me."

They cheered once again. The ancient pine trees lining the Forum swayed as citizens rocked them back and forth as an interesting display of praise.

I stole a glance down at Arrea, whose wide smile and proud eyes filled me with courage.

"For those of you who do not, I am a husband, father, and veteran of the Roman legions."

"Hero more like!" The newsreader interrupted me and encouraged the crowds to continue their praise.

I held a hand to my heart and bowed my head. My actual intention was to stall for a moment and remember what I'd planned to say. I hadn't expected this reception. I'd been gone for so long, fighting in this campaign and that, that I had no notion Rome celebrated my deeds.

"I am humbled by your kindness."

I looked down at Arrea again and she tapped her eye to remind me of my speech.

"I gave my eye for Rome in battle," I said. "Now I offer to give Rome everything that remains. I stand here today to announce my bid for the tribunate."

They cheered louder now. Fathers propped sons on their

shoulders to see me more clearly. Young men climbed up old arches and columns to show their support.

Courage, devotion, and honor. We'd chosen the words carefully over the past few weeks as I practiced.

"With courage, devotion, and honor, I fought for the safety and prosperity of Rome's people in countless battles. I vow to do the same in the tribune's toga if you elect me."

Another glance at Arrea and Barca reminded me to focus on the people. Apollonius was correct when he once said people do not vote for those they simply admire, but for those who will bring them the most benefit.

"With my election, I promise to stand for your rights against all those who would try to diminish them, whether they are within the senate house or outside it. Your friends will be my friends, and your enemies will be my enemies. I hope to represent you in a new age of Rome that harkens back to a time when we were strongest."

I could have ended my speech there. Perhaps I should have.

Arrea and I had discussed which topics I should cover in this introductory address. We decided my proposed legislation wasn't one of them. The people wouldn't want to hear about war or my desire to stop it. They yearned to hear declarations of power, glory, and all the good things we could achieve if they elected me. No, speaking of war would do nothing for my reputation or my odds of victory.

But as I looked out over Rome's people, I felt love for them. The men who spoke from that platform usually told them only half-truths and lies, masking their intentions with flattery, promises, and elegant oratorical gestures they learned from the most expensive tutors in Greece.

The Roman people deserved honesty. They deserved to have candidates look them in the eye and tell them the truth.

"Countrymen, perhaps I am about to commit political suicide. How? Because I will do the thing that politicians are typically forbidden to do: tell the truth."

There was a stirring in the crowd at the accusation, followed by anticipatory silence.

"The Republic is enslaved. Not to one master, but to several suitors who are currently bidding for our soul."

I forgot all about rhetorical devices and the structure of a proper speech. I addressed the people now like I spoke to my friends.

"At all times, civilization is on the brink of collapse. We are ever at risk of falling into the hands of the tyrant, a corrupt government, or the man with the most coin. Each of these poses a unique and perilous threat to our Republic, but they share one thing in common. The despot, the immoral regime, and the highest bidder can only thrive during constant civil strife and war. When individuals can make careers on exploiting conflicts with foreign nations . . . when your elected officials can bolster their power by requiring you vote them unprecedented powers to stop conflicts they built . . . when the rich own mines from Hispania to Egypt, ones only profitable when we wage war after war and need a constant resupply of arms and armor with which to fight them . . . we are doomed to be trapped in an endless cycle of strife."

There were some hecklers spread throughout the crowd, but most listened intently.

"I am a simple soldier, not an orator. But I have fought beside your sons, brothers, and husbands, and I have seen the eloquence of their courage. I am here today to ensure they didn't die in vain. We've lost too many of Rome's sons so that ambitious men can tilt the scales of justice in their favor rather than to protect our citizens or for the glory of our great Republic.

"My desire is to break that cycle. I want to end the war that currently besets our path and stop those who would seek to conjure up another for their own gain. We cannot avoid conflict if we wish to protect our borders, but we can eliminate meaningless conflicts of wealth and power when it is our young men who die in these wars and only the old and rich who prosper. We should have ended the war with the Italian tribes long ago. If I am elected, that's what I intend to do. After that, I will do whatever I can to save Rome from the enemies—foreign or domestic —who threaten the freedom, prestige, and safety of our Republic. I can do very little alone, but together we can liberate Rome from any who would seek to buy us. With discipline and courage at home, and fairness and justice abroad, we will create a better world. Thank you."

Heartfelt applause sounded from various pockets in the crowd, but overall, the people were quiet. A slow murmur developed, and it threatened to turn into jeering. I wasn't surprised. Most of Rome's citizens wanted to hear only of how we would punish the rebels for betraying us. Even whispering about peace was tantamount to weakness, a lack of patriotism, or outright treason. But I was confident I'd done the right thing. I didn't regret it, even if it resulted in being heckled.

But before the crowd's animosity escalated, something distracted them. The people fell silent as a massive throng of cloaked men forced their way through to the rostra. There must have been four hundred of them if my quick estimation was sufficient.

I descended from the speaker's platform. I struggled to keep my footing as the cloaked men forced their way up the steps.

When I arrived at the bottom, Arrea threw her arms around my neck.

"You were marvelous, Quintus!" she said.

"I know we decided not to—"

She shook her head. "We were wrong," she said. "It was perfect."

Barca clapped my shoulder. "Excellent work, Roman," he said. "Now, we leave. I don't like these." He nodded to the cloaked men, many of whom were now on the rostra.

I considered it but shook my head. "No, I should wait to greet citizens after the assembly is concluded," I said.

"Very well."

One of the cloaked men stepped to the front of the rostra. He unbuckled the cheap gray cloak and let it fall to the ground, revealing a patrician's toga beneath. One would not expect to find a high-born citizen with such a retinue.

His hair was long and boyish, in the day's style. Gold and jewels adorned his wrist, neck, and fingers. His eyelids were darkened like a courtesan's, but there was an aggression to the way he moved that was unmistakably masculine.

The crowd's silence seemed to please him. A charming but dangerous smile spread across his face.

"Another round of applause for the legionary," the man said. He clapped his hands slowly and looked directly at me.

His voice was like honey pouring from his lips. There was an aristocratic tinge to his words, but it was the effortless resonance of his voice that made him so enthralling. He spoke as calmly as if addressing friends around a dinner table but with the authority of a battlefield commander.

"Much like him, I am here to state my intention for the tribunate."

Arrea took my hand and squeezed it. Should I be concerned?

No, no. Rome elected ten people's tribunes each year. We could both be elected without any problem, and it didn't hurt that he made a gesture of goodwill with his opening line.

"My name . . ." he paused from dramatic effect, "is Publius *Sulpicius* Rufus."

The crowd now cheered him like they'd initially cheered me. I wondered why the newsreader hadn't introduced him, and why the crowds hadn't recognized him by sight if his name was so revered among them. I assumed he'd yet to do anything particularly noteworthy, but whispers of his aims or reputation were beginning to spread.

He spoke with the perfect cadence of a poet or a marching legion, emphasizing certain words and allowing them to linger. He moved his arms to the left and right in perfect oratorical form. I'd forgotten much of my rhetorical training but knew my delivery wasn't as polished as this man's. "Also, like the one-eyed tribune-elect, I fight for the rights of the people. Ignore this *cursed* toga I'm forced to wear." He gestured to his pristine toga as if it were rags.

The people guffawed. There was nothing they liked more than a patrician shunning his heritage. In all my years, I'd never seen it done so flagrantly.

He continued. "Unlike Quintus Sertorius, though, I will not be doing so alone." He gestured to the men behind him and the other cloaked men throughout the crowd. "This is my 'anti-senate.'"

The laughter continued, despite the men pulling back their cloaks and revealing clubs and other makeshift weapons hanging from their belts.

I pulled Arrea closer to my side and exchanged a quick look with Barca.

"You see, the tribunate is not a position like any other along the cursus honorum." He shook his head. "No, no. It's a *weapon* to wield. First, a shield in defense of you fine Romans. And second, a sword to destroy all those who stand against you."

The tribunate held no military power; the position was solely designed to protect the rights of the people. If he wielded the tribunate as a weapon, the victim could only be the senate.

The people relished his threats.

"Quintus Sertorius desires first and foremost to end the war with the rebels."

The crowd jeered.

I remained resolute as the people turned their gaze on me. Arrea tightened her grip around my hand.

"Sertorius, we go," Barca said.

I shook my head and kept my gaze fixed on Sulpicius.

"Instead, my focus is not on the pitiful excuse for a war with the milk-drinking rebels but on the great war to come."

"Mithridates!" The crowd shouted.

Sulpicius nodded. "Rome has never seen a war like this.

We've never seen an enemy like this. No man here can so much as *fathom* the sheer wealth we will obtain in this war . . ." he trailed off as if in deep thought. "They say the Pontic army embeds diamonds in their shields because they've run out of space around their necks for jewelry. I've heard tell that even the poorest of Mithridates's people have *hoards* of gold stored up in their shabby huts. They have so much, it means little to them. But to you . . ." He licked his lips, imagining it.

"We want it! We want it!" The people shouted. They reached out and begged for it, as if the gold of Asia were his to bestow.

"The war is coming, whether tired old veterans want it or not. We will fight Mithridates, and we will conquer him. His wealth will become *ours*. But . . ." He raised a finger. "Quintus Sertorius is right about one thing. If you do not have a tribune who will fight for you—not simply with words but with clubs if necessary—we all know whose pockets will be lined with this wealth."

"The senate!"

"The aristocrats!"

"Patricians!"

The crowd shouted out in consensus.

He nodded. "Without me, the old and rich will grow older and richer with this wealth, passing it on to their hapless, *worthless* children to do the same."

I found it ironic that this man would say such things while clearly a patrician himself. Was I the only one thinking this? Roman crowds aren't known for their deductive reasoning, but perhaps they simply didn't care. The claims he was making would make him a target among his own kin. But with hundreds of armed men at his side, I suppose he feared nothing.

"I will ensure this great wealth goes to you. The people! Those who provide your sons to fight in our legions and who bake the bread that feeds us and build the aqueducts that quench our thirst. Mithridates's gold belongs to you!"

The people cheered louder than ever before now. They

clapped against the marble columns and stomped the ancient stones of the Forum. I told the people what I thought they needed to hear, but Sulpicius told them what they *wanted* to hear.

Wielding his power like a sword would be the only way he could fulfill even a fraction of this declaration. The crowd either didn't comprehend or didn't care about the cost.

Before the cheering reached a crescendo, another man forced his way onto the rostra. Unlike Sulpicius, this man's flawless patrician's toga could be seen from the first moment he stepped up. His golden hair radiated under the June sun.

Lucius Cornelius Sulla had arrived in the Forum.

Sulpicius's "anti-senate" surrounded him and held fast to their crude weapons. Sulla stared them down, unblinking, until Sulpicius nodded for his men to let the legatus pass.

"And look who it is that joins us," Sulpicius said. "One of the very men who would *strip* that gold away from you if he's able."

For the first time since Sulpicius began his speech, I turned away from the rostra. What if Gavius was here? What if he'd returned with Sulla?

Some of the crowd continued to cheer; others grew quiet. They were unsure what to do now.

Sulla was Rome's hero of the day. His role in the war against the Italian tribes had earned him the people's adoration.

But he was an unapologetic member of the aristocracy. An *optimate*, as they called themselves. One of the "best men."

Sulla towered over the skinny Sulpicius and shook his head.

"Of all the degenerate miscreants who've run for the tribunate in Rome's history, you might be the worst, Sulpicius." Sulla's words reverberated throughout the Forum. He was one of the most eloquent speakers I'd ever heard, but even he seemed uncouth and coarse compared to Sulpicius. "Who among them could boast of being three million sesterces in debt before even coming of age?"

Jeers and curses spread throughout the crowd. I wasn't sure

if this was an objection to Sulla's insults or to the man he aimed them at. Either way, Sulla paid them no mind.

"Worse than your warmongering and your threats to Rome's most august body is this . . . you're a liar. A pandering liar. Any man here with a hair or two on his chin has seen your ilk before and knows that every word spewed from your lips is dripping with poison."

Sulpicius continued to stand in Sulla's shadow with an amused smile on his face.

"You think I'm a liar?" Sulpicius shrugged and turned to his anti-senate. "Do you boys think I'm lying?"

They brandished their clubs and gnashed their teeth.

Sulla only shook his head. "I am unafraid of your thugs. A little history would tell you that each and every one of them will end up floating lifeless and bloated in the Tiber before this year is done."

Sulpicius's piercing laughter rang throughout the Forum. "And he says *I* am the one making threats!"

"They aren't threats. At worst, they are an educated guess, but I would call it prophecy."

Sulpicius held his stomach to control his feigned laughter. "Well, tell me, seer, what will become of me? Will I become the people's tribune? That's what you want, isn't it, Romans?"

The people shouted out, angrier this time. An unambiguous, undisputed cry of support for Sulpicius.

Sulla pointed up toward the Capitoline hill. "There lies the Tarpeian Rock. If you continue down this path, you'll be thrown from it to your death. Thus is the special fate reserved for traitors and would-be demagogues."

At this, the anti-senate sprang into action. Sulla's men reached the rostra with the speed of Jupiter's lightning. The crowd cried out, this time in fear, and stormed in every direction to get away.

"Quintus!" Arrea shouted, pulling me back from the rostra.

I turned to Barca. "Take her home!" I said. "Go!"

I pushed my way onto the steps, along with Sulla's supporters and more men of the anti-senate. I was unarmed, but this was my Republic. I'd seen men slain in the Forum in these types of political brawls before, and I wouldn't stand idly by while it happened again, even if the most endangered was my enemy.

SCROLL XX

GAVIUS SERTORIUS—THE Kalends of June, 665 Ab Urbe Condita

I charged up the rostra steps, and fortunately I was not alone. Ten of our men escorted us back to Rome, and they were just as ready for this skirmish as any battle we'd fought. We'd relinquished our weapons at Rome's sacred boundaries as is customary, but I still liked our odds against these criminals.

"Legate, fall back to us!" I shouted over the ensuing chaos. "Legate!"

One of Sulpicius's cloaked men clambered up the side of the steps. A quick kick to the chin was enough to push him back down.

"Sulla!" I shouted over the din of clubs against flesh.

I caught sight of his golden hair in the center of the melee. He stood tall, defiant, and completely still.

This "anti-senate"—as Sulpicius had called

them—weren't quite ready to assault someone of Sulla's stature, despite their need to show violence. Instead, they rushed us.

One ruffian hoisted the broken arm of a chair and swung for my head. I dodged but it connected with my shoulder. Pain reverberated through my arm, but it was nothing compared to what I'd faced on the battlefield.

I struggled to grab the attacker's wrist. "Legate, please!" I shouted.

He cast his gaze over the fleeing people. "Is this the Rome you hope to leave your children?" His voice belted out over the crying throng. "Is this what we have fought for?"

We had no shields among us, but we formed a wall of flesh and pushed as far onto the speakers' platform as we could. Sulla finally fell in behind us.

Sulpicius was standing nearby and watching the melee unfold like a drunken spectator of gladiatorial games. His eyes were hungry, ravenous, marveling over the blood spatter on his white toga.

One of the unarmed legionaries at my side collapsed under a club blow to the side of his head. They pummeled him to the point of unconsciousness before I could push back one of the men responsible. I wrenched a mallet from his hand and then thrust it at his chin. Blood spewed from his mouth as he fell back.

Sulla's words echoed in my head as I struck the next man. Is this what we fought for? Is this what the Republic really was?

My father told me tales of rapacious, violent politicians when I was a child, but I thought they were cautionary tales. Perhaps they were lived experiences.

The jagged edge of a wooden plank clipped the flesh of my neck. Sulla must have seen it, as he jumped into action for the first time since the chaos began.

Sulla grabbed the closest man by the neck of his tunic and threw him like Hercules from the rostra.

I sent a knee into the groin of a burly anti-senator nearby and kicked him in the back for good measure once he collapsed on top of his fellows.

Their ranks thinned out on the platform, but we'd seen how many of them gathered in the Forum. We were Rome's greatest legionaries on the field, but we could only do so much if all those angry thugs attacked at once.

I turned back toward the stairs to see how many were rushing us, but there were a handful of loyal Roman citizens standing in the fray. One in a senator's toga led them. Shouting orders to the anti-senate to stand down in the name of Rome. Even muffled by the sound of angry curses, I could tell the voice was my father's. I wondered why he wasn't back on his farm. Where was my sister? Where was Arrea?

I would have fought my way to him if I could've, but he didn't seem to need my help.

He turned back toward me in a moment of reprieve, and I think he saw me.

"Father!" I shouted.

Blood dripped from his nose and stained his toga, but otherwise he appeared unharmed, unfazed by the violence.

"We'll see how this ends, legate," Sulpicius spit out the words like sour wine. "We'll save this for another day. Anti-senators, to me!"

The man leapt from the rostra and strode away

at an even pace as his hundreds of followers flocked to join him. They headed back down the Via Sacra, and I wondered where they would go. What does one do after assaulting Rome's favored son in the Forum and disrupting a sacred political assembly?

But I didn't care so much about them.

My father was here.

Our legionaries, at least the ones unharmed, cursed them as they fled. I checked on Sulla to make sure he was unharmed, and instead I found him enraptured.

"Well done, my boy." He grabbed me by my face.

"Are you well, legate? I am sorry I did not reach you sooner."

"Thanks to you, I'm more than well," he said. "The whole city will know of what you've done today. And what that rapacious little *scelerum caput* Sulpicius did. We've already won the year, Gavius, I tell you."

"Gavius?" A voice came from behind.

"Father."

I turned and pushed through our men until I could embrace him.

"What are you doing here? Are you hurt?" I said.

He said nearly the same thing.

We laughed and embraced again.

I didn't like how I'd left him the year before. He wanted me to retire from the legion and return home. I declined. I swore an oath to Sulla, to the legion, and to Rome. But I wanted him to know under different circumstances I would have joined him.

"The legatus is running for consul," I said. "We've come to announce his bid for the upcoming elections."

He made an odd face, then smiled. "I came for the same reason . . . well, not for consul. For tribune. I'm going to run for tribune."

I slapped his shoulder. "Father, what excellent news! You'll make a fine tribune. Surely better than that miscreant."

I felt Sulla's presence behind me.

"It's been a long time since we've seen a politician like that one in Rome, hasn't it, Sertorius?" Sulla said.

Father released me and stretched out his hand. "It has."

"And we all remember what happened last time."

Father no longer smiled, but Sulla still was.

I looked between them. "What happened? I'm too young to remember, I suppose."

"Ask your father sometime," Sulla said. "He can tell you."

My father turned his attention back to me. "Are you able to join me for dinner? Your mother will skewer me and serve me up like wild boar if she finds out you're here and I don't bring you to see her."

I considered it, frowned, and looked at Sulla.

Father continued, "Of course, you're all welcome. I'd be honored to host the consul-elect."

Sulla threw his arms around my father, and for the first time I realized the height difference between them. They'd both always been giants to me, though my father and I were of equal height now. "Delightful!" Sulla said. "We'd love to join you."

"Good, good." Sertorius dabbed at the blood of his nose. "Give me some time to clean up and prepare a worthy feast. Gavius, would you like to help me?"

"I need him with me," Sulla said. "Who knows what Sulpicius and his playthings will attempt?"

I nodded. "Yes, I should protect the legatus."

"Sertorius," Sulla said, "I should mention, I had dinner guests planned for this evening. I suppose it wouldn't be a problem if I brought them along?"

"Of course not. Bring whomever you'd like, and I'll honor them properly."

"Excellent. We'll see you soon then. *Vale.*"

SCROLL XXI

QUINTUS SERTORIUS—THE Kalends of June, 665 Ab Urbe Condita

The low dining couches circled a dark wood table laden with platters of food and amphorae of wine. An evening breeze from the peristylum gently swayed the linen drapes.

Arrea had done an excellent job decorating the *domus* while I was in Greece, and our *servi* had kept it in fine condition despite our absence. Still, I could only imagine what Sulla and his guests would say when they arrived.

Barca, sitting on the couch to my right, noticed my tapping feet. "Drink a cup or two of wine," he said. "Helps with patience."

"Thank you, Barca," I said. "But I need to keep a clear mind when Sulla is present."

"You do not trust this man?"

The clinking of plates and cutlery sounded in the kitchen, where Arrea and my mother were assisting the *servi*. I told them our staff was more than capable of handling it, but they were determined for everything to be perfect for our guests—and for Gavius.

"I trust few men in Rome, to tell you the truth," I said. "But him least of all."

"Why? What has he done?"

They could arrive at any moment, and I didn't have time to give details. Sulla and I had a long and sordid past, from service beside each other in the legions to arguments in the senate house. I saw in him the most dangerous man alive. One only need look into the pools of his blue eyes to see the boundless ambition there. And beyond that, he had my son at his hip.

Barca leaned forward on his couch. "Look here." He reached under the fold of his ornate toga, revealing the gilded hilt of a dagger. "He tries anything, I cut his throat."

I smiled. "Thank you, *amice,* but that shouldn't be necessary. That's not the kind of threat this man poses."

Barca narrowed his eyes, but there was no time for further explanation. My doorman was already beginning to announce our guests.

"Legatus Lucius Cornelius Sulla, commander of the southern legions!" He projected as well as a centurion.

I nodded to Barca and hurried to greet our guests. I took a deep breath as we walked. I had no desire to share bread and wine with Sulla or any of his companions. But if that was the price I must pay for a few hours with my son, I wouldn't hesitate.

When he saw me, Sulla said, "What a lovely, simple home you have, brother Quintus." He released the hand of a tall, thin woman and embraced me with a firm kiss on either cheek.

"I pray you find it to your liking," I said. "This must be your wife, Cloelia."

Sulla laughed. "Not quite. We divorced three days ago," he said. "Well, that's when I sent her the letter."

"Oh . . . I apologize then."

"No need. We haven't formally announced my new betrothal. This is Caecilia." He stepped aside and allowed me to take her hand.

"*Ave*, Caecilia. You grace our home with your presence," I said.

She smiled coyly and allowed me to kiss her hand. Her eyes were emerald jewels, as shrewd and calculating as they were inviting. She covered her face in white powder like most noblewomen but couldn't conceal her olive skin. Red hair, styled to perfection in tight ringlets and flowing curls, hung down behind the gold earrings dangling near her shoulders. It must have taken her servants hours to style her hair like this floral arrangement. I'm sure the slave girl whose hair was taken to craft this wig was just as beautiful.

"I'm delighted to finally meet you in person," she said. Her voice lingered on the precipice of laughter. "I've heard so much about you."

"All of Rome has heard much about this one, my dear," Sulla said. "The one-eyed warrior has become a modern legend to rival Cincinnatus and Horatius Cocles."

"I'm sure there were people who spread foul rumors about them in their time as well," she said.

Clearly, she was as versed in veiled, insulting repartee as her betrothed. I ignored the comment.

"Come, let me show you to the triclinium," I said.

Sulla followed behind me. "Cloelia was as barren as one of the rebel strongholds I've conquered, and Sulla needs a son. Caecilia made for the perfect candidate," he said, half to me and partly to her. "I believe you know her brother, Quintus. What do they call him in the legions, dear?"

"Metellus. Metellus Pius," she said.

A marriage and alliance between Sulla and Metellus Pius . . . How fitting. I could only imagine the schemes they would conjure together. Sulla's boundless ambition and Metellus's complete disregard for Roman life was a perilous combination.

"Here we are." I gestured to the dining room. "You and your bride can take the couch of honor, here."

"Nonsense," Sulla said. "It should be your son, whenever he arrives. He was the one who saved the day."

A generous offer for a patrician, but that couch was the farthest away from my own, and he knew that.

"You are very considerate," I said.

"Besides, I want to sit beside you!" He threw an arm around my shoulder. "We have much to catch up on."

"Of course," I said. "When will Gavius arrive?"

"He's taking care of a few things on my behalf at the moment." Sulla released me and plopped down on the couch of his choosing. "He'll be here with a few friends of mine in a moment."

He turned and noticed Barca, who was doing little to conceal the disgust in his eyes. "Who is this?" Sulla asked me.

"A friend, my neighbor in Nursia. Rebels were in the area, and he protected my wife, mother, and daughter while I was away fighting."

Sulla considered it. "Interesting. I did the same for you and your family while you were in Greece, didn't I?"

He did, but not without an agenda. He never failed to mention it when he could.

I nodded. "You did."

"Interesting." He leaped up and moved over to Barca. "Lucius Cornelius Sulla." He extended a hand.

For a moment I was afraid Barca would dishonor him by remaining seated, but he was accustomed to mingling with the rich and powerful as a *lanista*. He stood and addressed him properly.

Sulla pinched some of Barca's toga between his fingers. "Fine cloth! How do you afford such material? Do you make your wealth hosting refugees?"

Barca's strong jawline flexed. "I earn my coin from arena."

Sulla clapped his hands. "Very good!" He turned to me. "I enjoy the company of actors, pantomimes, poets, and the sort at dinner parties. Makes for more amusement, nay? I'm sure gladiators are just as entertaining."

"He no longer fights," I said before Barca could respond. "He runs a school. One of the finest in Italy."

Barca blinked for the first time at those words. That statement was likely untrue since the betrayal of his men.

Sulla turned to me and lowered his voice. "Careful, Quintus. Voters might not look kindly on gallivanting about with gladiators at your side. You might appear like another Sulpicius, nay?"

My mother and Arrea entered in time to spare us any more of this.

"My dear Arrea," he said. "You are as lovely as always. A flower." He kissed both her hands.

"You honor us by being here." She bowed until he lifted her chin with a single finger.

"And you must introduce me to this beauty at once," he gestured to my mother.

"This is my mother-in-law, Rhea." Arrea smiled.

Sulla threw a hand over his chest and looked back and forth between my mother and me. "It couldn't be," he said. "Impossible."

"It's true." I feigned a smile. "A creature like me came from a woman like her." I played along as well as I could and would continue to do so for my son.

Sulla kissed her hands with the same familiarity as Arrea's. "The very image of Venus."

"I prefer Diana, the huntress," she said. Rhea was a shrewd woman. Sulla's attempts at flattery and charm wouldn't work on her.

Arrea sprinted away from them, and it was then I saw Gavius standing in the doorway with two other men.

"Mother!" he said.

She jumped into his arms. Many Romans would have considered the display to be emasculating, but I taught Gavius to ignore such social conventions. Love was love. That's what my father taught me.

The room clapped for the reunion, led by Sulla, who blinked absent tears from his eyes.

I said, "The last time I saw you two together, you were half her height." I made my way to them.

"Much has changed," Gavius said. He released Arrea and embraced his grandmother. A few tears stained the shoulder of his toga.

I tried to settle into the moment. We were all together. In our home. For the first time in as long as I could remember.

Then Gavius met his sister for the first time. She was sleeping in the crib suspended from the wall in a dark, calm corner of the room. Typically, I would have forbid waking her or disrupting her rigorous sleep schedule, but Gavius was an exception.

Love was apparent in his eyes the moment he saw Toria. With the calloused hand of a warrior, he gentled touched her cheek. As if he feared hurting her, he stepped back.

"She has your eyes, father," he whispered.

"You can hold her if you'd like," I said, hoping he would accept the offer.

"Let me introduce you to my good friends, Quintus," Sulla said.

He again referred to me by my praenomen, typically reserved to my wife and mother, but this was not the time to mention it. That this intrusion distracted Gavius from his sister bothered me most.

"This is Quintus Pompeius Rufus. He is running for consul alongside me."

He was a rather unassuming man, average height with the build of someone leisured. His hand was soft as butter when he shook mine.

"Call me Rufus." He gestured to his red hair, which fled from the crown of his head.

"Any relation to Pompeius Strabo?" I asked.

"My cousin." He smiled and raised his chin. "I understand you've been serving under him with some distinction."

Caecilia giggled.

They weren't very close cousins if that's what Strabo told him. But I could tell the man was a seasoned politician and knew how to flatter, prattle, and lie.

"Young Pompey showed great promise," I said, avoiding any comment on Strabo in particular. "I think he will make a fine general one day."

Rufus nodded. "He certainly will. As will my son, Rufus Minor." He gestured to the eager young man behind him.

"Pleasure to make your acquaintance." He offered a much sturdier handshake than his father. "I've heard much about your accomplishments." There was something in his eyes that seemed more honest than his father.

Both seemed like a strange fit for companions of Sulla. I imagined he would keep company with the ambitious scions of the *Claudii, Servilii,* or another powerful patrician family. I suppose for a political ally he valued a simple and docile man, one who would follow his orders.

"Please come, sit, sit. All of you," Arrea said.

The *servi* entered with the main dish as we found our seats. Succulent lamb seasoned with cumin, coriander, and cloves to "delight the palate," as my cook told me. I wasn't sure what any of those tasted like, and I preferred my lamb plain, but I didn't want to offend anyone's patrician sensibilities.

Most of the meal was without consequence. Sulla had a plate piled high for himself and then barely touched it, too busy regaling us with stories of his exploits alongside Gavius.

I watched my son from across the room as he chuckled and nodded along, a familiarity in the looks shared between them.

Of all the vices a stoic must avoid, envy was normally the easiest for me to resist. Wealth, fame, power, prestige . . . they meant nothing to me. But this I envied. I was jealous for the affection of my son.

Arrea tried to engage with Caecilia in the brief interludes between stories, but Sulla's bride made it clear with single word answers she had no interest in discussion. She refused to even look at my wife when addressing her.

I assume Sulla told her about my wife's past. To someone like Caecilia, the thought of engaging with a freedwoman was a disgrace to her family name.

When she became irritated by the frequent attempts at levity, she turned her attention to me.

"Is it true you lost your nerve in the recent battle?"

My grip tightened around the stem of my cup. "Is that what your brother told you?"

"He said you wept when they executed the rebels and immediately relinquished your position."

I took a sip of wine to consider my response. How could I tell the truth without accusing her brother of lying? The last thing I wanted was to give Sulla a pretense for leaving and taking my son with him.

I'm sure he told her about the siege equipment I destroyed and the confrontations between us.

Caecilia sat up, leaned forward, and crossed her legs, waiting for my response with glee. Gavius watched with the same interest but with a different look in his eyes. Arrea and mother looked away, and Barca crossed his arms.

"In a legionary camp, embellished tales spread like an insula fire," I said. "I'm sure someone recounted the story to him this way."

She exhaled in relief. "I knew it couldn't be true! A warrior like you could never be so womanish. Tears on the battlefield?" She plopped back on her couch and laughed at the thought. "Absurd."

"My father has conquered a dozen cities or more," Gavius added quickly. "Scaled the walls first during a siege in Gaul and received military decoration for it." His gazed moved back and forth between Caecilia and me.

I think he wanted me to defend myself, but I refused to be goaded by this noblewoman.

"My father is the bravest man in the legion, I'd wager," he went on. "If you hear tales of him crying, you can assume at once they're lies."

"Hear, hear!" Sulla raised his wine.

Everyone's gaze turned to me again. They wanted to hear me confirm it.

I met Gavius's gaze and offered a gentle smile.

"If ever I was to cry, I could easily hide it," I said. "All I have to do is move the eye patch from one eye to the other."

Everyone laughed, Sulla most of all.

The tension in the room eased, and Barca sat back. Caecilia's insinuations might have been enough to make him draw his dagger if I'd so much as given him a nod. He didn't yet realize this was standard procedure in the Eternal City.

As the dinner continued, Rufus interrupted occasionally but offered little in the way of meaningful conversation. He told a few jokes he'd heard in the Forum, which no one laughed at except his son. He spoke of the unnaturally warm weather of the summer and asked if it had affected my harvest.

"I wouldn't know," I answered. "I have been away fighting."

Sulla snapped his fingers for another cup of wine. He was bored with this conversation, so he raised his voiced and interjected. "So, tell me, Quintus . . ." He accepted the cup and reclined on his couch in my direction. "What makes you desire a position as troublesome as the tribunate?"

Everyone looked at me.

Again, I needed to choose my words carefully. I was not among friends. "I serve the Republic," I said. "The tribunate is where I can serve Rome best at this time."

"I think my husband will make a fine tribune." Arrea took my hand.

"Well, he can't be any worse than that rapscallion Sulpicius,"

Rufus said. "I don't know what that man is up to, but it isn't good."

Sulla continued to analyze me, searching my face for answers I didn't give. "It's an awful burden, from what I'm told."

"Perhaps. One I'll gladly bear for the Republic if I'm elected."

He swirled his wine around in the silver cup. "The *Republic*," he whispered.

Caecilia, who'd barely touched her meal, set aside the plate in contempt. She rested her head on Sulla's shoulder and said, "When we return home, can you have your cook prepare that flamingo's tongue you told me about?"

"Of course, my dove." He kissed her head and settled in to tell another story while Rufus and Rufus Minor finished their meals. When they finished and set down their plates, Sulla stood and left the story unfinished.

"Unfortunately, we must depart," he said. "I wrote a letter announcing my bid for consul. Tomorrow we will nail it to the senate house doors and be on our way."

"Leaving so soon?" I stood.

Gavius said, "I'd like to teach Toria all those games you and I played when I was a boy, but we have more battles to win." Pride glimmered in his eyes.

"Nola will not conquer itself," Sulla added.

"Perhaps Gavius could stay with us tonight?" Arrea asked.

"Your room is just as you have left it," I added.

For a moment, I noticed a longing in Gavius' eyes. I thought it might encourage him to change his mind and stay.

He looked to Sulla, who considered it for a moment.

He frowned. "I'm afraid not. There is too much to do, and we must prepare for our departure."

Gavius nodded, neither disappointed nor relieved by the answer. He simply accepted Sulla's word as law. He came to my side and placed a hand on my shoulder. "Don't worry, father, I'll be back soon."

As I walked them to the door, Sulla smiled. "Oh, yes," he said. "We'll be back very soon."

SCROLL XXII

QUINTUS SERTORIUS—TWO days before the Ides of June, 665 Ab Urbe Condita

For the two weeks following that dinner with Gavius and Sulla, I campaigned for election. It was no simple task. Rome is a complex organism with thousands of moving parts. Ignore any one of them, and your odds of success decrease dramatically, no matter how Fortuna favors you.

I missed Apollonius's wisdom and guidance now more than ever. He would have been a brilliant campaign manager, but I was happy for him to be away. He deserved a holiday away from me and the strife that seems to follow me like a plague.

Tasks filled the day from dawn to dusk, each more pressing than the last. Most days began with greeting my clients for the morning levy. I had few compared to most of Rome's politicians, but I'd inherited my father's clients, and many Sabines who found themselves in Rome were happy to pledge themselves to my patronage. They offered votes for me; I offered favors to them.

There were still two weeks before the election, and the list of obligations was endless.

After I tended to my clients, I would go and speak to one of Rome's various factions, encouraging them to vote for me. There were dozens of collegia on each of the seven hills, and they all demanded attention. Two days before the Ides of June, I was scheduled to meet with the Triumph Organizers Guild. The group dedicated to planning a parade once every few years held significant voting power, to my chagrin.

Their office was on the lower level of the Villa Publica. I made my way to the Field of Mars, wearing my freshly laundered senator's toga and thinking about all the times I mustered with the legions here. Now I prattled with voters, but it would be worth it if I were elected and could end the war.

The building was older than almost any in Rome. If the plaque by the entryway was to be trusted, it was built just a few years after we overthrew the kings and established the Republic. It was easy to believe with the amount of dust inside. The building was mostly wood, held up over the years with patchwork stucco and chipping scarlet paint to keep it more in line with the state buildings in the Forum.

I found my way to the proper office and announced my entry. "Quintus Sertorius, tribune-elect for head of the Triumphal collegium, Opimius Critor."

A weary-eyed, dark-haired man looked up from his cluttered desk. "I am he."

The room was damp and small but filled to the brim with the trappings required for a triumph. Bird cages, wicker baskets filled with rose petals, cheap silver goblets painted to look more exquisite than they were.

"*Salve.*" I bowed. "I am here to speak with you about my bid for tribune."

Critor leaned back in a squeaky wooden chair and kicked his muddy sandals up on the desk. His untrimmed toes wriggled and he squinted his eyes. "Did you arrange this meeting?"

"Yes, last market day," I said.

"I see." He exhaled and rubbed his eyes.

He wasn't the first important man to greet me this way. I'm sure I wasn't the only candidate for office pestering him, but from the look of the place, he had little else in the way of responsibilities.

"I will make this easy for you, then," he said. "Do you plan on increasing the price of rose petals?"

"Uhh . . . no."

"Sacrificial lambs? Doves? Fabrics?"

I shook my head. "No plans to raise prices. If you would allow me to—"

"Good," he said. "Then you may have my vote."

"Would you like to hear about what I *am* planning to do?"

He shrugged. "Not really, but I won't stop you."

I inhaled and prepared to give the rehearsed speech I'd been giving to collegium leaders.

He raised his hand and cut me off. "Actually, never mind. I'm quite busy here if you can't tell. You're already going to win the election. Why waste your time?"

"What do you mean?"

He waved his arms around above his head. "You are the great Quintus Sertorius, slayer of gorgons and lover of Artemis. The city sings your praises to the point I have a headache. Even with that anti-war blathering, the people love you."

"Honey water is said to help with headaches," I said. "But as a legatus, I learned you should never ride into battle with any possibility for failure. If I can ensure voters like you and your clients are on my side, I should feel much more confident on election day."

"Well, be assured then. Rome elects ten of you each year, and I've not had ten men wasting their time coming here. All the men of substance are fighting in the war or already died in it. I hardly recognize most of the names on the ballet."

"Very well then. *Vale.*"

"If you would like to leave me with a token of gratitude . . ." he rubbed his forefinger and thumb together. "That would certainly help me remember this promise I'm making. My wife says I'm a forgetful man."

"I would not," I said.

"On your way then. Hopefully those other tribunes don't show up feeling more generous."

Most of the collegia heads had made similar veiled demands. Apparently, bribery was routine in the electoral process, but I wouldn't contribute to it. Besides, what coin I'd earned in my years of service rested in the home my wife and daughter now slept in and in my empty farm with unattended fields.

Hopefully Critor was right and my popularity with the people would see me to victory.

My next appointment was with the lictors' guild, located on the Quirinal hill. I set off in that direction and hoped my next encounter would be more productive.

As I crossed the Field of Mars toward the city walls, a horse and rider nearly trampled me.

I dove out of the way. "Be mindful of your steer," I said.

I couldn't make out the rider from the June sun glaring behind him but could tell he was older. Overweight through his belly but the muscles of his chest and arms were powerful despite his age.

"Do you not remember me?" he asked me.

I shielded my eye from the sun, but still I could not see him.

I didn't need to. Despite the age and weight of the man before me, he was unmistakable. Years could not take away the power in his voice.

Gaius Marius.

"Of course I remember you!"

"No, I think you've forgotten," Marius said, a tinge of sadness in his voice. "Hertensius would not have forgotten me."

"Hirtuleius? Do you mean my friend Lucius Hirtuleius?"

"That's what I said." He grunted as he threw himself off the horse and extended his hand. "How many years has it been now?"

"How many years since what?"

Closer now, I could see the old general better. The past few years had done him no favors, but he was still there. Beneath the wrinkles and the excess, Marius was still there.

He did not reply.

"Since I first served under you?" I said.

"Yes. How many years has it been?"

I genuinely smiled as I considered it. "I first marched under your banner fourteen years ago if my memory serves me. I suppose we—"

"Ahh! I recall. You were little more than a suckling babe then. But by the gods you've grown."

There was nothing in his eyes that revealed our more recent history. He didn't mention fighting together the year prior. He failed to mention Saturninus and Glaucia, the violent revolutionaries he released on Rome. He didn't address what we went through together ten years before, how our close relationship had fallen apart.

"The years will do that, I suppose," I said. I wanted to say more, but something kept me from it. He responded, but hushed and monotone, almost to himself.

"Let me introduce you to my son," he said. "Boy! Come, come."

A young man hurried closer.

"Yes, father?" the young man said.

The boy looked nothing like Marius.

Marius had always been a severe-looking man. Regardless, one couldn't deny his rugged handsomeness, especially when he was at the height of his fame and power.

This son lacked any such quality.

He bore a pockmarked face with a nose too small for the rest. Blanched skin stretched out over flappy muscles. Beady, dull eyes. An overgrown beard that was too long on the chin and lips but absent on the cheeks.

"This is my former protégé," Marius told him. "Had he been any less scrupulous, he might now be your brother-in-law."

Marius the Younger furrowed his brows. "He refused my sister?"

"Of course not," Marius said before I could respond. "He refused *me*."

"General, I did no such thing," I said.

He closed his eyes, let his head fall back, and smiled. "Call me that again," he said.

"I'm sorry?"

"General . . ." he said. He abruptly turned and grabbed my shoulders. "We conquered nations together! We saved Rome!"

I wondered if he were drunk, but there was no smell of wine on his breath. He was prone to drunkenness in the past, but that didn't seem to be the cause for his odd behavior today.

"We did. Yes, we did," I said. "We conquered many foes together."

And that was true. When I reflected on Marius without the stain of the past ten years, I couldn't help but consider him fondly. I worshipped him in my youth, served him as a young man, and learned from him as I grew. But after everything he'd done in his pursuit of power and praise, I resented him.

I wished it were different.

Marius threw his arm around his son's shoulders. "This is my boy. I'm happy for you to meet him."

We'd met before, if I recalled correctly. But neither Marius seemed to remember, so I didn't mention it.

"It's a pleasure to meet you." I extended my hand.

Marius the Younger accepted the gesture reluctantly, as if my hand were covered in snot. "And you," he said.

Marius smiled. "That's why I want the war with Mithridates," he said. "I want to teach my boy how to be a general. I want Rome to always have a Marius to rely on."

I should have left at that moment. The lictors' guild was waiting, and nothing good would come out of talking to Marius in this state. But I couldn't ignore his last comment.

"You want the war with Mithridates? What do you mean?"

"Of course I want it," Marius said. "What man wouldn't? But I am the savior of Rome. I'm the Third Founder of Rome. The war belongs to me."

It took a few moments before realization dawned on me. He didn't simply want the war with Mithridates to take place, he wanted command of the legions sent against him.

Looking at the shirtless, barrel-chested, hairy old man before me, it was hard to see a general capable of handling a war against Rome's most dangerous enemy since Hannibal. But still, he was Marius.

"Who deserves it more than I?" he said.

"I wouldn't presume to know the answer," I said. "It was nice to meet you." I nodded to Marius the Younger and hoped to make my escape.

"Ser . . . Ser . . . this man was one of my finest officers when I fought against the northern invaders," Marius told his son.

"Like a centurion or something?" the son said.

Marius nodded.

"Not a centurion," I said. "But I did serve on your father's staff. General, I heard you bought a home in Baiae and retired?"

"I did," Marius said. "But I will always come back when Rome needs me." He became sullen. "This war with Mithridates is serious. Not some pissing fight with jealous allies. None in Rome could hope to win such a war but Marius."

There were many things I wanted to say but chose not to. "I only hope Rome is victorious," I said. "If you offer the best chance of survival for our people, you can count on my support." I clapped Marius on the shoulder and hoped that was enough.

Everyone in Rome knew the battle command would go to one of the two consuls elected for the next year, and Marius couldn't hope to be elected after the debacle that was his last consulship. He unleashed Saturninus and Glaucia, a tribune and a praetor, to tyrannize the Republic with corruption and mob violence, only to betray them and deliver them to death when they no longer suited him. No, he would never be elected again. Most agreed the office and command of the war already belonged to Sulla.

I disliked the prospects of either man leading the war against such a powerful foreign king. But the notion of Marius commanding an army at this juncture of his life was almost enough to make a man laugh.

Was this just the misguided ramblings of an old man? Despite our past and the anger I felt, it saddened me to see him fall so far. He was once a great man.

"I must lead," Marius said. "Otherwise, we will have no Marius to protect the Republic after I am gone. I must teach the boy."

He wrapped his arm around his son's shoulders and held him tight. I thought of Pompey. I couldn't imagine Strabo displaying such affection, though he deserved it. I admired Marius for loving his son, despite Marius the Younger displaying none of the characteristics men often desire in their heir.

"It was good to see you, general Marius," I said, and I partially meant it.

A shadow grew behind me. "Conspiring with my rival, dear Marius?" came the unmistakable voice. Sulpicius joined us.

"Rival?" Marius the Younger tilted his head.

"You are running for tribune?" Marius asked me. For the first time since he'd arrived, his eyes reflected clarity and awareness.

"I am."

"Mmm. Very well." Marius nodded and turned his attention to Sulpicius.

They embraced as warmly as Marius and his son.

"Quintus gave a *rousing* speech at the *comitium* last market day!" Sulpicius said. "Had the entire gathering in tears and thumping their chests for Rome."

Marius grunted. "I taught him a thing or two about giving speeches."

"He was riveting, Marius. Unfortunately, I spoiled the whole thing." Sulpicius frowned and shrugged. "I may have been a *touch* dramatic for that specific audience."

Marius the Younger chuckled. Even if he wasn't present, I'm sure he'd heard rumors. They spread through the city like a plague.

"Nothing that can't be undone, I'm sure," Marius said.

"I meant you no disrespect, by the way," Sulpicius said. "Dirty business, politics. Oh, the things we do for victory."

"Your words did not insult me," I said.

He exhaled and placed a hand on his chest. "I'm relieved to hear it. I'm actually quite fond of you, you know? Your career has been a spectacle to behold from a distance, and I wish our first encounter had been more pleasant."

The sun had shifted from when I first ran into Marius. I needed to leave soon or disrespect the lictors' guild by tardiness.

"After the elections, perhaps we'll meet under more amicable circumstances," I said. "In the meantime, go with fortune."

I extended a hand, hoping to end the conversation, but Sulpicius pretended not to see it.

"Marius and I had half a mind for you to join us in our endeavors," he said. "You were at the top of our list, be assured, but we decided you might not want to wade in the filth beside us." He winked. "It wouldn't go to have a hero like you tarnishing your good name!"

I lowered my hand. "What endeavors?"

He frowned. "I'm not at liberty to say, I'm afraid," he said. "What kind of politician would I be if I went about divulging all my secrets? And to my rival, no less!" He patted my shoulder affably.

"Not a successful one," Marius grunted.

It was no wonder why Sulpicius could afford to be so fearless. He had the backing of Gaius Marius. And his coin, too, I assumed, which I'm sure was useful for bribes and hiring thugs to intimidate detractors. I wondered if some of Sulpicius's anti-senate were former Marian legionaries, men I served with.

"I should go," I said. "I have a meeting."

"With the lictors' guild, yes," Sulpicius said.

My jaw tightened.

"I've spoke with them myself. Lovely fellows. Do me a favor, could you? Tell Eppius the shipment of wine his wife requested should be arriving from Greece any day."

"*Vale*," I said. This time I didn't offer my hand.

"I shall sacrifice a bull that you and I are both elected, and we can serve the Republic together," Sulpicius shouted after me as I turned away.

I made for the Quirinal hill. I could feel their gaze following me as I departed.

Sulpicius's casual acknowledgment of his alliance with Marius consumed my thoughts. The old general was not the man he once was. He'd always been reckless and dangerous to those he considered enemies, but Rome could always rely upon his noble intentions. Was that still the case? With a man like Sulpicius at his side, he could re-create the same havoc that nearly destroyed Rome ten years before. Or worse.

And what could they be planning? What could have brought the two of them together in common cause? The two men made unlikely allies. The war with Mithridates alone made sense to me, though I knew their schemes were even higher.

Rome wouldn't have to wait long to find out. Only two weeks remained until the election.

SCROLL XXIII

Q<small>UINTUS</small> S<small>ERTORIUS</small>—<small>THE</small> Kalends of Quintilis, 665 Ab Urbe
Condita

They built the makeshift wooden voting structure overnight.
Impressive, given that it was large enough to host twenty-four
tribune-elects—each with a *servus* except myself—and several
magistrates, priests, and young scribes. A separate stairway led
to a covered pen, where tribal elders could cast their votes in
private.

It was here, on the Field of Mars, that I greeted voters on election day morning. I arrived early, but already my skin prickled
with sweat under the burgeoning Quintilis sun. Wisps of dust
swirled up underfoot, kicked up by the restless shuffle of thousands of sandals. Fortunately, a breeze was present to hold off
the stifling heat, carrying with it the faint smell of the nearby
Tiber and the adjacent livestock farms.

Here, my fate and the fate of the Republic would be decided.

As much as possible I greeted each citizen by name and refer-
enced some aspect of their life I was familiar with: interests,
hobbies, patron deities. The other tribune-elects all had a nomen-

clator, a *servus* specifically tasked with remembering as many citizens as possible, standing behind them. I didn't. I hoped remembering voters without any aid would earn their respect, but only a few hours remained before I would know if that was enough.

The presiding magistrate, Lutatius Catulus, tapped his ceremonial staff on the wooden voting structure to announce it was time for us to join him on the stage.

"It is time," I said to Barca.

He nodded. "I remain here. We are with you." He gestured back to his gladiators and the few dozen clients of mine who joined us that morning.

I longed to embrace Arrea one last time before the voting began, but Rome didn't permit women to attend. The senate made exceptions at times, but with so many voters flocking to the city for this election, the Field of Mars could barely host the thirty-thousand male citizens, let alone their families.

I settled for a handshake with Barca and ascended to the voting structure. Twenty-four backless wicker chairs were spaced out on the stage. I fell in line with the rest of the would-be tribunes and stood before an empty seat.

I focused my attention on the crowd and did my best to acknowledge each citizen who shouted my name. Thus distracted, I hadn't seen Sulpicius take the seat directly to my right.

"It's a wonderful day for democracy, isn't it?" he said.

He smelled of olive oil and lavender perfume. He surprisingly wore more jewelry than the first time I'd seen him. His *servi* had coifed and oiled his hair, delineating each strand and combed it just to his liking. Sulpicius looked the part of a victor before voting even began.

"It is," I said. It felt unnatural to agree with him about anything, but he wasn't wrong on this point.

Even with all Rome's faults and all the struggles besetting our path, the freedom of our people justified it all.

Scarlet banners with ancient symbols flapped in the summer breeze, heralding the tribal groups as they formed orderly queues. Disputes over position in line caused sharp, heated exchanges, but officials quickly silenced them.

Catulus raised his staff and shouted, "Greetings, Romans! Today, we weave another thread through the Fates. You are about to write history. But first, let me introduce your illustrious candidates!"

He went down the line, announcing one by one, referring to a piece of parchment for the names of obscure candidates.

When he announced my name, the crowds cheered. I lifted an open hand to greet them. I would serve them as best I could if elected.

But Sulpicius was introduced next. Catulus uttered his name like it was poisonous to his lips, but the applause of the crowd was rapturous. The support they showed me was miniscule by comparison.

As the cheering died down and Catulus moved on to announce the next candidate, Sulpicius leaned toward me. "Don't worry, good fellow. There are still nine more positions available."

Whether or not I was victorious, I would accept the gods' will. It was the thought of Sulpicius's imminent election that concerned me.

Catulus instructed us to take our seats. He didn't want the older candidates falling over from the heat.

Instead of responding to Sulpicius, I looked out over the gathering. Voters stretched back all the way to the city, a mosaic of humanity under the Roman sky. Olive trees lined the boundary of the field, their silver-green leaves shimmering in the early sunlight.

As I marveled at the site, intent on ignoring Sulpicius, the voting began. Catulus announced the first tribe, and its elder entered the covered voting pen with the cheering support of his allies.

"That's the Collina tribe," Sulpicius whispered. "They were *particularly* expensive."

The sun reached its zenith by the time the second tribe moved forward to vote. The pervasive scent of baking earth mingled with the sweat of closely packed bodies. Togas become quite burdensome in the heat. Grains of sand and dirt cling to it and the sweaty skin beneath.

The third tribe stepped forward. Gatherers shouted out occasional endorsements for various candidates—usually Sulpicius—but the voters had likely known for weeks who they would support. All the work we'd put in since I arrived in Rome, it would be enough to earn my election or it wouldn't.

Time would tell, but I began to feel less than confident. The fourth tribe to vote was my own, Quirina. The elder gave me a nod as he ascended the steps. Of the four tribes to vote so far, he alone looked my direction.

Sulpicius reclined as best he could in a backless chair as his *servus* waved him down with an ostrich-feathered fan.

"One day I should like to build an *indoor* voting structure," Sulpicius said. "This heat is ghastly."

"The people have voted here for centuries. If the Field of Mars was good enough for our ancestors, it's good enough for me," I said.

He chuckled. "Our ancestors were also quite fond of their sheep, from what I've heard. I shouldn't suppose *everything* good enough for them is acceptable today."

The next tribe stepped forward. In the brief moments of quiet, I could hear merchants shouting from their stalls on the perimeter of the parade field, hawking all kinds of goods. Watered wine was the most popular, but the wafting scents of roasted meats and fresh bread tempted voters as well.

Sulpicius picked up his chair and moved it closer to mine, determined to chatter whether or not I engaged. "That's Suburana. Do you know what they asked for when I spoke to them? They wanted a *lion*." He chuckled and shook his head. "'*A lion?*'

I said. Apparently, they run the Esquiline hill with an iron hand. They fancy a caged beast would keep their people in line." He found the story quite humorous, unashamed at the flagrant admission of bribery.

Each tribe was called up in turn as I awaited the tally, and Sulpicius made ceaseless trifling comments. Thirty-four tribes stepped forth, and only when each placed their vote in the ceremonial urn did Catulus announce the results.

He announced each, one by one. It was clear immediately Sulpicius would be elected. Each of the first ten votes contained his name. Catulus became increasingly frustrated with the results, but he could do nothing to change them.

Sulpicius didn't appear surprised or elated by his pending victory. He was more interested in how rarely Catulus called my name. Fourteen candidates were ahead of me by the tenth reading.

"Perhaps Catulus announced all the naysayers and unpatriotic tribes first?" Sulpicius pretended to comfort me. "Surely the remaining votes will contain your illustrious name."

Whether or not he believed that, he was wrong.

By the fifteenth vote, I was falling out of contention. The odds of my election were slim.

I spotted Barca among my supporters. He furled his brows and crossed his arms. He scanned the crowd as if looking for those responsible for this betrayal. Perhaps I simply had not done enough. Perhaps I believed my reputation as a warrior and a man who strove after honoring our past was enough to earn me the tribunate. Maybe I overestimated my esteem with the people.

The twenty-seventh vote officially eliminated me. Even if the remaining seven votes included my name, it would not be enough to earn me a seat among the ten tribunes.

I sat, defeated, and looked out over the people who rejected me. Shame, relief, disappointment, anger . . . all these and more came over me. I asked the gods why this had happened. They led me to Rome, or so I believed, to help end the war and serve the Republic. Had I misjudged them? Or perhaps this was what they intended all along. Maybe I needed to taste this defeat before I'd allow myself to return home and stay there. Without it, perhaps the incessant need to interfere in state affairs would continue to draw me away.

The thought of taking my family back home was enough to quash the disappointment and embarrassment growing my chest.

I did my best. I hadn't resorted to bribing tribes with gold and lions. Now I could only accept my defeat with dignity.

After Catulus announced the thirty-fourth vote, he formally introduced the ten victors, Sulpicius among them. The magistrate dismissed the crowd and encouraged them to enjoy the feast soon to take place in the Forum. Priests would make further sacrifices and additional auguries, but otherwise the rest of the day would be devoted to revelry and celebration.

I addressed each of the new tribunes. "Congratulations on your victory. Congratulations. Good fortune." I embraced each of them, saying a silent prayer that they would protect the Republic in my stead.

I'd hoped to avoid Sulpicius, but he blocked the stage exit until I addressed him.

"Congratulations on your election, tribune," I said. With a curt nod, I attempted to step past him.

He grabbed my arm with more strength than I expected from someone his size. "I am *deeply* grieved by your defeat," he said. "You would have made a fine tribune. Brothers-in-arms, we could have created a new Rome together."

We didn't need to create a new Rome. We needed only to serve and protect the one we had.

I squared myself with him and met his gaze. "I appreciate your sympathies, but my election is not the will of the people. I accept that."

He chuckled. "The will of the people, the will of the gods . . . we often write our *own* fate."

I thought of how the fate I would be a part of writing was to accept the people's decision and return to my farm. I was content with that. The dread in my heart was only for what would become of Rome in my absence.

"Congratulations, again." I stepped past him.

I heard his words trailing after me, "I believe the gladiator retinue might have been a touch dramatic for the people's liking. I would leave them in the arena if you run for office again."

Those words stopped me.

I faced him.

He went on, "The people won't tolerate armed thugs unless they're the *people's* armed thugs. You'll find plebs will tolerate any amount of corruption and violence if one wields it on their behalf."

"Threats and bribery make us a weaker Rome, not a stronger one."

"Honorable. Respectable. That's why I like you, Quintus Sertorius," he said. "I spoke in jest. You didn't lose the election because of gladiators." He waved away the silly notion.

I looked at the retreating crowd. Barca waited below, his gaze fixed on my conversation, ready to strike if the tribune tried anything untoward.

"Why did I lose then?"

"Oh, it's simple, really. The people love you. This alone should have guaranteed your victory. A powerful man must have opposed you and you have no powerful man of your own to offset the sabotage efforts." He pantomimed balancing a scale. "Everyone has known about the resistance to your election since the day you put your name forth. But you weren't even aware of that, were you?" He whistled low and shook his head slowly. "Candidates should have *networks* of spies throughout the city reporting to them."

Sulpicius was as deceptive as he was charismatic, but I had

no reason to distrust what he said. Who had opposed me? And why?

Only one name came to mind.

Sulla.

Sulpicius continued his monologue. "If you'd known about your detractors, you could have bribed voters. If you're too *honorable* to cajole them with coin, with entertainment." He abruptly laughed. "You have a famous *lanista* in your retinue and a dozen gladiators at your back, and you didn't even sponsor games!" he said. "Nothing sways voters more than cheap wine and a spectacle of blood sport."

I wouldn't ask Barca to sacrifice even more of his damaged gladiatorial school just to improve my likelihood of election, but the thought hadn't even crossed my mind. It probably should have.

Sulpicius gestured to his fellow tribunes, who were now off the platform and celebrating with their associates. "Most of them, the people haven't even heard of before the campaign. The few who are known are disliked. Your standing with the plebs should have been a bounty, but these reprobates, degenerates, and unworthy sons of more illustrious fathers did everything I mentioned. Spies, bribery, entertainment . . . and coin. Oh, coin!" His eyes widened, presumably recalling the vast sums spent over the past month. "Do you truly think I could afford this election on my own?"

"I'm not abreast on your financial capabilities, tribune."

"You *really* do need some informants, Sertorius. I'm telling you this as a favor . . ." He emphasized his point. "My ruinous debt is a commonplace discussion throughout the taverns and gambling dens of the city. A matter of public record, really." He raised his chin, almost proud of the omission. "I couldn't have done this alone."

"I'm assuming a powerful benefactor supported you." Marius, my old mentor, and a man I once worshipped, clearly funded Sulpicius. I'd suspected as much since the day I saw them together.

The tribune nodded. "Covered *all* the costs of my campaign and erased my debts as if they were little more than a pittance. Let me assure you, they were more than that."

"Gaius Marius isn't known for his charity," I said. "What did he stand to gain?"

Sulpicius didn't blink at the mention of Marius's name, nor did he attempt to deny it.

He shrugged and looked at me blankly. "The man wants a war. I shall give him one."

My blood ran hot. I reminded myself this wasn't the battle-field. I exhaled and unclenched my fists.

"This has been enlightening, tribune, but I must go," I said. "My farm calls to me."

"The tribunate passed you by, but you can still wield its *power* and serve Rome."

I stole a glance at Barca. He searched my eye for any sign of warning. I shook my head and returned my attention to Sulpicius.

He continued. "My cause could use a hero like you, Quintus Sertorius. I may be in the people's favor *today*, but my plans will test the limits of their loyalty." He smiled and placed a hand on my shoulder. "Your shining name and faultless reputation alone would convince the people of the purity and virtue of our efforts."

I took the first step down the stairs. "Goodbye, tribune."

"You haven't heard my offer yet," he said. "Everyone knows you want to offer the rebels amnesty and citizenship. I can end the war like *that*." He snapped his fingers. "The people want the rebels annihilated. Removed from Terra Mater's earth. You sympathize with the prodigal tribes for your own rural heritage or because of their service beside you in years past. Without me, I regret to say the Republic will decimate your distant kin and former companions. To the last man, woman, and child."

Rage boiled in my chest. Perhaps he spoke true, but if he wielded the power to end the war, and would only do so with my complicity, he was even more corrupt than I realized.

"We can only hope the Republic's new magistrates will govern with honor and foresight," I said.

"Even if Rome had elected you, the assembly would have annihilated your proposal," he said. "But I *control* the assembly. I can guarantee the bill passes into law. The people won't like it, but with a hero like you supporting my efforts, I can stand to ruffle their feathers." He winked. "In addition, the next time you run for office, I can teach you how to play this game of thieves and brigands. And *win*."

Many men had tried to buy my loyalty, but it wasn't for sale. It belonged to my family and to the Republic, and no bribes could change that.

"I will return to my farm, Sulpicius."

He clicked his tongue and frowned. "All that wasted potential . . . disappointing." He shrugged. "No matter. Do stay for my inauguration, though. I have some real *theatrics* planned."

Rome's newest tribune smiled. This time when I stepped away, I didn't stop.

"What does he say?" Barca asked.

I set off toward home, my disappointed retinue trailing behind me.

"He thinks he can buy the heart of Rome. He thinks violence and intimidation will allow him to rule the Republic," I said. "I fear he is right."

SCROLL XXIV

GAVIUS SERTORIUS—SIX Days before the Nones of Quintilis, 665 Ab Urbe Condita

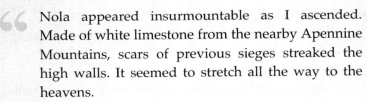 Nola appeared insurmountable as I ascended. Made of white limestone from the nearby Apennine Mountains, scars of previous sieges streaked the high walls. It seemed to stretch all the way to the heavens.

The time had come.

When war season began, I asked Sulla if I could be the first Roman to scale the walls of an enemy stronghold. I regretted the question now but refused to break my word.

With the next ladder rung in hand, I pulled myself up. *Don't look down, Gavius.* Instead, I turned my gaze above, where spear tips glistened like Jupiter's tears in the morning sun. That was more terrifying than the fall back to earth. I kept my eyes directly on the ladder.

Sulla's Fist roared below, eager to follow me.

The enemy matched the ferocity of our war cries from the wall.

Had my father really done this before? Hard to believe. It didn't seem possible to survive the walls with so many enemies waiting to strike me the moment I arrived at the top. How had he lived? Perhaps his patron goddess, Diana, protected him. I prayed she would extend her protection to his son.

I tried to take the next step up the ladder, but my shaking foot refused to move.

"Do you require assistance, tribune?" the legionary beneath me asked.

I thought of telling him that I didn't like heights but held back.

"No," I said, then summoned all the courage I could and hoisted myself up.

The entire war came down to this engagement. Nola was the last major enemy stronghold standing. With its collapse, Italy would once again be ours. Some rebels would carry on the fight despite their certain destruction, but they would no longer threaten Roman sovereignty. Mutilus waited for us on the other side of that wall. So did the Numidian cavalry. Either we would be victorious and have our revenge, or our defeat would set back the Roman war effort by months, maybe even years.

We couldn't allow that to happen.

I couldn't allow that to happen.

Projectiles whistled past me and struck companions below. I was almost to the top, a few more steps.

The sunbaked ledge scraped my hand as I fingered for a hold. The first glimpse over the high walls revealed a chaotic tangle of defenders preparing to strike.

With one hand white-knuckling a grip on the wall, I reached back and grabbed my shield with the other. I slung it around and held it before me. My life depended on the quality of its construction.

Swords and spears jabbed at me. The force against the shield nearly forced me from the ladder and to a certain death, but I held on.

I couldn't brandish my sword, though. A third hand would have been useful. I waited for an advantage, the perfect time to leap over the ledge, but if I held on too long I would lose my grip.

Now or never, victory or death.

I threw myself over the crenulated battlements and onto three of the nearest attackers. The legions below cheered for me. If I died, at least that praise would echo in my ears for eternity.

Three more ladders crashed against the walls. The distracted enemies struggled to topple the ladders, not aware that they were on dollies and wouldn't budge.

Thank you, Diana.

I took advantage of their lapse in judgment and found my footing. Before I brandished my sword, another Roman joined me on the walls. Then a third legionary followed him. I wasn't alone.

Stabbing into the melee, I struck someone. I couldn't see or make sense of much, but the screams indicated the blow was lethal. If I died, at least I'd take a rebel with me.

I stole a glance over the top of my shield. The rebels appeared emaciated and weak. Their skin was ashen, stretching taut over brittle bones. But their eyes contained the rage of Mars. They would fight until their last breath.

Steel flashed as more Romans took the wall and

the battle began in earnest. The metallic ring of blade striking blade, followed by the low hiss of puncturing flesh.

"Form up! Find your footing!" I ordered.

I foolishly hoped Sulla could see me from his vantage point. His pride meant as much to me as our victory.

My blade connected with enemy armor, sending a wave of vibration up my arm. No time to recoil, I struck again and found my mark in the exposed flesh between the helmet and chain mail of the rebel. Modeling their armor after ours was useful to them but allowed us to exploit the weaknesses we were all too familiar with.

The speed of Sulla's Fist was remarkable. Already we nearly matched the rebels, man for man, on the battlements.

Our odds of victory improved with each passing moment. I might even survive. If I did, the men might elect me for a military decoration. Sulla would be proud, and so would my father.

A blow to my left shoulder distracted me from my vain imagination. The pain seared, but the wound wasn't deep, my chain mail taking the worst of it. A hot iron or some stitching would fix me up if I lived, but the grip on my shield weakened.

I didn't know who struck me, but it didn't matter. I focused my attention on the nearest rebel and stabbed him above the knee.

Slick, wet blood dripped over the hilt of my sword, making it as difficult to grasp as my shield.

The struggle for space and footing resulted in chaotic pushing and shoving from the tightly packed bodies of both armies. My feet threatened to slip on the blood-slick stone, forcing me to adjust or risk falling.

And falling meant death. The precarious drop on either side of the wall was a constant threat to both armies of combatants.

"Remember your training! Discipline and courage, men!" I shouted.

Earthy smells of stone and mortar, freshly chipped by weapons and projectiles, covered the struggle on the wall. This and the subtle scent of nearby olive groves faded beneath the stench of human waste and decaying flesh.

The coppery mist of blood in the air overcame all the senses, though. The gritty taste of the battle itself.

I'd fought in many battles, but never one so concentrated, so isolated to one location. If we won on the walls, the city was ours. If they fought us back, we'd be forced to withdraw and break the siege. They could replenish their supplies and their forces, and the war would continue.

Everything hinged on the walls.

The rhythmic drumming of soldier's boots against the limestone sounded as more Romans took the walls. We outnumbered them now.

From the corner of my eye, I saw the glint of a sword careening toward my face. I dodged back but the blade caught my cheek.

Unlike the stab to my shoulder, the wound numbed instantly, and I felt nothing but the warmth of blood rushing down my face.

The rebel attacked again like a rabid dog. I brought my shield up in time to deflect his sword this time. Despite my weakened grip, the rebel's blade twirled through the air and clattered into Nola.

Disarmed, he reached out and clutched for my throat. Before he could reach me, I severed three of his fingers. A small injury compared to the limbless and disemboweled men around us, but he would be no more threat to Romans today.

In a pain-fueled delirium, he stumbled back into the ranks of his allies and off the wall to his death.

The rebels should have retreated then. Perhaps there was a citadel or capitol where they could make a final stand. But they didn't budge. No horns sounded a withdrawal. Their last struggle for freedom would take place here.

The city would be easier to take afterward, but there would be no opportunity to reform and plan the next wave of our assault. There would be only one.

Battle cries swelled around me; a chorus as fervent as the hymns sung in Minerva's temple. Many wounded fighters cried out for mercy, brief and doomed, before they were swallowed up by the clamor of conquest. But the thud of my own heart pounding in my ears was louder than anything, a drumbeat calling me to glory or to the River Styx.

The most pleasant sound, however, was the rattle of chains. A few legionaries found a way to open the gates. Sulla and Crassus's cavalry could soon enter in triumph.

Desperation and terror shone in the eyes of the next rebel to assault me. If hatred and fear could win a fight, if a desire to live at all costs was enough to win a battle, he would have defeated us single-handedly.

But that wasn't enough. Malnourishment and

puncture wounds weakened him, and his thrust was too slow. I batted his spear away like an errant fly and thrust my blade into his throat. He wouldn't suffer long enough to scream.

The rebels lost their footing. Scores of them fell back into their city and to swift deaths as Sulla's Fist closed in around them. The charging cavalry swiftly consumed any who survived the fall.

I stole a glance over the city. Nola stretched back as far as I could see, a sprawling metropolis built on commerce and luxury. For four hundred years, Nola had been the jewel of the Campanian coast, competing only with Capua in grandeur, and none as a military stronghold.

But on that Quintilis day, Nola would fall.

Bodies smacked against stone with sickening thuds as the last of the rebels fell. Sulla's Fist alone remained on the walls. Victorious.

All that remained was Sulla's revenge.

 The once bustling city streets were like a theatre stripped of its actors and audience, desolate and forlorn. All the living citizens hunkered in their homes, temples, sewers, or anywhere else they deemed safe. But nothing could protect them from our wrath. They betrayed Rome and took up arms against us. We would punish them thoroughly enough that no one else would be tempted to do the same again.

We were eager to reach the city center to discover what remained of the enemy resistance, but Sulla was cautious. Refusing to be ambushed, he ordered us into proper ranks.

Several legionnaires clapped me on the back and praised my actions on the walls. I beamed with pride. I made the mistake of reaching up to inspect the wound to my cheek, only to find a loose flap of skin hanging down over the bone. The injury wouldn't heal handsomely. But my father lost his eye in battle, it was only right for me to earn a scar to match his bravery. The sagging flesh made my head spin, but I was as honored by the wound as the legionaries' words.

"Let's end this," Sulla said from his tall horse.

He led the way toward Nola's heart as Crassus's cavalry and our ranks thinned out and adapted to fit through the narrow city streets.

Ghosts seemed to haunt the desolated buildings. Each home, insula, and temple bore the scars of siege. The columns and facades were covered in soot. Animal waste littered the streets, but I saw no animals. During a siege, any creature with a heartbeat was subject to consumption when supplies ran empty. Livestock, sacrificial birds, house pets, and guard dogs. What had Nola's occupants resorted to when all these were eliminated?

The ground beneath my feet, trampled and filthy, provided an unsteady foundation, like the shifting sands of the arena. Fortunately, we marched slowly. Centurions kept their eyes on the rooftops, preparing for rebels to appear at any moment.

My chain mail burned against any flesh not covered by my tribune's tunic, but despite the heat the hilt of my sword was still cool to the touch. I wondered if I would use it again that day or if the battle was over. Either fate suited me.

Up ahead, Sulla exited from the shade of the tall buildings flanking the street. We'd reached Nola's Forum.

The acrid taste of smoke invaded the air, and the faint taste of ash filtered through my teeth. Why? We hadn't set any fires yet.

Arriving in the vast city center, the source burned in my eyes.

The flames licked the sky as if trying to devour the gods themselves. It only grew as the cornered rebels hurled anything flammable they could find onto the blazing inferno. Chairs, tables, lecterns, and temple pews stoked the flames.

Mutilus, consul of the Italic League and leader of the rebel cause, stood before the flames. A few hundred of his surviving warriors remained on either side of him.

The Numidians who had betrayed us mixed with their ranks. I'd expected to meet them in a cavalry charge, but not a horse was in sight. Apparently, the finest battle steeds in the world didn't escape the city's famine.

Sulla raised his fist. We came to a halt a few hundred paces away from the rebel survivors.

Mutilus turned to his men. "Higher," he said before stepping toward us.

We watched. They were cornered. They could not escape. Sulla savored the moment of his triumph.

"Rome is victorious again," Mutilus shouted. "I've imagined this moment daily since I took up arms against you."

Sulla didn't move. "If you predicted your defeat, why go to all this trouble?" he said.

Mutilus straightened. His hair was mangled and his flesh dirty, but the nobility in his gait and the resolve in his eyes proved how he convinced thousands upon thousands to betray the strongest power in the world.

His eyes narrowed. "To watch the Republic squirm. If only for a short time." He turned back to his men. "Higher!"

Sulla's laughter was the only sound to match the roaring flames. "Any regrets?" he asked.

"Not killing more Romans."

Sulla leaped from his horse with effortless grace. "Your defeat is sweeter to me than the finest wine, your failure more pleasing than a virgin nymph. Truly, Mutilus, I will enjoy this."

The rebel commander considered the flames and seemed to find it adequate.

"One day," Mutilus said, "the Roman Forum will look like this. Your people will suffer the same inequities you've perpetuated on the entire Mediterranean. On that day, I will rejoice from Hades."

"I hope you're patient, dear Mutilus. You may be waiting a long time." Sulla raised his fist again. "Prepare to advance."

Mutilus's eyes revealed no fear as he stepped back. "These flames will burn just as hot when they devour you."

Before Sulla could respond, Mutilus stretched his arms out like wings and dropped backward into the fire.

The flames engulfed him, but no screams rose from the makeshift pyre.

Legionaries gasped, but the rebels didn't respond. They'd seen worse than this during the siege.

"I actually respect that," one legionary said behind me.

"I respect it, but I'm unlikely to imitate it," said another.

Sulla stood silently until the last of Mutilus was consumed by the fiery debris around him. I wondered what went through his mind.

"Advance," he ordered.

The remaining rebels brandished their swords and prepared to meet their fate.

"Wait! Wait! Wait!" A young Numidian ran out from the rebel ranks with his arms stretched out.

I'd never seen him among our former cavalry. Thin, young, and smooth faced, this boy had never seen battle. This was Juba, prince of the Numidians.

"We surrender," he said. "Please. We surrender." Juba addressed his subjects. "Lay down your arms."

"I say we fight them to last man!" one of his warriors shouted.

The prince knelt first. One knee, and then the second. He unsheathed the sword on his hip and placed it on the ash-covered stone before him. He stretched out and lay prostrate before Sulla's Fist.

Reluctantly, the Numidians soon joined him, followed by the remaining Italian rebels.

Sulla cast his gaze across the cavalry who served him in so many battles. "I thought I taught you better than this," he said. "Break formation."

The commander's first order was to confiscate their weapons. The legionaries stacked the *khopesh*, swords, and spears by my feet before separating the Numidians and the Italians.

Once disarmed and packed in among their own, Sulla ordered the first cohort to eradicate the Italians.

It's no simple task to slaughter a few hundred men, even those starving, disarmed, and supplicating.

The occasional collapse of timber and debris punctuated their screams. I felt little as I watched their fate. They chose this path. They betrayed Rome and butchered our people. Reestablishing order required consequences. I simply wanted this to be over.

When the first cohort finished their grim task, they returned to formation painted with rebel blood from helmet to boot.

Satisfied, Sulla turned to the Numidians. Their suffering would not end so quickly. The commander planned something special for them.

"On your feet, princeling," Sulla said.

Juba pulled himself up but refused to meet Sulla's gaze. The royal son awaited his fate as obediently as an old *servus*. He bore none of Sulla's courage, or he would have fought back. The Numidians were foolish for following him.

Sulla threw his muscular arm around Juba's slender shoulders and turned him to face his defeated followers.

"What shall become of them, prince?" he said. "How should Sulla repay treachery?"

"Please . . ." Juba's lips quavered. "Show them mercy. Take my life if you must but spare these warriors and they will serve you faithfully for the rest of their days."

I pitied him. I hadn't expected that.

Sulla clicked his tongue. "That wouldn't do, your highness," he said. "Mercy, you see, is not given freely. It is earned." He gestured back to me. "Return their weapons."

The legionaries looked at him like he was mad.

"Do as the commander orders," I said.

The Numidians hesitated to reclaim their weapons. Was this a trick?

Sulla pulled Juba closer to him. "I came to value your subjects in the many years they served me. I even came to love them. But they showed great weakness, in mind and forethought, when they betrayed me." Rage lingered on the edge of his words. "The weak do not deserve mercy. The weak exist only to be eliminated." He almost snarled now. "But I could still make use of the strong."

Fear radiated from the Numidians as sure as heat from the still-blazing fire. But frightened men are dangerous. I steadied my sword and moved to Sulla's side.

"Are they strong, princeling?" Sulla asked.

Juba swallowed and tried to steady his trembling hands. "They are strong. Fierce in battle. And loyal to a fault. Their loyalty was misplaced, but they will not make the same mistake again."

His Latin was more polished than any Numidian I'd met. I wondered if he'd ever set foot in his own country, or if he'd spent his entire life as a royal hostage in Italy.

"I cannot trust your word, dear prince. You've also proven to be disloyal as of late," Sulla said. "I require proof."

The Numidian captives glimpsed hope for the first time. Could Rome truly pardon them?

Sulla offered leniency when none expected it, and retribution when it seemed unnecessary. His capriciousness sowed terror into the hearts of any at his mercy. None could know which way a flight of fancy would carry him.

But I knew his acts were not random. Each decision was calculated. And I also knew the Numidians would not escape punishment. They likely understood this as well, but one can only hope when death stares them in the face.

"How many of these warriors remain?" Sulla asked.

A single tear streaked down Juba's face. "Two hundred and eleven."

"You were once as sons to me," Sulla said. "And my sons fight by my side and conquer in my name. They obliterate my foes." He stepped away from the prince. "Look to the man on your left and right. He betrayed me."

What little hope blossomed in their eyes withered just as swiftly. Now they understood.

"Two hundred and eleven of you remain. Only forty will leave Nola alive. Forty of you will be given safe passage to your homeland. Forty of you will receive my blessing, my protection, and my forgiveness. Decide."

All of Nola was frozen and silent until the first blow was struck. When the first body fell, utter chaos ensued.

Sulla turned away from the violence, not out of remorse, but to watch young Juba's reaction.

My eyes marveled at the spectacle, the horror. I'll speak no more of it.

"Please, lord, I beg you . . ." Juba wept.

Sulla ignored him. "See, your highness? These

men fought beside one another for years. Not so loyal, are they?"

The Numidians slew one another much quicker than we'd dispatched the other captives. By the time Sulla ordered a halt, only thirty-three remained. They'd been overzealous in their desire to live.

"Look again to your left and right. The man standing there, who called himself your brother, would have taken your life without second thought if it meant keeping his own. Remember this: loyalty to anything but me is meaningless. Never forget who spared your lives."

The survivors were too distraught to properly thank their savior. But Sulla had made his point and asked nothing else of them.

"Those of you who remain, you may seek water and bread in our camp. Then you will take the king and return to Numidia."

They stared back at him blankly.

The commander smiled. "Did I forget to mention? Your father is dead. Your older brother, too, is now ash and bone. You are the rightful king of Numidia."

Juba's eyes fluttered and a low moan escaped him. The news wounded the captives more than the swords of their brothers. But Sulla's glee wasn't diminished.

He pinched Juba's chin and forced the prince to meet his gaze. "Let me assure you, King Juba," he said, "if your father and brother had not died, you would join Mutilus in the fire." The flames raged in Sulla's eyes. "But I have use for a king."

Sulla refused to release him until Juba nodded his acknowledgment.

"Go," he said. "All of you. Get out of my city."

The wounded Numidians, the finest cavalry in the Mediterranean, sulked away from us and the fire raging in Nola's heart.

The commander turned back to us with a smile on his face and no more flames in his eyes.

"We have done it," he said.

For the first time since we entered the Forum, the men erupted in applause.

"Rome is victorious. You, Sulla's Fist, are the mightiest conquerors in the world."

After long months of hard fighting, sacrifices, and slaughter, we had won the war. I bellowed until my voice was hoarse and Sulla ordered us to listen.

"Like the Numidians, we are leaving this place." He raised his eyes to the heavens and basked in this moment. "For I received news this morning. Lucius Cornelius Sulla has been elected consul of Rome."

We cried out as if each of us had been voted to rule the Republic.

Somehow, Sulla's commanding voice rose above the praise. "Mithridates's gold awaits us!"

The prospects of returning to another war so soon after finishing this one discouraged none of us. Unfathomable wealth and glory awaited, whatever sacrifices remained would be worth the reward.

"But before we go, let's enjoy the spoils of our victory, shall we?" Sulla said. "Burn every building, bind every captive, and take whatever you want!"

A blur of legionaries burst in every direction as Sulla delighted in the spectacle.

Unwilling to miss out on the excitement, I

hurried to the pyre and engulfed the broken leg of a chair in flame.

Then I set off toward the nearest building to do Sulla's bidding.

SCROLL XXV

Quintus Sertorius—Three Days before the Nones of Quintilis, 665 Ab Urbe Condita

With the fall of Nola, the rebel cause would collapse. The war would end soon, and we would exterminate our former allies. Cities would be leveled. Captives would be bound and crucified en masse. Entire tribes erased from the annals of history in the blink of an eye.

I knew this to be true but resented that fact.

As tribune, I would have assimilated the defeated back into the Republic. I could have protected them from Rome's wrath. But I lost. Without accepting Sulpicius's insidious offer, I couldn't save the supplicating rebels. Even if I prostituted my name to Sulpicius and his conspirators, I knew they wouldn't fulfill their end of the bargain.

I could do nothing else for the rebels, so I would return to my farm. I could salvage what remained of my fields and finally give my family peace. Perhaps I could write Apollonius and encourage him to return. We could read Zeno and Aristotle in the evening. I could take Pollux and go hunting, just me and my dog, with no fear of rebel scouts lurking in the shadows. I wouldn't miss Toria's first steps or her first words. She would know the scruff of her father's beard on her cheek and the strength of his arms.

A few more hours and I would return to my wife, pack our things, and leave. Barca would return to his *ludus*, and our lives would return to how they'd been. Perhaps we'd join each other for dinner a few times each month, avoiding any mention of the trials we endured together.

But there was one last thing I needed to do before we departed. Three days before the Nones of Quintilis, the senate convened to usher in the new magistrates. Most of the also-rans refused to attend after a loss, but I wasn't one of them. I would congratulate the victors and retire with grace.

I arrived early and took my seat before any others. This would be my last meeting with the senate for some time, gods only knew how long. I drank in the moment.

The early morning sunlight poured in through the high, open rafters and cast a celestial glow on the raised podium where the new consuls would soon take their place. There stood the statue of Lady Justice. Blindfolded, she held aloft a scale. On one side, she balanced all the actions of the Senate and People of Rome, and the other, the consequences. She clutched a sword in her other hand, symbolizing that justice would be swift and final.

Other senators trickled in. Some laughed among their peers, already celebrating their own victory or that of their allied candidates. Others hung their heads and sulked to the benches in disappointment.

A voice echoed throughout the mostly empty chambers. "Sertorius, it is good to see you after so long."

It was Cinna, the father of my old friend Equus.

"Dear Cinna," I stood and made my way to the senate floor, where I embraced him. "How many years has it been?"

He was much the same as the last time I'd seen him. Ruddy, thinning hair. A curly beard that gave evidence to his connection to our ancestors. Wrinkles crawled out from his eyelids and smile lines etched his cheeks. He'd always looked older than he was, but now age suited him.

"Ten years or more, I have to imagine." He placed his hands on my shoulders and studied me with a smile. "I thank the gods for protecting you."

"How is Equus?" I asked. "I've missed his wit and charm these long years."

"The same as ever, I'm afraid," he laughed. "Cynical, too smart for his own good, and his wit still as sharp as a dagger. He should return to Italy within the next few months."

Equus arrived in Greece shortly after I left and had served there ever since.

"I look forward to our reunion." I nodded and prepared to return to my seat, but he squeezed my arm.

"Condolences for your loss," he said.

I stared back, perplexed.

"The election, I mean." Cinna shook his head. "It's a shame. You would have made a fine tribune."

"No condolences necessary," I said. "I placed my fate in the gods' hands. Now they beckon me back to my farm."

He seemed not to hear me. "It seems we may have hitched our wagon to the wrong horse," he said.

I knew he meant Marius, the only political connection we ever shared. The smile fell from my face.

"I am not a wagon, Cinna," I said. "I am the horse. I will return and run again one day if Rome needs me."

He nodded. "I'm pleased to hear it," he said. "Just don't leave me alone in this place with the likes of our new consuls for too long."

I returned to my seat. I didn't recall him being so forward, but remarks like that on the senate floor in today's climate were dangerous.

The seats continued to fill, and now the chamber was humming with the chatter of gossip and political discourse.

There was tension in those hushed murmurs. What would Sulla do as his first act as consul? His unpredictability was equal parts admired and feared. What would Sulpicius do with the power of tribune now in his grasp? Would he disband his anti-senate now that he'd won the election, or would he wield them as a weapon, like he'd threatened?

And what would Marius strive for with his pet tribune doing his bidding? The senate may not have known of their alliance, but I did. That concerned me as much as anything else we expected that day.

Sulla's friend and proud co-consul Rufus soon arrived. The senate house erupted with applause at his entry; this for a man they likely considered irrelevant before Sulla put him up for election. The power Sulla had over the senate was palpable.

Pompeius Strabo entered next, a broad smile on his face as he waved to the clapping senators, despite this being his last day as consul. He seemed content with his lot of glory, respect, and plunder.

Of course, where Strabo went, there, too, was Metellus Pius, Rome's newly elected praetor. With the arrogant swagger of a politician in his natural habitat, he joined his kinsmen and other aristocrats on the opposite side of the senate house from me.

Marius arrived next, much later than was his custom. He was usually the first man at the senate house, as he was the first soldier awake in camp. I wondered if something had stalled him, or if he was he slipping in his old age.

My side of the senate house erupted in applause as if Marius was arriving from a great victory instead of exercising on the Field of Mars. Metellus Pius and the other nobles crossed their arms, shook their heads, or leaned back. I recalled similar displays among school children when I was growing up.

The new tribunes arrived together—all ten of them—marching in order. Many senators jeered. And they obviously meant their insults for one man.

Sulpicius led the way, grinning and bowing lowly as if receiving praise.

If I'd been elected, I would have entered with them. I wouldn't have been afraid of Sulpicius or his schemes, I could have resisted him. From the timid looks on the faces of the tribunes behind him, I doubted these other men could. I tried to remind myself the gods had chosen another path for me.

They took their seats on the long bench near the front of the senate house, just beneath the consuls' platform. Sulpicius reclined and kicked his legs out lackadaisically.

Conveniently, Gaius Marius was the man right behind him.

The newly appointed Father of the Senate took the center of the Curia and raised his arms. "Conscript Fathers! What a glorious day for Rome this is," Catulus said. "With these elections, the gods have guaranteed another strong year, one of protection and glory for Rome."

Both sides of the senate house stomped their feet in approval, and so did I.

"Today, we formally pass the power from last year's magistrates to this. May we begin by welcoming our new consul!"

Rufus stood from his curule chair and bowed as the senate chamber praised him.

"My colleague is on his way. No messenger has arrived to announce his coming, but if he travels as quickly as he marches to battle, he shall soon arrive. He is eager to greet you."

The senate house cheered even louder.

Many began to chant his name. "Sulla! Sulla! Sulla!"

Once Catulus quieted the chamber, the official transfer of power took place. Strabo handed over his badges of office, and a priest of Jupiter said a prayer.

Next, Catulus presided over the appointment of the new praetors. They drew lots to decide what roles each of the four would be responsible for during their term of office. Metellus Pius appeared thrilled, but unsurprised, by his lot. Perhaps

Sulla, his brother-in-law, was already pulling strings to benefit those he favored.

Rays of sunlight shifted over the senate house with the passage of time. Aediles next, then quaestors, and finally Catulus came to the tribunes.

The ten tribunes stood up from around the chamber and came to the senate floor where they exchanged their badges of office. A priest declared the new tribunes to be sacrosanct, meaning they could not be touched, harmed, or hindered in any way while their appointment remained.

Sacrosanctitas hadn't saved tribunes from being murdered in the past. But Sulpicius's face, basking in the moment, revealed he was unafraid of such a fate.

Catulus continued until Sulpicius stepped away from the rest of the tribunes and demanded the floor.

He had no right to do so, not at this time, but he refused to relent as the senate cursed him and shouted for him to sit down.

"I demand the floor! I demand the floor!" he continued to bellow.

The display continued for several minutes. He refused to relent. And with the power of sacrosanctity, no one could force him to sit. Many of us would have liked to.

Catulus threw his arms up in exasperation. "I concede the floor."

Sulpicius smiled and clapped his shoulder, the manner condescending to one so prestigious as the Father of the Senate.

"Good senators! How long have I waited for this day?" Sulpicius said.

"Since Marius put you up to it!" an *optimate* shouted.

Apparently, some were just as privy to their schemes as I was.

There were no attempts to deny the hecklers.

Sulpicius shouted, "Rome has waited on bated breath, *pregnant* with anticipation for this moment." He took a deep breath, drinking in the air like honeyed wine. "So much that has been wrong will be made right."

"To the brothels and gambling dens with you, leech!" someone shouted, and others stomped their feet.

Sulpicius whipped in the direction of the voice, still wearing his charming smile. "Unfortunately for you senators and for the brothel whores, I am here to stay for the next year. The dice games will have to wait."

"What is it you wish to share, tribune?" Catulus said. "Say your piece and sit down."

"Unlike many of you, who lie, deceive, and flatter your way to an election, I intend to follow through on my promises. I told the people I would see them represented in the war to come with Mithridates, and I shall. Next market day, I will call a *comitium* of the people, where we will vote on who will lead our *glorious* legions into battle."

"Sulla!"

"Sulla!" many shouted.

Sulpicius wagged a finger with them. "It is not for you or me to say, dear brothers, but the people. They will decide who will lead the war in their best interests!"

Catulus waited until his strained voice could be heard. "Rome has already decided. This august body declared that one of our two consuls would lead our armies against the Pontic king. We declared it!"

Sulpicius laughed and shook his head. "Your age has afflicted you, dear Catulus," he said. "Perhaps frailty and age has done the same to *all* of you. For you've forgotten your place! This august body *declares* nothing. We advise. We recommend. The senate does not speak its will into the law. The *people* do. And have long since been worthy advisors! It is time the will of the people is heard!"

Metellus was on his feet, a finger aimed at Sulpicius the way he'd so often pointed at me. "The people already voted! This was their decision. Insult this gathering no longer because you dislike the outcome!"

For the first time, Sulpicius's smile faded. He glared in Metellus's direction. "They voted once, yes, *misguided* though they were. They realize now how you have all *lied* to them, and they wish to set things right."

Marius stood to his feet. "I put my name forward." His booming voice barely rose above the hecklers.

"Honorable Marius, even in his old age, is willing to save Rome once more!" Sulpicius shouted above them.

If they still intended to conceal their alliance, Marius and Sulpicius failed miserably. This performance was as poorly acted as an amateur production in the Forum. So carefully orchestrated, so dreadfully executed.

I lowered my head and rubbed my weary eyes. What had become of Rome? The Eternal City, the light of liberty, the jewel of the Mediterranean?

"One more thing," Sulpicius raised his voice and repeated himself a few times as senators threatened to storm the floor. "We will first be enrolling all Rome's new citizens. They shall have their voices heard as well."

With so many thousands of new voters owing them patronage, there was no telling what kind of power they would wield. This would guarantee Marius's command of the war. Anything Sulpicius brought forth during his term of office would easily pass into law.

The senators couldn't tolerate this. The Three Furies were about to be unleashed on Rome. They clambered over one another and stormed the floor, hurling insults instead of fists. Fingers pointed at Sulpicius's face, where they'd like to strike him. But they couldn't.

He smiled, basking in their anger and his divine protection.

Rufus watched, helpless and perplexed.

"Order, I call this chamber to order!" Catulus shouted.

But no one heeded his feeble, old voice.

"Demagogue!" they shouted.

Sulpicius let his head back and laughed. "A demagogue would use his anti-senate more directly. Instead, I let the sovereign people of Rome decide. If that makes me a demagogue, so be it."

A hush fell over the senate house. Everyone's eyes turned to the doorway. I strained my eye to see what it was.

I prepared for Sulpicius's cloaked thugs to rush in, but only one man stood at the door.

Senators returned to their seats.

Sulla strode through the door and headed directly to Sulpicius, the sweat of hard riding still damp on his brow.

"Our consul has arrived!" Sulpicius clapped. He continued to grin, but it was clear to see his confidence waning.

No one else moved.

I didn't know what Sulla would do, but I prepared for the worst. This reminded me of the tumultuous election ten years prior when blood filled Rome's streets. With Sulpicius's anti-senate waiting in the Forum, the possible devastation was unimaginable.

When Sulla spoke, his voice carried the weight of sadness. "I am grieved," he said. "That I should fight alongside our legionaries through so much toil to find Rome in this state. If only I had been here, this sad day should never have come to pass."

"The people have spoken," Marius shouted. "You have no right to stand in the way."

Sulla did not remove his gaze from Sulpicius. "The people have been deceived. They are lambs being led to the slaughter with the promise of a meal." Sulla continued. "But I will not allow this to happen! No, I will protect my people, even against their own wishes."

"Tyrant!" a few of the senators shouted, but Sulla paid them no mind.

A resounding thud echoed throughout the Curia. Once, twice, then a third time.

"Do you hear that?" Sulla asked. "That is a *justitium* being nailed to the doors of this august building. A state of emergency. I am suspending all civil and political business effective immediately—" A great clamor rose from both sides of the senate house, some cheering, some cursing, but Sulla continued. "The courts, the treasury, everything—suspended until order is restored."

For the first time, Sulpicius could find no words, no reason to smile smugly. He turned to Marius for guidance. The old general's veins were bulging in his forehead and neck. Neither seemed to expect this, nor did they appear to have answers.

I moved to the edge of my seat. When men like that lose all other recourse, they resort to violence.

"I will veto the motion!" Sulpicius said in a moment of realization. "I use my tribune's veto on the motion!"

All fell silent. Only Sulla laughed.

"I am not proposing a law. This is a decree and not subject to your veto. Return to your seat."

Sulpicius looked around and scanned the faces of his supporters, unsure if this was true.

"Sit down!" Sulla roared.

Sulpicius recoiled and returned to his seat, if only to strategize with his ally.

"I have restored order throughout Italy, and I will restore it here in Rome," Sulla said. "Now, good Catulus, I believe you have a few other matters to attend to."

Marius stood and stormed from the senate house.

Laughter and heckles followed him.

Only a few moments passed before Sulpicius departed as well.

"Run! Run!"

"Whipped dog!"

"Coward!"

Catulus raised his hand to calm the chamber, but the *optimates* were too busy basking in their moment of triumph.

Other senators made their way to the exit. My side of the Curia was thinning considerably.

Sulla thwarted so many plans with just a few words, and for once, I was glad of it.

We could accomplish nothing else after the confrontation. Catulus dismissed us before the hour passed.

I exited out into the Forum, where pockets of gathered citizens argued about what had just happened. Men and women of every tribe, race, and creed were present. The only thing they shared in common was a reliance on Rome for their lives and their freedom. I felt sorry for them. All that they loved and held dear held in the balance, protected only by the thin cord holding the Republic together. They could do nothing to save it, they were powerless to heal the growing rift. They could only wait and argue among one another.

"Quintus Sertorius, I'm surprised to still find you here," Sulla said, joining me on the steps of the senate house, his retinue close behind.

I turned and extended my hand to him. "Congratulations on your consulship, Sulla," I said. "I hope you use your authority wisely. These are tumultuous times."

Rufus and Rufus Minor joined us.

"Your defeat disappointed me," Rufus said. "I'm sorry the elections didn't go as you hoped."

"Thank you," I said. "Congratulations to you as well." I shook his hand and turned back to Sulla.

"I'm sure you're disappointed by the results of today's meeting," Rufus Minor said.

"We've heard you stand for the cause of the people," his father clarified.

"I have no political affiliations," I said. "Especially not to those who would sow chaos into the Republic, no matter the veil they use to disguise it. I'm relieved to see Sulpicius repudiated, though I suspect this turmoil is far from over."

Sulla smiled. "Sertorius is too virtuous to muck about with the likes of these, dear Rufus. He's too scrupulous for all of us, unfortunately. But I keep trying to sway him." He winked.

"I respect you, Quintus Sertorius," Rufus Minor said. "There aren't enough Romans like you left."

I turned to Sulla. "Is my son with you? I shall be returning to my farm soon and wish to say goodbye."

Sulla seemed pleased by the news of my retirement. "He is not. I trust none but him to manage the legion in my absence. But I will pass along your message."

"Gratitude," I said. I turned to leave but then stopped. "I spoke with several of the *collegium* heads, and many of them said my election was nearly guaranteed."

Sulla nodded. "Aye. A hero of the Republic like you? I would have said the same," he said. "Someone powerful and influential must have opposed you."

"If you'll forgive me, I must ask . . . was it you?"

Rufus looked appalled.

Sulla placed a hand on his chest and gasped, but soon abandoned the act. "You're a shrewd one, Quintus Sertorius," he said.

I took a deep breath. I was confused but unsurprised. "Your efforts would have been better spent fighting him." I pointed across the Forum to where Sulpicius conspired with his supporters.

Sulla shrugged. "Some matters must be brought to a head before they can be rectified. His appointment was necessary for me to remove the blight. Permanently," he said. "But I hope to keep you from doing anything foolish until you finally decide to be my friend." He smiled, clapped my shoulder, and leaned closer to whisper. "I may have opposed you, but your old friend Marius didn't stop me, and he could have. You should keep that in mind."

SCROLL XXV | 275

The admission dismayed Rufus. "I did not partake in this," he said. "Can you tell him that?"

Sulla nodded. "Good Rufus took no part in my opposing you. It was purely political, but entirely personal, if you take my meaning."

"I don't, but it will suffice."

I followed their gaze to the rostra. Sulpicius climbed the steps and stood at the center of the platform.

"Perhaps we should leave," Rufus Minor said. "I don't like the look of that crowd."

Sulpicius's anti-senators gathered beneath the rostra and listened to their leader. Marius wasn't in sight.

"These reprobates will not intimidate me," Sulla said.

"Perhaps you should listen to the wise counsel," I said. "He must feel cornered and without recourse. Such a man may attack his enemies in such circumstances."

Sulla smiled. "You should know. I am not an enemy to be taken lightly."

"I will take my leave then," I said.

Before I could take the first step, the anti-senate turned and charged in our direction.

"Stop! Stop! The rule of *law* must be heard!" Sulpicius shouted after them.

He remained a poor actor.

"Father, we must go," Rufus Minor said.

Out of bravery, stupidity, or the grip of fear, the surrounding senators stood in place. I did the same. I'd seen bloodshed in Rome before and would fight back against it no matter what.

But the anti-senate charged on.

"Father!" Rufus Minor shouted again.

When neither his father nor Sulla moved, the young man ran. Not away from the charging horde, but toward it.

"Stop!" Rufus Minor shouted as loud as his lungs would allow. "I order you to stop in the name of Rome."

The mob was undeterred.

"This august body is protected by Jupiter Capitolinus and—"

A dagger sliced through his throat.

He spun around and fell to his knees, clutching the wound with a wild look in his eyes.

They trampled Rufus Minor before the light died out of his eyes.

A guttural moan escaped Rufus as he watched his only son fall. He lunged toward them. Only Sulla's grip saved Rufus from meeting his son's fate.

Daggers and swords appeared in the clutches of the angry mob. They left the clubs and sticks at home. Their purpose was no longer to intimidate but to kill.

Rage gripped my chest as the charging crowd consumed the twitching body of Rufus Minor.

I ran to meet them.

The first man lunged at me; his dagger aimed for my ribcage. I sidestepped the attack and wrapped my arm around his. With an upward motion, I snapped his elbow, the bone nearly puncturing the skin.

He shrieked as the dagger fell from his grasp.

I might have picked it up if I was able, but already two or three others set against me.

"Protect the senate house!" I shouted to rally the few brave enough to fight alongside me.

"For Rome! For the Republic!" The anti-senators shouted, the irony lost on them completely.

Another swiped viciously at my side, but I stepped back in time to avoid it. When he advanced, his feet came tangled up with the men beside him and he lost his balance.

I wrapped my arm around his neck and spun him to block the stab intended for my back. The man cried out as his friends recoiled. I kicked his body into their midst, then turned to find no one else was there with me.

Senators and citizens were fleeing in every direction, fighting one another to escape rather than fighting the attackers. Sulla and Rufus had disappeared.

I was alone.

Many of the anti-senators rushed into the senate house, looking for any cornered prey who remained.

I thought of Arrea and Toria. They needed me. I needed to get home immediately. Who knew where this chaos would stop?

I ran without looking back, although I was keenly aware of the stomping feet behind me.

They likely didn't even know who I was, but my resistance to them drew their enmity. They would not stop until I lost them, or they killed me.

I headed south toward the Temple of Castor and Pollux, hoping to escape my pursuers on the Via Sacra.

Sulpicius's anti-senators followed in pursuit and shouted, "Come back, you coward!"

I shuttled in and out of scurrying crowds, hurdled a fence behind the *Regia* and took an overgrown dirt path nearby.

Leaning against the back of an old column, I caught my breath. Perhaps I lost them.

"Come here!" I heard the same man shout as his footsteps drew near.

A dagger careened toward my stomach. I jumped to the side, the blade grazing off my hip.

I punched the attacker in the jaw with all my strength. Despite the blood and teeth dripping to the stone beneath us, he maintained his balance and poised himself to strike again.

Before he could, I kicked his knee and sent him to the ground.

His friends were close behind, so I set off.

My toga slowed me down, so I ripped it off and discarded it, leaving only my tunic to conceal me. A stone ledge was nearby, and I jumped and pulled myself to the top.

They were still close behind.

What to do now? I could not lead them to my home.

I continued running, in no particular direction now save the one that led me away from my pursuers. Turning a corner, before me I saw the tall, opulent villa Marius had purchased with his war plunder to overlook the city.

He was party to Sulpicius and this violent mob, but surely he would shelter me.

"He's that way!" an anti-senator shouted. They were close.

I had no time to consider it.

I hammered away at the door and shouted for aid. Before my fist could reach it the third time, the heavy iron entrance swung open, and I fell into Marius's home.

"Shut and bar the doors," Marius said.

A man with his back to me said, "Why? Surely, you're in no danger. They're your dogs after all." He sounded like Sulla, but that was impossible.

I picked myself up off the floor and strained my eye to see in the darkness of Marius's atrium.

There they were. Marius and Sulla. Standing across from each other.

Marius crossed his arms and leaned forward, his posture rigid and alert. His gaze was sharp, darting between Sulla and me, never lingering but always searching.

Sulla was out of breath. His perfectly coiffed blond locks hung down over his brow. The mud of Rome's streets stained his legs. I'd never seen him in such disarray.

"Careful, or I'll open those doors and throw you back out." Marius made a knife with his hand and pointed it at Sulla like an angry centurion.

"I'm surprised to find you here," I said to Sulla.

Slaves busily boarded the doors behind us.

"It seems both of us had the same idea. Taking shelter in the aggressor's home is either brilliant or idiotic," Sulla said. "Unless you two are still closer friends than I had realized?" His cold eyes narrowed.

"I was running for my life, same as you," I said. "Marius, those men killed the son of consul Rufus. They tried to kill me. I could not risk leading them to my home."

There was a twitch in Marius's eyes. He didn't appear to know of Rufus Minor's fate. Even if he endorsed the anti-senate's actions, he wouldn't have desired the young man's death. Perhaps he would have accepted the death of his father, or his father's consular colleague, but not the boy.

Marius did his best to veil any reaction. "So instead of leading the attackers to your home you bring them to mine?"

The doors behind us shook as the anti-senate thrashed against them. Was Marius's home less safe than I'd hoped?

"Cease the act, Marius," Sulla snarled. "You unleashed this chaos. This was your doing, and you alone in Rome know these reprobates pose you no threat."

Marius turned his back on us. "I do not command them. I do not command Sulpicius. I only want command of the war. I only want to lead Rome one last time and teach my son how to fight before I die."

The old general admitted far more than he realized with those words.

Sulla and I both knew it. All of Rome knew it. But Marius now admitted his complicity openly.

"So, what was the deal then, aye? What did you promise Sulpicius in exchange for shedding blood in Rome's streets?" Sulla said.

Marius whipped back around. "I promised him nothing. Everything the tribune does is of his own accord."

"Listen." I gestured back to the quaking doors. "There is nothing we can do to prevent your measures now and no reason you shouldn't tell us the truth."

Marius's gaze bounced between the two of us. "Six million sesterces."

Sulla buckled over and placed his hands on his knees. "*Cac*! To teach your useless son how to fight you would leave him bankrupt?" he shouted. "Of course, that's just a pitiful excuse regardless."

"I have more coin than you realize."

"So, you paid off his considerable debts and more . . . to buy yourself a command." I shook my head. "But the true cost was not to your coffers but to the Republic. Listen to the chaos outside your doors. You have caused this for your own vanity and boundless ambition."

"You are smarter than I thought," Sulla said.

"I should have known you two were in league together." Veins bulged in Marius's forehead and neck. His outbursts were increasingly erratic and unpredictable.

"You know that's not true, general," I said. "You know he resisted my bid for tribune. He still harbors hate for me for my ties to you, and yet you did nothing to help me. Because you know I wouldn't support this treachery."

Sulla composed himself. "The man has a point," he said.

Marius grunted, another tacit admission.

"What do we do now?" I said.

"I could make you walk out those doors, since you've both arrived with nothing but accusations and insults."

"You could, but you won't," Sulla said.

"Or I could have you both killed here and now."

Marius's slaves steadied themselves.

"You could, but you won't." Sulla seemed less sure this time.

I would've never believed Marius could do something like that, either, but there was something different in his eyes now. A wildness, something absent, foreign.

"Why wouldn't I?" Marius asked.

"You wouldn't kill me because I'm the only means to your desire."

Marius cocked a brow.

Sulla continued. "If you kill me, my *justitium* will remain in effect until long after the war with Mithridates begins. Rufus or whoever replaces me as consul will take the command, and you will gain nothing."

"Get to your point," Marius said.

Sulla took a deep breath. "See me safely from the city, and I will recall the decree. You and Sulpicius can go about your plans."

Marius's eyes sparkled with renewed hope. And then he turned his eyes to me.

Sulla looked my way also, as both wondered what I could offer in exchange for my life.

"Kill me if you must," I said. "I will die with a clean conscience. I served you loyally all those years and have never fought against you, even when men like Sulla have attempted to bribe or threaten me into betraying you." I looked between the two of them. "The two of you have sought to hinder or destroy my career at every turn because I refuse to be bought." I stepped within arm's length of Marius. "If all the blood we spilled together is not enough to stay your hand, then do what you must. I count six slaves awaiting your orders. You've seen me in battle. I'll accept my odds against them. You decide, *general.*"

Marius's gaze softened before he laughed. "Sulla, if only we had a thousand men like this one, we could have conquered the entire Mediterranean," he said.

"That's why I've fought so hard to buy his loyalty," Sulla said sincerely.

Marius clapped me on the shoulder. "Of course, I will not harm you, my boy." He turned to Sulla. "Write a letter to rescind the *justitium.*"

"Bring me pen, parchment, and wax. I will steal it with my signet ring."

One of Marius's slaves hurried off at the command. I doubted Sulla's sincerity. He had the cunning of a fox, and I knew he was already calculating a way to reverse the tide. I'd never known him to admit defeat before, and I didn't expect him to now.

But there was no doubt in Marius's eyes. "Very good. I'm glad we could come to this arrangement peacefully."

"Not peacefully, sir," I said. "The consul's son is dead in the Forum. It will be days before we can tally up how many others have fallen."

Marius's good cheer was undiminished. "Now that I have my command, how about you join me in the war? You can be a tribune, legatus, whatever you desire. What say you? Like old times," he said.

I ground my teeth to keep from saying something I shouldn't. To promise such a position as the rightful consul of Rome wrote a letter against his will beside us was too much to bear.

Was Marius always this way? Had he changed, or had I been remarkably naive? Perhaps both.

"Sorry, general," I said. "I am returning to my farm. I have no desire to fight. I have no desire to sit in the senate house if this is the way we conduct our Republic."

Marius shrugged. "More fool you then," he said. "Your son serves in Sulla's legion, correct? I'll be leading him into battle, then. Don't worry, I'll keep an eye out for him."

From one man's pawn to another. If I could have done anything to stop it then and there, I would have. But I couldn't. Gavius would have to discover Rome's true nature the way I did. I could not spare him the disillusionment.

Marius turned to one of his *servi*. "Bring them cloaks. Escort them from the back door. See Sertorius to his home, and Sulla to the Caelian gates. Ensure no harm comes to either of them, or I'll feed your children to my eels. Understood?"

"Yes, *domine*," the *servus* replied.

With Marius distracted, Sulla turned to me. With a grin, he said, "Oh, how the cubs will roar when they hear how the old lion suffered."

Before I could ask for clarification, the *servus* returned with cloaks. I threw it over my shoulders and pulled the hood over my head.

Sulla sealed the letter with wax and handed it to Marius. "Give it to one of my lictors. The *justitium* is over. Let this be the end of the turmoil between us. Let no more sons die."

Marius grunted and snatched the letter from Sulla. "Many more sons will die," he said. "Let's just hope they aren't ours."

SCROLL XXVI

GAVIUS SERTORIUS—FOUR Days before the Ides of Quintilis, 665 Ab Urbe Condita

 Lucullus was giddy. "Ha! The gods love me today," he said after counting his die.

"The gods are making up for that ugly face and boring personality they gave you," I said.

There was little to do in camp since Sulla left us. We would have stayed in Nola and enjoyed the spoils of victory, but there was none of it left.

We bound every citizen in chains and took them away. We scorched every mud brick with flame and reduced every building to rubble. There was nothing else to enjoy in Nola, nowhere even to lay our heads.

So, to the camp we returned, and idled away our days with dice games like *Tessera*.

Lucullus laughed and swept the two denarii at the center of the table into his lap. "They must have something special in store for you then," he said.

Our tent opened and Crassus stepped inside.

"Come to give me some of your coin?" Lucullus said. "Dear Gavius is running out."

Crassus reclined on a cot beside us. "I think not. It's a game of probabilities one cannot control. There is no real profit to be made."

Lucullus jingled the coin in the folds of his tunic. "I disagree. If the gods are on your side, as they are on mine, the profit is inevitable."

Crassus stopped frowning, which was as close as he came to ever smiling. "Surely you don't think so little of our gods as to believe they oversee petty gambling?"

Lucullus looked confused. "Come, have some wine."

Crassus joined us. He didn't make for pleasant company, but I didn't mind his presence either. We'd fought in many battles together now. Shed and sacrificed much blood beside each other. That's a bond that overcomes personal affinities.

"His trick, Crassus, is to ply you with wine." I took another sip of my own. "And then he takes your coin when your not looking."

The horn sounded outside.

We looked among one another.

"I didn't call an assembly. Did you?" Lucullus said.

Crassus sat up. "That is no assembly."

I sighed. "Perhaps it's one last assault from the rebels. Let's get it over with."

I grabbed my sword and buckled it around my waist but didn't bother putting on my armor. The rebellion was broken. They could pose little threat to us now.

We made our way through the fort to the closed gate where the trumpet's blare continued sounding.

"Let's have a look," Lucullus followed me up the stairs.

We reached the precipice. "Legionary!" I plugged my ears and shouted at the trumpeter. "We've heard you. What is it?"

He pointed off toward the north, away from the coast and the destroyed city of Nola. The legionary had better eyesight than I did. There was nothing to see at first, but eventually a faint silhouette appeared on the horizon.

"It's but a single rider." Crassus crossed his arms. "Truly, this is no reason to cause such alarm."

"He's wounded, sir."

"You can't possibly know that." Lucullus squinted.

"Wait . . . he's right. I see blood," I said.

"I still see no reason to sound—" Crassus stopped mid-sentence.

The wounded man was coming into view. Riding bareback, he slouched to the side of his horse, barely holding on.

Blood or paint covered his face and toga. Mud stained the hem.

"That's a senator," Lucullus said to himself.

Despite the soot and the blood, I could see the golden hair of our general.

"No. It's the consul," I said.

We sprinted back down the stairs and out of the opening gate.

I reached Sulla just as he released the reins. He fell into my arms.

"Consul, what has happened?" I helped him to

the ground. "Get the *medici!*" I ordered anyone listening.

His voice was hoarse and shallow. "No time. Sound assembly."

"General, you need aid." Lucullus knelt beside him and checked him for wounds. Despite the blood on his face, I couldn't find its source.

"I'm not so bad as I look," he said. "Help me to my feet."

I shared a look with Lucullus and Crassus as we tried to decide what to do.

"That is an order. There is no time."

We did as he commanded. The three of us pulled him to his feet and held on until he could maintain his balance.

"No time for what?" I asked.

"Sound. Assembly."

"Sound assembly! Everyone in formation!" Lucullus shouted back to the fort.

I rarely saw Sulla without a smile on his face, without a gleam in his eye. It was not present now. His ice blue eyes were stained pink. His lips were cracked. A gash along his forehead had clotted with dirt.

"Sulla if you would but tell us who did this, we will find them and annihilate them," I said.

He cast down his gaze, something he rarely did. "I'm afraid that won't be possible, young Gavius."

Word was passing through the camp about Sulla's arrival and the state he was in. I'd never seen the men rally so quickly. I pitied whoever did this. Sulla wasn't thinking right, but when he cleared his mind and tended to his wounds, he would lead us to kill them. We would destroy whatever rebel band attacked him. The carrion birds would feast on their flesh, and their bones would serve as a reminder for generations to come.

The centurions ushered the men into formation on a high, rocky place, the only location along Nola's coast large enough to accommodate the twenty thousand legionaries of Sulla's Fist.

A *medicus* arrived. "Consul, let me help you," he said. "I will clean and dress your wounds." He began to dab at Sulla's head with a wet rag until Sulla pushed him away.

"No, let the men see the truth."

I hesitated to make sure he could stand on his own, but then turned to join the formation.

"Wait," Sulla said to me, Crassus, and Lucullus. "Stand beside me. I want to share this moment with you. One last speech, one last time. All of us together . . . Sulla's Fist."

"Consul, what are you . . ." I stopped. We would find everything out soon enough.

But my mind was racing as fast as my heart. Sulla had departed a week prior to accept and celebrate his election as consul. Rome voted for his friend Rufus to be his co-consul. The war with Mithridates would come soon, and we relished its arrival. We conquered the rebels and felt like the conquerors of the world, like Alexander's generals.

What had happened?

The men were still forming up as Sulla led us to the center.

"Brothers, I bring you grave news . . ." Sulla said. His voice did not carry as it usually did, so powerfully and effortlessly. He repeated himself. "I bring grave news."

I searched the faces of the men, and they looked terrified. Colorless, wide eyed, trembling. Battle had never stirred them to such concern, but the sight of their bloody commander did.

"I was attacked," he said. "In Rome."

Gasps and murmurs spread through the ranks.

My heartbeat thrashed against my breastplate. Had rebels infiltrated the capital?

"Who? Who did this?" some whispered.

Sulla took a deep breath. "Romans did this."

Silence fell over the entire assembly.

"A mob, ordered by a newly elected tribune. A man named Sulpicius."

"Why?" a centurion shouted.

"He sought to strip me of my command," he said. "I outwitted him, so a mob under his control stormed the senate house."

He continued speaking, but even beside him, I could not hear him over the legion's roar. Every legionary of Sulla's Fist made their rage known.

Sulla closed his eyes. "I fought back, Rufus and me. We held them as long as we could, but no one aided us. Most of the senators fled, some watched from a safe distance and laughed at our plight."

"No!"

"Cowards!"

Sulla hung his head. For a moment I feared he might fall or faint. When I turned to him, I saw tears streaking paths down the blood on his face. "And I held . . . I held . . ." He lifted trembling arms. "I held my co-consul's son in my arms. He died valiantly defending the Republic, slain by this brutal mob."

The legions cried out. Pain, fury, remorse. I saw

men weep who casually joked about the deaths of their friends.

Tears welled up in my eyes. My throat tightened like a noose.

I thought of all the men we'd lost, all the battles we'd fought, the suffering we'd endured together. This is how Rome repaid us? This is how Rome honored sacrifices?

"I fled from Rome. I lost Rufus along the way. They pursued me as far as they could, but I lost them on the road." Sulla took a deep breath and looked over the city of Nola, the great rebel stronghold we'd conquered together. "But they will be here soon," he said.

"We will kill them all!" The legions shouted in unison.

"Not the attackers—they've done their master's bidding. But delegates from Rome. They will come to relieve me of my duties. Gaius Marius is taking over your command. He is to lead you to the East."

Legionaries fell to their knees. Others tore their tunics. Some stomped their feet and bashed their shields.

"No!"

"No!"

"Never!"

"We will only fight for you, Sulla!" the legions shouted.

I nodded.

We were Sulla's Fist. We fought for him. I would not serve under this Gaius Marius, who I'd heard so much about. None of us would.

Sulla raised his hand to placate us. "You are Rome's best legions. The Republic will need you in the war, but Gaius Marius will lead you. Sulpicius was successful, and he has stripped my command," he said. "There is nothing more I can do."

"Where will you go? What will you do?" a legionary shouted.

"I am still consul of Rome, as far as I know. I will return to the city and serve my term of office, though I don't know how to lead with such violence and corruption around me," he said. "I wonder if Sulpicius's dogs will not kill me when I return. But I have my orders, and you have yours."

"Save yourself!"

"Do not return!" the legions begged.

He bled beside us, and we loved him for it. He made us greater than we were. Sulla made us all who we'd become. None of Sulla's Fist, including myself, could imagine fighting without him.

"Do not weep for me, brothers!" Sulla shouted through cupped hands to make himself heard. "Cry now only for the people who are enslaved by a tyrant and his mob."

The unified, deafening, defiant cry of twenty-thousand men had not dissipated as horsemen appeared on the horizon.

Most of the riders came to a halt, while two of them galloped on. It was clear to see from the spotless togae of the riders that these were the delegates Sulla mentioned.

The legions finally fell silent as the two men leaped from their horses and strode toward us. They came to a halt directly before Sulla and turned to face the legions.

One unfurled a long scroll and cleared his throat. "The Senate and People of Rome do hereby command Sulla to relinquish command of his four legions, effective immediately, to Tribune Rancullus, who is he reading this message. Tribune Rancullus will hold authority of the southern legions until such time that the elected imperator of the emergent war against Mithridates is available to command. By order of the Republic of Rome, the Nones of Quintilis, 665 *Ab Urbe Condita*."

He rolled up the scroll, turned, and extended it to Sulla.

The second tribune spoke just directly to us. "Effective immediately," he reiterated. "You must collect your things and vacate the fortifications by nightfall."

The first tribune's eyes widened when he saw the wounds Sulla sustained. "Who did this to you?" He looked over his shoulder, as if he thought the legions were responsible.

I said, "The same whose orders you now bear." My sadness evaporated with the tribune's poisoned recitation. Now only rage filled my breast.

It was wise of Rome to send tribunes to deliver such a missive. If they were not sacrosanct, I might have killed them myself.

"That's impossible. We were assured no harm came to you," the second tribune said. "Marius gave an order of protection."

Lucullus snarled and stepped closer. He could not touch them, either, but he came as close as he could without doing so. "What has befallen Rome that a private citizen should have to offer protection to the rightful consul?"

They did not answer.

The roars of the legion had stirred again.

"No!"

"Only Sulla!"

The various cries turned into a chant.

"Sulla! Sulla!" they shouted.

The tribunes spun back around to the legions.

"It is not your place to decide who leads you!" one bellowed. I heard him, but the legions refused to listen. "You are soldiers of Rome! You swore an oath, an oath of loyalty and one unto death. Not to him!" He pointed back at Sulla. "Not to him, not to me, not to one another, but to the Republic!"

They shouted louder.

"You will do as you are told! As Rome commands you!" the second tribune shouted.

Lucullus took a step toward them, but Sulla caught his wrist.

He nodded for us to follow him away from the formation.

This was it, then? The end of Sulla's mighty Fist? I'd never seen my commander despair, no matter the dire straits we faced. Had he no more tricks? No clever ruse by which we could outwit the enemy, as we had so many times before?

The tribunes continued their tirade against the men.

Sulla stopped and turned back to the legions. One last look at the masterpiece of war he'd built.

"Let me say it again so that you may understand: BY ORDER OF THE SENATE AND PEOPLE OF ROME!" the tribune shouted. "I will not tolerate the—"

A rock struck his face.

All fell silent.

The legions stopped chanting Sulla's name and the tribunes ceased their insults.

The tribune dabbed at his lip and marveled at the blood.

I turned to Sulla. He looked on with blinking but unemotional eyes.

"Execute him!" The tribune pointed at the man he believed responsible with a forked left hand, a potent curse. "Execute him! I am a tribune of Rome and sacro—" The second rock struck him in the head.

Then a third.

The breath caught in my lungs. My vision swirled before me as the legions broke ranks and charged, the stones of Nola's coastal cliff in hand.

Lucullus picked up a rock. Sulla did not, but neither did he do anything to stop him.

I looked down and found a stone in my hand. I could hardly remember picking it up.

It was heavy, jagged. I turned it over in my hand. Rocks continued hailing down on the two tribunes as if from Mount Olympus by order of an angry god.

My father's face flashed before my eyes, but I couldn't focus on it.

I had no love for these tribunes. Their cries stirred nothing in my heart.

I had no love for our magistrates, our senate, even our people. My love for Rome paled compared to the bloody general beside me, to the legionaries before me.

My allegiance was to them and to no one else.

The tribunes were on their knees now. They tried to protest but couldn't.

Bruises and welts spread over their flesh like the fire that consumed Nola. Their teeth chipped. Their eyes swelled shut.

I ran forward and threw the stone with all the strength in my limbs. It struck one of the tribunes between his eyes. He collapsed, curled up into a ball.

It did nothing to shelter him. The volley continued.

The second tribune fell and wrapped his arms around his colleague. They cradled each other as the blows continued.

What have you done? I heard a voice in my head. It was familiar and louder than all the chaos.

But I picked up another stone.

When it struck the second tribune, he did not recoil or flinch. Neither tribune moved now.

"Consul!" a centurion shouted. He marched to the dead bodies of the fallen Roman delegates and stood over them. "Lead us to Rome!"

"Lead us, Sulla!"

"We will follow you!"

The triumphant shouts carried and echoed throughout the twenty-thousand.

No armed legion had ever set foot within the sacred boundary of Rome. But to my surprise, the words did not abhor me.

"Lead us, commander!" Lucullus shouted, dropping the final stone still in hand.

I turned and found dust rising in the sky where the tribunes' retinue had fled, abandoning them.

Word of our deeds would spread quickly.

"Lead us!"

"We will crush them, consul!"

Sulla simply watched. His heart did not seem to beat like ours. His breath was steady and unlabored.

His gaze turned to me. With a blank stare he seemed to wait for me, merely curious.

I unsheathed my gladius and extended it to the

heavens. "Let us liberate Rome from her oppressors!"

The metallic song of swords filled the air as the legions followed my example.

For the first time that day, a smile spread across Sulla's bloody face. "To Rome then!"

SCROLL XXVII

ARREA—THE Ides of Quintilis, 665 Ab Urbe Condita

We passed by the cloth dyers and the door makers, the potters and the fruit merchants. The wheels of our wagon rumbled over the ancient stones of Rome's roads, lulling Toria to sleep.

The rising sun gleamed on the damp roofs of the Palatine, illuminating the paths where so recently armed thugs killed honest citizens. My husband was nearly one of them.

I leaned over toward him, thankful to feel his warmth beside me. His eye was fixed ahead, the reins held tight in his grip.

Rhea gently bobbed Toria beside me. Barca and the dozen gladiators who came with him to Rome walked beside the carriage, prepared to defend us if they must.

Quintus and I told them over and over they owed us nothing more, and they could return to the *ludus* anytime they wished. Barca refused. He would not leave us there with the city in upheaval, not until we returned to the safety of our farm.

Servi swept the road before us and stepped out of our way, citizens watched our departure. I felt the weight of my husband's thoughts, the tension in his shoulders.

I wrapped my arm around his.

Leaving was difficult for him. He wanted to stay and do what he could to prevent more violence. He wanted to save his country. I sometimes wondered why.

What did he owe Rome? He'd sacrificed everything since he was a young man to his Republic. And how was he repaid? An election stolen from him by bribery and deceit, forced to flee from armed men on the steps of the senate house.

Sometimes I wondered why he loved Rome as he did. To a foreigner like myself, it was sometimes difficult to understand. Corruption, greed, excess, boundless ambition, selfishness. That was the character that ruled Rome, and Quintus possessed none of them.

As we gathered the last of our possessions the night prior, I asked him about this. He told me, "I love Rome for what she was, and what she will be. For what she could be, for what she should be. For what we all should be."

I didn't seek clarification. I would never understand, and he wouldn't be able to articulate such a thing.

"I'm looking forward to seeing the farm," I said. "Perhaps we can send for Apollonius soon?" A group of laughing children scurried out of our wagon's path.

He smiled at the thought of his old mentor. "I'd

like that. I miss him. The farm will be too quiet without his lessons and the patter of Pollux's paws on the mosaics."

The election results disappointed him, but I also sensed relief. He ran for office not out of ambition but out of duty and a desire to follow the gods' will. His time as tribune would have been a sacrifice, just as when he served on the battlefield, delaying the peace he yearned for most. But Rome didn't elect him, and now he was free.

"What does that say?" I said to Barca and pointed at a road sign nailed to a wooden post before us.

He studied it for a moment. "The... to the Via Salaria."

I nodded. "Very good."

He smiled in triumph. "I will be greatest reader in Italy," he said. "One day, I teach Toria."

But I watched as his face hardened. Barca raised a fist for us to halt and stepped forward.

A cloaked man stood in our path. He watched us for a moment before saying anything.

"State your business," said my husband.

I moved as slowly as I could and took hold of a walking stick near my feet. If my husband's attackers wished to finish the job, they would find us ready to fight.

Quintus reached over and squeezed my hand to steady it.

Barca approached the cloaked man. "Why hinder us?"

He looked past him to my husband. "You Quintus Sertorius?"

"I am he."

Barca's gladiators steadied themselves.

"I've been sent for you. The senate is convening at the Temple of Concord on the Fields of Mars," he said. "You're to come at once."

I could see the suspicion in Quintus's eye. "There is no meeting of the senate," he said. "I would have known about it."

"It's an emergency, and the intention is to avoid public attention. Otherwise, the consul would not have sent me in such a manner."

Barca said, "I do not trust him." He searched for armed men behind the messenger but found none.

"You are not required to trust me, but you are required to comply," the man said. "You are late already, as I've been searching for you nigh an hour. You must come at once."

Quintus took a deep breath. He looked at me, and I nodded.

"Lead on," he said.

When the senate met, hundreds of citizens gathered just outside the sacred boundary, listening to the day's proceedings so they could share the news with their associates.

Not today.

The slaves and retinue of the other senators stood nearby, waiting anxiously, but otherwise, no one else had come.

We might have turned and departed in disbelief, but the shouts of senators within echoed through the old Temple of Concord.

The hooded man gestured inside and stepped away.

"We wait here," Barca said. "I will protect your women."

Quintus left a lingering kiss on my forehead and

nodded to Barca. "I'll repay you in whatever way I can," he said.

He swept his legs off the side of the wagon and made his way inside.

My curiosity bade me follow him.

"Where are you going?" Rhea asked.

"Stay with Toria," I said.

I made my way closer to the temple and leaned against one of the massive columns supporting it.

Quintus found a seat among his peers as others continued shouting over one another.

It was difficult to understand what they were discussing with so many angry voices.

I noticed Rufus, Sulla's colleague and recent guest of our home, at the center of the torchlit temple. Nearby, that horrible man Sulpicius stood with the other tribunes. Two of their chairs were empty, but Sulpicius was loud enough to make up for their absence.

Rome again confused me.

This was the man responsible for the death of the consul's son, for an armed gang let loose on the city. And yet here he stood, mere feet from the consul himself. In Gaul, we would have killed him, and not easily.

There was another man standing between them who did not appear to belong. He did not wear the senator's toga, but the tunic of a servant covered in dirt. He bowed his head and clutched his trembling hands before him.

"You are sure? You are certain they are dead?" consul Rufus asked.

"Look at the man!" Sulpicius said. "*Of course*, he is sure. Why else would he return in such condition?"

"Yes, consul," the dirty servant said. "I watched them die. The soldiers picked up stones and . . ."

A collective gasp lingered in the temple.

"I cannot believe this," Rufus said. "I know Sulla, and he would not order the deaths of two tribunes."

"Perhaps you do not know your colleague as well as you thought," Sulpicius said. "We must bring him to Rome in chains for sentencing."

I didn't believe what I was hearing. Though my husband disliked him, I believed Sulla was an honorable Roman. His ambitions were clear to even an outsider like me, but killing two tribunes? Impossible. This was another trick of Sulpicius. His mob failed to kill Sulla, and now he hoped to destroy him in court.

"His term of office has just begun!" Rufus shouted back at him, the tension between them palpable. "He has immunity from prosecution until the year's end."

"This calls for a state of emergency." Sulpicius strode the temple floor and shook his head. "No man, not even the consul himself, may act with *impunity*. Murdering two magistrates requires a special court and special procedures. We cannot wait a year before passing down judgment. The gods *demand* justice!"

"I will not allow your coercion to corrupt this city further!" Rufus said.

The consul dabbed sweat from his brow. His meek temperament was ill-suited for this arduous task.

Sulpicius skulked toward Rufus and stared into his eyes. "You should be careful what you say next, lest I accuse you of *complicity* in these acts."

"It was you who forced us to this place!"

The senators on each side of the temple jumped to their feet and began shouting over one another. My husband was one of the few who remained seated, consternation in his eyes.

"Conscript Fathers, order!" An older senator forced his way between Sulpicius and the consul and held them apart. "Order! Order!"

Eventually, the senators complied, but the tension was tightening like a noose. One wrong move and I felt the entire senate might surge into violence. I felt compelled to storm the temple and grab my husband, to force him to the wagon and onward to our farm. Away from all this. But I couldn't.

The old senator turned to the servant. "Lad, did the consul *order* the deaths of the tribunes?"

He shook his head. "No, not that I could hear."

"See?" The senator looked relieved. "Perhaps he is decimating his legions as punishment for their actions."

"Already he has failed to punish his men for mutiny!" A random senator jumped up from the benches. "My cousin was commander of Sulla's fleet, and he was murdered by his men, and yet Sulla did nothing to avenge him!"

"Lies!" several shouted.

"This is no time for conjecture," the old senator shouted above them. "We must decide what to do now."

"We must send out guards to seize him. He must return to Rome for sentencing," another senator said. I identified the speaker as Gaius Marius, the man whom my husband served under for so many years.

I glowered at him. Roman politics made little sense to me, but I knew Marius was behind this trickery, the same as Sulpicius. He had the look of an eagle in his eyes, ravenous at the sight of prey.

Marius continued. "Lucius Cornelius Sulla should never set foot in Rome again, but in chains!" Spittle flew from his lips as he shouted.

That caused another uproar between the senators.

"Be reasonable!" Rufus shouted. "He has twenty-thousand armed men at his side! We should send a delegation to speak with him—to hear what he has to say and to see what he demands."

Sulpicius's piercing laugh rose above the tumult. "Was this your plan all along, then?" He turned around to the senators behind him. "Clearly, this man has a *vested* interest in Sulla's fortunes. He cannot be trusted to oversee the safety of the city in this hour!"

Senators began clambering down from their benches. Violence was imminent. More violence.

I prepared to run back to the wagon, to protect Toria, when I saw my husband stand.

"Send me." His voice, forged and sharpened by so many years on the battlefield, overcame the others.

He continued shouting until they listened.

"Send me to Sulla's camp," he said. "My son is a trusted officer in his legion. I will speak with them and learn everything we need to know."

"Why should we trust you?" someone shouted. "If your son is one of his officers, you might simply join the criminals yourself!"

Quintus turned toward the accuser. "My honor and my differences with Sulla are a matter of public record," he said. "I seek to stop this violence from escalating further."

"Or what? What will you do if Sulla refuses to listen to reason?" Sulpicius said.

My husband took a deep breath. "If the consul plans to use violence on more of Rome's people, I will kill him myself."

The senate was louder now than ever before. My chest ached. I clutched my heart with both hands as if I could still its beating.

Sulla would not harm Quintus. Even if the consul wanted to do so, Gavius wouldn't allow it. Quintus wouldn't harm Sulla; he wouldn't have to. I refused to believe it. This was just a politician's wicked scheme.

Still, I didn't want him to go. I wanted us to escape Rome and its clutches. Our farm beckoned me more than ever, away from this madness.

"No, no," the old senator shouted until he was heard. "Your honor is not here disputed, but you hold no authority. It must be magistrates of rank."

"That did not stop Sulla before," Marius shouted. "He will kill them the same way. We should prepare armed defense!"

"I will go!" A man jumped to his feet, a praetor by rank if I could tell by his toga. "I will go, and my lictors with me."

"Yes. It must be a praetor or a consul, and Rufus must remain here for the defense of the city. It should be you," the old senator said.

My husband sat back down, but it appeared that the decision offered him no relief.

Rufus nodded. "Ask him what he seeks. Say whatever you must, offer whatever you must."

This enraged Sulpicius, Marius, and their supporters, but Rufus refused to back down.

"I have spoken! Go and do not delay."

The praetor hurried out the door, passing right by me.

The shouting, cursing, and accusations continued after the senate dispersed.

I rushed into my husband's arm as he was one of the first to exit.

He wrapped his arms around me, but his mind was elsewhere.

"Quintus." I buried my head in his chest. "Let us go away now. We shouldn't delay."

He led me back to the wagon before speaking.

Toria was awake now and crying, the angry senators upset her as well. Rhea was pacing around and bobbing her granddaughter to no avail.

Quintus asked for her and held Toria close to his chest. He needed to comfort, and Toria stilled in her father's strong arms.

"The two tribunes sent to relieve Sulla of his legions have been killed," he said. "The senate is sending a praetor, but their efforts will fail."

"How do you know?" Rhea asked.

"I know Sulla far better than others." He looked down at Toria. "If he gives in now, his enemies will drag him through the courts and have him thrown from the Tarpeian Rock. He cannot relinquish control, and he won't."

Sour bile collected in my throat. What was my husband suggesting?

"Surely they are lying?" I said. "Sulla would not kill Romans. . . . Sulpicius is spreading lies."

Quintus frowned and shook his head. "I'm afraid not, my love."

"How can you be certain?" Rhea asked.

He took a deep breath. "All these years, I've been suspicious of Sulla, but I never knew exactly why. Now I know. Now I can see what he is capable of."

Realization was dawning on me. I placed a hand over my mouth to still my quavering lips. If the accusations were true, if Sulla's men killed two tribunes of the people, and he refused to back down . . . There was much about Roman politics I didn't understand, but I could imagine the repercussions on the entire Republic.

My husband continued. "I cannot abandon the city now. I can't. Barca, if I can ask something of you again after all you've done, would you and your men escort my family back to the farm?"

"No," I said. "I will not leave you."

"Arrea, I am—"

"We are not leaving, Quintus," Rhea said. "This is our Republic too."

When he failed to listen to me, Quintus listened to his mother. She was wise and strong. She would have been a consul herself if born a man.

Quintus nodded in acceptance.

Rhea added, "Much work is to be done if Rome is unsafe. We will speak with your clients and your allies. We will rally defenses."

He looked to me.

"I do not know Sulla as you do," I said. "I cannot believe all this . . . but I will not leave you again. We will do what we must."

Barca stepped closer and placed a fist on his breast. "I will fight beside you." He turned back to his gladiators. "Hear me now. This is not your battle, nor is it mine. But I fight beside Quintus

Sertorius and protect his family. Return to *ludus* if you wish. But, stay and fight, you are free. When battle is won, you are free men."

The gladiators clapped a fist to their chests as well.

"We will fight beside you, Barca," one of them shouted. "And you, Sertorius."

Quintus kissed Toria and handed her back to Rhea. "Then there is much to do."

SCROLL XXVIII

GAVIUS SERTORIUS—EIGHT Days Before the Kalends of Sextilis, 665 Ab Urbe Condita

"I beseech you to listen, consul," he said. "Rome will do everything you require. We will fight to return your rightful command of the war against Mithridates. We will establish tribunals to punish Sulpicius and anyone else complicit in his schemes."

Sulla sat tall atop his stallion and looked down on the magistrate in judgment. He'd yet to say anything. He left the praetor in suspense.

Behind the pleading man was a dozen lictors.

Behind Sulla and I were twenty-thousand legionaries, lined up in marching columns.

"Consul, what happened to you in Rome was unspeakable. We will punish the perpetrators. I will oversee their execution personally. Rome will restore to you everything that is rightfully yours.

Please do not allow bloodshed to reach Rome's door for the sins of a few miscreants!"

I remained in place beside Lucullus and Crassus, as Sulla kicked his horse to a trot. He slowly circled the praetor.

"By all the gods, if you would only tell me what it is—"

"What do you think, men?" Sulla shouted.

"To Rome!" we shouted.

The praetor looked up at Sulla with trembling lips.

"So, you intend to lead this army against your own city?"

Sulla ignored him. "Shall we listen to the praetor? Shall we listen to his honeyed promises and allow courts to decide Rome's fate?"

"No!" we shouted.

Sulla brought his steed to a halt before the magistrates.

"On your knees."

The praetor took a few steps back. "I am a praetor of Rome. I bow to no one."

"I do not intend for you to bow." He clicked his tongue and the first cohort stepped forward.

The lictors hurried to surround the praetor.

Although they were well-trained in fighting back angry crowds of citizens, they were no match for the legionaries of Sulla's Fist. Only moments passed before they were beaten back. No swords even needed to be drawn. We took their fasces, the ceremonial rods symbolizing authority and invulnerability, and broke them.

"Please, for the love of all the gods, do not do this, Sulla!" the praetor cried out as legionaries took him by both arms.

"On your knees," he said.

The legionaries forced the praetor to the Italian soil and ripped off his purple-edged toga.

"Please, please, I beg you!"

I watched. I scratched Bucephalus behind his ears to comfort him. The sight of this would have horrified me even a few months before. Two tribunes stoned to death by Roman soldiers, and a praetor assaulted. I would have wept at the thought then, but no longer. I felt nothing as I watched legionaries destroy the praetor's badges of office.

As they continued their grievous work, Sulla said, "I had a dream last night. Bellona came to me on a mountain overlooking the city of Rome. She requested my hands. Outstretched, she placed in one thunder and in the other lightning. Then she pointed toward the city with her great spear and listed my enemies. Sulpicius, Gaius Marius, Quintus . . . Tranquilius. She bade me strike them down. When I did, she rejoiced, and I awoke."

The praetor cried out as the legionaries removed his tunic, leaving him naked and ashamed in the dirt. "The gods will punish you for this! Jupiter will strike you down. Mars will annihilate your legions."

One legionary slammed his boot on the praetor's back, forcing him back to the dirt. "Commander, let us kill him!" he shouted.

Sulla raised his hand and shook his head. "No, the praetor need not die," he said. "Return to Rome, magistrate. Tell them Sulla is coming to save them."

The praetor wept. "No Roman has ever marched an army on the city before. Never! How could you—"

A kick to the ribs silenced him.

"Go," Sulla said. "Rejoice and thank the gods you leave with your life."

There was nothing else for the praetor to say. He covered himself with his torn toga the best he could and crawled back on his horse.

Dust shrouded the road as they sped off to report the news.

Sulla returned to us, and the first cohort returned to formation.

"There is no turning back now," Sulla said. "Are you prepared for what's to come?"

"Yes, consul," Lucullus said. "Lead us."

"We will do what must be done." Crassus spoke of attacking Rome with as little emotion as he spoke of the grain provisions.

"And you, Gavius?" Sulla asked.

I needed no time to consider my answer. "I am ready to free Rome."

He nodded. "Very good. I am sending you and Lucullus in first. I want you two to command the initial breach of the Esquiline gates."

Something about those words sent a shiver down my spine. This was real. We were really doing this. I didn't doubt Sulla or myself. I didn't doubt the virtue of our cause, but my stomach churned regardless.

"As you command," I said.

"We will prepare the way for you, commander," Lucullus said.

"Take no life you aren't required to take, but spare none who resist you," Sulla said. "Understood?"

Bucephalus swayed beneath me, sensing my fear.

"Understood, consul."

SCROLL XXIX

QUINTUS SERTORIUS—SIX days before the Kalends of Sextilis, 665
Ab Urbe Condita

The bells were louder and more persistent than I'd imagined.
They started the moment the praetor returned and continued
several hours later.

Unlike most Romans, I had considered this moment before.
When an army would march against the city, guardsmen
flocking to the walls, the people taking shelter. It was treason just
to admit the possibility, but I'd considered it many times before.
Perhaps it could have been the Cimbri, or more recently, the
Italic league.

The thought had long haunted me, but never in my worst
nightmares had a Roman army marched against us. And even
after all my doubts and fears of Sulla's ambition, I underesti-
mated what he was truly capable of.

I thought of Gavius as we organized our defenses on the
Capitoline.

What was he thinking now? I pictured the young boy who
used to get angry with us when we chastised the horses, who

thought endlessly of his mother's feelings, who loved deeply and longed for goodness. I worried for him. Was he afraid? Held captive by Sulla and the strength of his legions?

Or did he support this barbarity? Did he cheer as his fellows butchered the two tribunes and assaulted the praetor? Had he witnessed it all? Did he participate? I couldn't bear the thought.

Second only to my duty to Rome, I was determined to find him when the battle began, and I would save him.

Barca plugged his ears. "Battle is coming, yes. Why continue making such noise?"

"Rome itself is weeping, crying out," I said. "This has never happened before. Romans will now draw swords against one another."

I looked down over the Forum. Here the kings were overthrown and the Republic formed. Here liberty was born. In this open plaza, the people spoke each year and elected officials to represent them, to protect them. This was the seat of freedom, of democracy. The world outside was cruel and dark, but Rome served as a light. A beacon of hope that justified all the sacrifices we made to sustain it.

The system was flawed, certainly. The twisted hearts of man ever veers toward corruption. But at the core, the principles upon which Rome was built were good. That's why I loved Rome, that's why I continued fighting for her even when I preferred retreating to the peace of my farm.

What would happen if Sulla were victorious? What would Rome look like reborn in Sulla's image? Could the Republic survive such a fate?

I tried to block such things from my mind.

"We should be on walls." Barca leaned up against the Capitol beside us. "We should not allow traitors to enter."

"The forces of Marius and Sulpicius are defending the walls," I said. "The senate has ordered us to defend the Forum at all costs if Sulla's forces make it this far."

His eyes narrowed. "Of course they will make it. How can we hope to resist legions?"

I looked at the gathering militia before us. My mother was good on her word and rallied as many of my father's old clients as she was able. Bakers, flute players, and turnip farmers gathered around us in defense of the city. Other appointed defense leaders had brought their supporters as well, but not enough. If all of Rome unified to confront Sulla, perhaps the odds would have been in our favor. But many of those who were able fled. Some wished only to save themselves. Many others privately desired Sulla's victory, hoping he would crush their political enemies with swiftness and finality.

What remained of the senate rallied as many veterans and able-bodied men as we could. We even sent word to Pompeius Strabo and demanded he return to Rome with his legions. Days had passed, and still we heard nothing from him. His silence didn't surprise me, considering Strabo's relation to Rufus, and Sulla's betrothal to Metellus Pius's sister. Strabo would not defend the city.

We were alone, and the citizens here gathered were not enough.

But what else could we do?

"Marius gave a speech," I said. "He promised freedom to any *servus* in the city who takes up arms in defense of the Republic."

"How many joined?" Barca asked.

"Three, the last I heard."

He let back his head and laughed. "Cannot blame them."

I nodded. "One couldn't blame you for leaving either." I turned to him. "This isn't your battle, Barca. You owe nothing to me, and nothing at all to Rome. I do not know why you stay here."

He sobered, his eyes growing as stern as the ancient statues on the Capitol around us. "I spent my whole life fighting for Roman entertainment. I was cowardly. I should have fought my captors. Avenged my ancestors," he said. "But now I am free man. Now I will fight a battle I choose. I dreamed of honorable combat. Now I have it."

"That doesn't explain why you've given me so much since the day we met. You protected my family even when it was dangerous. You escorted us to Rome and have stayed here all this time when you have much to do in Nursia. Why?"

He smiled. "I ask this myself. I say it's because you are great warrior. I respect you. Admire you. I admire your women. They are strong. Warriors. And teach me to read," he said. "But that's not why."

"Why then?"

He looked at me curiously. "Because you called me *'amicus.'* No one ever called me friend. Only *servus* or *lanista.*"

I smiled and clapped him on the shoulder. "You told me once the first rule of battle was to never fight unless you can win," I said. "I don't know how we can win this one, *amice.*"

He shrugged. "Sometimes, losing battles still worth fighting."

I looked beyond him where his gladiators were standing, now fully armed. They nodded along with him.

"What about your *ludus*?" I said.

"I rebuild it," he said. "If I survive."

I closed my eye and said a silent prayer. I asked for the gods to protect Rome. Even as I recited the words, I felt the request was one even gods couldn't answer. I thought then of my family. The barred doors and shuttered windows would only protect them for so long. I prayed that even if the city fell and I along with it, that the gods would shield them and carry them to safety.

"Worry not, Quintus Sertorius," Barca said. "I ask my gods to protect your women also."

The sun was sinking in the west, casting a golden hue over the Forum. If the praetor was correct in his estimates, by the time the sun rose again, Sulla's armies would be approaching.

SCROLL XXX

GAVIUS SERTORIUS—FIVE Days Before the Kalends of Sextilis, 665 Ab Urbe Condita

 We had no need of torches. The moon lit our way. It was high and bright in the sky that night.

My father's patron goddess was Diana of the moon. Her presence was auspicious.

"I'm coming, father," I said beneath my breath.

Rome would expect us from the south, but we would enter the city from the east, through the Esquiline gates.

Lucullus and I, and the three thousand infantrymen at our command, would take the gates and open the way for Sulla and the rest of the legions when they arrived in the morning.

We would liberate the city and kill those who cast Rome into such chaos. I knew my father would cheer for our arrival, if indeed he witnessed what happened to Rufus Minor, a man who dined in our home just weeks prior.

"Quietly," I said as I ushered men toward the gate.

They were closed, as I expected, but I saw no guards posted nearby. They must have moved everyone to protect the southern gates. Or had they abandoned the city?

I would kill Sulpicius myself if I could, and Marius as well if he resisted. Rome would consider me a hero for saving them. Well, Sulla would be the hero, but perhaps my name would enter the annals of history as well.

My men placed the ram's head against the wall. As if activated by touch, bells began ringing throughout the city.

Panic clutched my chest. No time for introspection or dreams now.

"No use in discretion, men, hit it hard!" Lucullus shouted.

The gate groaned as the ram smashed into it.

I spotted movement above and looked up in time to notice a handful of archers there.

"Shields!" I shouted.

I ducked beneath the shield wall of the legionaries closest to me as the arrows rained down on us.

One arrow splintered straight through the shield above me. It stopped just inches away from my cheek. I marveled at the sharp tip so close. Why did it go only as far as it did and no farther? Perhaps the gods were protecting me? I knew it was Diana. She saved my father once, and now she protected me.

"Pila, pila!" I shouted as we opened the shield wall.

It was no small task to hurl javelin up those high

walls, but we outnumbered the resistance significantly. A few found their mark, and the archers shrieked and fell back.

There was no more than twenty of them. We'd faced stiffer resistance from even the smallest of rebel strongholds.

We'd taken them by surprise, and perhaps more resistance would be waiting for us as we moved into the city. But for the senate to leave the city so vulnerable during a time of war . . . shameful. Sulla, when he was back in command of the Republic, would fix all this.

The ram struck again.

A well-placed arrow from one of the surviving archers pierced the neck of a legionary manning the ram. He writhed and fell away.

I broke away from formation, stepped over the dying man, and took his place.

"Heave!" I shouted.

The alarm bells were deafening, as was the ram's thud against the gates. Even as my ears rang, I could hear the faint cheering of crowds as they welcomed us as saviors.

"One more!" I said.

I pulled back with all my might and let out a lion's roar. We sent the ram back into splintering gates.

We released the ram and pulled the gates apart by hand.

"Into the city!" Lucullus shouted.

I fell in line with the legionaries as we marched through the broken gates.

Where was the resistance? Why was there no one here to push us back?

Perhaps Sulpicius's men had fled in terror at our coming. No one else had reason to fear our arrival.

I thanked the gods. This was going better than I'd expected. Not only would the people love me, but I would permanently earn Sulla's trust and respect.

"Establish a perimeter," I said. "I want a century on every street corner. I will not allow us to be ambushed here."

The men split up at my command and spread out. The rest of the archers were easily dispatched.

Ancient statues lined the Esquiline streets. My forebears stood in silent witness to Rome's liberation as the heroes depicted celebrated in Elysium.

"Traitors!" I heard a cry and looked up.

Hundreds of citizens crawled out of windows and onto their roofs.

"What did they say?" Lucullus asked.

"They called us traitors," I said, just as perplexed.

I heard clattering around me, but before I could realize what happened, something jagged struck my cheek. I recoiled as blood dripped down my chin. A broken roof tile laid by my feet.

More roof tiles rained down over us, along with anything else the citizens could grab ahold of.

"Shields!" I shouted again.

"Cowards!"

"Traitors!"

I didn't understand; I couldn't still my thoughts. We had saved Rome from the rebels. We were saving them now from criminals and usurpers. Why did they call us cowards? Why did they not cheer us as we entered?

"Charge!" a voice came from the west, followed by stomping feet. The voice was unmistakably that of Gaius Marius.

Resistance had arrived.

SCROLL XXXI

Quintus Sertorius, Five Days Before the Kalends of Sextilis, 665 Ab Urbe Condita

"They are here," I said.

"Impossible," Barca shook his head. "They could not arrive so quickly."

I looked out over the city. Even from the height of the Capitoline, I could see no warriors, no fires. The sound came unmistakably from the Esquiline. Clever. We expected them at the southern gate, so that's where Marius and Sulpicius had led the anti-senate and all the citizens who volunteered to fight. The traitors would have been able to breach the walls before the resistance realized their error.

"Sulla sent a forward party to breach the walls," I said. "The rest of his forces will be here before the sun comes up."

Barca unsheathed his curved blade. "Time for fighting, then."

Romans were required to leave their swords before entering the city, but gladiators had no such restrictions. Barca's weapons would be useful.

"Quintus Sertorius!" a voice carried in the night.

It was Cinna. He was one of the few senators willing to lead in the defense of the city. He had military experience under Marius, but nothing noteworthy. He wouldn't have been my first choice to defend the Capitol, but that was the senate's orders.

Cinna blinked sleep from his eyes as he hurried toward me. "What's happening?"

"They have entered the Esquiline," I said.

His jaw dropped. He shook his head in disbelief but listened to the chaos and knew I was right.

"Move your men down the hill. We must protect the Temple of Saturn at all costs." Cinna's eyes shimmered with panic.

The Curia Hostilia held the symbolic power of Rome, but Saturn's temple contained the practical power: the treasury. If the state coffers fell into Sulla's hands, his power would be unlimited. With control of the city, all of Rome's gold, and an army at his back, he could make himself king if he desired.

"Let's move," I said.

Barca rallied the gladiators, and together we marched down the hill, no more than fifty of us.

We passed by the rostra, where I spoke two long months prior, and Sulpicius followed with promises of anarchy. I could almost see the ghosts of Sulla and Sulpicius arguing on that day and wished I'd known then what it would mean for Rome. We passed the Curia Hostilia. Barred and silent, the senate house stood as a mute witness to the Republic's darkest hour. For nearly seven hundred years this building had been the seat of democracy, proof that law and order ruled Rome rather than the tyrant, the sword, or the mob.

But already the blood of a consul's son stained the stone steps. How many more would fall here? Would I?

I called for a halt in the center of the Forum, surrounded by the monuments to Rome's eternal victory. "Romans," I said. "Here is where we will meet them," I said. "They will arrive on the Argiletum, on the Via Sacra. They will pour over this place like a flood." I met their frightened gaze. "We cannot defeat

Sulla's forces, I admit it. But if we fight them back long enough, they may consider the cost of their treachery and turn back. If not, we will resist them until our last breath so that any man who hopes to take Rome by force will reconsider. We will not give in to traitors. We will fight them with all we have to give. Your courage and bravery will live on as long as Rome herself. Take heart."

The gladiators chanted. At first, this startled the frightened citizens, but then they joined in. I did too.

I met Barca's crazed eyes as we chanted and beat our chests. He gave me a nod. We would not give up without a fight.

But visions haunted me even as we chanted. I recalled the destruction of Asculum and could see the same chaos spreading throughout Rome's streets. Soldiers would punish old lovers who spurned them. They could hunt anyone they envied. They could erase their debts with the murder of their debtors.

Sulla did not understand the anarchy he had unleashed on Rome. Or perhaps he did not care.

SCROLL XXXII

Gavius Sertorius, Five Days before the Kalends of Sextilis, 665 Ab Urbe Condita

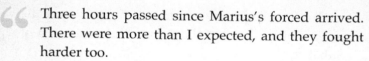 Three hours passed since Marius's forced arrived. There were more than I expected, and they fought harder too.

They couldn't break our shield wall, but they hammered away at us regardless. Angry citizens aided them, hurling stones and broken roof tiles into the dark fray where we toiled. The animosity in their eyes was more painful than a crack on the head. Was this how the tribunes felt as we killed them?

We couldn't break our formation or take an offensive position, so the stalemate continued.

Marius was at the forefront, his age no deterrent. He fought with wild eyes and reckless abandon, like a man possessed. By either a god or a demon, I did not know, but even our most formidable legionaries could do nothing to stop him.

But as the third hour came and a sliver of silver light appeared in the sky, the men in the back of our formation began to cheer.

"Sulla! Sulla has arrived!" they shouted.

No sound had ever been sweeter than the ringing of the trumpets and buccinae. It completely eclipsed the alarm bells and the sound of fighting.

The pressure against our shield wall eased.

"What are you doing?" Marius roared. "Come back and fight, you cowards!"

"Rome will *not* forgive you!" came the voice of that treacherous tribune, Sulpicius. I hadn't seen him among the fighters, but his posh voice was unmistakable.

Marius and his companions fled as their forces crumbled.

We chanted our commander's name as he arrived at the head of the twenty-thousand men of Sulla's Fist.

Sulla himself led the way. His eyes were piercing and stark against the sacrificial blood smeared across his face. His high plumed helmet made him a target for the citizens who refused to relent even as Marius fled, but there was no fear in the consul's gaze. He carried no shield or sword. Only a burning torch in hand, as if he would perform a ritual cleansing of divine importance.

The trumpets continued to announce his arrival as he passed through the gates. We maintained position as Sulla's force split and passed by us on either side.

"You're a traitor, Sulla!"

"You betrayed Rome!"

"To Dis with you, traitor!"

The citizens continued pouring insults down on my commander.

Sulla looked up at them with a blank expression and held out his torch. The fire took hold on the wooden door.

Smoke billowed out as those on the roof screamed.

"Legionaries!" the commander spoke at last. "I want Gaius Marius and Sulpicius alive. Kill any who resist. Archers, light your arrows!"

Dozens of legionaries passed us with torches and wasted no time burning nearby buildings.

Flaming arrows shot up overhead, crashing down on the rooftops and striking citizens.

"Gavius, let's go," Lucullus said.

I realized our column was already advancing.

"We have to keep moving," he said.

I nodded to him but couldn't move my feet. My gaze fixed on the burning homes, and I could not tear it away.

Lucullus grabbed me by my shoulder and hauled me along.

The flames singed my flesh as I followed, my sword still dripping with the blood of Romans.

The moon was no longer in the sky. Morning light replaced it. Diana was no longer with us.

SCROLL XXXIII

QUINTUS SERTORIUS, Five Days before the Kalends of Sextilis, 665 Ab Urbe Condita

"Peltasts," I shouted and looked up to the Basilica Aemilia where citizens gathered on the roof with rocks and sticks in hand. "Prepare yourselves."

We packed ourselves in between throngs of statues. The Roman heroes depicted gave their lives for Rome's freedom and protection. The stone must have wept as they saw the failure of their sacrifices.

I could hear the marching of Sulla's legionaries through the Argiletum. They drew close.

"Arms," I said. The militia prepared themselves beside me.

The first legionary turned the corner. Four shields appeared, with dozens behind them. Roman blood dripped from their distinguished white tunics.

"Chariot," I ordered.

The Temple of Vesta contained a ceremonial chariot, a relic of the past enshrined there for centuries. It was sacrilege to use it, but the gods would understand. Nothing was too precious to sacrifice for Rome's freedom.

Several militiamen covered the chariot in pitch and hurled a torch on top. The sudden eruption sent the horses charging.

Chaos ensued among Sulla's forward party as they scrambled to avoid the fiery chariot. The tactic effectively disrupted them, but it wouldn't be enough. Scores of legionaries continued to arrive on the narrow Argiletum.

"Forward!" I shouted.

I charged the disordered line with a mallet in hand, Barca beside me and the others close behind.

I thrust my shoulder into the regrouping shield wall with the force of a battering ram.

Their centurion barked orders. The rooftop citizens pelted the invaders with rocks, like Sulla's Fist allegedly stoned the tribunes.

Barca leapt forward and hooked his curved *khopesh* around a legionary's throat and slashed it.

The man's eyes looked familiar as he collapsed into the shields of those behind him. Had we served together long ago? Had we broken bread together or shared a cup of wine?

Perhaps my son knew him. Perhaps all these men were his comrades.

I cursed Sulla for bringing us here. Sulpicius and Marius were guilty of their actions as well, but only Sulla marched a legion against Rome.

My militiamen crashed against the enemy line beside me, beating against the shield wall with all the strength they could.

"Make known the price of treason!" I shouted.

The wild, desperate cries of the defenders juxtaposed the disciplined chant of Sulla's legionaries. The grim command of their centurions cut through the turmoil, precise and chilling, orchestrating the onslaught with brutal efficiency.

I cracked my mallet against the helmet of a legionary. He

staggered back along with his fellows. They had not expected to find resistance here. They should have.

As we pushed them a few steps back, I stepped on the handle of a sword. I picked it up. It was a fine gladius and had doubtlessly slain many of Rome's enemies. It would continue serving that purpose today.

The legionaries raised their shields in a *testudo* at the centurion's command. The peltasts could no longer help us, but they continued their work as citizens with no other recourse.

One of Barca's gladiators threw himself over the line and crashed down on top of the shields, momentarily breaking the protection and causing the legionaries to panic. He clawed, punched, and bit at their legs until their swords silenced him.

A legionary impaled the militiaman to my left. He bore no armor to protect him. The sword drove the breath from his body. He died without so much as a scream or a whimper.

The cobblestone path of the Forum, worn and smooth underfoot from a ceaseless current of Roman feet, was now treacherous and slippery with the blood of Rome's defenders. One of my men slid on the bloody stone of the Argiletum. Three gladii skewered him before he reclaimed his footing.

Barca continued to fight on in the face of sure defeat, as if this was his Republic to defend.

I could do no less.

But we could only hold them off for now, and no one was coming to help us.

Sulla's trumpets drew closer, announcing his arrival on the Via Sacra.

Soon, they would surround us.

SCROLL XXXIV

GAVIUS SERTORIUS, Five Days before the Kalends of Sextilis, 665 Ab Urbe Condita

"More and more citizens flooded into the streets to resist us. Why? There was nothing to gain by fighting but a swift death. If only they remained in their homes, they could live. Sulla wouldn't hurt anyone but those attacking us. Sulpicius and Gaius Marius were the only two men who needed to die.

But we continued to carve through the resistance like a warm knife through butter. They fell to our blades as easily as so many rebels before them.

I was sick with the sight of it. The smell of death had never seemed so foul. The taste of blood never as repulsing. It'd only been a few months since these same citizens cheered our arrival at the rostra.

How had it come to this?

"Gavius, you are falling behind." Lucullus grabbed me by my breastplate again. "You desired to march on Rome. This is it. This is what that looks like." He leaned in closer. "The men are watching you. You cannot waver now."

I found no words but nodded. Taking a deep breath, I steadied my sword.

The gods would forgive me. They knew my heart. They knew I only desired what was best for Rome, and for all those who sacrificed in her name.

Lucullus hurried forward to Sulla, and I followed him.

Sulla's voice echoed through Rome's streets. "I slayed your enemies. I conquered for your glory. I saved you from the Marsi and the Samnites! And this is how you repay me?"

I coughed, the acrid smoke filling my lungs with every breath, but I told myself to keep going. A little longer, a little farther, and Rome would be ours. Sulla would reestablish order. He would execute the tyrants. Everyone else in Rome would be safe. But first we had to win the day.

The legionaries around me gasped. I didn't see why at first.

A roof tile had struck Sulla. Fresh blood dripped from his lips.

"Protect the consul!" I shouted.

We rallied around our commander.

"Burn it! Burn it down!" Sulla was enraged. "Execute them!"

We pushed forward, lighting fires and killing any who resisted. The Forum was just ahead, and soon the day would be done. All this would be over soon.

SCROLL XXXV

QUINTUS SERTORIUS, Five Days Before the Kalends of Sextilis, 665
Ab Urbe Condita

Our backs were to the rostra now. Half our men had fallen. The
rooftop of the Basilica Aemilia roared with flames. Those above
burned alive or jumped to their deaths.

The sun beat down mercilessly, the weight of the Sextilis air
almost as oppressive as the dread filling it.

Echoes of each clang and clash reverberated through the
Forum's corridors, seven centuries of liberty crying out to protest
this sacrilege.

Barca continued to hold the line beside me but said, "Sertorius, we go. Nothing left to prove today."

The sharp stench of human death and disembowelment
completely masked the Forum's familiar aroma of commerce
and luxury. The fray's sour reek erased the comforting scent of
the Tiber. The acrid smoke of burning temples drowned out the
smell of sacrificial incense within.

Sulla's army poured in through the Via Sacra. I could see his high-plumed helmet above the rest. If only I could have made it to him, I would have gladly given my life to take his.

"Go," I said. "Take my family to Nursia."

"If you fight, I fight."

"I cannot leave until I find my son," I said.

It was a fool's hope. With any luck, he had long since abandoned his treacherous commander. If the boy I knew still lived, he would have turned away from this path and fled.

But I could not leave without knowing.

"Up steps!" Barca roared.

The few of us who remained climbed onto the rostra.

I tasted blood—my own or a foe's—a coppery reminder of the slaughter that follows defeat. The dryness of my cracked lips mirrored the parched desperation of the city, thirsting for deliverance from this onslaught and finding none.

Horns sounded from the Capitol. I assumed Cinna would finally march down from the Capitol and aid us. But as I looked up the hill, I found them retreating. They were leaving us. Who could blame them? Sulla's victory was certain. So close to Rome's heart, the traitors would not relent now. Resisting further only meant death.

"Sertorius!" Barca kicked a legionary from the rostra. "We must go. Now!"

Dust kicked up by thousands of marching legionaries and the few hundred defenders shrouded us. I glared at Sulla through the murky veil. "No, I cannot—"

The breath caught in my lungs. The sword slipped from my fingers.

There he was. My son. Gavius. My boy. He marched beside Sulla with a bloody sword and the wounds of combat on his face.

Agony gripped my chest like a serpent's snare as I watched my son slay a Roman citizen.

"Retreat! Flee for your lives!" my weak voice shouted.

I pulled Barca away, and we jumped from the back of the rostra.

Sulla's legions fixed their sights on the Temple of Saturn. With the treasury within their grasp, they had no interest in pursuing us.

My son's image still burned in my eye. Gavius . . . what have you done?

"The *cloaca maxima* contains a secret passage out of the city," I said. "We will help as many citizens escape as we can."

"Sewers?" Barca said.

Sulla's forces ignited with cheer as they broke through the gates of Saturn's temple. We had no time to consider alternatives.

"Lead," he said.

The invaders had yet to reach the Palatine hill. We could still reach my family in time to escape.

We would leave everything behind. We could take no wagon with us through the sewers, no family heirlooms, no trinkets to remind us of home.

My family and I would lead others into exile while Rome burned down behind us.

To receive Vincent's spinoff series "The Marius Scrolls" for FREE just scan the QR code below!

GLOSSARY

GENERAL

Ab Urbe Condita—Roman phrase and dating system "from the founding of the city." The Ancient Romans believed Rome was founded in 753 BC, and therefore this year is AUC 1. As such, 107–106 BC would correspond to 647–648 AUC.

Acropolis—The ancient citadel of Athens.

Agnomen—A form of nickname given to men for traits or accomplishments unique to them. Many conquering generals received agnomen to designate the nation they had conquered, such as Africanus, Macedonicus, and Numidicus.

Amicus (f. Amica)—Latin for "friend." The vocative form (when addressing someone) would be amice.

Arausio—the location of a battle in which Rome suffered a great loss. Numbers were reported as high as ninety thousand Roman casualties. Sertorius and Lucius Hirtuleius barely escaped with their lives, and Sertorius's brother Titus died upon the battlefield.

Ave—Latin for "hail" or "hello."

Balatrones—"jesters," an insult.

Boni—Literally "good men." They were a political party prevalent in the Late Roman Republic. They desired to restrict the power of the popular assembly and the tribune of the plebs while extending the power of the Senate. The title "Optimates" was more common at the time, but these aristocrats often referred to themselves favorably as the boni. They were natural enemies of the populares.

Buccina (pl. Buccinae)—A C-shaped Roman military trumpet.

Cac—Latin for "shit."

Caldarium—hot baths.

Carcer—a small prison, the only one in Rome. It typically held war captives awaiting execution or held those deemed as threats by those in political power.

Carnifex—Latin for "executioner."

Carthage—an ancient city that struggled against Rome for supremacy of the Mediterranean Sea until it was completely destroyed in 146 BC.

Carthago delenda est—"Carthage must be destroyed," a saying made famous by Cato the Censor.

Centuriate Assembly—one of the three Roman assemblies. It met on the Field of Mars and elected the Consuls and Praetors. It could also pass laws and acted as a court of appeals in certain capital cases. It was based initially on 198 centuries, and was structured in a way that favored the rich over the poor, and the aged over the young.

Century—Roman tactical unit made of eighty to one hundred men.

Cimbri—a tribe of northern invaders with uncertain origins that fought Rome for over a decade. Sertorius began his career by fighting them.

Client—A man who pledged himself to a patron (*see also* **patron**) in return for protection or favors.

Cocina—Latin for "kitchen."

Cognomen—the third personal name given to an ancient Roman, typically passed down from father to son. Examples are Caepio, Caesar, and Cicero.

Cohort—Roman tactical unit made of six centuries (*see also* **century**), or 480–600 men. The introduction of the cohort as the standard tactical unit of the legion is attributed to Marius's reforms.

Collegium (pl. Collegia)—Any association or body of men with something in common. Some functioned as guilds or social clubs, others were criminal in nature.

Comitiatus (pl. Comitia)—a public assembly that made decisions, held elections, and passed legislation or judicial verdicts.

Conium Maculatum—hemlock, used as a poison.

Contiones (pl. Contio)—a public assembly that did not handle official matters. Discussions could be held on almost anything, and debates were a regular cause for a contiones to be called, but they did not pass legislation or pass down verdicts.

Contubernalis (pl. Contubernales)—A military cadet assigned to the commander specifically. They were generally considered officers but held little authority.

Contubernium—The smallest unit in the Roman legion. It was led by the decanus (*see also* **decanus under Ranks and Positions**).

Cum Ordine Seque—lit. "follow in good order."

Denarius (pl. Denarii)—standard Roman coin introduced during the Second Punic War.

Dignitas—a word that represents a Roman man's reputation and his entitlement to respect. Dignitas correlated with personal achievements and honor.

Dominus (f. Domina)—Latin for "master." A term most often used by slaves when interacting with their owner, but it could also be used to convey reverence or submission by others. The vocative form would be domine.

Domus—the type of home owned by the upper class and the wealthy in Ancient Rome.

Ede Faecum—lit., "eat shit."

Elysium—concept of the afterlife, oftentimes known as the Elysium Fields or Elysium Plains.

Equestrian—Sometimes considered the lesser of the two aristocratic classes (*see also* **patrician**) and other times considered the higher of the two lower-class citizens (*see also* **plebeian**). Those in the equestrian order had to maintain a certain amount of wealth or property to remain in the class.

Es mundus excrementi—lit. "you are a pile of shit."

Faex—Latin for "shit."

Falernian wine—The most renowned and sought-after wine in Rome at this time. The grapes were harvested from the foothills of Vesuvius.

Filii Remi—lit. "Sons of Remus," a name used by Roman citizens who opposed Roman rule during the Social War.

Filius Canis—lit. "Son of a bitch."

Garum—fish sauced beloved by the Romans.

Gerrae—"Nonsense!" An exclamation.

Gladius (pl. Gladii)—The standard short-sword used in the Roman legion.

Gracchi—Tiberius and Gaius Gracchus were brothers who held the rank of tribune of the plebs at various times throughout the second century BC. They were political revolutionaries whose attempts at reforms eventually led to their murder (or in one case, forced suicide). Tiberius and Gaius were still fresh in the minds of Romans in Sertorius's day. The boni feared that another politician might rise in their image, and the populares were searching for Gracchi to rally around.

Ides—the 15th day of "full months" and the 13th day of hollow ones, one day earlier than the middle of each month.

Impluvium—A cistern or tank in the atrium of the domus that collects rainwater from a hole in the ceiling above.

Instate Hostibus—lit. "Chase the enemy!"

Insula (pl. Insulae)—Apartment complexes. They varied in size and accommodations but generally became less desirable the higher up the insula one went.

Jupiter's Stone—A stone on which oaths were sworn.

Kalends—The first day of the Ancient Roman month.

Latrina—Latin for "bathroom."

Latrunculi—lit. "Game of Brigands," a popular board game of sorts played by the Romans. It shares similarities with games like chess or checkers.

Lorica Hamata—chainmail armor worn by Roman legionaries

Lorica Musculata—anatomical cuirass (breastplate) worn by Romans made to fit the wearer's male human physique.

Mos Maiorum—lit. "the way of the ancestors," this is the unwritten code of social norms used by the Romans.

Murum Aries Attigit—lit. "the ram has touched the wall." This expression was used to indicate that it is time to strike, or that it is too late to turn back.

Nomen—the hereditary or family name of the Romans. Examples are Sertorius, Julius (as in Julius Caesar), or Cornelius (as in Lucius Cornelius Sulla).

Nones—the 7th day of "full months" and 5th day of hollow ones, 8 days—9 by Roman reckoning—before the Ides in every month.

October Horse—A festival that took place on October 15th. An animal was sacrificed to Mars, which designated the end of the agricultural and military campaigning season.

Optimates—*see* **boni**.

Oscan—a language spoken by several Italian tribes.

Passum—a raisin based wine, originally developed in ancient Carthage.

Pasteli—honey cakes with sesame seeds, a beloved Greek pastry.

Paterfamilias—the male head of the family or household.

Patrician—a social class made up of Rome's oldest families.

Patron—A person who offers protection and favors to his clients (*see also* **clients**), in favor of services of varying degrees.

Peristylum—An open courtyard containing a garden within the Roman domus.

Pilum (pl. Pila)—The throwing javelin used by the Roman legion. Gaius Marius changed the design of the pilum in his reforms. Each legionary carried two and typically launched them at the enemy to begin a conflict.

Plebeian—Lower-born Roman citizens, commoners. Plebeians were born into their social class, so the term designated both wealth and ancestry. They typically had fewer assets and less land than equestrians, but more than the proletariat. Some, like the Metelli, were able to ascend to nobility and wealth despite their plebeian roots. These were known as "noble plebeians" and were not restricted from any power in the Roman political system.

Popular assembly—A legislative assembly that allowed plebeians to elect magistrates, try judicial cases, and pass laws.

Posca—vinegar wine, typically consumed by the lower class and considered to be of poor quality.

Praenomen—the first name given to Roman males, generally eight days after their birth. Examples are Gaius, Quintus, and Lucius.

Proletariat—one of the lowest social and economic classes, comprised of the poor and landless.

Res Publica—"Republic," the sacred word that encompassed everything Rome was at the time. More than just a political system, res publica represented Rome's authority and power. The Republic was founded in 509 BC, when Lucius Brutus and his fellow patriots overthrew the kings.

Roma Invicta—lit. "unconquered Rome," an inspirational motto used by the Romans.

Salve—Latin for "hail," or "hello."

Salvete—a casual, familiar greeting.

Sancrosanctitas—a level of religious protection offered to certain political figures and religious officials.

Saturnalia—A festival held on December 17 in honor the Roman deity Saturn.

Scutum (pl. Scuta)—Standard shield issued to Roman legionaries.

Servus (pl. Servi)—Slave or servant.

Sesterces—an ancient Roman coin, roughly $.50 in today's value.

Sibylline Books—a collection of oracular texts the Romans considered to be prophetic.

Sinite Milites Exsultare—lit. "Allow soldiers to rejoice."

Stola (pl. Stolae)—the traditional garment of Roman women, similar to the toga worn by men.

Taberna (pl. Tabernae)—Could be translated as "tavern," but tabernae served several different functions in Ancient Rome. They served as hostels for travelers, occasionally operated as brothels, and offered a place for people to congregate and enjoy food and wine.

Tablinum—A form of study or office for the head of a household. This is where he would generally greet his clients at his morning levy.

Tata—Latin term for "father," closer to the modern "daddy."

Tecombre—The military order to break from the testudo formation and revert to their previous formation.

Tesserae—a common game of dice. Rolling three sixes was called a "Venus" and was considered the highest score one could achieve.

Testudo—In military terms, the "tortoise" formation. The command was used to provide additional protection by linking scuta together.

Teutones—a tribe of northern invaders with uncertain origins that fought Rome for over a decade. Along with the Cimbri, they nearly defeated Rome. Sertorius began his career by fighting these tribes.

Toga virilis—Lit. "toga of manhood." It was a plain white toga worn by adult male citizens who were not magistrates. The donning of the toga virilis represented the coming of age of a young Roman male.

Torna Mina—lit. "Turn and charge!"

Tribe—Political grouping of Roman citizens. By Sertorius's time, there were thirty-six tribes, thirty-two of which were rural, four of which were urban. This term is also used to describe the various Italian tribes, some of which were Roman citizens, others were allied with Rome but not citizens, and others still were hostile toward Rome.

Triclinium—The dining room, which often had three couches set up in the shape of a U.

Triumph—A parade and festival given to celebrate a victorious general and his accomplishments. He must first be hailed as imperator by his legions and then petition the Senate to grant him the Triumph.

Vale—Latin for "farewell," or "be well."

Valetudinarium (pl. Valetudinaria)—a hospital, typically present in Roman military camps.

Via (pl. Viae)—Latin for "Road," typically a major path large enough to travel on horseback or by carriage.

Zeno—The founder of Stoic philosophy. Sertorius was a devoted reader of Zeno's works.

DEITIES

Apollo—Roman god adopted from Greek mythology. Twin brother of Diana. He has been connected with archery, music and dance, and the sun.

Asclepius—The Greek god of medicine. There was a temple to Asclepius overlooking the Tiber River, and this is where Rabirius and many other wounded veterans congregated.

Bacchus—The Roman god of wine, orchards, and fruit. Sometimes connected with madness, ecstasy, and fertility. His Greek equivalent is Dionysus.

Bellona—The Roman goddess of war and the consort of Mars (*see also* **Mars**). She was also a favored patron goddess of the Roman legion.

Bona Dea—the "Good Goddess," she was connected with chastity and fertility among married women. The term was occasionally used as an exclamation.

Castor—Along with Pollux, twin half-brothers in both Greek and Roman mythology. Sometimes both are referred to as mortal, other times they are both considered divine. Most often, one is considered to be born mortal and the other divine, with the latter asking Jupiter to make them both divine so they could stay together forever. They were eventually transformed into the constellation Gemini (meaning "twins"). Their temple in Rome's forum was extremely important and sometimes facilitated meetings of the senate and elections.

Cybele—*see* **Magna Mater**

Diana—The Roman goddess of hunters, the forest, and the moon. Twin sister of Apollo. Quintus Sertorius gives her credit for saving him in a previous battle, and therefore he considers her his patron goddess. Her Greek equivalents are Artemis and Hecate.

Dis Pater—The Roman god of death. He was often associated with fertility, wealth, and prosperity. His name was often shortened to Dis. He was nearly synonymous with the Roman god Pluto or the Greek god Hades.

Fortuna—Roman goddess considered to be the personification of luck, chance, and fate. Lucius Cornelius Sulla believes he is beloved by Fortuna.

Gaia—Greek Goddess considered to be the personification of the earth.

Hermes—The Greek god of messengers, travelers, orators, and occasionally thieves. His Roman equivalent would be Mercury.

Janus—the Roman god of beginnings, gates, duality. He is depicted with two faces, one looking back and the other forward. The month of January was named after him, which represented an opportunity to reflect on the previous year and look forward to the next.

Jupiter—The Roman king of the gods. He was the god of the sky and thunder. All political and military activity was sanctioned by Jupiter. He was often referred to as Jupiter Capitolinus for his role in leading the Roman state, or Jupiter Optimus Maximus (lit. "the best and greatest"). His "black stone" was something to be sworn on.

Magna Mater—"Great Mother," she was adopted by the Romans in the late third century BC from the Anatolians. She was connected with and sometimes assimilated with aspects of Gaia and Ceres.

Mars—The Roman god of war. He was the favored patron of many legionaries and commanders. Unlike his Greek equivalent, Ares, he was respected and considered a "pater" of all Romans.

Mercury—*see* **Hermes**

Pluto—the Roman god of the underworld and the afterlife. His Greek equivalent was Hades, but Pluto often represented a more positive concept of the god.

Pollux—*see* **Castor**

Proserpina—the Roman goddess of the underworld. Her Greek equivalent was Persephone. She was connected with female and agricultural fertility, as well as the springtime.

Saturn—God of the Roman Capitol, time, wealth, and agriculture. He was the father of many Roman gods, including Jupiter. His Greek equivalent was Cronus. His temple in Rome's forum at the base of the Capitoline Hill was extremely important throughout Roman history.

Somnus—Roman god who was the personification of sleep. His Greek counterpart would be Hypnos.

Tiberinus—the god of the Tiber river.

Venus—The Roman goddess of love, beauty, desire, sex, and fertility. Her Greek equivalent was Aphrodite.

Vulcan—The Roman god of fire, metalworking, and the forge. He was often depicted with a blacksmith's hammer and a lame leg due to a childhood injury. He was considered to be the ugliest of the gods but was at times a consort of **Venus**, the goddess of beauty.

Zephyrus—Greek god of the West Wind. He was associated with flowers, springtime, favorable winds, and speed. His Roman equivalent was Favonius.

BUILDINGS, ROADS, AND LANDMARKS

Appian Way (Via Appia)—the oldest and most important of Rome's roads, linking Rome with farther areas of Italy.

Aqua Marcia—the most important of Rome's aqueducts at this time. Built in 144–140 BC.

Argiletum—a route leading to the Roman forum.

Basilica Aemilia—located at the juncture of the Via Sacra and the Argiletum, this was one of the most celebrated buildings in Rome.

Basilica Porcia—the first named basilica in Rome, built by Cato the Censor in 184 BC, it was the home of the ten tribunes of the plebs.

Basilica Sempronia—built in 170 BC by the father of Tiberius and Gaius Gracchus. It was a place often used for commerce.

Circus Maximus—a massive public stadium that hosted chariot races and other forms of entertainment. It's speculated that the stadium could have held as many as 150,000 spectators.

Cloaca Maxima—the massive sewer system beneath Rome.

Comitium—a meeting area outside of the Curia Hostilia. The rostrum stood at its helm.

Curia Hostilia—The Senate House. The Curia was built in the seventh century BC and held most of the senatorial meetings throughout the Republic, even in Sertorius's day.

Forum—The teeming heart of Ancient Rome. There were many different forums, in various cities, but most commonly the Forum refers to the center of the city itself, where most political, public, and religious dealings took place.

Field of Mars—"Campus martius" in Latin. This was where armies trained and waited to deploy or to enter the city limits for a Triumph.

Fucine Lake—known as Fucinus Lacus to the Romans, this was a large lake in central Italy.

Liris River—one of the primary rivers of central Italy.

Mare Nostrum—the Roman name for the Mediterranean Sea. This means "our sea" in Latin.

Ostia—Rome's port city, it lay at the mouth of the river Tiber.

Pillar of Hercules—a phrase used to describe the promontories that flank the Strait of Gibraltar, which connects Spain to Africa.

Porta Triumphalis—the triumphal gate. Triumphing armies would ceremoniously enter here.

Regia—a building just off the Via Sacra, the Regia was originally the main headquarters for the kings of Rome. By the late Republic, the Regia was used as the residence for the Pontifex Maximus, the highest religious official in Rome.

River Reno—a river in northern Italy, near Mutina.

Rostrum (pl. Rostra)—A speaking platform in the Forum made of the ships of conquered foes.

Senaculum—a meeting area for senators outside of the senate house, where they would gather before a meeting began.

Servian wall—the defensive barrier around the city of Rome, constructed in the 4th century BC.

Subura—a rough neighborhood near the Viminal and Quirinal hills. It was known for violence and thievery, as well as for the fires that spread because of the close proximity of its insulae.

Tarpeian Rock—a place where executions were held. Criminals of the highest degree and political threats were thrown from this cliff to their inevitable deaths.

Temple of Asclepius—located on the Tiber Island, it was a temple of healing. The sick and ailing made pilgrimages here in hope of healing.

Temple of Bellona—dedicated to the consort of Mars and goddess of war, this was a temple often used for meetings of the Senate when they needed to host foreign emissaries or meet with returning generals awaiting a triumph. It lay outside the city limits but close to the Servian wall.

Temple of Castor and Pollux—oftentimes referred to simply as "Temple of Castor," it remained at the entrance of the Forum by the Via Sacra. It was often used for meetings of the senate, as it was actually larger than the Curia. Speeches were often given from the temple steps as well.

Temple of Concordia (Concord)—a temple devoted to peace and reunification in the Roman Forum. It often held meetings of the senate.

Temple of Jupiter Capitolinus (Optimus Maximus)—a temple devoted to Rome's patron God, which resided on the Capitoline hill. It was sometimes referred to as the "Capitol."

Temple of Saturn—a temple of deep religious significance that lay at the foot of the Capitoline hill in the Roman Forum. Sacrifices were often held here following a triumph, if the generals didn't surpass it to sacrifice at the aforementioned Temple of Jupiter.

Tiber River—a body of water that connected to the Tyrrhenian Sea and flowed along the western border of Rome. The victims of political assassinations were unceremoniously dumped here rather than receive proper burial.

Tullianum—a prison for captives awaiting death. (*See* **Carcer under General Glossary**.)

Via Appia—*see* **Appian Way**.

Via Cassia—the northern road from Rome, this road passed through Etruria and was one of the main routes for travelers heading north.

Via Latina—"Latin road," led from Rome southeast.

Via Sacra—the main road within in the city of Rome, leading from the Capitoline hill through the forum, with all of the major religious and political buildings on either side.

Via Salaria—"Salt Road" led northeast from Rome. This was the path Sertorius would have taken to and from his home in Nursia.

Via Triumphalis—the "triumphal way" leading from the Field of Mars to the Capitoline hill. Roman generals awarded a triumph would take this road during their triumphal ceremony.

RANKS AND POSITIONS

Aedile—Magistrates who were tasked with maintaining and improving the city's infrastructure. There were four, elected annually: two plebeian aediles and two curule aediles.

Aquilifer—the eagle bearer of each Roman legion.

Augur—A priest and official who interpreted the will of the gods by studying the flight of birds.

Auxiliary—Legionaries without citizenship. At this time, most auxiliaries were of Italian origin but later encompassed many different cultures.

Centurion—An officer in the Roman legion. By the time Marius's reforms were ushered in, there were six in every cohort, one for every century. They typically led eighty to one hundred men. The most senior centurion in the legion was the "primus pilus," or first-spear centurion.

Consul—The highest magistrate in the Roman Republic. Two were elected annually to a one-year term. The required age for entry was forty, although exceptions were occasionally (and hesitantly) made.

Decanus (pl. Decani)—"Chief of ten," he was in a position of authority over his contubernium, a group of eight to ten men who shared his tent.

Evocati—An honorary term given to soldiers who served out their terms and volunteered to serve again. Evocati were generally spared a large portion of common military duties.

Flamen Dialis—Priest of Jupiter Optimus Maximus.

Hastati—Common front line soldiers in the Roman legion. As a result of the Marian Reforms, by Sertorius's time, the term *hastati* was being phased out and would soon be obsolete.

Imperator—A Roman commander with imperium (*see also* **imperium**). Typically, the commander would have to be given imperium by his men.

Immunes—those who were exempt from physical labor within the Roman legion.

Legatus (pl. Legati)—The senior-most officer in the Roman legion. A legatus generally was in command of one legion and answered only to the general. The vocative form would be legate.

Legion—the largest military unit of the Roman military. A legion was comprised of roughly 4,800 men at the time of Sertorius.

Legionary (pl. Legionarii)—soldiers which made up the Roman legion.

Medici Optimi—the senior most medicus.

Medicus (pl. Medici)—The field doctor for injured legionaries.

Military Tribune—officer of the Roman legions. They were, in theory, elected by the popular assembly, and there were six assigned to every legion. By late second century BC, however, it was not uncommon to see military tribunes appointed directly by the commander.

Optio (pl. Optiones)—second in command of a legionary century, they served directly under a centurion and were generally considered next in line if the centurion was to fall.

Pontifex Maximus—The highest priest in the College of Pontiffs. By Sertorius's time, the position had been highly politicized.

Pontiff—A priest and member of the College of Pontiffs.

Praetor—The second-most senior magistrate in the Roman Republic. There were typically six elected annually, but some have speculated that there were eight elected annually by this time.

Prefect—A high-ranking military official in the Roman legion.

Princeps Senatus—"Father of the Senate," or the first among fellow senators. It was an informal position but came with immense respect and prestige.

Proconsul—A Roman magistrate who had previously been a consul. Often, when a consul was in the midst of a military campaign at the end of his term, the Senate would appoint him as proconsul for the remainder of the war.

Publicani—Those responsible for collective public revenue. They made their fortunes through this process. By Sertorius's time, the Senate and censors carefully scrutinized their activities, making it difficult for them to amass the wealth they intended.

Quaestor—An elected public official and the junior-most member of the political course of offices. They served various purposes but often supervised the state treasury and performed audits. Quaestors were also used in the military and managed the finances of the legions on campaign.

Rex Sacrorum—A senatorial priesthood, the "king of the sacred." Unlike the Pontifex Maximus, the rex sacrorum was barred from military and political life. In theory, he held the religious responsibility that was once reserved for the kings, while the consuls performed the military and political functions.

Tribune of Plebs—Elected magistrates who were designated to represent the interests of the people. Sometimes called the Plebeian Tribune or People's Tribune.

Tribunus Laticlavius—lit. "the broad-stripped tribune" the senior of the six tribunes assigned to each legion.

CITIES AND NATIONS

Acerrae—A Roman colony in Campania. Acerrae would serve as a base of operations for the Romans throughout the war. Samnite general Papius Mutilus besieged the city early in the war.

Aesernia—An important Roman colony in Samnite territory, it remained loyal to Rome despite being surrounded by rebels. It was quickly besieged by Samnite armies, and those within were faced with starvation and disease.

Alba Fucensis—sometimes called Alba Fucens and othertimes referred to simply as Alba, this city was located near the Fucine Lake and Marsi territory. The city remained loyal to Rome but was swiftly attacked by the rebels.

Asculum—The city situated in Picenum was the first to rebel against Rome. They rounded up and butchered all Roman citizens, which sparked the Social War. This city was a target for both sides throughout the duration of the war.

Capua—the primary city of the Campania region and therefore an important stronghold for Rome during the war. The city was specifically known for its gladiator spectacles.

Cisalpine Gaul—The portion of Gaul on the Italian side of the Alps. Sometimes referred to as "Nearer Gaul." It was conquered in the third century BC. Although it comprised much of what is today northern Italy, it continued to be administered as its own province.

Corduba—A city in Hispania, it was originally conquered by the Romans in 206 BC. A Roman colony was established there roughly fifty years later.

Corfinium—A city situated within the tribal territory of the Paeligni (and close to the Marsi), it was chosen as the new "capital" for the Italic League when they rebelled against Rome. It's military positioning was the cause of this distinction. It was renamed **Italica** at the onset of the war.

Firmum—An important city within Picenum. It was sometimes called "Firmum by the sea" as it was a coastal city. Several battles took place near Firmum during the Social War.

Genua—The capital city of Roman Liguria. It was originally destroyed by the Carthaginians during the Second Punic War but was rebuilt and received municipal rights from the Romans following the destruction of Carthage.

Herculaneum—a city in Campania, near Pompeii. It was either taken quickly by the rebels or joined willingly after the onset of the war.

Italic League—The name for the fledgling nation of Italian tribes who were united against Rome. Their aims were likely on achieving the citizenship, at least originally, but after the onset of the war, the Italic League likely sought to destroy Rome and replace her entirely.

Italica—*see* **Corfinium**

Lusitani—The Lusitanians were a collection of tribes native to Hispania that fought many wars against Rome. Although the most notable Lusitanian general, Viriathus, was betrayed and assassinated in the mid-second century BC, the Lusitani continued to oppose Rome.

Mutina—A city in northern Italy, which was made a Roman colony in 183 BC. It served as a citadel throughout several wars, as its high walls were difficult to penetrate.

Numidia—An ancient kingdom comprising much of northern Africa. Gaius Marius and Lucius Cornelius Sulla both earned a great deal of prestige for their parts in defeating the Numidian king Jugurtha. The notorious cavalry of Numidia thereafter served Rome in battle.

Nursia—Sertorius's home, located in the Apennine Mountains and within the Sabine tribes. It was famous for turnips and little else until Sertorius came along.

Pompeii—A city located in Campania, Pompeii joined the rebellion soon after the Social War began. Pompeii had a large port that was very important during the war.

Salernum—A city located in Campania, Salernum fell to the Samnite armies under the command of Papius Mutilus soon after the onset of the Social War.

Stabiae—A city located in Campania, Stabiae was quickly captured by the Samnite armies under the command of Papius Mutilus soon after the onset of the Social War. Like Pompeii, it was a port city and therefore of strategic value to both the Romans and the Italic League throughout the war.

ABOUT VINCENT

Vincent B. Davis II writes historical fiction books to keep the past alive through the power of storytelling. He is also an entrepreneur, speaker, and veteran who is a proud graduate of East Tennessee State University and was honorably discharged from the US Army in 2022. Armed with a pen and an entrepreneurial spirit, Vincent quit his day job and decided it was as good a time as any to follow his dream. He's since published several historical fiction novels, most of which have become Amazon International Best Sellers.

When Vincent isn't writing stories and traveling back through history, he enjoys the present with his wife and their three little legionaries, their two rescued pups, and two kittens. Vincent is also a devoted and depressed Carolina Panthers fan.

Join Vincent in celebrating the past through the pages of his books. His newsletter, The Legion, is more than just another author email list. It's a community of readers who enjoy free additional content to enhance their reading experience—Maps, family trees, free eBooks, and more. You can join the community and snag your freebies at vincentbdavisii.com.

Printed in Great Britain
by Amazon

57795525R00219